Spirit Me Away

Jade Luck

Brickworks Publishing

Dedication

For Matthew

You've spirited me away, body and soul.

Contents

Chapter One

Naming the House Ghost

Harley

I wasn't sure if I needed to call a handyman, a matchmaking service, or an exorcist. There had to be something defective with my inn if the bottom cabinet in the bathroom kept swinging at my kneecaps at the exact moment that I walked by. Logically, I thought a handyman would come in—well—handy if I ever had enough money to quit fixing things around here myself. As it was, most of the items I "fixed" at the inn lately were really hanging on by a strand of duct tape and a prayer.

Of course, if I hired a matchmaking service, maybe I could find a relationship with a man instead of with a house, and then I could focus on fixing a human instead of a building. Was it sad that my connection to my bed and breakfast was the closest relationship I had, especially since my inn was an ass sometimes? Probably.

And naturally, an exorcist would be necessary if the house was truly as haunted as my realtor insisted when I bought the Burnt Creek Bed and Breakfast. Also, us being separated by spiritual planes of existence has made it difficult to break up with the ghost of the house over dinner.

Rubbing the knot on my shin where the cabinet door had made its impact, I contemplated naming the house ghost. On one hand, it would give me something other than curse words to shout whenever the house misbehaved. On the other hand, curse words seemed to take the pain out just a bit.

But as I stood up and made my way down the stairs to the front desk, I realized that it was times like this when I may have officially hit a new low. My closest relationship was with an imaginary house ghost, and I didn't even know its name.

The stairs creaked beneath my feet, evoking a new set of choice words.

Great. Just great.

"If you don't stop muttering like an angry old man, we're never going to have guests," Maggie called up from the front desk on the first level. I paused, my hand on the polished curve of the grand staircase, to call back to her.

"The house is being snarky about my life choices again!" I protested. I could feel Maggie rolling her eyes, even if I couldn't see it. My sister Maggie helped a few times a week at the front desk of the inn and even helped get it on the map as the oldest building in Burnt Creek. Thanks to my hard work on the renovations to restore it back to the original style, I reasoned the seven bedroom, eight-and-a-half bath bed and breakfast was probably the most beautiful as well.

Although we were sisters, Maggie was the opposite of me in nearly every way. Where I was tall and athletic, Maggie was petite with feminine curves. Where I had long, dark hair, Maggie had short blond curls. But us Malone sisters both had attitude in spades and no problem letting it come out when necessary.

"It's an old house," Maggie reminded me. "It's normal for the stairs to creak."

"They never creak after I have a salad! But let a girl have pizza *one night* and suddenly the house has a foundation problem!" I knew it was irrational to blame a two-hundred-year-old house for making strange noises beneath my feet, but I was pretty sure the house enjoyed baiting me, so who was I to deny the building its fun? I paused on the bottom step.

"Mags, I think we should name the house ghost."

Maggie looked up from her laptop behind the ornately carved wooden desk that I rescued from the old dining room. She pushed her horn-rimmed reading glasses up and brushed a blond curl behind her ear. "You want to name a figment of your imagination?"

I paused for a moment, deciding if I wanted to brush it off like I was joking to avoid being sent to a mental institution. But after a moment, Maggie just shrugged.

"How about Winston?" she suggested.

"Richard?" I asked with a returning shrug.

"Thomas?"

"William?"

"Frank?" Maggie offered, turning her attention back to the computer. I paused, mulling it over.

"...Frank." I rolled it around in my mouth and smiled. "Yeah, Frank. Opinionated, obstinate Frank."

Maggie clicked a few times on the computer. "Hey, didn't you have that date with the plumber's grandson on Saturday?"

I cringed. "Ew, yes, please don't remind me."

Maggie swiveled the chair to face me. "Don't be dramatic, it couldn't have been that terrible. Paul's such a nice guy."

Paul, the plumber who did all of the work on my bed and breakfast, was a seventy-five-year-old man whose wife wanted him to retire. He was the only plumber in Burnt Creek, and I desperately needed his help during the renovations. Because the residents of Burnt Creek were always in everyone else's business, Paul's wife had heard that I was single and decided that she would allow Paul to work on the bed and breakfast if I went on a date with her grandson. At the time, I thought it was a small price to pay for excellent plumbing, and if I got my own pipes cleaned, so to speak, all the better.

"Let's just say I should have questioned why a grown man needed his grandmother to get him a date."

"Details, Harley," Maggie demanded.

I groaned and leaned against the desk. "Well, first he picked me up in his car and went to open the door for me, which I thought was really sweet until he hacked up a wad of snot and spit it at my feet before I stepped in."

Maggie gasped. "He did not!"

"It gets worse. So, so much worse." I rubbed my hands over my face, remembering the awful date. "He told me he was trying to stay in shape and asked if he could take me to a place that's a little cheaper but with healthy food options, and I said sure because I didn't really care. I mean, it was a blind date, why would I expect him to splurge on a stranger? He took me to the fast-food joint just outside town and ordered chicken nuggets. Then, he spent the next fifteen minutes loudly complaining in the dining room that he didn't get the barbeque sauce he ordered."

"I don't even know where to start unpacking that. Why didn't he just go ask for more barbeque sauce?"

"I asked the same question. He said that if it was a good establishment they should be checking with their patrons." Maggie's eyebrows raised, matching my expression. "Yeah, like he was appalled that some maître d' wasn't walking around with a white napkin to wipe the floor he walked on."

"Oh, my gosh that's horrible."

"I'm not done," I said with a chuckle. "You wanted details."

"There cannot possibly be more."

"His ex-girlfriend worked there, and when she came into work, which is the only thing that cut off his sauce rant, he spent twenty minutes trying to win her back. I texted Brandon to pick me up."

I remembered how my cousin Brandon started laughing the second I got into his car. The only way I escaped without him texting my mother was by threatening to make him have Thanksgiving with his parents instead of with me.

"You could've called me. I would've gotten you."

I sighed. "I know, but you bail me out of everything, and I'm supposed to be the big sister. I'm sort of failing on that part, but I'm not going to interrupt your night off to save me from a garbage blind date. Besides, Brandon owed me for getting rid of Crazy Rita."

"Oh, God, I remember her," she said with a shiver. Rita had been the saleswoman who sold Brandon his latest car. Brandon's mother went with him when he signed the final papers and invited her to the family picnic as a punishment for Brandon not having given her grandchildren yet. Aunt Shelly miscalculated though because Rita ate all the potato salad straight out of the serving bowl and proceeded to invite herself to the next three family functions before I intervened.

"What happened to her anyways?" Maggie asked.

"I found her a nice transfer position in another state." Although it sounded menacing when I said it, the truth was that Crazy Rita had always wanted to sell cars in New Jersey. And if it kept her greasy paws out of the potato salad bowl, I was willing to make any number of miracles happen.

Maggie leaned back in her chair, and I glanced around the organized desk before my eyes landed on a little league trophy. A small brass-colored batter adorned the top and a matching brass plate on the bottom had an inscription that read "Maggie Malone – Employee of the Month" with the bottom line reading in smaller print "Hitting it out of the park every day."

"Really?" I deadpanned. Maggie beamed.

"Isn't it cute? The sports store was having a sale."

Burnt Creek was unique in the sense that the entire town pretended it was autumn all the time. New England was famous for its activities in the fall from apple picking and long drives to enjoy the fall colors, to the occasional pumpkin festival. But all of that paled in comparison to Burnt Creek. We were so dedicated to autumn that our town mandated that every business name needed to have a reference to the town or the season. Often the business names would lean towards Halloween or Thanksgiving, which is how we ended up with adorable and quirky store names, like our sports store Team Spirits, or Trick or Treat Bakery, or classic and boring names like my own Burnt Creek Bed and Breakfast.

Glancing between Maggie and her discount tee-ball trophy, I raised an eyebrow. "This says 'Employee of the Month.'"

"So?"

"So, you're my only employee, Mags."

She harumphed. "Which is why it's my job to tell you that I took an employee survey, and the results came back that morale really sucked."

"Well don't go bragging about that trophy to the vacuum, since it's the only thing that actually works around here, I don't want it to get jealous."

I turned around and scurried away before the paper ball Maggie threw at me could hit and climbed back up the stairs with a laugh to do a final check on the room before the only guest was set to arrive. I had done the final check four times already, but it was a nervous habit since I had only opened the inn six months ago. Glancing inside the room, I noted the linens were fresh and pressed, the towels perfectly folded in the bathroom, and there was a full roll of toilet paper and a backup. By the time I headed back downstairs, I heard another voice talking with my sister. When I got close enough to recognize the voice, I had to stifle a full-body cringe.

"Ms. O'Neal," I said, plastering on a fake smile as she walked into the foyer. "Are we making a reservation for you and your sisters? Or for you and a lucky plus one?" I gave Ms. O'Neal an exaggerated wink and watched as the eldest Ms. O'Neal's cheeks went red. The three O'Neal sisters were either in their early sixties or late nineties—no one could really tell—and none of them had ever preferred the long-term company of a man the way they enjoyed the bonds of sisterhood. This was especially because that bond enabled them to fake psychic intuition by texting each other information that they could later feed to unsuspecting tourists. This Ms. O'Neal was named Dorothy, and she was the oldest and shortest of the trio, unless you counted the hair teased on top of her head.

"Oh, no, I was just looking for you and had a *feeling* you would be here." She accompanied the word "feeling" with a knowing look and a slightly other-worldly air to her voice as if she had divined my location from the spirits.

"Of course, I'm here, Ms. O'Neal," I stifled a sigh. "I live here."

"Hmm," Dorothy muttered impassively. Dorothy's gray hair was kept teased and hair sprayed to add another three inches to her height, and her clothes were basic. Well, basic compared to her sisters who insisted on dressing like fortune tellers at a county fair. Dorothy's personality, however, was the exact opposite of basic. While her exterior exuded low maintenance, her interior was a charming collection of seldom-satisfied grudges and a constant stream of gossip ready to give and receive at a moment's notice. She opened her eyes and looked behind the desk to the many sets of keys waiting for visitors to check in. "How's business?"

Maggie and I pursed our lips as Maggie discretely pushed the envelopes labeled "final notice" under the computer keyboard. Business was awful, but if we told one of the O'Neal sisters that the newly reopened B&B was struggling, there would be a town-wide meeting to try to funnel every available citizen to our doors. I wasn't sure if the boom in business would be worth my neighbor's pity glances for the next two years.

"Business is great," Maggie piped up from behind the front desk. I waited for the nervous tick that I knew was coming. Any time Maggie lied, it was as if the heat from the lie fogged up her glasses, making her pull her glasses off and wipe them with the edge of her shirt. Sure enough, a moment later Maggie pulled the horn-rimmed glasses away from her face as she continued talking. "We've actually got a guest checking in today scouting out the inn for a YouTube channel about ghosts."

The second part wasn't a lie, but it wasn't anything I was excited about. I loved my inn, even the judgmental creaks of the floorboards. Actual blood, sweat, and tears had been poured into every refinished antique and window trimming. It was because I loved my inn that I didn't want it pimped out to an amateur ghost-hunting sideshow.

"Ooh," Dorothy said with wide eyes. I could already sense the wheels turning in the old woman's head. Dorothy had already started digging in her multi-pocketed beige purse for her phone, likely so she could text her sisters. Whoever taught the O'Neal sisters how to group text deserved a swift foot up the ass.

"Ghosts are good for business," Dorothy stated with rapid nodding as she typed. "My cousin Lenny died of a heart attack while he was cheating on his wife with a prostitute. His wife gives ghost tours of his office space now. Every now and then patrons will say that they can feel a quivering in their anus from the ghost of his vibrator."

"How much are tickets?" Maggie asked, wiggling her eyebrows.

Kill me, now.

"Is there something I can help you with, Dorothy?" I asked pointedly. The last thing I needed was a potential guest walking in to hear a senior citizen discussing anal vibrations.

"Oh, of course! I was coming by to ask if you would be willing to host this year's Haunted Trail. The kids just love it, and I'm sure it would bring the inn a lot of extra money."

"What happened to Joe's Apple Orchard?"

Ever since Maggie and I moved to the town as children, the town had always had the Haunted Trail at Joe's Apple Orchard because he was the only one in town with a large enough parking lot for the hordes of tourists who came to Burnt Creek in the fall. It was officially called In-Cider's Orchard, but the locals dealt with the jokes all through high school and got sick of them pretty quickly.

"He's being a bit of a party pooper at the moment. Apparently, he finally dug in his heels when one of the teenagers tried to burn down his orchard last Halloween. But you know, kids will be kids," she said with a flippant wave of her hand. "Anyways, thank you for letting us use your property for the Haunted Trail, the town council is in your debt."

"I didn't actually agree—"

"We can discuss the particulars at the next town council meeting," she said, hurrying out the door with more speed than I thought was possible for such short legs.

"Ms. O'Neal, I didn't—" the door shut with a click, and I could already tell the finely practiced art of manipulation that Dorothy and her sisters had become accustomed to doling out had finally reared its ugly head in my direction. Rolling my neck against the oncoming headache, I pondered asking Joe how he'd finally gotten out of hosting the Haunted Trail. Hell, maybe I could sweet-talk a few firefighters to come out for the big night just in case. Now that I had ruled out hiring a matchmaker, maybe hosting the disaster that would be the Haunted Trail could be just what I needed to hook a hot fireman.

"You are so screwed," Maggie sang.

"Yes, yes, I am," I sighed. "And on top of all that, now I have to go play nice at a town council meeting."

Chapter Two

A Beautiful Con Artist

Malcolm

Once upon a time, I had been a man on a mission, and now I was a man on a back-alley road in the middle of nowhere. My GPS had taken me off the interstate forty-five minutes ago, and I wasn't sure when I was going to see signs of life. On my right, a hand-painted sign welcomed me to Burnt Creek with a motto claiming it as the "Home of the Perpetual Autumn," whatever the hell that meant.

The phone rang over the car stereo, and I clicked a button on my dash.

"Ben, where the hell did you send me?"

"Ahh, so you *are* alive!" Ben mocked over the phone. My best friend since grade school had cashed out his stock options in his tech startup company that exploded before he decided to start a YouTube channel dedicated to finding and identifying ghosts.

Yeah, *actual* ghosts.

This all came to pass around the time that my career and my life came crashing down around me and Ben called to say he wanted me in on the ghost-catching action. I can't believe the timing was a coincidence, but it was harder for my conscience to believe my friend gave up an amazing life to give me a perfectly suited research position and a purpose after life as I knew it disintegrated.

So we joined up to create *Spirits, Seekers, and Skeptics*, a ghost hunting show that went from state to state investigating and debunking paranormal encounters. Ben was the "Seeker," I was the "Skeptic," and the "Spirits" would either be found in old buildings, or we would consume them in bars after a case.

"I might not be alive much longer if the Children of the Corn jump out and murder me," I told him, glancing warily out the windshield. "Seriously, why Burnt Creek? This place is in the middle of nowhere."

"Yeah, but it's supposed to have a lot of ghost activity, and the town is really into it. Just give it an honest shot."

"Who's my contact?" I asked. That was one of the conditions Ben gave me. I couldn't know the history until I got to the location, I had to go in blind. Ben said it was harder for me to form pre-conceived notions until the ghosts 'got to me.'

"Harley Malone," Ben said after shuffling around some papers on the other end of the line. "She's the owner of the Bed and Breakfast that you're staying in, which is also the place of the main haunting."

"Alleged haunting," I corrected. Not only was I a skeptic when it came to ghosts, I was also pretty cynical when it came to people trying to drum up tourism dollars by scamming people into believing there was something other-worldly in a regular place.

"Yeah, sure, alleged. But she seems helpful, so *be nice*."

"I'm always nice."

"You're always an ass," Ben corrected. "I'm going to be there in two weeks to get the equipment set up and the inn better not be a war zone when I get there. Harley is the owner and she's part of the historical society, so she should be able to get you the hookups you need for your research."

I blew out a breath as the road narrowed in front of me. Small shops lined the street, and I barely caught what Ben was saying as I made out some of the names. Har-Vest Secondhand Clothing Store was across the road from Witches' Brew Bar and Grille. There were a few couples standing in line at the Hallo-Weenie Hot Dog Stand.

"Is this place for real?" I asked Ben.

"Sure is! I gotta go, but call me if you find anything interesting. This location is going to be our Halloween special on the channel, so we've got to make it stellar. Try to research some other places in the town too. If it's exceptional, we can turn it into a multiple-episode deal."

I promised to call with updates and agreed reluctantly to not be an ass. When I pulled off the main strip and drove a few minutes down a winding road, my GPS chimed announcing my arrival at the Burnt Creek Bed and Breakfast. The inn sat on a rolling estate with acres of trees surrounding it. Two stories with a possible basement, if those were windows I saw near the ground, standing proudly. Large windows from the second floor had private balconies every so often. The house was idyllic, white with red trim, and a prominent wrap-around porch on the first level.

It was everything you'd expect from a historic New England inn, complete with a run down carriage house out back.

Just as I parked, my phone vibrated once more, the screen flashing a New York phone number that had hounded me for months last year. Anger flared in me from the trigger that often ranged from irritation to just short of fury. The anger worked through my mind before I took a deep breath. I hit 'ignore' with more force than necessary. I then reprogrammed the name before getting out of the car.

After briefly registering the chill of early October as it hit my face, I saw a short, elderly woman come bustling out of the front door of the inn, pausing a moment when she saw me. She was dressed in loose clothing in earth tones with a string of rough cut crystals around her neck that made her look like she belonged to a hippie cult or a yoga retreat, neither option garnered much confidence. I slowly pulled my luggage out of the trunk and walked toward the inn.

"Hello there!" The woman smiled brightly, bringing a lift to the wrinkles on her face while her eyes assessed me. She eyed my tee shirt that had our *Spirits, Seekers, and Skeptics* logo on it. "Welcome to Burnt Creek, I have a feeling we'll have a lot to discuss. Here's my card."

She unceremoniously snagged a card from her beige purse and handed it to me. When I set my bag on the sidewalk and grabbed the card, our fingers brushed and the old woman slapped a hand to her heart, making me jump.

"Ooh!" she exclaimed, bringing one hand to her temple. I frantically reached for her in case she dropped before my eyes.

"I've got you. Are you okay? Should I call an ambulance?" *Or a shaman, whatever the hell this woman used as a doctor.* Dropping the card I held in the hand that wasn't anchoring her, I started patting my pockets for my phone. My first day in town and I was going to be a witness. That did not bode well for small-town grapevines.

"No, dear, I'm quite all right," she said breathlessly. "Sometimes the spirits just take me as they want."

"You just look a little—I'm sorry did you just say 'spirits'?" I asked, holding her a tad farther back from me to take in her demeanor. "Maybe we should have a doctor look at you."

The little old lady's hand still danced at her temple. "You come to our town seeking to learn more of the afterlife, of those who have not yet passed over."

I could feel the color drain from my face before hearing the door to the inn open and a woman hollering out the door. "Dorothy, leave the man alone, and quit peddling business from the inn!"

The old lady, Dorothy, I surmised, straightened suddenly with an air of annoyance when she glanced back at the door. She then smiled gently at me and patted my hand. "We're in town if you ever need our services, dear. We'll even do ten percent off your first reading."

With that, she waltzed down the sidewalk to a little scooter with a neon green helmet and took off out the driveway. I stared after her wondering what had just happened. Remembering the card, I glanced around until I found it on the ground.

"Three Sisters' Psychic Services," I read aloud. When I picked up my bag and headed through the door, the look on my face must have told the woman standing at the base of the stairs everything she needed to know.

"She's not psychic; she's just nosy," she insisted, a hand rubbing her forehead in annoyance. When she released her forehead and looked up at me, words left my mouth as I took in green eyes that lit up the room. She smiled at me, soft lips parting over straight white teeth, her eyes crinkling a little as if smiling was what her eyes were made for.

The woman extended out her hand, and I tried not to make it obvious as I raked my eyes from her face, down her chest, down the dip of her waist, flare of her hips, down to her hand.

Huh, no ring.

"I'm Harley. Ben said I should be expecting you."

I could feel my expression immediately cool as I shook her hand. She didn't look like a charlatan ready to hustle customers through the door with promises of haunted experiences, but the best liars are the ones who looked like her. Beautiful. Innocent. I wasn't about to let her get the drop on me, too.

"Malcolm Jones," I said in the cold, detached persona I had mastered.

Harley must have noticed the shift in my demeanor because she cocked her head to the side as her smile slowly retreated behind a mask of efficiency.

"Right, let me get you checked in. We have you set up for the month. We practice environmentally friendly housekeeping, so we normally wash towels and sheets every four days for long-term guests. If you need us to wash something sooner, don't hesitate to let me know."

I nodded slowly, watching her eyes as they looked over the shoulder of the blonde in front of the computer screen and back to me. The blonde was pretty in a quirky, off beat way, and if it were any other day, she would've captured my attention. Much to my annoyance, the woman with the long brown waves and stunning green eyes who was trying to con people into believing there were ghosts in her inn was the only one who sent a surge through my blood. God, she was pretty, and it was infuriating as hell.

Harley wore a moss green blazer over a frilly white shirt that complemented the color of her eyes and the swell of her chest. Her pants were straight and black, ending at the ankle where I could just see the sparkle of an ankle bracelet above black flats. My mind immediately wondered what that ankle bracelet would look like with her legs wrapped around my back. I cursed my stupid brain and forced myself to stay focused.

Ben had apparently already paid up for our stay, so all I had to do was get settled in for the night. Harley spun around and reached up toward the old-style keys hung on hooks on the wall behind her. Her shirt and blazer rose slightly, revealing a small sliver of pale skin that made my eyes tingle in delight. The younger woman sitting behind the desk cleared her throat, and I tore my eyes away from Harley, realizing my eyes had been all over her backside as she stretched to reach the keys. I could feel my face flush red as the young woman glared at me behind horn-rimmed glasses that reminded me of a librarian from the fifties.

"Hi there," she said, flashing a deadly smile. "I'm Maggie, Harley's sister."

"Oh, right, nice to meet you," I replied. *Get it together, man.*

Harley spun around, having finally secured the key from the top hook. "Right, let me show you to your room. Can I get your bags?"

"Oh, no, thanks, I've got them." I was all about professional courtesy, but I wasn't about to let her carry my bags. They were heavy with research books and office supplies.

She led me away from the check-in desk and up the grand staircase. The staircase creaked and I thought I caught her mumbling something about pizza.

"So," I started. "'The Town of Perpetual Autumn.' What's that about?"

Harley smiled at me, and it did something to my stomach. "Burnt Creek was founded in the autumn. The founder named it because when the trees change to reds and oranges, the creek that runs through the town reflects it and makes it look like fire. So, the founder named it Burnt Creek. Now everything we do stems from autumn. We have a massive festival coming up in a couple weeks, and we carry autumn themed food and drinks all year round."

"Autumn-themed drinks?" I asked. "Like what?"

"Like apple cider, pumpkin-spiced lattes, that sort of thing."

"But how do you have pumpkin-spiced lattes in the summer?"

"We add ice to them," she replied, dipping her head, but not before I caught a glimpse of her wry smile. I shook my head, telling myself I wasn't allowed to find her funny. I had to remain objective. Even if she was probably swindling money from poor souls hoping for a glimpse of the "beyond."

Harley led me down to a plain door with a plaque that had the number four on it. Twisting the key in the lock, she swung open the door and revealed my room for the next month. The room was stately and comfortable, which was not what I was expecting. Other inns we've stayed at that tried to boost sales by linking themselves to "spirits of the past" put gaudy wallpaper everywhere and deep floral patterns that made me dizzy. This room had wallpaper, but it was a cream-colored stripe with navy accents. The soft colors carried throughout the room to a couch beneath the window and a bathroom off the room. It was just...pleasant.

And standing in the middle of it all was a woman I already knew was going to be a problem.

My suitcase was spread out over the bed, papers and notebooks littered every available surface, and I'd barely gotten started preparing questions for the infuriatingly attractive Burnt Creek Bed and Breakfast owner when my cell rang. I pushed my glasses further up my nose and shuffled around clothes and books until I found my phone tucked against the bedspread. When I saw the name across the screen, I decided it was time to bite the bullet. I had waited long enough.

"Hi, Mom."

"As I live and breathe, is that my son?" The familiar voice that sang me to sleep at night as a child and called me out on my bullshit during my teenage years made my throat close like a vice grip.

"Yeah, Mom, it's me."

"Are you sure? Because it's been so long since my son has answered his phone when I've called, I thought he'd been kidnapped by some South American drug lord, forced to mule drugs across the border or sell his body to prostitution. My baby boy!"

"Jeez, lay it on a little thicker, would ya?" I said, smiling.

"I'm just glad you answered, Malcolm Jones, or my next phone call was going to be the American embassy."

"I've literally never been out of the country."

"How was I to know that? You keep everything else from me."

Silence permeated the phone and I thought I could hear a sniffle. This is what I had been avoiding.

"Mom," I started. "Mom, I'm so sorry."

"It just would have been nice to know, that's all," she said quietly. My mind flashed back to the look of shock and fear when she opened the door to find that her entire life was about to get turned on its head two years ago. "Anyways, I wasn't calling about that."

I nodded silently. Maybe she thought it was best not to talk about it. Maybe it was easier to love a son when she could pretend his sins never existed.

"I've seen some of those episodes you and Ben put up on the YouTube."

I grinned. "Yeah? What'd you think?"

"It was nice! That Benjamin always had such charisma. And you look so excited explaining the history of all of these places. You know, your father was quite the history buff back in his day—"

"Hey, Mom, I actually need to get going," I lied, not wanting to take a walk down Dad's past.

"Oh, right, of course," she said. The dejected voice nearly broke me. I had done that to my mother. "Well, I love you very much, and please make sure you let me know if you plan to come into contact with any cartels or drug lords."

"You'll be my first call," I promised.

Chapter Three

An Unplanned Interview

Harley

As Malcolm got settled in his room and Maggie manned the front desk, I spent my time checking tasks off my list to prepare for more guests. The lock on room five needed to be tightened, the TV in room seven was stuck on French subtitles, and the bathroom of room two had a slow drip in the tub. I wasn't going to risk another date with Paul's grandson, so I was going to have to figure out the plumbing myself. When I made my way back downstairs, I found myself facing the raised eyebrows of my sister.

"Don't look at me like that," I said with a sigh.

Maggie schooled her expression into one of innocence with a smirk just under the surface. "Like what?"

I rolled my eyes. "Like Malcolm Jones is not just another customer."

"Have you *seen* him? He looks like he just stepped out of a GQ magazine! And he was looking you over like he wanted to eat you for breakfast."

"He was not," I argued, a flush rising up my cheeks. Maggie wasn't wrong about his looks. Light brown hair artfully mussed and a five o'clock shadow dusting his squared jaw, framed by glasses that gave him a hot professor vibe, Malcolm Jones was a gorgeous man. I thought back to the moment when I was getting his key. When I had turned back toward him, it was as if he had yanked his gaze away a smidge too quickly. Was Maggie right? Was he checking me out as much as I was trying to avoid doing the same?

No, of course not, I thought. Maggie was a romantic at heart, and I loved her for that. But the experiences that had jaded me weren't going to go away overnight, and I knew better than to get interested in a man who would blow out of town in a month.

"Besides," I huffed. "He's a ghost hunter. Like, that's his *actual* profession. He might as well be a vampire slayer or a sasquatch tamer."

Maggie ignored my rebuffs. "When is he going to start interviewing you for the Spirits channel?"

"I'm not sure. I figured I'd let him get settled in and he could ask me about the inn whenever he needs answers. I don't know how his process works."

Maggie shrugged, eyeballing me one more time. I shrank back toward the kitchen to avoid her gaze. "I'm going to get the menu ready for the week. If he comes back down, can you ask him if he has any allergies or breakfast dislikes?"

"Sure can." Maggie pulled her glasses from her eyes and wiped them on her shirt. My warning bells immediately started ringing.

"So, Maggie," I hedged. "Anything...interesting...happen today?"

I leaned against the desk, watching as Maggie's lips pursed.

"Um, nope. Not a lot happening around these parts. I mean, I really should find some stuff to do. You know what they say about idle hands and all that. Well, actually I don't know what they say about it but I gather that it's really bad—"

"Maggie," I interrupted before she filled the next half hour with ramblings. "Whatever it is that you don't want to tell me, just tell me, and you'll feel a lot better."

Maggie breathed out a sigh and bowed her head. "The Red Hat ladies canceled their monthly meeting reservations here."

My mouth fell open. "When did this happen?"

"When you were getting Malcolm checked in. I didn't want to tell you right away, I thought I could find a way for us to recoup the costs."

I sighed and rubbed my head. That was the third reservation to cancel in so many weeks. "Did they say why?"

She shook her head. "Nothing specific, just that they would be having it at their new member's house."

I dropped my head in my hands, wondering what I had done in a former life to warrant such things. Our rates weren't crazy expensive, our accommodations included pastries and drinks. By all accounts, our inn should be the place where these groups are flocking to, but every time a group reserved the conference rooms, they called and cancelled within the week.

I walked back to the kitchen, grateful to be away from my sister's prying questions and sullen news. Once in my kitchen, I let myself relax against the counter with my recipe book. Out of all of the renovations I had done to the inn, the kitchen was my favorite. Open and airy with an old farmhouse table serving as a kitchen island for prep work, I spent many hours tediously working to give the room an old-world feel while trying to keep the aura cozy and fresh. Green hanging ivy planters hung from the ceiling near the windows that flanked the small breakfast nook that I used as a makeshift office during most mornings when my pastries were baking in my state-of-the-art convection ovens.

The kitchen was also the only place I seemed to be safe from the house-ghost Frank. I drew a line at my opinionated ghost douche coming in and messing with my kitchen. A woman has to have standards.

Evaluating the ingredients in my fridge and dry storage, along with my available freezer space, I pulled out a large mixing bowl and lost myself in the process of creation. Mixing and forming sausage patties from scratch to freeze for later and a batch of cookie dough for the historical society meeting, I threw myself into the chopping, rolling, measuring, and blending side of prep work. Then, possibly one of my favorite parts, was the storing and labeling—creating order from chaos.

Most importantly, it allowed me to focus on something other than the bills I couldn't afford to pay, the guests who weren't coming in, and the ghost hunting entertainers who might be my last hope to keep the doors to my inn open.

Forty minutes into recipe prep, a knock happened outside the swinging door. The door swung open, and Malcolm stuck his head in. *And my, what a gorgeous head it was.*

His soft honey-brown hair fell onto his forehead as he tilted his head down. In this light, I could see how his stubble that dusted his jaw framed soft, kissable lips. I blamed my childhood crush I had on Clark Kent for the obsession with his glasses. I had to brace my hands on the counter to stop myself from swooning.

"Mr. Jones, come in," I said, trying to keep the breathiness out of my voice.

"Please, call me Malcolm," he said, bringing his tall frame into the room. Somehow the room seemed to shrink around him. "Sorry to bother you. I just wanted to see when you were free for some interview questions for the video segment?"

"No bother, I'm free whenever. I'm just prepping stuff for the morning. Do you have any allergies? Breakfast dislikes?"

"No allergies, and I generally eat anything."

"Awesome," I said, placing the pastries that were ready to put in the oven in the morning in the cooler. I turned back around toward him and placed my hands back on the counter before glancing down at the flour-coated shirt I was wearing. "Oh, are we doing a video thing now? Because your viewers might be disappointed."

His eyes pierced me as he took me in, pressing his lips into a firm line as if trying not to say something. His lips tilted up at the corners.

"No video today, that's more Ben's wheelhouse. I'm just the researcher so I ask prep questions," he said, lifting a bag I didn't realize was hitched over his shoulder onto the counter. He pulled out a notepad, pen, and a recorder. "Is it okay if I record this?"

"Go for it, although I should warn you, I'm pretty sure I sound like Jabba the Hut on recording devices."

A corner of his mouth lifted before he schooled his expression. "Jabba the Hut?"

"Yeah," I said, "You know, the chunky Star Wars dude that held Princess Leia hostage? He was the one who put her in that outfit that placed her squarely in the eternal spank-bank of teenage boys everywhere."

Malcolm's head tilted to the side as he evaluated me. I used to be one of those girls who shrank under the weight of inspection, only to look up behind eyelashes with uncertainty, but that only got me assholes like my ex Connor who wanted a submissive housewife. Instead, I stared back at Malcolm, matching his gaze with a raised eyebrow.

"I'm familiar with said spank-bank moment," he said finally with a quirk of his brow. "Ready to get started?"

I nodded and directed him over to the breakfast nook so we could sit. He sat his phone and a recorder down, pausing as his phone started vibrating on the table. I couldn't see the screen, but when he saw who the caller was, his lips formed a thin line and his jaw clenched. Ignoring the call, Malcolm shook his head and slid the phone back into his pocket. When he returned to me, the lightness I saw earlier was gone, and instead a tightness came over him as he pressed the record button on his little device, uncapped the pen and jotted down some things as he spoke directly to the recording device.

"Interviewing Harley Malone, owner of the Burnt Creek Bed and Breakfast, who claims to have ghosts present in the inn for her customers to experience."

Wait, what?

"Actually," I started, looking at his eyes which seemed harder than before this interview started. "Sorry—I'm not sure how this works—but I don't actually claim to have ghosts here."

"Come again?" he asked.

"Yeah, I mean, it's an old house and all, and sometimes Frank likes to mess around, but this isn't like a ghost attraction or anything." I rubbed my hand over the back of my neck.

"Who's Frank?"

"Oh, he's my ghost."

"So, you do have a ghost."

"Yeah, but like, he's *my* ghost. He doesn't really exist for everyone else." *Dear God, I sound like a crazy person.* "Like he's sort of a Murphy's Law ghost. When something shitty happens around here, I just sort of shake my fist at the ceiling and say, 'Damn it, Frank.' Actually, I just named him this morning. He didn't even have a name."

"So, you're admitting to making up a ghost," he asked, his eyes cold.

Jesus, am I in court? "What? No. Forget about Frank. Who told you I have ghosts?"

"You did!" he said, incredulous. "What the hell am I even doing here if you aren't trying to scam people with shitty ghost tales?"

I lurched back in my seat. I tried to be kind, telling myself he was a guest who held the future of my inn in his fingertips. But this was the last thing I needed to be told today. "Scam people? Is that what you're all doing here? You've come to crucify me on the internet by telling the world that I'm *scamming* people?"

He ran a hand down his face. "Shit, I'm sorry, I didn't mean to say that. I'm sure you really believe you're bringing people here to see actual ghosts."

"What the hell are you talking about, Mr. Jones? Look, when your guy Ben called me, asking to poke around a bit, I said fine because I thought, no harm no foul. But I'll be damned if you and your cronies are going to come here and try to scare off my customers by screaming 'ghost,' and I'm certainly not going to stand around while you accuse me of scamming my customers!"

I felt the blood rush to my face as I stood and prepared to walk away from this asshole. *What the hell had I gotten myself into by letting these clowns run rampant in my inn?*

"What do you mean, Ben called *you*?" he asked, shuffling quickly to follow me. I was annoyed at myself when I turned around and caught a sniff of him. Ink and leather and pure man scent. He gave me a strange look, and I prayed he hadn't noticed me sniffing him. I spun on my heels, doubly annoyed now.

"Talk to your boss, Mr. Jones," I called over my shoulder on my way out. "I've got some errands to run."

I walked out of the kitchen with my hands balled into fists and walked promptly over to the desk where Maggie was hunched over the computer with her face scrunched in concentration.

"No," I said, without waiting to explain.

Maggie pulled her face up from the screen. "Huh?"

"No, this ghost hunting thing isn't going to work out."

"Harley," she started, but I cut her off.

"Maggie, that guy Ben sent here just accused me of scamming people to bring them to my inn. He basically said I was making up ghost stories to give them an excuse to come here. So he thinks I'm a conman *and* a liar."

"He did *what*?" she asked, lips thinning in anger.

"We have a hard enough time keeping our doors open as it is. If those guys go on the internet and blast the inn, I'm going to be lucky if I have enough time to sell the building before going bankrupt."

Maggie held her hands up. "Harley, I will talk to Ben."

"I don't want them here. They're going to ruin everything I worked so hard on." I tried to blink back the tears. I hated crying. It was a wasted action and accomplished nothing.

"Or they could save everything you worked so hard on. Just let me talk to Ben and make sure we're on the same page, okay?"

I sighed and reluctantly nodded. "Fine, but if I get one whiff that they're out to ruin us, they're out." She nodded, and I looked at the screen she had been so focused on. "What are you working on?"

"I'm doing a social media deep-dive on the three groups that canceled their meeting rooms here."

"Mags, I really can't afford bail money, so please tell me you aren't planning something crazy."

She waved me off. "Nothing like that," she said. Then lowered her voice and mumbled, "yet." I raised an eyebrow at her, and she continued. "Don't you find it strange that these businesses are booking with you then canceling almost right away because something better came along? It might have been a coincidence the first two times, but maybe not anymore."

I sat down behind the desk with her and groaned. I had a grumpy ghost hunter in my kitchen who smelled really nice but was probably trying to ruin me, and now I had some sneaky saboteur trying to sink my business. Or maybe I was the problem all along. I didn't get into the habit of blaming others for my problems, and I wasn't about to start now.

"I hate to think the worst of people, but if you find something just let me know."

Maggie nodded, straightened her "Employee of the Month" trophy, and started typing. I cast one more glance towards the kitchen where Malcolm Jones was and turned on my heel to look up plumbing tutorials.

Chapter Four

Phone-a-Friend

Malcolm

What in the actual fuck just happened?

I turned off my recorder, shoved my notebook in my bag, and sat back down at the breakfast nook. Pulling out my phone, I called the only guy who could tell me what just went down.

"You got something already?" Ben asked as he answered the phone.

"You wanna explain to me what I'm doing here?" I asked, blood boiling to the surface. It wasn't often that I got pissed off—well, okay, I wasn't exactly the epitome of chill, but I didn't get mad often—but nothing ground my gears like not knowing what's happening around me.

"Malcolm, my man, what are any of us doing here?"

"Don't give me that philosophical bullshit, Ben. I just got finished with a really interesting interview with the owner of this B&B who says that *you* called *her* asking for us to come here and seemed genuinely surprised when I asked her what ghost scenario she was using to lure her customers here. Also, she thinks you're my boss, but I guess that's not as important."

"Fuck, Malcolm, I specifically told you not to be a prick to her."

"Who said I was a prick?"

"You did, like five seconds ago, ass hat." Ben sighed into the phone. "I was the one who called asking to do the Halloween special there. Harley's sister Maggie used to date my brother. She'd seen some of our YouTube episodes and reached out to tell me about the town. She mentioned in her emails that the inn wasn't doing as hot as Harley wanted it to, so I volunteered to have us come scope it out for the channel."

"Jesus Christ, Ben. You didn't think to tell me anything of this before I made an ass of myself?"

"You making an ass of yourself is totally on you, and you fuckin' know it. I told you to be on your best behavior and to treat this like any other case where you do the research. Nobody told you to go in guns blazing accusing our gracious host of being a crook."

Damn. I wasn't sure if I was more pissed off that I screwed the pooch or that Ben called me on it.

"Just tell me, how bad was it? Am I going to be coming into a war zone?" he asked.

I sighed and ran my hands over my face. "It's two weeks before you're here. I'll fix it by then."

"Good, do that. And besides, the B&B is ancient, and the town is too. Use that big research brain of yours to find something interesting. I'm sure there's something we can use when we film."

"Ugh, fine."

"It's Halloween, baby!" Ben hollered into the phone before hanging up.

He was an idiot sometimes but damned if I could find a better guy to work with. I, on the other hand, am probably the worst guy to work with. I tucked my phone in my pocket before slowly pushing the door open to the lobby area. Harley wasn't behind the desk, but based on the glare that her sister Maggie shot my way, I guessed she had been through there. I took the coward's way out and simply went up the stairs to my room. I consulted my list to take a new approach to the research.

Normally, we would go into a place that a person claimed had "haunting" activity. Ben would get excited. I would call bullshit. The crew would take some spooky shots while I did background research on the location to give them some information on any deaths. Then, Ben would use that information as fuel to jump at shadows and all that other crap. It was a concise formula, one that got millions of views on the internet and paid my paychecks.

But if Harley wasn't going to claim a haunting, we were going to need a new approach. I scribbled out the old list that mostly consisted of burrowing into Harley's mind when I interviewed her. I flipped the page and scratched out a new list.

1. Apologize to Harley.
2. Dig up info on building origins.
3. Get info on town history. Historical society?
4. Find local bakery.
5. Type up information.

I set the pen down and read through my list. Apologizing to Harley had to be done first, otherwise, my stay here was going to be awkward as hell. The memory of her green eyes widening in shock when I tried to interview her made me wince. Just for verification, and to see how much of an apology I was going to need, I pulled out my recorder, rewound it, and listened through our conversation. The sound of the recorder turning on came over the speakers followed by the sound of my own hollow voice.

"So, you're admitting to making up a ghost."
"What? No. Forget about Frank. Who told you I have ghosts?"

"You did! What the hell am I even doing here if you aren't trying to scam people with shitty ghost tales?"

"Scam people? Is that what you're all doing here? You've come to crucify me on the internet by telling the world that I'm scamming people?"

"Shit, I'm sorry, I didn't mean to say that. I'm sure you really believe you're bringing people here to see actual ghosts."

"What the hell are you talking about, Mr. Jones? Look, when your guy Ben called me, asking to poke around a bit, I said fine because I thought, no harm no foul. But I'll be damned if you and your cronies are going to come here and try to scare off my customers by screaming 'ghost,' and I'm certainly not going to stand around while you accuse me of scamming my customers!"

I listened as the recording ended and put my head in my hands. Fuck, I was really an ass to her. This was going to need to be some apology if I was going to get any of her help. I had stupidly forgotten that she was also my contact with the area's historical society.

I ran it through in my mind again. Did she sniff me before she stormed out? I didn't know what to make of that. But I do remember that I wanted to smell her too. God, I was a mess.

Drumming my fingers on the desk, I picked up my phone and dialed the one guy on the team who knew women better than anyone.

"Malc, I thought I wasn't gonna hear from you for another two weeks," Davis said, his cool voice damn near lulling me to sleep over the airways. Davis was one of the five other crew members of *Spirits, Seekers, and Skeptics*. When he was on location, he manned all of the sound equipment with the utmost professionalism you would expect from an ex-Hollywood movie sound producer. When he was off location, however, he was using that Hollywood charm to talk his way into the pants of any single woman around.

"I need apology ideas," I grumbled.

"You mean, aside from saying 'I'm sorry?'"

"Yeah, a little more impressive than I'm sorry."

I could practically hear him smirking over the phone. "For a woman?"

I scowled. "Obviously. I wouldn't have to pull out all the damn stops if it was a dude. I'd just buy him a beer and let him razz me a bit."

Davis laughed. "How bad of a fuck up was it?"

"Pretty bad."

"Did you sleep with her?"

A vision of Harley sprawled across the plush blue comforter in my room, a finger crooked beckoning me closer flashed through my mind. "What? No, I didn't sleep with her."

"Ooh, but you want to."

"Will you just tell me what I need to do? Preferably without being a dick in the process."

"Well, you could always do flowers, those are the go-to. You could also do wine but make sure she's not a recovering alcoholic first, otherwise, trust me, that ends badly."

I quirked an eyebrow, wondering how many apologies this guy has had to come up with over the years.

"You could also offer to take her somewhere," he continued, "like an apology lunch or dinner. Then you can pull some smooth moves and turn it into a date."

"I don't need a date; I need access to the town's historical society."

"You need to have some fun, especially if you're going to be there for a whole month."

"Yeah, I'll take that under advisement."

"Is she hot?" he asked. Irritation rose in my chest from nowhere.

"She's not a baked potato; she's a woman," I snarled. "But yes, she's...pretty."

"Awesome. If you don't make a move, I'll be sure to give her some comfort when I roll into town."

A wave of jealousy that I had no right to rolled through my stomach. "She's not your kind of girl, Davis."

"If she has the right equipment between her legs, no wedding band, and she's of age, she's my kind of girl, Malc," he said. I pulled the phone away from my ear and gave it the finger.

"I'm hanging up now," I said. Not waiting for a response, I hung up the phone and looked up florists in the area. I'd figure it out in the morning. The growling in my stomach had no plans to go away and after a seven-hour drive from the last film site in Massachusetts, I was going to need a cheap meal, a long shower, and a deep sleep before I tackled today's screw-ups.

The next morning, I went downstairs for breakfast at eight-thirty on the dot. The card on the side table in my room stated breakfast was served in the dining room downstairs at eight sharp each morning, and after yesterday's brush with stupidity, I figured Harley wouldn't take it well if I showed up late to the breakfast she made. Also, I'd be lying if I said I didn't change my shirt twice, as if Harley would only listen to my apology if I was wearing gray instead of blue.

When I made it down to the dining room, I faltered in the doorway when I saw Maggie at the table, and Harley nowhere in sight.

"Where's Harley?" I blurted out.

"Good morning to you too, Mr. Jones," Maggie said, her blonde eyebrow quirked.

"Oh, um, Malcolm is fine. Good morning. Sorry about that. I'm a little flustered this morning."

"Mm. To answer your question, Harley is busy avoiding you."

"I see," I said.

Maggie passed me the pastries and pot of coffee in silence while she looked at her phone. After a few moments, I cleared my throat.

"Can I help you?" she asked, not looking up from her phone. I was beginning to think Harley told her everything I had said yesterday. I hadn't known that Maggie and Ben were old friends, but now I felt like an even worse asshole.

"I...uh...need to know what kind of flowers Harley likes."

Maggie once again raised an eyebrow behind her glasses as she looked my way. Tucking her phone in her pocket, she reached for her coffee. "Why do you need to know?"

Of course, I had to ask the leader of the inquisition this question. I probably should have just grabbed a pre-done flower arrangement, but something told me that wouldn't go over too well.

"As I'm sure you've heard, I was kind of an ass to her, and I need to apologize."

She looked me up and down for a long moment, not bothering to hide her obvious evaluation. "Harley filled me in on your...conversation. But before I tell you anything, I need to know, are you a good guy or a bad guy?"

"Um...what?" I shook my head at the question that came out of left field.

"It's not a hard question, are you good guy or a bad guy?"

"I mean, I guess I try to be a good guy. Hence, the flower question."

She paused as she weighed my answer. "She doesn't like flowers. The way to get on her good side is pastries." I looked down at the pastries on the table and Maggie shook her head, rolling her eyes. "Pastries she doesn't have to slave over. Take her out for pastries, and she'll probably forgive you in a heartbeat. But don't tell her I told you that. I just need her to stop avoiding you because I have better things to do with my mornings than to have awkward breakfasts with her guests."

I pondered that for a moment and nodded. She was right; this was awkward. "Do you know where she went?"

"Yeah, she went to the pumpkin patch out back," she said with a wave toward a door leading outside, abandoning her sisterly loyalty before downing the last of her coffee and walking out of the dining room.

I braced myself for the upcoming apology, but I figured I shouldn't do it on an empty stomach. I grabbed the pot of coffee and an up-turned mug and filled it nearly to the brim. Pastries littered the table with different toppings and icings swirled on them. I had seen Harley making them in the kitchen the day before and even then my mouth was watering. I grabbed one that was puffy with some sort of yellow dollop on top and bit into it. Lemon and crème flooded my senses as buttery dough melted over my tongue. I moaned louder than a man not in the throes of sex should.

The universe was cruel. How was I supposed to resist a woman as beautiful as Harley who also was a damn good baker? It was downright unfair. I tried to remind myself that she, like her bed and breakfast, was a subject to study, and I needed to be professional. But when another bite of her pastry went down my throat, I began to wonder what that lemon crème would taste like with me licking it off her skin. Mental flashes of her sprawled out on her kitchen island popped up faster than I could stop them. Unfortunately, the same could be said of my dick.

God, even when the woman wasn't in the same room as me, she was infuriating.

I shoved the pastry violently in my mouth, threw the scorching hot coffee down after, then forced myself to head outside.

Chapter Five

Professional Airs

Harley

The sound of vines and dust from stiff dirt stirring underfoot turned my head toward the inn. Malcolm Jones, gatekeeper to the world of hauntings and self-proclaimed charlatan police, stood unfairly attractive in a gray button-down over jeans that seemed to hug his hips like a woman's grasp. I tried to ignore the fact that my knees were coated in dirt from playing with pumpkins all morning. The pumpkins really didn't need any attention, but I needed Maggie to believe they were in dire straits if she was going to take over for me this morning.

Apparently the guilt I was harboring for putting Maggie between Detective Ghost Buster and me was for nothing, since it seems that she sold me out.

'Employee of the Month,' my ass.

"Hey, Harley, do you have a minute?" he asked, edging closer and rubbing the back of his neck. A flush crept up my neck when his shirt lifted, revealing a toned stomach. I looked away for my own sanity, standing to brush the dirt off my knees.

"Sorry, I'm a bit busy setting up Ouija boards and lighting candles for seances."

He rocked back on his heels, his hands shoved in his pockets. "Yeah, I probably deserved that."

I snorted in a way that was probably unladylike. "What do you need, Mr. Jones?"

"Please, call me Malcolm." I raised my eyebrow at the nerve of him. "I was wondering if you happened to know where I might find a decent bakery in town and if you would also like to accompany me to it."

I stared at him, trying to pick my jaw off the floor. "You want me to take you to a bakery."

"No, *I* want to take *you* to a bakery," he said. "I owe you an apology for what I said yesterday, and I thought baked goods said, 'I'm sorry' better than words."

I pondered this. "Well, start with words, and I'll see about the food."

He nodded, and the expression that came over his face seemed to be genuine in its remorse. "Harley, I'm sorry for accusing you of scamming people to get guests. I didn't know that Ben had reached out to you. Normally, when we get called to a business to do an episode on it, the place is just a tourist trap, and they call us there to help them bring in revenue. There are some greedy people who will tell patrons just about anything for the almighty dollar, and I'm sorry that I ever thought you were one of them."

I waited a moment, weighing the words before nodding. "And this apology has nothing to do with the fact that I'm the contact you need at the historical society?"

I was pushing my luck, and I knew it, but I liked pushing his buttons.

He smiled at me, and it took the wind right out of me. "You really would have made a killer reporter. But no, despite the fact that it would be helpful to have you in my corner with the historical society, my apology to you is genuine."

"Thank you for saying that. I forgive you, but mostly because Trick or Treat has some killer blueberry scones."

"Wait a minute, '*Trick or Treat*?'"

"Yeah, cool name, right? There was actually a huge conflict a few years back because a new spa wanted to open named *Trick or Treat Yo' Self* but it was too similar, so they had to settle for Burnt Creek Spa."

"Man...this town." This earned him a smile.

Mr. Jones, or *Malcolm* as he wanted me to call him, walked me inside to let me get changed before leading me outside to his car, a luxury black sedan with tinted windows. I raised my eyebrows at him.

"What?" he asked.

"I didn't realize ghost hunting paid so well," I answered honestly. He laughed, and the sound of it tore through the air and landed squarely in my chest.

"You'd be surprised," he said as he walked to the passenger side of the car. He leaned over and opened the door for me, the smell of leather and ink making an appearance in my nostrils. I smiled at him and sank into the car to escape the intoxication. No sense in getting attached to this gorgeous man. He was temporary, he was a guest, and he was kind of a jerk.

Yeah, keep telling yourself that.

But trying to get away from his aroma didn't work so well when I sank into the car that screamed of opulence and smelled just like him. He closed my door, effectively sealing me in with his enchanting scent. Instead of fighting it, I decided to indulge myself. As he walked around the car, I tried to discreetly lean onto the center console and sniff the driver's seat to figure out what hair gel or body soap he used. I jumped back and looked out my window as he opened his door.

Sinking down behind the steering wheel, I could feel his gaze on me. When I glanced over at him, a self-righteous smirk graced his face.

"What?" I asked him. His smirk blossomed into a full smile.

"You could just ask me, you know," he said, humor dancing in his eyes. Even through the tinted windows, his honey hair seemed to light up in the daylight. It gave him the renegade look under all the sexy nerd vibrations he gave out. My eyes scanned down and locked with his, nearly stealing my breath. *Wait, did he ask me something?*

"Sorry?" I asked softly, wondering where my voice went.

He chuckled. "I saw you smelling my seat. That, paired with the sniffing you were doing in the kitchen yesterday makes me think you want to figure out what I smell like."

Could a person die from embarrassment? Asking for a friend.

"I wasn't—I don't—" My face felt like a million degrees.

"It's that inquisitive side of you, Harley. You've just gotta know, don't you? Go ahead, ask."

He waited, drumming his fingers on the steering wheel with a smirk.

I took a deep breath, hating him for being so smug, and hating myself for being so curious. "Ugh, fine. You smell like leather and ink and something else and it's been really annoying me. Since you have a tendency to annoy me, I think it's par for the course."

He laughed, his voice carrying through the car as he started the engine and pulled out of the driveway. "Glad to know I have such an impact."

"I didn't say that," I protested.

"You didn't have to," he said, his grin still splitting his face. "It's probably old books that you're smelling. I spend a lot of time in libraries and records rooms doing research. Paper breaks down over time, the age of the paper gives it different scents."

I nodded, forcing my tongue to untie. "That explains why you smell like an antique. I was starting to think you might be a vampire."

He laughed again. I was starting to enjoy how free he was with his laughter. Most guys tried to look cool and sophisticated, not allowing themselves to just feel joy.

"Not a vampire," he said, directing my attention to the road. "Which way am I going?"

I directed him back toward town. The town was filled with its usual suspects this time of day, a few day tourists checking out the shops, a few locals grabbing a bite to eat, and a few senior citizens sitting on benches looking for fresh gossip. Pulling up in front of the bakery with its classic black awning and white block font, we got out, and I led him inside.

The interior of Trick or Treat was modeled after a Parisian bakery, giving a nod to the French Quarter of New Orleans where Jaynie, the owner, came from. Small tables and chairs sat on brick flooring, a clear display case showed colorful macarons, cupcakes with flavored frosting, and scones with fresh berries. The familiar scent of warm sugar surrounded me, and I breathed in the smell of my happy place.

"Harley!" A voice called from behind the counter. "I've been wondering if you forgot about us!"

Jaynie emerged from the kitchen, the white flour coating her arms in stark contrast to her deep brown skin. She maneuvered her curvy body with the grace of a dancer around massive mixers.

"I haven't forgotten about you; I've been trying out baking myself to save some money at the inn."

"Good for you, traitor," she said with a smile. "And who is this handsome fella?"

"Malcolm Jones, meet Jaynie Romero. Mr. Jones is in town for a bit doing research for a YouTube channel."

"Please, call me Malcolm," he said with a smile. "I keep telling Harley to, but she's hellbent on keeping it formal."

I rolled my eyes. Jaynie shot me a knowing glance.

"It's because she finds you attractive," Jaynie stated matter-of-factly.

"Is that right?" Malcolm asked, cocking his head at me with a smile.

I shook my head, but I could feel the traitorous blush coming up. "Nope."

Jaynie tossed her head back and cackled, working her way over to an oven that just beeped. "Look at your vanilla skin getting all red like a cherry!" She pulled out a baking sheet from the oven and slid the baking sheet on a cooling rack and turned back to them, addressing Malcolm.

"She does this every time she's sweet on someone, thinking that if she keeps up 'professional airs' that she won't get too attached."

"Okay, your friendship has been revoked," I stated resolutely. "I brought Mr. Jo—*Malcolm* here to try some of your blueberry scones and maybe some of your beignets, but if you're too busy spouting off gossip..."

I got a knowing look from Jaynie. "I ain't too busy, but if you're revoking my friendship, I'm revoking your friendship discount."

"Ugh, fine, friends for life. But you're on thin ice, missy."

She laughed again and turned to pull some fresh beignets out of the fryer. After piling the sweets coated in powdered sugar onto plates, pouring an apple cider for me and another coffee for Malcolm, and Malcolm insisting on paying, we settled into a small booth in the corner.

"So, tell me, *Malcolm*," I started, enunciating my informal use of his name while I dipped a beignet into raspberry sauce. "How does one get into ghost hunting? It's not a profession you see every day."

He smiled. "No, it's not. I actually used to work in New York at one of the major newspaper conglomerates. I started off in research and worked my way up. By the time I left, I was one of the leading editors gunning for Editor-in-Chief. I grew up with Ben, the one you talked to on the phone, and when things went south at the newspaper, we teamed up to make the Spirits Channel."

I studied him for a moment, wondering how far to push my questions. "Why not go work at another newspaper? New York is filled to the brim with them."

He sighed, rubbing one hand down the scruff on his chin. "There's a lot of politics in newspapers of that size, especially in New York where the competition is so stiff. I had offers, quite a few of them honestly. But I needed to get out of that world for a while."

"For a while..." I said slowly. "So, you're thinking of going back?"

He cracked a grin. "Anyone ever tell you you'd make a damn good reporter?"

"Anyone ever tell you that your deflection skills could use some work?" I shot back with a grin of my own.

He laughed. "Okay, okay. The truth is, I have a standing offer to come back if I chose to. And I don't know if you noticed, but I'm sort of the skeptic on the ghost-hunting team."

"You don't say," I said wryly.

"It's true," he said with a smirk of his own. "It's just...complicated. Ben could manage without me, and the job I've got back there is nothing to turn my nose up at, but I feel like this business with Ben is something I've helped build. I like the idea of building something of my own instead of being another cog in a machine."

I nodded, thinking it over.

"But enough about me," he said, rubbing the powdered sugar off his hands. "Tell me all about Harley Malone, the infamous owner of the town's B&B."

I laughed and tipped my head. "Well, there's not much to tell, I'm afraid. I went to college for hospitality and tourism management. I've always wanted to work in hotels, much to my mother's annoyance. I interned with the Monterey Hotel Group and decided to open an inn of my own. So, I saved up and bought the B&B when it was in awful condition and fixed it up, and here we are."

"Huh, you're right, totally boring."

"Hey!" I said with a chuckle.

"No, that's actually really impressive. You're not even thirty yet and you've built your business from the ground up."

I shrugged. "I guess I haven't thought of it like that. I've been so busy trying to figure everything out, reach for the next milestone and all that. I guess I forget how far along it is."

"Your mom's not supportive of the hotel life?" he asked.

I dipped my head a teensy bit. "She's supportive, I guess, in some ways. She's always valued ambition. She and my dad got divorced because he wasn't moving up the chain at his job as fast as she wanted. When I was interning at Monterey Hotel Group, she thought I would climb the ladder and get into management. When I turned away from that to explore something of my own, especially something that might not be as lucrative...I think she feels like I'm a failure. Lately, I have a hard time thinking she's wrong."

"Can I ask something?"

"Shoot."

Malcolm looked like he was trying to figure out the best way to ask his question without offending me. "Your inn is the only hotel in miles, and it's gorgeous, but yesterday Ben said that you've been struggling to keep it filled. How is that possible?"

I sighed, familiar frustration running through me. "Nobody knows that it's here. I took some bad advice about where to allocate my money when I was building the business, so now my budget for advertising has dried up. But on the upside, I've got a killer movie room for my imaginary guests. Plus, I keep meeting resistance for hosting town gatherings and the like there because my ex's family is influential and people are worried about choosing a 'side,'" I said with an eye roll. "And recently I've been getting a number of reservations for small groups to use our conference room, only for them to cancel within the week. Maggie's looking into why that keeps happening, but it's so frustrating."

"Well," he said, seeming to sort through all of the information I word-vomited. "I, for one, am thrilled you have a movie room. I'm a sucker for a good movie night."

"What kind of movies?" I asked.

"Horror, mostly vampire flicks. You know, because I'm a *sucker* for them?"

I paused. "That was the best worst joke I've ever heard, and I live in the town of perpetual pun names."

"I aim to please," he said with a laugh.

"Well, I happen to hold a black belt in popcorn making. Maybe the next time Valerie, my mom, comes over for a movie night, I'll bribe you to act as a buffer."

"It's a date," he said. The twinkle in his eye left me wondering if it was just a saying or if he actually meant it.

Chapter Six

Spit-takes and Handshakes

Malcolm

How is it possible that an apology pastry has turned into what feels like a date? And why am I not upset about it? Maybe Davis really does know what he's talking about, even though taking his advice was the result of an accident. As I held the door of the bakery open for Harley, I caught a whiff of her perfume, the smell of wildflowers and honey. I suddenly realized why she was so obsessed with how I smelled. I could get high from the scent of her hair alone.

When she invited me to act as a buffer between her and her mom, I hadn't meant to insinuate a date would come of it. But at the time, the only thing I could think of was having this curious, funny woman alone with me on a date. As she stepped into the daylight, a smattering of light freckles I hadn't noticed before danced across her nose, barely visible. As she smiled, they rearranged on her cheeks like wayward constellations.

"Harley!" A woman called from behind us as we stepped out onto the street. I broke out of my study of Harley's face when I heard her curse quietly. As we turned to look at the object of Harley's frustration, I saw an older woman carrying a shopping bag next to a man closer to Harley's and my age. The woman had Harley's same brown hair that the wind had carried out of her secured bun, and she waved with the shopping bag in her hand like a debutant on a parade float.

The younger guy held a smug smile and wore an outfit that looked freshly ironed and a pair of shiny black shoes. I didn't know what it was about guys who wore shiny shoes, but I just didn't trust them.

"Mom, hi," Harley said with a smile at the debutant, but I noticed a vein ticking near her temple. "What brings you out on the town?"

I found myself straightening up unexpectedly. I've never been nervous about meeting a woman's parents before, not that there had been a lot of that in my life. But I suddenly felt the strangest desire to impress Harley's mom. Harley's mom looped a free arm around the man affectionately, and I felt Harley tense beside me.

"Connor was just taking me shopping for the day. Isn't he the sweetest?" she crooned.

"He's something," Harley snarled under her breath, her hand gripping her cup of apple cider tighter. The smug smile that cascaded over Connor's face reminded me of a sports fan whose team had won by cheating. It slipped slightly into more of a scowl when he looked my way.

"Who's your friend, Harley?" Connor growled; his arm still wrapped by Harley's mother. Harley tensed again before a smile overtook her face. I watched as a mischievous glint took her eye, and she wrapped her free hand around my arm, mirroring her mother and Connor's movements.

"This is Malcolm Jones," she said, nearly reverently. I wasn't sure what dynamic I had walked into, but I sure wasn't going to complain at the warmth radiating off Harley. It certainly was better than the icy distance I had gotten when I put my foot in my mouth at the interview yesterday. And as much as I didn't want to admit it, I'd sell the clothes off my back if I could get Harley Malone to look at me like that every day.

Instead, I extended my hand toward Harley's mom as Harley took a drink. "Nice to meet you. You must be Valerie. I've heard a lot about you," I said with a smile, only lying trivially. She took her hand out of Connor's arm and politely shook my hand. I extended my hand toward Connor even though I wasn't sure I wanted this smarmy guy to shake it.

"And Connor," I said, searching my mind for the right words to say as Connor gripped my hand tightly in a show of macho. It was near bone-crushing, but aside from a raised eyebrow, I wasn't going to give him the satisfaction of reacting. He was shorter than I am, something I didn't normally notice, but at this moment I gained immense satisfaction from. "It's nice to meet you. I'm still learning the ropes here; Harley didn't mention Valerie dating anyone."

Beside me, Harley sprayed hot apple cider out her mouth in a spit-take that would rival Hollywood. The liquid shot through the air and coated the front of Connor's much-too-expensive pants. Connor yanked his hand back from me like it had been burned, and Valerie's cheeks tinged red. I handed Harley a napkin from my bakery bag and watched as she wiped her chin with a smile that I hoped would never go away. I didn't bother giving one to Connor. I didn't like his vibe, and it's not like one measly napkin was going to do much against the rendition of the exorcist Harley just gave his wardrobe.

"Oh, no," Valerie said, waving me off. "I'm not dating anyone. Connor and Harley are dating."

My eyebrows furrowed as I looked at Harley. If she told me she was dating this dude, I may spit my drink out, too.

"Nope," Harley said with a shake of her head, fisting the used napkin. "No, we are not."

Connor's eyes lit with fire as he redirected his gaze toward me. "We're high school sweethearts. One of those on-again-off-again kinds of things."

"They're just meant to be," Valerie chirped with a wistful smile.

Something churned in my stomach about the idea of Harley having ever dated this guy, much less being "meant to be" with him. It seemed I wouldn't have to worry though as I noticed anger radiating off Harley as her hand shook. She redirected her attention toward me, where I selfishly felt it better belonged. "Connor and I dated in high school. We broke up *once* in high school, got back together *once* after graduation, and haven't dated in years. So, we're not an on-again-off-again kind of *thing*. We're not any kind of *thing*."

Warmth and relief spread through me, followed by confusion on why her testament made me so damn happy.

"Harley," Valerie scolded, putting her shopping bag fist on her hip. "That's enough."

"Exactly my thought," Harley said sharply. "This has gone on long enough."

"Valerie was just inviting me to family dinner on Saturday," Connor added quickly, nearly talking over Harley. "I'm looking forward to spending time with you."

Like hell, I nearly growled.

Harley's lips formed a line as she glared at her mother but tipped up on the side after a moment. "That's nice, but I'll be pretty distracted. You see, Dad and Miranda are going to be there this Saturday, and I haven't seen them in a bit."

I watched as the color drained from Valerie's face. "Why would your father and that woman be there, at *family* dinner, Harley?"

"Well, up until now I've resisted inviting them because I thought inviting your ex to a family function, despite him being *my* family, might make you uncomfortable. But now that you'll have Connor to keep you company, I think you'll be just fine."

Valerie sputtered on her words and looked up at Connor to say something.

As I watched Connor go from angry to cocky as he wrapped his arm around Valerie's shoulder in a comforting way, something snapped inside me. As proud as I was that Harley stood up for herself, were they really just going to ignore that Harley didn't want to be with this guy? I wrapped my own arm around Harley's shoulders in a move that widened the eyes across from them. I felt Harley tense beneath me for just a moment before her shoulders loosened. I dragged my lips down near her ears while I tried to fight how good it felt to act this intimate with her.

"Baby, relax," I said lovingly in a voice loud enough that Connor and Valerie could hear me. I felt Harley shiver beneath my lips and a jolt of electricity went beneath my belt. "Let them have their day. I promised you a movie night, remember? And you promised to make your special popcorn."

I could feel the anger exuding from Connor and something like confusion from Valerie, but my only focus was Harley. This gorgeous, spunky woman. I was stepping way out of line here, but I hoped that Harley would wait to deck me until after the peanut gallery was gone.

After a beat, I felt Harley twist her body into me until our faces were merely inches apart. She moved so smoothly it was as if we did this every day. I could feel her breath on my chin as she wrapped her arm around my waist. "Does that mean I get to pick the movie this time? I know how much you love your sappy rom-coms, but I'm feeling an action flick."

A chuckle broke from my throat. This girl was a spitfire, and I loved it. "Action flick it is." I tested my luck further by kissing her forehead, her skin soft beneath my lips, before turning back toward the two people I wanted away from Harley. Connor's hand was a fist at his side and his eyes narrowed. Valerie just looked bewildered.

"Well, it was nice meeting you both, but Harley and I have plans."

"See you Saturday," Harley said with a bit of cheer and a wiggle of her eyebrows. "But give me a call, Mom. Maybe we can set up a double date before then."

As Harley pulled from my embrace, she wove her fingers through mine and guided me back to the car holding my hand. Though I could feel the weight of the stares on my back, I noted the smile bursting on Harley's face and felt like no matter the consequences, this would be a win.

As we drove away from the main street of Burnt Creek in silence, I chanced a few glances at Harley. Was she mad at me for insinuating that we were dating? Was she missing Connor? That thought alone made me cringe. Her quiet words broke me from my thoughts.

"Thank you for stepping in back there," she said, still looking out the window.

"Thank God, I thought you were going to be super pissed at me for that."

She laughed, and the sound shot relief through my body like nothing else I've ever experienced. I didn't know what it was about this woman that made me want to chase away her shadows, but hearing her laugh because of me, after she was so stressed, was a high I could ride for life.

"Not pissed, no," she said, finally looking at me with a grin. "Although I did sort of dig myself a hole. My dad and his wife will have no problem coming to family dinner, but now I'm going to have to explain that you and I aren't actually dating when you don't show up."

I rubbed the back of my neck as I put the blinker on to head down the road to the inn. "Well, here's an idea—and I'm just spitballing here—but why don't I come with you?" I said, glancing at her out of the corner of my eye.

"To family dinner?"

"I mean, I don't know how sacred family dinners are, but I assume they can't be that exclusive if that douchebag Connor is going to be there." I nearly growled his name and a giggle escaped Harley.

"You didn't like him, huh?"

"Honestly, I'm a little floored that *you* liked him at one time. The guy seems like a total tool."

"Yeah, I'm not super proud of that one," she admitted. "Honestly, if you're really offering to stand in as a buffer for me at family dinner, I would absolutely take you up on it. But only if you mean it."

"Oh absolutely," I said, surprised at how excited I was to make sure Connor kept his distance. "But I need to make sure before I go in there defending your honor and all that shit that you don't actually still have feelings for this guy. Because I don't want to get in the way if you want to be the future Mrs. Sleaze Ball."

"Yeah, no. No feelings for him, no future with him. I just want him out of my life."

I nodded, pulling into the parking lot of the inn, nodding toward the building. "Okay, how about this: I'll be your pretend love interest at family dinner if you save me some research time by giving me a tour of the inn and telling me about the history."

"It's a deal."

After Harley spent some time prepping the next day's breakfast, we met up in front of the main entrance of her inn to start the tour. I only had my notebook, not needing to have a word-by-word playback that the recorder would provide. Harley had pulled her hair up on top of her head, giving me a front-row seat to the delicate curves of her neck, something I never found particularly interesting in anyone else.

Hell, maybe I am becoming a vampire.

"Okay, so the history of the inn," she started, snapping me out of my reverie and walking me through to the sitting room as if she was leading a tour at the White House. "The Burnt Creek Inn was built in 1892 and is the oldest building in the county. It was originally the hotel and tavern, serving people passing through from Baltimore and Catonsville down to Annapolis, as well as the local population who settled here. It was pretty successful, especially when the local population started thriving in wheat production," Harley paused, cocking an eyebrow at me. "But the part that *you're* going to be interested in happened in 1926."

I leaned in to see the picture that she had walked toward on the wall, surrounded by various old documents and records framed up neatly. A proud, robust man with slicked-back hair and a thin mustache posed for a picture in front of the inn. The front porch was still in place and the inn looked nearly the same now as it did back then. It was hard not to feel proud of Harley's ability to maintain the past during her renovations.

"Who is this?" I asked, jotting down some notes.

"This is Elias Johnson. He was the owner of the inn and tavern back in the twenties after inheriting it from his father in 1916. However, he didn't count on prohibition happening when he took over the business. Maryland, as a whole, had mixed responses to prohibition, but in Burnt Creek they didn't really enforce the laws against consuming alcohol. However, they didn't like people making their own alcohol, something about people going blind."

I raised my eyebrows at this. Harley just shrugged. "Some people were dedicated to drinking. Anyways, Elias couldn't get alcohol shipped in anymore and he wasn't supposed to make his own, so he told people that he found a supplier of moonshine and started serving that. In fact, he was making it himself in the basement."

"People had no idea he was making it himself?"

"Oh, I'm pretty sure they suspected. I mean you couldn't get it anywhere without bootleggers which were expensive and dangerous. But as long as they didn't see it happening, people didn't care. That was, until Jeremiah Little came to town."

"You should narrate documentaries. You have a gift for cliffhangers."

"Shut up," she laughed. "Keep writing your notes, ghost hunter. This is where it gets interesting." Harley wiggled her fingers together in excitement and her genuine joy around the history of this inn was so endearing.

"Jeremiah Little," she explained, "was a preacher who had come from a nearby town. He had heard of people still consuming alcohol out of the Burnt Creek Tavern and came out to have a little chat with Elias. He made a lot of threats, and Elias promptly threw him out. However, Jeremiah was a man of the faith and had this unshakable belief that alcohol was the entrance of sin into the lives of the people of Burnt Creek and the surrounding areas. So, he came to the tavern every single evening for months, berating Elias and guilting the patrons of the tavern until they left each night.

"Now, Elias was annoyed, sure, but it wasn't until Jeremiah went snooping in the basement and found Elias' operation where he was creating his own moonshine that events really took a turn. Jeremiah decided he was going to hold a town meeting revealing Elias' alcohol-making treachery, which would bring the feds down on the tiny town of Burnt Creek. But the night before the town meeting, Jeremiah disappeared."

I had to hand it to her, Harley knew how to tell a story. I waited for her to tell me the rest, but she just leaned forward with raised eyebrows looking so damn adorable, it was hard for me to ask her to keep going. "So, what happened?"

"Nobody knows," she finally said with a wistful voice that could rival Dorothy O'Neil. "There was never a body found, and no one had heard from the clergyman again. But everyone suspected that Elias had murdered poor Jeremiah Little, but nobody could prove it. No body, no crime, and all that. Instead, the people of the town were so conflicted about the idea that the innkeeper had murdered a man of the cloth that they decided that alcohol maybe *did* cause people to turn to sin. They stopped going to the tavern, travelers were warned away from the inn, and Elias eventually had to shut down. He tried to sell it at first, but everybody was convinced it was haunted by the ghost of Preacher Jeremiah Little, so no one would touch it. It became an abandoned building."

"Until you bought it."

"Yep, nearly a century later."

"Do you think that I could scan in some of these pictures and documents that you have hanging up for the channel?"

Harley laid a finger lovingly on one of the photographs. "Sure, just be careful with them. A lot of these are originals and the only ones in existence."

"From one researcher to another, I promise to take care of them." This earned me a smile, and damn if it didn't warm me to my bones.

Chapter Seven

A Friend Outing

Harley

Malcolm and I spent the next few hours sorting the articles, photos, and letters I had hanging up and another half-an-hour scanning the important ones. Every now and then he'd ask me a question that would launch me into an excited historical rant, but for the most part, we worked in quiet companionship.

When six o'clock snuck up on us, alerted only by my stomach loudly rumbling, I started hanging the framed articles back on the wall.

"It's getting kind of late," I said, toying with a frame against the wall to disguise my nervous energy. It had been a while since either of us had eaten anything, and we were both in the same location, so it made sense that if I was going to get food, he should come along, right?

Sure, keep telling yourself that, Harley.

I pushed the annoying voice out of my head. "I was thinking about heading out to the Witches' Brew for dinner, if you want to come with. I don't know if you've been there yet, but it's a great local place—good food, decent beer, and weird artwork."

I was still avoiding his gaze when he nudged my shoulder with his. "You had me at 'weird artwork.'"

I breathed a sigh of relief and turned to face him, only to find him grinning at me. I tried not to read too much into it, but my brain didn't want to listen. Did I just ask him on a date? Were we two friends hanging out? Or was I just an innkeeper showing a guest the local dives?

"My car or yours?" he asked. This was a much simpler question than the ones bouncing around in my mind.

"We can take mine," I said, grabbing my keys. We headed to my car, a Reliant Aries K that was manufactured in the late 1980s and was a gift from my dad when I was still in high school. It had the look of an old boxy police car, so I think he bought it out of nostalgia for his job. Malcolm knocked on the metal top of the gray car.

"I don't know if I've ever ridden in a car this old before," he marveled.

"Not old," I protested, stroking lovingly along the square frame of my door. "Vintage."

He slid inside and took in the pink plaid ceiling and covered seats. "Did the pink come standard?"

I laughed. "No, I remodeled it after I saw a bug crawl out of the old fabric. I couldn't get in my car for a few days, so I just stripped it all out."

I pulled out of the driveway, the car making a high-pitched squeal every time I turned my wheel far enough. Malcolm raised his eyebrows at me but wisely said nothing. As the speedometer hit forty-five, the engine started making a *thunk-thunk-thunk* noise. I turned the radio dial to the "on" position and raised the volume a notch to drown it out.

"Harley, I think something's going on with your car."

"Oh, that noise? You get used to it," I said with a nonchalant wave that I didn't fully feel. "Give it a few minutes and it just becomes white noise."

"When was the last time you got the oil changed?" he asked with a raised eyebrow.

"I don't really get it changed. I just add more oil to it when I remember."

Malcolm's mouth gaped open. "Harley, you've gotta get the oil changed."

"I will, it's just going to be a bit. I was going to get it done two weeks ago but the washing machine stopped working and my cousin tried to fix it but instead made it worse, so I had to buy a new one or else I wouldn't be able to wash the linens."

"And before that?"

"Before that I was going to fix it, but a pipe burst in room four and I had to pay Paul to come check the plumbing and replace that part of the floor."

"I see," he said, running his finger over his lip, probably to stop himself from telling me something I wouldn't want to hear.

The drive continued with the only sound being the radio and the thumps from the engine to fill the silence. Luckily, I pulled in front of Witches' Brew in time to secure a parking spot nearly right at the front. The brakes squealed loudly as I put the car in park. I didn't miss Malcolm's wince as he eyed the car that he probably thought was a death trap.

Witches' Brew was a bar and grille tucked along Main Street, sandwiched between Burnt Creek Insurance Company and Sweater Weather, a local outdoor clothing store. The outside looked non-descript to match the cheerful small-town street, but once inside, the entire vibe changed.

The doors opened to an assortment of tables on the left and a long bar to the right. Behind the bar were the usual bottles of liquor and a mirror, but flanking the mirror were rows of realistic-looking skulls embedded in the walls. A few well-placed fog-makers were set just under the bar top to make give the illusion of a cauldron. The effect was fun, spooky, and downright cool. I checked Malcolm's expression to find him equally impressed.

Artwork of varying degrees of strangeness hung all over the walls, with one section dedicated to black light art. My eyes gravitated as they always did to the painting tucked into the corner. It was a relatively normal painting compared to the artwork of skeleton dogs playing poker and a whole jack-o-lantern eating a pumpkin pie, but it always spoke to me.

A few locals were already lined up at the bar, so we grabbed a table against the wall. Before too long, a tall guy was handing us menus.

"Hey there, trouble," he said to me. I looked up to see my cousin Brandon wearing a black waist apron and a self-satisfied smirk.

"Whoa, you work here now?" I asked.

He shrugged. "Temporarily, just while Mom's getting back on her feet."

I turned to Malcolm. "Malcolm, this is my cousin, Brandon. My Aunt Charlotte usually works here but she broke her ankle doing..." I paused as I checked with Brandon. Aunt Charlotte is as wild as they come, and her exploits often landed her in hot water.

"She was trying to do yoga on a paddleboard," Brandon explained. Malcolm nodded as though it was a normal activity for those over the age of fifty to partake in. Brandon scanned Malcolm. "Is this the same guy I had to rescue you from last weekend? Because I gotta tell ya, he doesn't look like he'd ditch a girl for fast food on a first date."

"Oh, my God, shut up, Brandon," I gritted out.

Malcolm didn't seem to mind as he extended a hand. "Not the same guy, although we're gonna circle back to that," he said, chuckling. Brandon shook his hand.

"So is this a date, then?" Brandon asked, fishing his pen and paper from his pocket to take our orders. I cut my eyes over to Malcolm who was glancing at me before looking down at the menu with rapt attention. I was going to kill my cousin.

Instead of answering, I quickly scanned the list of bar drinks.

"Brandon, I'm gonna have the Poisoned Apple," I said, giving him my best "drop it" look. He grinned in response.

"Malcolm?" Brandon asked.

"Just a bourbon for me, thanks."

As Brandon scurried away from the table to fill our drink orders and avoid my burning glare, Malcolm shifted in his seat to give me his full attention.

"So, I noticed you didn't answer him," he said, wearing an earnest expression, but I caught a teasing glint in his eye.

"Hmm?" I pretended ignorance.

"He asked if this was a date, and you didn't answer."

"You noticed that, did you?" I asked nonchalantly, pretending to read the menu that I'd practically memorized. "And how would you classify this outing?"

"Oh, no," he said, holding up his hands. "You asked me to come with you. Since *you* asked *me* out, *you* are the one who defines it."

"Well that hardly seems fair," I protested. "I asked and you agreed before we set parameters on what this was. If I define it as one type of occasion now, it might not match the expectations that you held when you agreed."

"I'm confused, so let's just define it together."

I could feel my stomach flipping. Did I want this to be a date? He was attractive. Hell, who was I kidding? The man was hot. Strong hands and sculpted forearms, plus the sexy as hell glasses? If this was a date, I was certainly batting above my regular dating game.

But Malcolm was only here for a short while, and in the small amount of time I had known him we had argued, bickered, and faked a relationship. Not exactly events leading to a strong foundation for a relationship.

Seeming to sense my inner turmoil, he extended a hand across the table. Not quite touching my hand, but close enough to get my attention. "How about this," he proposed. "We call this a friend outing with the option to change the title later. Less pressure now, and if we decide later that it was a date, then we hold the right to alter our previous assertions."

I smiled. "You could've been a lawyer."

He mock-shuddered. "It's a good thing this isn't a date, Innkeeper, because that right there is some fighting words."

I laughed, feeling more at ease. By the time Brandon brought our drinks and we placed our orders, Malcolm and I had fallen into a comfortable back and forth, which allowed Malcolm to circle back.

"So, your last date ditched you at a fast food joint?"

The next day still held no new visitors at the inn, but I did manage to book a lovely couple for Saturday night. If everything went well, they'd check in before everyone arrived for family dinner. If everything went *really* well, I figured I could use the fact that I had guests to prevent my mother and father from murdering each other, or to prevent me from murdering Connor. Only time could tell.

Meanwhile, Malcolm had taken the information I gave him the night before and went on an internet deep dive of all things Burnt Creek. At least, that's what he said he was going to do when we got back to the inn after dinner. Last night wasn't a date. Although he paid for dinner insisting it was the least he could do for me helping him research the inn, there was no goodnight kiss, not even an affectionate hug when we got back. He thanked me for inviting him along and said goodnight.

I hadn't seen him at all the next day, and I couldn't tell if he was avoiding me because he thought I read too much into last night, or if he really was just busy researching. It was three in the afternoon when I knocked on his door with a basket of sandwiches and a tight chest filled with nervous energy.

Opening the door, Malcolm was shrugging a tight t-shirt over his bare torso, leaving nothing to the imagination. I had no words for the work of art that was Malcolm Jones coming out of a research binge. Low-slung plaid pajama pants exuded comfort and smudges of ink covered the sides of one hand from him furiously jotting notes. He adjusted his glasses before leaning against the doorframe and smiling at me.

"Morning, sunshine," he said. I shook my head at myself. *He's a guest. He's a guest. He's a guest.* Although after dinner last night, despite there not being anything more than some great conversation and a few sparks, it was getting really hard to not blur the line from friendly acquaintances to something more.

"Only if you're nocturnal, ghost hunter," I said, annoyed that my words sounded breathy. He seemed to notice it, too, because his eyebrow quirked, and his smile grew.

"You doing okay there, Harley? You seem a bit out of breath."

Heat flooded my cheeks. I shoved the basket from my hands to his chest and became particularly fascinated with a spot on the wall beside him as words tumbled out of me. "You missed breakfast. I thought you might be hungry. Also, there's a historical society meeting tonight at seven. You're welcome to ride with me if you want. I'm leaving at six-thirty."

"Harley," he said quietly, but he still hadn't taken the basket from my hands.

"Um, it's a few sandwiches, I didn't know what you liked, and some cheeses, but are you dairy intolerant? I should've asked. There's a mini-fridge in your room if you don't want to eat them now."

"Harley," he said again, still with the same quiet determination.

"Please take the basket," I whispered.

I felt fingertips brush along the bottom of my chin, guiding my eyes to his. His smile was gone now, and a warm sincerity reflected in his eyes.

"Harley," he said again. I swallowed hard as his fingertips shot jolts of electricity straight to my heart and his thumb traced invisible lines along my jaw. "I'm sorry I missed breakfast." He trailed his fingertips to the side of my face and tucked a lock of hair behind my ear, his golden eyes never leaving mine. "I had a great time last night." He then drifted his fingers down my neck, across my shoulder, and down my arm, finally meeting my hand where it was holding the basket. "You look amazing today."

Allowing my hands to drop when I felt him holding the weight of the basket, I stood grounded to the spot, my heart fluttering quickly as he leaned his face toward mine with a grin and whispered, "And there's no way in hell we're riding in that death trap you call a car."

I snapped my gaze to him to find him grinning. I rolled my eyes and marched back toward the stairs, willing my heart to go back to its normal rhythm. I could feel the boring of his eyes behind me until I heard his door close, and I finally allowed myself to take a breath. Even when he was annoying me, he was making my lady parts sing. I mean, was this guy even human?

For the next two-and-a-half hours, I busied myself by washing the windows in the lobby and painting my fingernails purple based on a horoscope quiz from an expired magazine. When I still had an hour before I was set to leave, I decided to paint my toes, too. When Malcolm found me, I had gotten all of one toe sloppily done and was upside down on the couch in the sitting room trying to find the perfect angle to finish the rest of them. The sound of his chuckling nearly made me drop the nail polish.

"Should I ask what you're doing?" he asked. I tilted my head back on the couch and noted that even upside down he looked amazing.

"Um, well, I was going to paint my toenails, but I think I've been out of yoga for too long."

"You've done yoga?" he asked.

"Um, well, no, never."

He walked over to me and held out his hand. I furrowed my brows in question, and he merely took the nail polish out of my hand.

"Hey!" I said, trying to figure out how to get out of the position I was in. He sat down and gently grabbed one leg and pulled me until my back rested against the seat of the couch and my feet were in his lap. I watched in wonder as he dipped the brush in the nail polish and began expertly painting my toenails. "Is this real life?"

He pulled the brush across my toenail and chuckled. "Yes, it is."

"How do you know how to paint toenails? Do you have some secret fetish I'm not aware of?"

"No, but if I did, you'd be the first to know," he said with a wry grin. I didn't even know how to take that, but my body sure had some ideas. "I have a sister, Victoria," he continued, "and when she was pregnant, she was put on bed rest for two months. She was really bored and emotional, so once a week she would ask me to come over and paint her toenails that she couldn't reach. It was really just an excuse to shoot the shit, but we had fun. Her belly was so big at the time that she couldn't see how horrible of a job I did but after the third time I started to get pretty decent at it."

"I just...you're like the unicorn of men. Like, you don't exist out in the wild."

"I can assure you I was born in captivity," he said with a grin, but there was something in his eyes that was guarded like he truly believed that.

I watched him as he finished, painting delicate swipes with the brush in quiet concentration behind his glasses. He twisted the brush back on the nail polish and began blowing softly on my toes. The moment his breath touched my skin, it suddenly felt so much more intimate, and I clenched my thighs together as I watched him.

"I can feel you staring," he said with a quirk of his mouth.

"Does it make you uncomfortable?" I asked.

"Not in the slightest," he said, "I think if anything, I make you uncomfortable."

I looked away, frustrated again and the heat spreading up my neck. He had no idea how he made me feel. How *much* he made me feel. I tried to figure out the words to answer him.

"Not...uncomfortable." I said quietly, still looking away. "You make me confused."

I gathered the courage to look back at him and found him tilting his head to the side. Not wanting to have this conversation, I pulled my feet from his lap and sat them delicately on the floor. "Come on, we don't want to be late, and I still have to grab a bottle of wine."

"A bottle of wine?" he asked, his head still cocked to the side.

"You'll see."

Chapter Eight

Release the Goose

Malcolm

On the way to the historical society meeting, Harley filled me in on the inner workings of the women who made up the group. According to Harley, the Burnt Creek historical society met on the first Thursday of each month and the location rotated between each member's home.

"Why not just have it at the inn?" I asked, stopping at the only stoplight in town.

"Mabel was behind that decision," Harley said, blowing out a breath. "She said it was to keep the cops from breaking up our 'fun' as if it was an illegal craps game, and the rest of us indulged her because she always brings the best wine."

"Where is it at this month?"

"It's at Penny's garage."

I started scanning the streets for a car shop. "Is Penny a mechanic?"

"No, she's a seamstress and costume designer. But she wants us to meet in her garage because she said there was no way she was risking the drunken lushes of the historical society near her prized sewing creations."

I raised my eyebrows but kept driving until Harley directed me to pull up to a small one-story house with a brick façade and a detached garage. Just as we were about to get out of the car, my phone rang in my pocket. I pulled it out, and the look on my face as I saw who was trying to reach me again must have pulled Harley up short.

"I'll let you get that, just meet me inside," she said with a small smile. Before I had to chance to ignore the call, she was already closing the door. I wavered between answering it or going inside, but the grinding I was already doing on my teeth made my decision for me. I hit ignore, left my phone in the car, and grabbed my notebook and the bottle of wine Harley forgot in the front seat.

The door to the garage was open a crack, allowing me to hear snippets of conversation from the women sitting around an old card table.

"Why are you looking at me like that?" I could hear Harley ask someone.

"Because word on the street is that you have a new boyfriend. And we want details. Spill," another woman's voice added. As tempted as I was to hear what Harley would say, I figured it might be a dick move to feed her to the wolves by herself.

I pushed the door open and walked in with the bottle of wine extended to her. I didn't miss the flash of relief on Harley's face as she avoided the inquisition.

"You left this in the car," I said with a grin, grabbing a fold-up chair from the wall and sitting next to Harley, pretending to be completely oblivious to the stares we were getting. Harley smiled back at me before clearing her throat.

"Ladies," she started, addressing the three women at the small table. "This is Malcolm Jones. He's in town for a bit researching the town for the Spirits, Seekers, and Skeptics YouTube channel that's coming in a couple of weeks."

"Oh! Just in time for the Autumn Festival!" a woman exclaimed. She spoke in exaggerated hand gestures and had a New York accent that was bigger than the dark curls piled on top of her head.

"Malcolm, these are the women of the historical society. This is Miranda, my stepmother," she said, gesturing to the New Yorker.

"Uh huh," another woman said, motioning for us to get on with it as her eyes bounced back and forth between Harley and me. She was closer to Harley's age and had long, straight, black hair with bangs covering her forehead and bandages covering two of the fingers on her right hand. "And how do you know Harley, Malcolm?" I cocked an eyebrow at Harley with a grin, and I saw her shifting a bit in her seat.

"He's staying at the inn while he's in town," Harley said delicately, her cheeks lighting up pink. She cleared her throat. "Malcolm, this is Penny Wayward, owner of Doom, Gloom, and Groom Costumes."

"Groom?" I asked Penny, thinking it was strange that people dressed as a groom for Halloween.

"I do Halloween costumes, stage costumes, and I'm the only wedding outfitter around here."

"I see," I conceded with a smile.

Harley extended her hand toward the oldest woman across the table from us. She was dressed in dark patterns with large bangles adorning each wrist. She reminded me of a fortune teller animatronic I had seen at a gas station once. "This is Mabel O'Neil. You met her sister Dorothy outside the inn on your first day."

I extended my hand to the older woman, but instead of shaking it, Mabel grabbed my hand with her wrinkled ones and flipped them over, jingling the bracelets up and down her wrists. "You have wonderful palms. I'd love to read them sometime."

I could feel my eyebrows rise as I put the pieces together. "Ah, the psychic sisters."

Mabel beamed at me, quickly retracting her hand and diving it not-so-covertly under the table, which seemed odd until Penny clicked her teeth at the old woman. "Mabel! We agreed. No group texting during meetings!"

Mabel's eyes widened as her hands slowly emerged from beneath the table, still typing with her thumbs efficiently before she hit the send button. "All done, dears."

Harley groaned. "This better not be the buzz of the town within minutes because one of your sisters has a "revelation" in the supermarket about Malcolm being here," she warned.

Miranda waved her off. "It's so nice to meet you, Malcolm!" she said, extending her hand and shaking mine enthusiastically. Looking at Harley while she did so, she mouthed 'Oh, my gawd!'. Only, I could still clearly see her, and I had to suppress my chuckle as Harley's face lit bright red.

"Um, Miranda," Harley said, probably trying to distract her from the eyebrows Miranda was wiggling my way. "I was hoping you and dad could come to family dinner on Saturday night."

Miranda dropped my hand. "Really? But your mom's going to be there, and you know she's not going to like that."

"I know, and I hate to put you and dad in a weird situation, but mom invited Connor."

The women around the table collectively gasped. Penny placed her hands flat on the table. "No, she did not!"

"Oh, but she did," Harley sighed. "So, of course, I told her since she was okay with exes being in attendance that you and dad were going to be there. I shouldn't have done that to you guys."

Miranda paused for a moment and burst out laughing which sounded more like a witch's cackle. "Gawd, you're such a hellcat! I just love it! Of course, we'll be there, and I'll be on my best behavior.

Although, I can't speak for your father when he sees Connor. I still don't know why he hates him so much, but I look forward to meeting the man who was responsible for your father's high blood pressure for so long."

Penny scoffed and folded her arms in front of her. "I still don't know what you saw in Connor."

Mabel pulled a wrinkled hand from the phone she was furiously texting on and waved it in the air. "She saw a hot piece of ass."

"Well, she needs a hot piece of ass attached to a good heart," Penny said.

I can't say I was thrilled with the group agreeing that the douchebag Connor was a hot piece of anything, but I worked to keep my opinions to myself.

"And an intellectual brain, we all know how argumentative she is. She needs someone to keep her on her toes mentally," Miranda threw into the mix, giving me a look that made me think she had a certain guy in mind.

Harley grabbed the bottle of wine I had handed to her earlier and pointed the neck at the three of them. "*She* is sitting right here and the only thing I need is for all of you to stop acting like I need anything from a man," she eyeballed the three ladies. "And for the love of pumpkins, Mabel, stop texting your sisters!"

I gently pried the bottle of wine Harley was currently using as a weapon from her fingertips with a chuckle. The three women were looking sheepish, and Mabel had stopped texting, but the moment the bottle was out of Harley's hands, Mabel lifted the phone at me, and I heard the sound of her camera feature going off.

"Mabel," Harley growled.

"It's fine, Mabel," I said grinning. "Just make sure you get my good side."

Mabel, for her part, had the grace to look slightly embarrassed. I opened the wine and poured Harley a glass, offering wine to the other ladies. Harley took a deep swig of her wine and set her glass back down.

"Look, I know we love to girl-talk during most meetings, but this week Malcolm really needs some information on the town for the Spirits channel."

Penny nodded. "What do you need to know?"

The next thirty minutes were spent gathering information on the town, although little information was usable for the show. Although, I did discover that Mabel was the head of the Burnt Creek Museum, and she invited me to come by and take a tour on Monday. Also, when Harley got up to grab another bottle of wine, Miranda whispered that she had an 'in' with the Sheriff and she'd set up an appointment for me to come scope things out the next day.

As the night drew to a close, I helped Harley up from her chair. Three glasses of wine in and she was a smidge tipsy. I walked her to the car and helped her in.

"I'm really sorry that you didn't get more information," Harley said as I got into the driver's seat.

"Are you kidding me? Coming to this meeting was like drinking from the fountain of knowledge," I said with a wry grin. "Before I came here, I had no idea that Bo Zamford's girlfriend was the one who insisted he wears a toupee."

"You're hilarious," Harley said dryly.

"Seriously, though, I got some good contacts here. I've got a tour guide at the museum, and I'm meeting the sheriff tomorrow."

Harley noticeably winced. "What was that face for?" I asked her.

"Um, it's just that the sheriff is a little...difficult...sometimes. Do you want me to go with you?"

"Nah, I can handle him. Besides, Maggie would kill me if I took you away from the inn for another day."

"I know, just...don't let him walk all over you. He doesn't like open challenges, but he doesn't respect pushovers either."

"How many times have you gotten arrested that you know this much about the sheriff?"

She laughed, and the sound washed over me. Being with Harley was so damn easy.

"I can't say that I've ever been arrested, but I spent a lot of time in the station growing up. What about you? Did you lead a life of crime before becoming a ghost hunter?"

My mind unwillingly flashed to the memory of handcuffs being tightened over an expensive suit jacket as the FBI agent recited the Miranda rights. A knot of tension coiled tightly in my stomach.

"Nope," I said, hoping she couldn't hear the strain in my voice. "Can't say I've ever been on the wrong side of the law before."

I spent the rest of the ride asking for directions even though I knew my way for the most part by now. It was better if Harley thought I was directionally challenged rather than diving deeper into my past experiences with criminals.

The next morning, I typed up my notes from the night before, took a shower, and headed down for breakfast. Harley was already there, sipping coffee and reading something on her iPad. When I walked into the room, Harley tore her eyes away and looked at me, a smile blooming on her face.

Damn, she's got a gorgeous smile.

I wondered if this was her normal innkeeper smile or if this was special for me. It felt special, which made me feel like an idiot. What could Harley possibly gain by smiling at me like that? And how much of a cynic have I turned into that I've started to believe people use generic smiles as a means of manipulation? Of course, there was nothing generic about her smile.

"Good morning," she said. I shook myself out of my thoughts.

"Good morning," I returned, sitting down to her right. Just then, Maggie breezed in carrying a travel mug and wearing a smile and her signature horn-rimmed glasses in bright orange today.

"Hey," she said to the two of us, and it was comforting to feel like this was going to be a new normal. It didn't often happen when I was researching for the YouTube channel that I was able to sit down and have breakfast with friends. At least, not until the rest of the crew got to town. "What's on the agenda today, Malcolm?" Maggie asked, filling up her mug with the pot of coffee on the table.

"I'm going to visit the sheriff, see about getting some background on local crimes."

Maggie's hand stilled on the pot of coffee as her eyes darted quickly over to Harley. "You're going to see the sheriff?"

I might have imagined the mischievous glint in her eye, but I definitely didn't imagine the warning glare Harley shot her.

"Am I missing something?" I asked, glancing between the two of them.

"Nope," Harley said, quickly. "Maggie just came by to steal the good coffee. Bye, Maggie. Enjoy your day."

Maggie chuckled and shook her head, blond curls bouncing around her youthful face before walking out the door with her coffee.

I put some eggs and bacon on my plate and started eating as I stared pointedly at Harley. She looked everywhere around the room except for me until she finally met my gaze.

"How's your breakfast?"

"Great, great," I answered, shoveling the eggs into my mouth faster than what would normally be polite. "So, you're sure there's nothing important I need to know before going to see the sheriff?"

Harley's face froze as she slowly shook her head, once again looking everywhere but at me. At least I knew now that Harley was a shit liar. There were worse traits in a woman.

"All right," I said slowly. "Well, I'm headed out then. I'll see you later."

I grabbed my bacon on the way out the door and munched on it as I got in my car. The sheriff was just a man. Maybe he was a difficult man, but I wasn't going to bend to the hype of other people's opinions and strange behavior. I was going to meet him and form my own opinion.

I pulled up to the police station and made my way inside. The lobby area had bright blue carpeting that had aged in different spots and a line of seats that appeared to be bolted to the wall. Against the far wall was an electronically locked door and a bulletproof window showcasing a pretty, young woman with a no-nonsense mask over her gaze.

"How can I help you?" she asked through the speaker on the window.

"Hi, I'm Malcolm Jones, Miranda said she'd set up an appointment this morning for me with the sheriff."

The woman's face broke into a clear smile, her façade of professionalism a distant memory. "Of course, Mr. Jones! When Miranda called this morning, I thought she was pulling my leg, but the sheriff is right through the doors in the bullpen. Give me a second to unlock them."

"Thank you..."

"Avery," she supplied.

"Right. Thank you, Avery."

She raised an eyebrow, and I ignored the thorough perusal she made over my body. When I would catch Harley sneaking peeks at me, my stomach flopped. But aside from feeling flattered when Avery looked, I felt...nothing.

The door clicked as the metal in the lock slid free, and I went through the doorway, down a hallway, and eventually ended up in the bullpen of the station. Two police officers, a man and a woman, were sitting in a corner talking to a civilian who was moving her hands wildly. A smattering of desks with chairs on either side were placed purposefully around the room. I scanned around, looking for the sheriff.

I heard Avery enter behind me, and she walked past me toward a desk with a stack of papers and no personal artifacts. "This is the sheriff's desk. We can wait here for him."

Avery leaned against the side of the desk, crossing her legs in a move that spoke of experience seducing men. At one point in my life, I might have fallen for it, and I would have been a happy man. Now, my mind barely registered Avery's presence as an eligible woman.

A broad man with dark hair, brows, and a thick mustache came out of one of the back rooms and descended on me slowly. A toothpick sat firmly in the corner of his mouth, and it would shake when he spoke if he actually said anything. The top left side of his uniform held the label "Sheriff."

I extended my hand first. "Hey Sheriff, my name is Malcolm," I introduced myself, forcing myself to slip into the casual acquaintance role. The sheriff stared at my hand briefly, a flash of what I thought was disdain ran across his face before he reached out and shook it.

"Name's Sheriff Charlie. You can call me Sheriff. Welcome to Burnt Creek. So, you're a TV personality?" his voice was gruff, and his toothpick bobbed in his mouth as he spoke. I found it difficult to focus on his words as the toothpick bristled under his mustache.

"No, actually, I do research for the videos before the team gets there. I'm not on camera very often."

"Hmm..." He tilted a coffee mug up. I didn't realize he was carrying it to his lips because his eyes never stopped appraising me. I had no idea how he managed to get it around the toothpick. "Miranda told me you'd be stopping by today to ask some questions. She said you'd been staying at the inn, spending time with Harley."

The way he said Harley's name put me on edge. He said it slowly, carefully evaluating my reaction to being associated with Harley. It was strange.

Avery cocked her head toward the sheriff with a grin. "Are you going to introduce him to Gus, Sheriff?"

I lifted my eyes and looked back and forth between the two of them.

"We'll see," the sheriff replied, and I realized meeting Gus must be some kind of test. Whoever this Gus guy was, I wanted to meet him. I needed to pass that test.

A light blinked above the door we entered through, and Avery stood up. "That's my cue, back to work." She popped up with a smirk in my direction before heading back to the lobby.

Trying my best to appeal to the sheriff's sense of duty to police work, I began asking my research questions. "I'd actually love to know some of the area's history from a police perspective. Some of the work we do is finding out about past crimes committed and seeing what links they have to historic buildings."

The sheriff's eyes narrowed. "I don't mind you asking some questions, but you keep in mind that this is a nice town, a peaceful town.

I'm not about to let some stranger paint this slice of paradise as some setting for a slasher flick."

"I wouldn't dream of it, sir."

The sheriff grunted and called across the room to one of the officers who had finished talking with the civilian. "Oliver, get over here."

As the younger officer walked toward us, his broad shoulders squared as the sheriff introduced him. "Malcolm, this is Oliver. He's the mayor's grandson and has a memory like a steel vault for facts on the town. Oliver, this is Malcolm. He's been staying at the inn with Harley."

Again, his voice changed when he mentioned Harley. It came out as a growl and his eyes cut to me.

Oliver slowed his gait with his eyebrows raised. "Huh. Do you need me to get Gus?"

Who the hell was this Gus guy? And what did he have to do with Harley?

"Not yet," the sheriff responded, eyes narrowed at me. "Oliver, how many unnatural deaths have occurred in this town in the last hundred years?"

My eyebrows furrowed. This wasn't how things were normally done, but Oliver answered anyways. "Seven. Four from the snowstorm of '83. Died of hypothermia, trapped in a car. Three unearthed during the flood of '72 after hurricane Agnes."

I quickly pulled my notebook out and started jotting notes. "What do you mean, 'unearthed'?"

Oliver stuck his hands in his pockets as he recounted from memory. "Three railroad entrepreneurs were looking for a quick buck and were scamming locals into believing a once abandoned railroad was going to reopen in the late '60s. They were getting local businessmen to invest in the railroad, taking an estimated one hundred sixteen thousand dollars before disappearing. When Hurricane Agnes came through in 1972, shallow graves were disturbed in an old cemetery and the flooding unearthed three bodies identified as the missing railmen."

Excitement coursed through my veins. This would make one hell of an episode for the channel. I furiously took notes with follow up questions that I would need to research.

"Were they murdered?"

"Yes, gunshot wounds for each of them."

"Did they find the killer?"

"Nope."

I continued my note taking, asking Oliver for the names of the deceased, which he rattled off without blinking. The guy's mind was seriously sharp. I wrote down locations for possible video sections, the cemetery where they were buried, the railway area they were trying to sell, and breathed out a sigh when I finished with the thoughts. Here was the part I always felt weird doing.

"Has anybody claimed to have experienced haunting activities in these locations after their deaths?"

The sheriff narrowed his eyes and flipped his toothpick to the other side of his mouth.

"The only person you're likely to find who claims to have much to do with the spiritual hocus pocus is the O'Neil sisters. And I can't say they're what we would call a reliable witness."

I nodded, understanding what he meant completely, as I penned the last of my notes.

"What does Harley think all this ghost hunting stuff?" the sheriff asked.

"Harley?" I asked, distracted by her name once more coming up out of the blue. The sheriff grunted with a raised eyebrow. "I mean, she doesn't think there are any ghosts in her inn, and she's not trying to like, scam people or something."

The sheriff's eyes narrowed. "How do you know she's not trying to scam people?"

"Well, I asked her," I said. I immediately knew this was the wrong thing to say.

"Oliver," the sheriff said to the young officer, but his eyes were still locked on me. "I think it's time this boy met Gus."

I breathed out a sigh of relief, thinking I had messed up massively, but if he was introducing me to the mysterious Gus, I must not have messed up as bad as I thought. "That would be great."

That was, until Oliver spoke up.

"Release the goose!" Oliver yelled to the other officer.

"Goose?" I asked, dumbfounded.

The officer across the station smiled and lifted a partition in the wall I hadn't noticed before. When he did, a long white neck bobbed into the room, attached to a head of a goose with the angriest eyes I had ever seen. As the goose waddled into the room, I saw a pouch attached to its butt.

Is that a diaper?

The thought barely entered my head before the goose whipped his head to the side, exposing one eyeball that looked at me, seeming to stare into my soul. The goose then let out an unearthly shriek, exposing a row of sharp teeth on the top and bottom of his beak, and a row of what looked like teeth along his tongue. I let out a lady-like scream as the goose spread his wings the width of a desk and charged at me.

"Fuck!" I yelled, scrambling to climb onto a chair and then onto the sheriff's desk. "What is that?" I screamed over the sound of the shrieking goose.

The sheriff howled with laughter and reached out to stroke the head of the demon goose.

"This is Gus," he said, calming the monster down in between chuckles. "He's our guard goose."

"Why are you saying that like it's normal? That's not normal!" I said loudly, still keeping my distance from the spawn of Satan that was still eyeballing me and honking aggressively. My eyes caught something shimmering on the backside of the goose. As Gus moved his body closer to the sheriff, I recognized a sequined police badge on his diaper. "And why is he glittery?"

The sheriff gave a shrug. "Miranda likes to bedazzle."

"How are you allowed to keep him here? And why the hell do you need a guard goose?"

My heart was still hammering as I still stood on the desk, ready to leap and run at a moment's notice if Gus kept looking at me weirdly.

The sheriff shrugged, still petting his monster's head. "It keeps us from having to keep an officer on-site at night to guard the place. Plus, the kids like him."

"You let that thing around children?" I asked incredulously. The officer who let the goose loose rounded the desk, ushering Gus back toward the door. I took the opportunity to grab my notebook tightly and shot a glare at the sheriff as I scrambled from the desk out the door.

"See you soon, Malcolm," the sheriff shouted after me with a laugh.

"Not if I see you first," I mumbled under my breath as I got outside the station. I decided it was safe to say the sheriff didn't approve of my being in Burnt Creek.

Chapter Nine

All Kinds of Guests

Harley

The next day was the family dinner I had been dreading. All day, I tried to focus on other things. I had a couple coming to check in and while I waited, I wondered what had happened with Malcolm the day before at the police station. When Malcolm came back to the inn yesterday afternoon, his clothes were disheveled, and he barely said two words before retreating to his room. I thought about calling Miranda, but I had a list of tasks to take care of, and I had given Maggie the weekend off, remembering she'd still be around for family dinner the next night.

Even worse, I had to remember that Connor was coming, and there was nothing that quite soured my mood like knowing that I was going to spend an evening with Connor.

The bell above the front door rang out as an older couple came in. A jovial old man, with a round belly and a balding head of white hair walked through the lobby delicately holding the hand of an equally white-haired old woman with wire-framed glasses. They smiled sweetly at each other before approaching the desk.

"Hi," the woman said. "I'm Wilma Rainer, and this is Doyle Rainer. We have a reservation for this evening."

Wilma's voice was high-pitched and sweet, making me nostalgic for all things grandmotherly.

"Of course!" I said brightly. "Welcome to Burnt Creek! What brings you up this way?" I asked as I got their information pulled up on the computer.

"My Wilma here is a sales lady, and there was a conference show-casing new products," Doyle said, his bright red cheeks beaming with pride. "Today was the last day, and we've been running ourselves ragged trying to keep up."

"We get to test out some of the new stuff tonight and see how we like it," Wilma chimed in. "It's always nice when we have new inventory."

"That's so exciting!" I said, wondering if it was cookies or other baked goods that she sold and if so, if she would be willing to recommend some products for the inn. But I could see Doyle biting back a yawn, so I quickly pulled their key and showed them to their room.

As the couple settled in for the evening, I prepped the dining room for the family coming over. I switched the tablecloth three times and spent half an hour trying to decide if the crystal candlesticks could be used as weapons. Playing it safe, I took them off the table and shoved them into a drawer.

I also spent far too much time trying to figure out how many chairs we would need, mostly because I was nervous that Malcolm might have changed his mind after yesterday's festivities at the police station. He hadn't talked to me at all when he returned last night, but that could just mean he was headed into another research deep-dive and would take a while before coming up for air. I reasoned with myself that if he decided not to come, I could always just remove a chair. I don't know why I made things more difficult for myself.

Choosing an outfit was another exercise in mental gymnastics. Choosing something relaxed enough to show Connor and my mother that I wasn't dressing up for my ex, while also looking attractive enough that Malcolm couldn't resist checking me out and deciding that he wanted to kiss every inch of me, was a tough balancing act. I ultimately decided on a dress with a high neckline that would give Connor nothing to ogle from across the table but was short enough that Malcolm could see the dress rise a bit on my thigh when I sat next to him.

When four-thirty rolled around, I went up and knocked on Malcolm's door, a little early in case he was in still research mode and hadn't gotten dressed yet. Or, worse yet, in case he changed his mind about pretending to be my date. When he opened the door, I was surprised to see him in a black button-down shirt tucked into black slacks. His top button was open, giving a casual look to his outfit and exposing a smidge of skin below his throat. Damn, this man was sexy.

"Hey Innkeeper," he said, and his voice was like gravel. His eyes scanned my body, lingering appreciatively at my legs, and I felt my stomach flip beneath the lace of my dress. "You look amazing. Are you ready for tonight?"

I nodded, not trusting my voice. "Are you sure you still want to come with me? I know it's probably not what you were thinking for a nice dinner."

He walked out of the room, shutting the door behind him and casually draping an arm over my shoulders. "What kind of fake love interest would I be if I left you to your ex at a family dinner?"

I breathed in the scent of him, and I swear, I would never get used to it. He chuckled under his breath, and I shrugged. "You know you smell fantastic. I'm just cashing in the benefits of having you as a fake boyfriend."

"Ah, so we're officially to the fake boyfriend stage. We've put a label on it?"

"Well, if you're meeting my family, I would assume our relationship had progressed far enough to put a label on it."

"Fair enough, fake girlfriend. So, what are the parameters?"

"What do you mean?"

"Like, how far are we willing to go to sell this to your mom and Connor? Holding hands? Hugging? Kissing?"

My whole body lit on fire at the thought of kissing Malcolm. "Um, I probably wouldn't kiss a boyfriend in front of my parents the first night they meet, so probably just casual touching."

"Got it," he said. I was hoping to hear disappointment in his voice, but he was all business. Was that all this was to him? Just business? I mean, I guess I was virtually a stranger to him.

As we made our way down the stairs, Malcolm helped me bring the food out to the table. I had put together a large salad, garlic bread, and shrimp linguini for everyone. Malcolm placed two bottles of wine on the table and made sure one of them was closest to me. I smiled gratefully at him.

The bell above the front door rang as it opened, and soon after, my mother shuffled into the room with Connor in tow. Show time. I felt Malcolm's arm circle my waist and leaned into him like it was the most natural thing in the world. Strangely enough, it felt natural.

"Hey Mom," I said, pulling her into a one-armed hug, not releasing Malcolm. I nodded to Connor. "Connor."

"Good to see you, Harley," he said, tossing his too-long hair to the side. I gagged internally. I could feel the microscopic tightening of Malcolm's grip on my waist.

Malcolm smiled at my mother. "Please, have a seat. Would you like a glass of wine, Valerie?"

My mother froze, contemplating Malcolm. "I'd love one, thank you."

Malcolm kissed the top of my head and released my waist. "I hope you like red. This one is Harley's favorite," he said, grabbing the bottle on the table. It was my favorite, but I was surprised he knew that.

"Red is great," my mother said, looking at Malcolm with a genuine smile. Connor, sensing Valerie's allegiance changing, cleared his throat.

"So, Malcolm, word around town is you're a ghost hunter, is that right?" he sneered. My mom's eyebrows raised, but before Malcolm had time to answer, the bell above the front door rang just a moment before Maggie came into the room, leading Miranda and my father behind her.

"Look who I found!" Maggie said with a wink at me. I melted internally at my sister. God, she was the best. She lived above our dad's garage while she was looking for a place to rent and it was nearly driving her crazy. I turned toward Malcolm only to find his eyes nearly bugging out of his head.

My dad's dark, thick mustache twitched at the side at seeing Malcolm's reaction. He walked over to me and kissed my forehead. "Hey there, pumpkin."

"Pumpkin?" Malcolm asked, his face painfully pale. My dad turned toward Malcolm.

"Don't look so terrified, champ. I left Gus at the station."

Now it was my turn for wide eyes. "Oh my God, Dad! Tell me you didn't sic Gus on Malcolm!"

Dad shrugged. Miranda made her way forward. "I already chewed him out for it, Harley."

My mother *harrumphed* at the table, drawing attention back to her.

"Charlie. Miranda," my mother greeted them icily. A large boulder of guilt sat in my gut for having asked Miranda and dad to come tonight. "I see you've made it to *family* dinner."

I rolled my eyes, but Miranda shrugged it off, looking at Connor. "And you must be—"

Connor preened under the attention, extending his hand. Before he got a word out, I volunteered, "This is mom's date, Connor."

Mom choked on her wine and shot a glare at me as her cheeks bloomed red. Understanding coated Miranda's face, and she quickly withdrew her hand from Connor's.

Connor chuckled. "You know our Harley, always a jokester." I glared at him, and silence descended on the room until Malcolm once more sidled up to me, slipping an arm around my waist. It was a comforting weight, anchoring me in the midst of chaos.

"How about we get seated for dinner, sweetheart?" he said quietly, but loud enough for everyone to hear it.

Maggie shot me a confused look as if she was going to say something, but I subtly shook my head to her. Instead, I sat down at the head of the table with my mother on my right and Malcolm on my left. Maggie sat on the other side of Malcolm, shielding him from the sheriff, and Miranda sat between the sheriff and Connor.

"So, Malcolm," Valerie said from beside me while everyone scooped food onto their plates. "what's this ghost hunting that Connor mentioned?"

Malcolm smiled, probably realizing that Connor most likely wanted to make him look like a fool.

"My job, actually. I work as the head researcher for a media company that specializes in identifying or dispelling spiritual activity. Then we put our findings on the internet for public consumption, which makes it quite lucrative."

I smiled at him. Only a journalistic wordsmith like him could turn a ghost hunting slam from Connor into a business model for a snob like my mother.

"That's fascinating," she said.

"He's a YouTuber," Connor said dryly.

"He works with Ben Glover," Maggie said quietly.

"Ben Glover?" my mother asked. "As in..."

"Yeah," Maggie said, "as in Archie's brother."

Silence descended once more over the table until Connor opened his mouth with a sneer.

"Who's Archie, Maggie? An ex-boyfriend?" I felt Malcolm tense beside me, but I put a hand on his leg, knowing Maggie could handle her own. But I realized that Malcolm wasn't just rigid in defense of Maggie. He had known Ben since they were children, which meant he had known Archie.

"Connor," Maggie started stonily, carefully placing her silverware down, "what the hell are you even doing here?"

"Language, Magdalene," our mother chided.

"Valerie invited me," he said smugly.

"Of course she did," Maggie snapped. "Because she's either desperate to marry her oldest daughter off to the sleaziest man in the state, or she's delusional about the kind of man you are that you would try to sleep with Harley's little sister *while you were still dating*. Either way, it's never going to happen. Harley doesn't want you anymore. Even before she had Malcolm, she didn't want you. You should leave."

Mouths around the table dropped. I had never told my parents, or Malcolm for that matter, why I broke up with Connor. I never wanted them to see me as the woman scorned, and I never wanted them to look at Maggie as some sort of homewrecker. I remember the night that Maggie came to me in tears, terrified to tell me what Connor had said to her. She was scared I wouldn't believe her, or that I would choose Connor over her. But I knew my sister, and Maggie would never lie about something like that. Dad, while never knowing the reason behind the breakup, saw Connor for the tool that he was and was happy I dropped him, no questions asked. But seeing the sheriff seething across the table, gripping silverware like weapons to scoop Connor's eyeballs out, was exactly the reason I never told him that Connor tried to deflower his baby girl while he was in a committed relationship with his other daughter. Malcolm had his hands fisted on his thighs at the revelation.

Valerie, finally overcoming her shock and embarrassment for not only bringing Connor to family dinner but getting called out on it, sat her wine glass down and stood up.

"Harley, thank you for dinner. I think it's time I walk Connor out. Have a good night, everyone."

After my mom dragged Connor out, there was a casual conversation on the surface, but my dad and Miranda left as soon as their plates were cleared, and I waved off their attempts to help with dishes. Maggie had been quiet through the rest of the night, throwing glances at me occasionally, but it wasn't until everyone left but Malcolm and me that she looked at me and kept her gaze.

"I'm sorry I ruined the night," she said, glumly. I couldn't help but laugh. She looked at me in surprise.

"Mags, Mom invited Connor and glared daggers at Miranda and Dad. Dad unleashed Gus on Malcolm yesterday. Dinner was a long-shot before it even started. You stood up for yourself, you stood up for Archie's memory, and you stood up for me. And I couldn't be more grateful."

"Thank you," she said quietly.

"Do you need to stay in a room tonight?" I offered. She shook her head.

"I should get home. Goodnight, you guys."

After Maggie left, Malcolm helped me clear the table and put away the leftovers, ignoring my insistence that I could handle it. We were quiet mostly, both lost in our own thoughts. When we were finished, he held out his hand and, after a moment's hesitation, I took it.

Malcolm led me upstairs to the door to my room before turning to face me.

"Well, how do you think meeting the parents went?" he asked, cracking a grin. I burst out laughing.

"I am so sorry for the most awkward dinner that ever went down in history," I said, biting my lip. "But I'd be lying if I said I wasn't happy you were there with me."

He squeezed my hand. "I'm happy I was there, too. Although, as your fake boyfriend, I should let you know that your father terrifies me."

I laughed; my head bowed in exhaustion after the night we shared. When I brought my head back up to look at Malcolm, his face was closer, and his eyes flicked from my eyes down to my lips. The air around us stilled, and I watched his gaze darkening as he stared at me.

Was he going to kiss me? Did I want him to?

Yes.

But he was leaving soon and from the way my stomach was already flipping, I knew that if I kissed him there was no way my heart wouldn't get broken when he left.

"Malcolm," I whispered, trying to convey the worry and the desire at the same time. It was as if a chord snapped in him and he leaned back, furrowing his brow at himself. Instead, he lifted his hand and caressed my cheek, running a thumb along my bottom lip.

"Have a good night, Harley."

Then he was gone, and the warmth of his hand was too. When I went into my room and climbed into my bed, recounting the way Malcolm looked at me, I knew he would hold a spot in my dreams.

Something dragged me out of my sleep. My bedroom was dark, barely any light filtering in from the window, but I knew that something had woken me up. My mind went to the last few hours—the disastrous dinner, Malcolm walking me to my door, Malcolm almost kissing me. I waited, allowing my eyes to get adjusted to the lack of light before I heard the noise.

A sharp snapping sound came from outside my door. Silence unfolded again as I listened intently.

Another snap, like the crisp cracking of a pane of glass, pulled me to my feet. I searched my memory for something to grab onto in the dark and settled on a high heeled boot from my closet.

Carefully pulling open my door, I waited for my eyes to readjust as the sound of the snapping grew louder. Although this time, it was followed by a high-pitched groan. My mind went to the elderly couple who checked in. Doyle had seemed nice, jovial even. But if he was putting his hands on his wife at my inn, this stiletto was going straight up his jovial ass.

I grabbed the ring of room keys from my bedside table then moved on my tiptoes to get closer until I saw something moving out of the corner of my eye. I startled when I saw Malcolm, bare chested with loose pants, holding an umbrella like a baseball bat. His broad shoulders were rounded with muscles that a researcher had no business having. Even in the dimness of the night, I could see his cut physique down to the delicious 'V' dipping into the pants hanging off his hips.

I saw the moment he recognized me, eyes skirting over what I realized was much too short of shorts and tight tank top that left little to the imagination. I flushed at the idea of him seeing so much of me before he eyeballed the boot in my hand.

"You going dancing?" he whispered with a smirk.

"You waiting for rain?" I retorted, eyeing the umbrella which was admittedly a much better weapon than mine. We were interrupted by another sharp crack and the sound of whimpering. There was light beneath the door. Someone was awake.

Malcolm met my eye and nodded. He had my back. I found the key to the room and knocked harshly. "Burnt Creek Inn, open up!"

An alarmed sound came from the other side of the door along with the sound of crashing glass. I turned the key in the lock and ripped the door open, completely unprepared for the sight in front of me.

Wilma Rainer kneeled on the end of the bed, a black hood covering her head like a leather ski mask, eyes wide, with her mouth zipped shut. Small white curls peeked out from the edges of the hood, but otherwise Wilma was naked as the day she was born except for a pair of black fishnet stockings. Gone was the meek church mouse of a woman, and in her place was five feet, two inches of a dominatrix, staring wide-eyed at Malcolm and me. In one hand she held a long riding crop, and in her other hand, she held leather leads attached to a very tied up, very naked Doyle Rainer. The leads were attached to nipple clamps, which held on impressively to his gray hair-covered chest as he lay ball-gagged and spread eagle on the bed.

A moment passed as we all stared at each other.

Wilma turned her head to sneak a glance at Doyle and slowly unzipped her mouthpiece with her riding crop hand.

"Extra punishments for squealing, mister," she whispered with a wink in my direction, delivering a quiet smack with the crop to his inner thigh.

I averted my eyes as soon as my brain caught up. I focused on the broken vase that must have gotten caught in the crossfire of the whip. I cleared my throat.

"Sorry, uh, for the interruption folks. Everything here, um," I paused, looking back over to the couple, "consensual?"

Malcolm snorted behind me, and I elbowed him hard in his sculpted abs.

Wilma gave a wide-eyed nod, prompting Doyle with a little tug on the leads. He let loose a high-pitched groan of what I assumed was pleasure, and I winced for him as he settled for supplying a thumbs up from his hand's location in the handcuffs.

"Right," I said, pulling the keys from the lock. "Well, um, carry on."

I quickly pulled the door shut, plunging Malcolm and me back into darkness. I waited a beat as the reality of what just happened dawned on me. I sank my face into my free hand as Malcolm's chuckles escaped.

"I'm gonna get such a shitty review," I said with a moan.

Malcolm wrapped his arm around my neck, still chuckling. "Come on, babe," he said, kissing my forehead. "We need a drink."

Chapter Ten

Wildflowers and Honey

Malcolm

"What is it with the old people in this town and their crazy sexual escapades?" Harley asked, leaning against the counter in the kitchen while burying her head in her hands. "The oldest O'Neil sister came by earlier this week talking about anal vibrators. Must be something in the water."

"Then it's a good thing we're drinkin' rum," I noted solemnly, pulling open a few cabinets in the kitchen. "Where do you keep the good stuff?"

She grinned mischievously and hooked her finger on the cabinet under the sink. When she pulled the cabinet open, I saw tall bottles of various liquor behind plastic bottles of dawn dish soap and bleach.

When Harley noticed my confusion, she laughed a little. "Maggie hates cleaning, but she loves good liquor. I keep the quality stuff where she won't think to look."

"Miranda was right, you are a hellcat," I said, laughing. I bent down and pulled out a bottle of rum. "Now," I said, examining the label and nodding approvingly. "I want to see this infamous movie room."

Harley grabbed two vintage snifters from a top cabinet and led to me a room towards the back of the inn. She pointed out the conference room that was filled with a large table and a set of comfortable but serious-looking chairs, before directing me further. It was then that I noticed an unmarked door just to the right of the conference room. Harley pulled it open, and I stepped inside.

The room was pitch black until she flipped a switch that illuminated not overhead lights, but three lamps set on small side tables. The walls were painted a dark muted gray that lent to the darkness of the room, and overstuffed loveseats with ottomans and fluffy chairs with pillows gave way to a comfortable feel. The lamps on the small side tables were covered in gauzy red fabric with tassels that looked like they could belong in a speakeasy in the nineteen twenties. The overall effect left me wanting a whiskey and a nap.

"This is awesome," I said, near breathlessly.

Harley sat on half of the loveseat directly in front of the screen. I noticed she left room for me next to her should I choose to take it. My nerves climbed like I was a teenager again. Instead of choosing where to sit, I walked over to the built-in bookcases surrounding the large screen. Stacks of movies arranged by genre instead of alphabetically showed that Harley was a movie enthusiast. I recognized familiar favorites and others that I wouldn't have imagined would be here.

"You really like horror movies," I noted, looking at the largest section. Harley laughed.

"I hate horror flicks, that's Maggie's section." I raised my eyebrows at her. She nodded. "I know, she seems like she would be into the Disney princesses, but I'm telling you, she loves blood, guts, and screams. Maggie's demented under all of that pep."

"Horror is Ben's favorite, too. He tries to get me to watch the gore and slasher flicks all the time, but I'm a big sissy."

Harley snorted. "You want to watch something?"

I shrugged and grabbed a random action film from the shelf. I really didn't care what we watched, my eyes would be on Harley the whole time.

I put the DVD in and tried to casually sit next to her. Her shorts barely covered any of her legs and her bare legs were folded in her lap. She took another sip of her rum and sighed contentedly as she sank back into the couch. I propped my legs up on the ottoman, my arms crossed over my bare chest. I could've put on a shirt before we came downstairs, but I saw the way she was checking me out when she thought I wasn't looking, and I wasn't going to pass up an opportunity. I turned the volume down and slid my eyes up her bare legs. I needed to talk about something that would distract me.

"You could rent this space out," I noted.

She cocked her head to the side. "What do you mean?"

"I mean the town doesn't have a theatre, does it?" I asked. Harley shook her head. "You could totally rent this room out for birthday parties or showings of popular shows for the town. Or hell, you could do movie showings here yourself and charge by the seat."

She rubbed her fingertips along the velvet on the arm of the loveseat. "Do you really think it would work?"

I looked at her quizzically. "Heck yeah, I do! This place is amazing, Harley. People just need to know that it's here. And you need to have more confidence in what you've created here." I paused a moment, looking at the woman I saw as a spitfire diminish into a small flame. "Who put that doubt there?"

She hesitated, then looked at her feet which were curled under her legs. "Connor had been the only person I ever told about my dreams when I was deciding if I should buy the inn. It took a long time, and a lot of pep talks from Maggie, to realize that Connor not only didn't support my ideas, he openly crapped on them."

I grunted. "Well, you already know how I feel about that moron."

Harley giggled and shifted in her seat. I decided to change the subject again, anything to get that look out of her eyes. "You said your mom comes around to watch movies with you?" I asked.

"Yeah," she said. "When she's not trying to set me up with Connor, she can be surprisingly good company. What about you?"

"Me?" I said, trying to deflect. "I can also be surprisingly good company. I'm appalled you have to ask."

She laughed. "No, I mean what about your mom? Are you close?" I took a swig of my rum, and she raised her eyebrows. "Oh boy, this sounds like a story."

I shook my head. "No story, we were close for a long time."

"Past tense?" she asked. I couldn't get a damned thing past her.

"I don't know. I guess it's past tense. I was really close with both of my parents, but I had kind of a falling out with my dad, and my mom got caught in the crossfire. Now, it's like I don't really know how to talk to her."

"Is she back in New York?" Harley asked.

I nodded. "Yeah, my dad's not really around anymore, but she decided to stay there."

"I bet she misses you," Harley said quietly. I looked at her, her face turned toward the screen but her eyes were unfocused.

"What makes you say that?"

"Because I'll miss you when you're gone." Her face still stared toward the screen, but I could still see her cheeks flush. I sank next to her until we were shoulder to shoulder, delving into each other's space. I wanted to let my body say the words my mouth couldn't.

I'll miss you, too.

I don't want to miss you.

I don't want to go.

As the opening credits came and went and Harley drank more of her rum, I saw her head turn to where it was only inches from my naked shoulder. I don't think she even realized she was doing it. I turned my head to face her. Harley looked up at me, her mouth only inches from mine and it was the purest form of hell not to close the distance. But she was now on her second glass of rum, and it was clear to me that she wasn't a frequent drinker.

"Hey, ghosthunter?" she asked quietly, still staring into my eyes. I muted the film that neither of us were paying attention to.

"Yes, innkeeper?"

"My realtor said my inn was haunted." Harley's eyes were wide, and her bottom lip jutted out the smallest bit.

"Is that so?" I asked, staring at her pout. She nodded slightly, jostling her long hair around her face, tickling the top of her tank top. I jerked my eyes back to hers. I had no business looking at the hard nipples poking through the thin sheer of fabric if I wanted to keep the inconsiderate animal in my pants on his best behavior.

"Not like Frank haunted, either. Like *haunted*-haunted."

"Do you believe it?"

"Are you asking me if I believe in ghosts?" she asked with a sudden smile that could melt the sun.

I tucked her hair behind her ear. "Sure."

She shrugged, then took another sip of rum, making a face like someone kicked a puppy in front of her. I chuckled. God, she was adorable.

"I don't know if I believe in ghosts. I've never been around death; nobody I've been particularly close to has died. And if there are ghosts here, they must like me a whole lot because they just go about their business and don't bother me none."

I smiled as Harley sat her drink down and cuddled back into the couch, now resting her head on my shoulder. I didn't want to breathe or move. I wanted to keep the weight of her head, the touch of her hair, against my skin forever.

"There are signs that a house is haunted, you know," I said, trying to keep the stirring in my pants under control.

"Is that so?" she parroted back to me.

"That's right," I said, picking up my own glass. I couldn't believe I was even asking Ben's ridiculous checklist. "For example, is there any place in the house where you don't like going?"

"I don't like going to the basement," she said, scrunching up her nose.

"Why not?"

She sighed. "Too many stairs."

I burst out laughing. I don't think there's a person on the planet who could make me laugh as much as this girl. "Okay, next question. Have you noticed any cold spots?"

"Mostly by the doors."

"Strange smells?"

She cracked a grin. "Mostly by the bathrooms."

"Strange sounds?"

"The stairs creak too much if I eat pizza. But I think they're just judgy."

I grinned. "Last question. Have you ever seen any odd or unsettling figures lurking around?"

"Malcolm, I told you that the oldest O'Neil sister came by this week," she gave me a quick pat on my thigh. "Keep up!"

I laughed again, a common occurrence around Harley. "I think it's safe to say your inn is ghost-free."

"Whew!" she said, wiping a hand across her forehead. "I'm not crazy about the idea of the ghost of a clergyman seeing all the shenanigans that happen around these parts."

I chuckled, finished my drink, and draped an arm around Harley's shoulders. She tilted her head to look up at me and we locked eyes. Her eyes were so green.

As her lips leaned toward mine, I smelled the alcohol on her breath and pulled back, running my thumb over her lip. "I think it's time we get you to bed, sweetheart."

Her eyes lowered and her mouth crinkled on the side. She nodded slightly.

I slid out of the loveseat and held my hand out to her. She took it, sliding out of the nook herself, and kept her hand in mine as we slowly made our way up the stairs. Harley tripped once on the stairs, saved by my hand wrapped around her waist, and she muttered a '*dammit, Frank*' before continuing carefully. As we reached the landing, I noticed there were no sounds coming from Wilma and Doyle's room, thank goodness, as I guided a stumbling Harley to her room.

Opening her door, I flipped on the light just long enough to locate a small lamp near Harley's bed. Turning on the lamp, I settled Harley into the bed and pulled the comforters up to her shoulders. Leaning over, I kissed her forehead and took a final sniff of her hair. Wildflowers and honey. Normally I'd feel weird about it, but at this point, it was kind of our thing.

And it didn't bother me the slightest that Harley and I had a thing.

"Malcolm?" she whispered as I walked out of her room.

"Yeah?"

"Thank you for being there for me today," she said, through a yawn, burying her head further into her pillows. Her breath evened out, and I could tell the alcohol had helped her go back to sleep easily.

"Always, Harley," I said quietly. As I closed the door behind me and made my way back to my room alone, I ran through the scenarios that would allow me to keep my promise. I traveled a lot with the Spirits Channel which made it difficult to maintain a relationship. Ben would be flexible about working around family life or even bringing a family or wife on the road with us, but I didn't want that life for my family. And I didn't want to say goodbye to a wife and child to go on the road.

I shed my pants and lay out on the bed. Barely one week with Harley and I was thinking about marriage and children. And it was Harley that I was picturing beside me. But what would that look like in reality? She owned this inn, she was a member of this town, and I couldn't ask her to give up her dream to run around chasing ghosts that I didn't even believe in.

What was I doing? These feelings were temporary. We were two ships passing in the night, not meant to be permanent. As I stood up to brush my teeth, my foot caught on the side table, and I stumbled forward.

"Dammit, Frank," I muttered.

Chapter Eleven

Sabotaging Social Butterfly

Harley

The light filtering through my window felt like I was getting beamed up by a UFO. I groaned, smashing the nearby pillow into my face to block out light, but the sound of the fabric rubbing against my face was like nails on a chalkboard. Looking slowly at my side table, so as to calm the rattling in my head, I saw a glass of water and a bottle of over-the-counter painkillers. Next to that was my alarm clock that read 12:54 PM. I shot forward, my head screaming in protest, as I quickly drank the water and downed two painkillers before rushing desperately into my clothes. I fell twice, cursing up a storm, and a knock came on my door.

"I'm coming!" I shouted, and I winced at the sound of my own voice.

"Harley, it's me," Malcolm said. I walked over to the door, gripping my head, and yanked open the door. "Whoa, where's the fire?" he asked.

"I slept in! I have to check out the Rainer couple and flip their room. I don't know how it happened—"

"Harley, breathe, I already took care of it."

I froze, looking up at Malcolm who looked at me through those dark framed glasses as he put his hands on my shoulders.

"You took care of it?" I squeaked.

"I called Maggie in this morning, explained that you might be a little under the weather, and she came in to check them out. I helped flip the room already. I was the one who turned off your alarm clock. I told you when I did it, but you must have forgotten. You needed your sleep after last night."

"But breakfast—"

"I make a mean pancake," he grinned.

I felt my shoulders sag in relief. "You did that for me?"

He shrugged sheepishly. "Yeah, but don't get any ideas. I do that for all my fake girlfriends."

I laughed quietly, gripping my head.

"Drink some more water," he said, rubbing circles on my shoulders with his thumb. "Take some time, Maggie and I have it handled."

I should have protested more; he was a guest after all. But he was starting to feel like so much more. Also, I caught a glimpse of my hair and a sniff of my clothes and decided if I didn't get a shower pronto, even Malcolm wouldn't want to be around me.

After taking my time in the shower, I got dressed in comfortable clothing and made my way downstairs to Maggie. She sat behind the desk, her blond hair braided away from her face and a pair of black horn-rimmed glasses adorning her face today. When she saw me, she smiled.

"Well, don't you look like death warmed over!" she said with entirely too much cheer and volume.

"As always, your enthusiasm is the bane of my existence," I responded, deadpan. She smiled wider and wiggled her eyebrows.

"I heard you had some excitement last night," she said, sliding me a small gift bag. "Wilma Rainer wanted me to give this to you to apologize for last night's...escapades."

I groaned, eyeballing the gift bag when Malcolm walked around the counter.

"What's this?" he asked, leaning against the counter next to me. His close proximity after last night made me painfully aware of every brush of our arms against each other.

"An apology gift from Wilma Rainer," I answered. "I hope it's cookies. Her husband said she was in sales. Hopefully, we can reap some of those benefits around here."

Maggie's shoulders shook in silent laughter. "I really hope you use some of what she's selling."

I eyed her, my confusion likely evident on my face. I opened the bag, shuffling around the tissue paper until my hand landed on a small package. Lifting it out, I read the label aloud. "Tropical Fruit Lubricants." My face turned bright red as I quickly peeked inside the bag, trying to read the labels silently away from Malcolm's prying eyes. A sample package of edible underwear and a pair of familiar rope cuffs which I had seen wrapped around the elderly Doyle Rainer's wrists the night before were also in the bag.

"What do you think, Sis?" Maggie asked, her laughter breaking through. "Think you can reap the benefits of what she's selling?"

"Oh, my God," I moaned. "She sells sex aids?"

Malcolm chuckled beside me. "At least we know she does thorough product research herself."

I shuddered. "Too soon, Malcolm." He laughed louder.

"What should we do with this stuff?" I asked. Beside me, Malcolm stopped laughing with a strangled groan. My face went red as I looked at him. "I didn't mean *we* as in...I just meant where should this stuff go—"

"Well I'm no expert, Harley," Maggie said in a fake whisper, "but there are a few places that stuff can *go* if you know what I mean."

"Yes, thank you, Maggie." I gritted through my teeth. I raised my eyebrows as I slowly backed away, looking everywhere except at Malcolm. "I'm going to get some food. I'm too hungover to participate in this conversation."

I walked into the kitchen, leaving the chortling laughs of Malcolm and Maggie behind me. Maggie or Malcolm must have cleaned up after the pancakes this morning, and seeing as it was nearly lunchtime, I threw together some eggs on toast.

Beside the toaster was a cell phone, maybe Maggie's. It started vibrating with an incoming call and the name flashed up 'DAD'S LAWYER – DO NOT ANSWER.' My eyebrows pinched together as I picked up the phone and inspected it. Definitely not Maggie's.

When the phone stopped ringing, an alert flashed on the phone that showed four missed calls from the same number. I brought the phone into the lobby where Maggie was on the computer looking for apartments in the area.

"Hey Mags, do you know whose phone this is?" I asked. "It was in the kitchen."

Maggie inspected it. "I think it's Malcolm's. He was making breakfast in there earlier."

My head tipped to the side. Why would his father's lawyers be calling him so much? A worry churned in my gut. Maybe something happened to Malcolm's dad.

"Is he up in his room?" I asked.

"Yeah, he said something about researching—" I didn't let her finish before I took the stairs two at a time, head still throbbing from the hangover, and knocked on Malcolm's door.

He opened his door, and I thrust his phone at him. His eyes look bewildered.

"Everything okay, Harley?"

I shook my head. "I didn't mean to look, but it started ringing and your dad's lawyers have called a lot. I think something is wrong with your dad!"

Malcolm's jaw clenched and his knuckles turned white as he gripped the phone. He turned and tossed his phone on the bed and turned back to me as it started vibrating again.

"Harley, take a breath," he said, as my eyes widened.

"But your dad, is he okay?" I asked, peering around his shoulder at the phone still ringing on the bed. He positioned his body in front of my gaze.

"My father is fine. Everything is fine."

I felt my eyebrows furrow as I looked at him. "But why would his lawyers be calling if everything's fine?"

"His lawyers want something from me and have a hard time taking no for an answer," his lips were set in a hard line, and I just wanted to smooth the tense wrinkles in his forehead.

"Oh, well maybe you can—"

"Harley, it's none of your business."

He looked at me pointedly, and I took a step back as his door closed in my face.

Embarrassment ballooned in my chest as I turned to go back downstairs.

At least now I knew that everything I was feeling for Malcolm was one hundred percent one-sided.

I blinked back my surprise and tears and kicked myself. Of course, it's one-sided. He's a guest. The last thing he needs is the owner of the inn he's staying at to be hitting on him. I played back our interactions from the previous night. I thought that he leaned into me the way I leaned into him. I thought he was feeling everything I was. But now I had to look at it through a different scope. Were his actions those of a guy who was flirting or were they of a guy who was spending time with a friend? Maybe he was just being supportive after we witnessed a disturbing scene.

I went to my room, grabbed my purse, and made sure I looked presentable. I needed some space from Malcolm to get a clear head. Clearly, he had no problem having distance from me. I checked my booking service, found no new reservations, and forwarded the calls from the inn to my cell phone before heading out. Maggie said she would be gone as soon as she updated some social media posts.

I sent a text to Penny, but I didn't have time to wait for her to tell me it was fine to come over. I needed to talk to her now. I needed my very sensible friend to tell me what to do with all these conflicting emotions.

I arrived to find Penny in a flustered state, which meant that instead of sitting in a comfortable chair, I was ordered to stand on a pedestal as Penny stuck pins into a costume that she had wrapped around me.

"Quit moving," she complained.

"What is this thing supposed to be anyway?" I asked, twisting to look at myself in the mirror. Long tendrils of purple draped loosely around me. Some had what looked like tentacles.

"The high school is putting on a production of The Wizard of Oz in space."

I whipped my head around to see her. "In space?"

Penny shrugged, sticking a pin in the large tentacle at my side. "Yeah, the director is some theatre school graduate who couldn't get a job because he's more obsessed with producing obscure social justice art than finding a good theatre company to be a part of, so now the simple high school costuming I've volunteered for has me turning out purple-people-eater suits." The frustration radiating from Penny was visceral. "But enough about me, what's going on with you and the YouTube guy?"

I groaned and shrugged my shoulders, earning me a pinprick to the thigh. "Ow!" I yelped. "I don't know what's going on with us. Well, that's not true, I know that nothing is going on with us. Sometimes it seems like he's sweet and he wants things to go places with us. The other night, I swear he was going to kiss me. But then other times he acts like I'm an annoyance and he wants nothing to do with me." I sighed. "Maybe that's not fair. I think he just wants to be friends."

"Well," Penny said, talking through four pins that sat in her mouth. "What do you want?"

"I don't know, Penn. I mean, I shouldn't want anything. He's only here for a few weeks, he's hot and cold all the time, and he's a ghost hunter and YouTuber for crying out loud. I mean, that's like one step above social media influencer, and one step below mermaid whisperer."

"That's a weirdly specific scale you have."

"I've put a lot of thought into it," I admitted.

"Okay, well, first of all, it doesn't matter what you should or shouldn't want. It matters what you actually want. Secondly, if Mr. Hot, Smart and Steamy is what you want, you need to recognize that he is a ghost hunter and a YouTuber. You don't have to like his career choice, because it *is* a career choice, but you do have to respect it. Of course, you could always just have a temporary roll in the sheets fling and get it out of your system before he goes anywhere."

The thought of Malcolm between my sheets had me feeling inappropriate things between my legs.

"But whatever you decide to do," Penny finished, grabbing my waist. "You need to quit moving before I pin this tentacle to your tail."

My phone rang from the table across the room, and I shot a desperate look at Penny who groaned and threw her hands in the air.

"Go ahead," she said. "Take the call."

I smiled gratefully and waddled off the podium and across the room. I looked at the caller ID and frowned. "Maggie? Is everything okay?"

"I figured it out!" she crooned loudly. I had to pull my ear away from the phone, and she celebrated.

"Figured what out?" I asked, glancing across at Penny.

"I figured out why all of these places keep canceling their reservations!"

My head snapped up. "Tell me," I demanded.

"According to the social media pages, organization websites, and the psychic sisters' gossip texts, Joanna Monterey has been quite the social butterfly these past few weeks."

"Joanna? Connor's mom?"

"The same one. She joined the Red Hat Society, the Modern Women's Book Club, and the local scrapbookers group all within the last month."

My mouth was set in a grim line. Those were the three organizations that called and canceled their conference room reservations.

"Why would she do this?" I asked. "I mean, Conner I get, and I know that Joanna never liked me, but this is kind of extreme."

"I don't know, Harley, but at least now we know so we can figure out what to do about it."

Except that I didn't know at all what to do about it.

Chapter Twelve

Why Does a Spirit Cross the Road

Malcolm

The next morning, I woke up ready for my meeting with Mabel O'Neil at the town museum. Harley wasn't anywhere that I could find. She wasn't at breakfast this morning, and I didn't want to ask Maggie and raise suspicion that I was looking for her. I really needed to apologize for being so short with her about the phone situation. And shutting the door in her face. It seemed like every time I was around this girl my brain stopped working.

I had been looking for her since the night before. I saw her car pull into the driveway and was prepared to offer my apologies then, but she had snuck in through the back door and managed to evade me. Even thinking about it made me feel equal parts a creep and an idiot. She was avoiding me, and I completely deserved it.

I drove my car to the museum. The building, like most of the buildings in Burnt Creek, was old. The plaster was falling off the faded side of the building, and the doors were clean enough to let in some light but not to see in. Faded letters hung over the door spelling "Burnt Creek Museum." The building was long, and I could see more faded letters imprinted on the dirty paint that outlined the words

"Burnt Creek Newspaper." I smiled at the luck. I'd have to check the newspaper after my tour of the museum.

Walking in the door, I found Mabel O'Neil on the other side. The middle Ms. O'Neil was a vision of crystals and beads clanging against every part of her and she was slowly waving around a burning sage bundle, leaving a trail of smoke that I had to wave my hand through to see straight. And, consistent with her reputation, she had her phone in her pocket, ready to whip it out at a moment's notice, like a sheriff drawing a gun in an old western.

Behind the welcome desk was another older woman with a long red scarf tied around her head, with beads and shells attached at the end that jingled as she moved. She looked like she bought a pirate costume and just added to it.

"Welcome," Mabel O'Neil said solemnly.

"Yes, thank you, Ms. O'Neil."

"Psh, please none of that Ms. O'Neil nonsense. It's Mabel, plain and simple. Over there is my younger sister, Bertha. Sorry about the sage, but I figure if you're going to talk to the dead in this building, I should have a smudging to be on the safe side."

The woman behind the desk didn't look up from whatever she was doing, but she nodded her encouragement emphatically.

"Um, of course. But Ms. O'—Mabel, I won't be talking to any dead, here or anywhere else."

Mabel broke her solemn face as her eyes snapped to me. "But I thought you were a ghost hunter?"

Bertha put down what I now recognized as tarot cards and matched Mabel's expression.

My head fell back, and I struggled to resist an eye roll. "I'm just here to do some research on the town."

Disappointment coated Mabel's face. "But...but I thought you were going to talk to the dead?"

"Sorry to disappoint," I said. "But I'd love for you to show me around, there might be ghosts around town that we need to report on, and I need to know the places in town that would have the highest likelihood of...activity."

"You mean you need to help the spirits cross to the other side," Bertha demanded.

"Sure," I said, trying to maintain my patience.

"How does that work?" Mabel asked, clutching a band of rough-cut crystals around her neck.

"How does what work?" I asked.

"Helping a spirit to cross to the other side?"

"Like a chicken crossing the road. Just with more humming and other spirit connection stuff."

"Fascinating," she said, wide-eyed.

"Right, well, I was told you give the best museum tours, Mabel," I said, trying to reclaim the conversation.

"Oh, of course! How about we take a mosey around the museum and then Bertha can give you a tarot reading! On the house!"

"That's not really necessary—"

"Our town was founded in 1899," Mabel interrupted, waving her hands like a flight attendant directing me toward the room to the left of the desk. "The Burnt Creek Inn was here before that, helping to house travelers on the road between larger towns and cities, and the population grew around that until we were officially founded as a town."

Mabel led me around the corner to a room with four large antique windows. "This building was originally built as a railroad station in the 1960s, but the railroad was never built to come through here. We still kept the original architecture, and you can see out these back windows and doors where the railroad would have gone, but now we use it as a bike path."

My eyebrows raised, and I scribbled notes and questions frantically as Mabel guided me around, pointing out various small artifacts and pictures, including the local cow that was in the Guinness Book of World Records for having the longest tail and the section in the museum dedicated to the yearly winners of the "Autumnest Businesses" in Burnt Creek.

As Mabel ended the tour back near the entrance, Bertha was still flipping tarot cards over like she was playing solitaire, I pulled out my note from earlier.

"Mabel, I was over at the police station last Friday—" I started.

"Oh, you were, were you?" Mabel asked, looking pointedly at Bertha behind the desk. Bertha pulled out her phone and quickly began typing, but being less experienced with technology than Mabel was, Bertha had to sound out the words she was typing.

"Bad...boy...ghost...hunter...got...arrested...last...Friday..."

"Whoa, I didn't get arrested! I was visiting the sheriff!"

Mabel patted his arm. "Of course, you were, dear."

I chose to ignore Bertha behind the desk. "Anyway, they said that in 1972 a flood following Hurricane Agnes unearthed three bodies. The bodies of railroad men? Does this museum have any connection to them?"

Mabel pursed her lips, clearly displeased by my question. "Why on Earth would you think that?"

I tilted my head at her and glanced down at my notes. "You said this building was originally created as a rail station in the '60s, did you not?"

"Well, yes," she admitted, glancing at Bertha who also looked displeased by this line of questions.

"Well according to the police records, the three railroad men were scamming locals into donating money to a proposed railroad to run through here, but there was no evidence of actual plans for a railroad. Since they were found dead in the same time period that this building was built, and both are linked to a failed railroad, can you see how a person would make a connection between the two?"

"I suppose," she admitted reluctantly. I waited for one of the sisters to add something, but they only stole guilty glances at each other. I felt the same tingle in the back of my mind that I always got when chasing down a lead as a journalist. These women knew something.

"Hey Bertha," I said, walking toward the front desk and leaning against it, flashing her my 'dazzle' smile. Her hardened countenance softened slightly as a blush tinged her wrinkled cheeks.

"How long have you ladies lived in Burnt Creek?" I relaxed my posture, aiming to be as conversational as possible.

"Oh, we've always been here," she said. "Born and raised."

"Well, far be it from me to guess the age of you young ladies, but I'm thinking you ladies might have been around town in the nineteen sixties?"

"Oh, yes, we were around then," she said, her blush deepening to the roots of her white curls. "We were quite the lookers then, too, you know."

I grinned at her. "Some things never change."

Mabel cleared her throat, and Bertha bobbed the tarot cards in her hand. She sighed heavily, then nodded at Mabel.

Looking down at her tarot cards, she said calmly. "We were around, and we knew the rail boys, but we don't like to talk about it because they caused quite a rift with us sisters. We decided after that not to let any man come between us, and we haven't spoken about those boys since."

"Right, well, I was more wondering if you had any information about their deaths that might help the team contact them in...the beyond...or whatever."

Mabel stepped closer with a sniff. "Well, like Bertha said, we don't like to talk about them. In fact, even having this conversation feels like a betrayal."

I gritted my teeth. "I see. Well, I'd hate to put you in an uncomfortable position." I looked around until I found a door along the far wall that she hadn't commented on during the tour. "What's over there?"

Mabel waved a hand dismissively. "That's a door to the old newspaper."

"Old newspaper?" I asked. "Where's the new newspaper?"

"There isn't one. The newspaper went bankrupt around ten years ago when the police busted the owner for using it as an illegal frog race gambling ring."

"I—wait, what?"

Mabel nodded sagely. "The sheriff has a soft spot for animals. The second someone let it slip that the old curmudgeon who owned it was housing poor, defenseless amphibians against their will to fight it out to the death on the racetrack for betting money, the sheriff swept in with the full force of the Burnt Creek Police Department! Of course, they also discovered some military-grade weapons and drugs and all that, but could you even imagine the damage that the frog racing could have done to our community?"

I had no idea how to respond to that.

"Um, so who owns that side of the building now?"

"The town does. Zippy was just renting the building. There's still a lot of office stuff in there, just sitting abandoned. The town auctioned off the computers and printers and stuff, but they left the desks and such in there hoping to draw another renter."

"Mind if I take a look?" She shrugged at me and waved me toward the door. I peeked in to find a collection of dusty old office furniture pushed up against a wall and some empty shelves. I closed the door and looked back at Mabel.

"Did Zippy leave any old newspapers? Or do you have any of them from the sixties?"

"Oh, heck no. The library might have some, but that's about it. Zippy didn't care one snot for the news. Us O'Neil sisters have been the main source of news around here for ages. It certainly helps that we can predict it before it happens," she said with a raised hand to her temple, a signature move for the sisters I was realizing.

I thought for a moment, trying to decide how I could find more information on the three dead bodies from decades ago which nobody wanted to talk about. With the newspaper out of commission, I realized I had to think outside the box.

Walking back toward the front desk, I adjusted my glasses and rubbed the back of my neck. I tried to look as small and uncomfortable as possible. Given the conversations I've had with these ladies, it wasn't that difficult. "Ladies, I'm finding myself in need of some psychic help."

Mabel perked up immediately. Bertha nearly rolled out of the office chair, and her tarot cards went flying as she quickly threw her hand up to touch her temple. "Yes, I sensed that you might."

"Right," I said, still shuffling from foot to foot. "So you'll do it, then?"

Bertha and Mabel looked at me confused. "Do what, dear?" Mabel asked.

"The séance," I said innocently. "As established as *Spirits, Seekers, and Skeptics* is, we've had a hard time finding psychic services with such...experience...to perform such a task. But I'm sure the Three Sisters' Psychic Services would be more than qualified to lead a séance."

Bertha smoothed her beaded scarf down the side of her shirt. "Of course, we are qualified," she said haughtily. "We merely need time to prepare."

"Yes," Mabel said quickly. "We need to purify our spiritual connection and purge ourselves of...waste...and such."

I tried to cover my grimace. "How about Saturday?" I asked. "Would that give you all enough time to purge your...waste?"

Both women nodded, and their hair bobbed around scarves.

"Wonderful," I said.

When I arrived back at the inn, Maggie was waiting behind the front desk with her high tops propped up on the desk and a shit-eating grin on her face. "Hey criminal, heard you got arrested last Friday."

Chapter Thirteen

Car-Napping

Harley

Malcolm finally found me in the laundry room adding bleach and softener to a load of towels. My attempts at avoiding him until I could figure out what either of us wanted from each other had been successful up to this point.

"Hey, Harley."

I gave my best hospitality smile, trying to ignore the shivers of electricity that started in my stomach and made their way down my arms. "Good afternoon, Malcolm. Is there something I can get you? Fresh towels? Sheets?"

An attitude adjustment?

He shook his head. "Forgiveness, if you have some to spare."

My hands stilled. I needed to keep up my walls. He was a guest, a temporary guest. He made it perfectly clear that I had no business sticking my nose in his life. I wasn't going to put my heart somewhere it wasn't wanted.

"No forgiveness necessary," I stated, closing the washing machine. "You've done nothing wrong."

As I turned to walk out, his large frame leaned against the door frame blocking my path with raised eyebrows.

"I call bullshit," he said simply.

I shook my head. "Malcolm—"

"We both know I was a jerk to you, and you pretending that I wasn't is your way of trying to pretend that it didn't hurt you. Because if hurts you, then it means that I matter to you."

How was it that I had only known this man for a few days, and he still managed to see me? Really see me? But I didn't want him to see me. I let my walls down around him once. I wasn't aiming to make that mistake twice.

"You're a guest, Malcolm. Guests have a right to their privacy, and a host should know better than to interfere with that privacy."

"Is that all I am? A guest?" His eyes bore into me, a challenge with vulnerability laced through.

"What else would you want to be?"

"I don't know, Harley," he said, running a hand over his head. "A friend, at least."

I felt my heart sink in my chest. "You want to be friends?"

"Yes. Friends who go to bakeries together and fake relationships and interrupt older couples' bold sexual encounters."

I tried to fight a smile and failed. "That's a very specific kind of friendship."

"You're a very specific friend."

I sighed. "You make it really hard to stay mad at you. And I should point out you never actually apologized for being an ass."

He pushed off the doorframe and stood in front of me, resting his strong hands on my shoulders. "Harley, I'm sorry I was such an ass last night. Things with my dad are complicated, and I have a hard time talking about it."

I nodded for a moment. "I forgive you."

"Good, because I have another outing I'd love to invite my friend to."

"Oh, yeah? What's that?"

"Wanna come to a séance with me on Saturday?" he asked. I raised my eyebrows at him and chuckled.

"Can't say a friend has ever invited me to a séance before."

He grinned and wrapped an arm around my shoulders as we walked out of the laundry room. "Honey, you need some new friends."

We ran into Maggie as we were coming out of the laundry room. I wasn't sure why she was at the bed and breakfast, she wasn't on the schedule for another two days.

"Harley, there you are! Have you figured out what we're going to do about the Montereys?"

I ignored the raised eyebrow from Malcolm about the comment, and I also ignored the raised eyebrow from Maggie about the YouTuber's arm around my shoulder. "I haven't really thought about it," I lied. Truthfully, when my mind wasn't consumed with thoughts of Malcolm, my mind was exclusively on what to do about the fact that my ex-boyfriend and his family were trying to sabotage my business.

"Well, we need to figure it out. I've been reaching out to local businesses that might need to use our conference rooms, and I've been checking out their social media accounts. There's already been an uptick in posts between Joanna and the businesses that seemed interested."

I tipped my head to the side. "You've been reaching out to businesses for the inn?" I took a good look at my sister. Her blonde eyebrows were furrowed in frustration and determination and her eyes were flinty. She wasn't just doing this to be a good sister or even a good employee. Maggie *cared* about this inn. She had reached out to local businesses. She had reached out to Ben. She had advocated bringing an entire YouTube circus here to save my inn. This meant if something happened to this inn, it wasn't going to be a loss of just a paycheck for her. Maybe I should get her a real employee of the month trophy.

She nodded briskly at me. "Yes, I've been trying to shore up additional income to keep us in the black, and I hope you don't mind, but I've launched some more social media posts and scheduled some more out."

She opened up her laptop and flicked through various screens showing different graphics.

"Maggie, this is amazing!" Malcolm said, working the touchpad. "You made all of these?"

She smirked. "I'm more than just a pretty face. But seriously, we need to address the poaching."

Malcolm dropped his arm from my shoulder. "What poaching?"

I was about to wave him off, but Maggie closed the laptop lid and spun to face him directly. "Douche-Face Connor's mom is joining or working with every organization that's been booking our conference rooms and they've been canceling within the week. It's bad enough that she and Connor don't let Maggie get any traction with the city council, but now they're blocking our bottom line."

Malcolm paused. "There's a lot to unpack there."

Maggie groaned. "Malcolm, Connor and his mom Joanna are Montereys, like the Monterey Hotel Group."

"Right, I got that, but do either of them actually work for one of the hotels? I don't remember seeing one near here."

"No, because three years ago the hotel group was trying to get permits to build in the town but the city council shut them down because the town prides itself on small business and Autumn-themed names. So when Harley got permission to reopen the Burnt Creek Bed and Breakfast, Connor and his mom claimed that she must have blackmailed the members of the city council to agree with her. Since then, Connor has always made a point to have a seat on the city council and his mom has made a point to destroy any opposition when he runs for city council."

Malcolm turned to me. "Seriously?"

I grimaced. "Unfortunately, yeah. But I'm trying to be the mature one and move past it."

Malcolm and Maggie exchanged a look. "We need a plan," Malcolm said finally. "And we need food while we do it."

"I'll text Brandon and Oliver to meet us at Witches' Brew," Maggie said, setting her laptop down and whipping out her cell phone. "Brandon's good at getting us into trouble and Oliver is good at making sure it's at least legal."

I rubbed my forehead. This was already getting out of hand. But something needed to be done, and I certainly had no idea what to do about it. I grabbed my car keys from behind the front desk and headed out to the parking lot, only to find my car was not where I left it.

I spun on my heels, searching in each direction. I racked my brain. I came home last night, parked it right next to Maggie's Volkswagon, and I haven't left since. "Um, have either of you seen my car?"

I turned toward them, expecting them to act like I was crazy. Honestly though, how does someone misplace a car?

"Oh, right," Malcolm said, swinging his keys on his finger. "I forgot to tell you, it's over at the Fall Apart auto shop."

I froze right in the middle of my parking lot as I ran through reasons as to why my car would have gotten sucked through the sky and dumped randomly at the auto shop. "Um, why? Did someone hit it?" I asked, staring at the nearly empty parking lot. Neither Malcolm nor Maggie had dents or scratches on their cars.

"No," Malcolm said, walking in front of me. "I called Jed and had him come get it."

"Why would you do that? I can't afford that!"

"Because as we just agreed, we're friends. And friends don't let friends drive death traps through town. Also, I covered the cost."

Maggie whistled low and wiped her horn-rimmed glasses on her shirt. "I'm gonna let you guys argue about this, and the rest of the gang and I will meet you there."

Maggie quickly jumped in the front seat of her lime green VW Beetle and pulled out of the driveway as I glared at Malcolm.

"I know we just cemented our friendship, Malcolm, but so far you kind of suck at it."

"I'll keep that in mind for our quarterly friend evaluations," he said, adjusting his handsome as hell glasses and putting a hand casually in his pocket. "Also, friend to friend, the proper response is 'Thanks, Malcolm. You're the best and most gorgeous friend I've ever had!'" He pitched his voice up in an annoying falsetto when pretending to be me, and I did not appreciate it.

"I don't sound like that," I grumbled.

"Harley, come on. Consider it my apology for me being a jerk yesterday."

"You already apologized for that. I don't need you swooping in and playing superman for me, especially with things that I can't reciprocate on."

"Get in the car, Harley. You can yell at me when I have a burger in front of me."

My stomach chose that annoying moment in time to growl loudly. He looked pointedly at my stomach then turned towards his car, opening the passenger door for me. I stomped like a toddler over to the car and made sure not to smell his intoxicating scent. "Just for the record, you are not the most gorgeous friend I've ever had," I grumbled.

Malcolm leaned into my space and buckled my seatbelt over my lap. My breath hitched as his lips grazed my shoulder. Then he paused inches from my face, eyes on my mouth. "Maybe, but how many friends get your heart rate up that much?" he asked with a smirk before pulling himself out of the car and shutting the passenger door behind him.

I took a full breath, willing my traitor heart rate to slow down.

Chapter Fourteen

Mother Dearest

Malcolm

When I pulled up to the curb outside Witches' Brew, Harley was still pouting in the front seat. Watching her have a temper tantrum to try to prove how grown up she is was probably the most adorable thing I've ever seen. Was it high-handed to have Jed from the auto shop come take Harley's car without her knowing? Probably. But Maggie had assured me that Harley didn't have any plans for the next few days, and I needed to apologize to Harley anyways. Might as well roll two apologies into one.

Also, I would be lying if I said that the idea of her driving that hunk of barely-there metal around town didn't leave me with nightmares of Harley trapped in a vehicle that could spontaneously combust. Somebody needed to look after her safety.

Buckling her into the seat was an exercise in restraint too. All I wanted to do was lean in and kiss those pouting lips. And when her breath hitched when my lips skimmed her shoulder, I wanted to see how her breathing would react if my lips were on another part of her body. I had to hurry to shut the door so I could discreetly adjust the raging hard-on pressing against the zipper of my jeans. I swear being around this girl makes me as hormonal as a teenager again.

I needed to keep my distance. That was the smart, responsible thing to do. But I didn't want to. I didn't want to act like Harley wasn't getting under my skin.

I put the car in park, and Harley was out of it before I could open her door. I shook myself. This wasn't a date, and Harley wasn't my girlfriend. We were friends.

Witches' Brew was busier than I expected it to be during a lunch rush on a Monday. The fake skulls and smoky bar top that looked nearly sinister the last time I was here looked fun and campy in the daylight. The art up on the walls showed brighter colors in the daylight as well.

I caught a glimpse of the piece of artwork that Harley had been staring at the last time. Only this time, I actually took the time to look at it. It was an impressionist painting of a woman in a red dress leaning up against a crumbling wall. Her head was turned, and her face was covered by cascading wild hair, and a bouquet of flowers hung loosely in her hand. It kind of reminded me of Harley in a way. A classy woman, all dressed up with nowhere to go. But maybe it was that the woman didn't seem defeated or downtrodden. She held herself like she was content in either world, crumbling ruin or fancy dresses.

A whistle cut through the air and drew my eyes away. Harley was already on her way over to Maggie, their cousin Brandon sitting at the table next to the blond-haired cop from the police station. He looked older here than he looked at the station, maybe it was the fact that he wasn't dressed in a freshly ironed blue uniform.

"Hey Malcolm," Brandon greeted, holding up a beer. It was one in the afternoon, and by all accounts from looking around the restaurant, that was five o'clock in Burnt Creek time. I gave him and Oliver a hello as Harley and I settled into our chairs.

A server came up with a messy bun scrunched up on top of her head and gave Oliver a shy grin. She got Harley's and my orders before be-bopping away. Oliver tried to be discreet when he checked out her ass and failed.

"Maggie was filling us in on the situation," Brandon said, nudging Oliver to get his focus back. Oliver dragged his eyes away from the server with the reluctance of a golden retriever turning away from a game of fetch.

"Oh, goodie," Harley mumbled.

Oliver tilted his head at her. "Harley, it's your inn and your reputation on the line here. We're not going to do anything you don't want us to do. But I'd hazard a guess and say that if your dad and Miranda had an idea what was going on, you'd have a lot less control over what actions were taken against the Montereys."

Harley narrowed her eyes at Oliver. "Ollie, are you threatening to tell my dad?"

I wasn't sure what familiarity took place for Harley to call him "Ollie," but I got more family vibes than anything which is the only thing that kept my hackles down.

He shrugged nonchalantly, but I could see him challenging her with his eyes. "Nah, I wouldn't tell your dad. But things get around, Harley. Maybe one day people are talking around the water cooler at the station and your dad overhears something. Maybe my mom gets wind that someone is messing with her goddaughter and suddenly Chad Monterey finds that all of his expensive ties have been mysteriously bedazzled with Miranda's signature bright pink 'F U'. I'm just saying, maybe you'd like to take control of the situation."

Silence lapsed over the table while Oliver and Harley faced off. Oliver, for his part, seemed to take in stride the glare that Harley was shooting him. He merely munched on the nuts sitting in the middle of the table.

The peppy server brought over our drinks, an apple cider bourbon for Harley, and a beer for me, bringing Oliver's attention back to her ass as she walked away.

"Fine," Harley said. "We can handle the situation ourselves, but I want to make sure there's no open combat. Just small things to get my business back."

Brandon clapped his hands together. "That's what I'm talking about!"

I pulled out my notebook, ready to play reporter, but Maggie beat me to it. "So, my first question is how is Joanna figuring out the businesses that are using our conference room? Is someone telling her, or is she a magical being that's somehow everywhere at once?"

Maggie looked cautiously over her shoulder just as Brandon shuddered.

"And," Oliver cut in, ignoring Brandon next to him. "What's the motive? Is it just her being spiteful? Is she joining these groups because she's lonely?"

"Is Connor involved?" I growled. Somehow, I had a feeling deep in my gut that the limp noodle of a man was involved.

Harley took a swig of her bourbon. "We either need to confront one of them or find someone close to them who could give us information."

We sat in silence for a moment before I cut my eyes to Harley, then Maggie. "Is your mom still trying to hook you two up?"

Harley and Maggie exchanged looks, equal parts horrified and hopeful. "It's possible," Maggie acknowledged. "She's spent the most time around Connor lately. She might know something."

Harley pulled out her phone and typed out a text. "All right, that part's taken care of. Now we at least have a starting point."

Our food arrived, and we settled into a comfortable conversation. It reminded me of the easy camaraderie of the Spirits crew. I actually missed my overbearing coworkers. Harley's mom texted back with an invitation for Harley to visit after lunch, and I grinned knowing that because I was driving, she had to bring me along.

Valerie Malone's house was a ranch-style bungalow twenty minutes outside of town. The front yard was covered in lush gardens carefully curated by someone obsessed with image and money. The front face of the house was glistening white as though it had recently been power washed, and the front porch had a matching patio seating set with perfectly fluffed pillows welcoming strangers.

As we stepped onto the porch, the door opened ominously, and Valerie stepped out in high heels and overly done makeup for someone just hanging out at home. It reminded me of the fake people my father surrounded himself with.

"Harley!" she crooned. When Valerie saw me, her façade cracked a little. "Oh, and you brought a friend."

'Friend' seemed like an odd choice of words, since the last time we saw each other, Harley introduced me as her boyfriend. I slipped an arm around Harley's waist and extended my other hand.

"Valerie, it's great to see you again."

Valerie nervously wiped her hands on the front of her dress in a gesture that reminded me of Harley. She extended a hand toward me and threw a guilty glance over her shoulder.

"Um, of course, it's great to see you as well."

"Mom, could we go inside? We were hoping to talk with you about some things."

Valerie wiped her hands down her dress again and glanced back towards the door. "You know, it's such a nice day out today, maybe we should just sit on the porch."

Harley's eyes narrowed. "What's going—"

A nasally man's voice boomed from inside. "Valerie, I've got the wine open. Is Harley here yet?"

"You have got to be kidding me!" Harley snarled before muscling her way past her mother. Connor Monterey stood in the kitchen with three wine glasses at the ready, wearing a smarmy smile that faltered when I came into view. "What in the hell are you doing here?"

Valerie quickly shuffled in behind me. "Now, Harley, Connor was just here to apologize for the misunderstanding that arose from your breakup."

"You mean the misunderstanding of where his dick was and wasn't supposed to wander off to?"

"I understand why you would be upset, but Connor has grown up a lot since then."

"Mom, I'm not upset with Connor." Harley stood in the center of the kitchen, hands on her hips. My eyebrows furrowed. Why the hell wasn't she upset with Connor? I was probably upset enough for the both of us and it wasn't my sister he tried to fornicate with.

"You're not?" Valerie asked, seeming relieved. Connor also seemed pretty pleased. He started filling the three wine glasses. That also brought my hackles up. Valerie was under the impression that I was Harley's boyfriend, and she was still actively trying to set her up with this guy right in front of me.

"No, I'm not," Harley confirmed. "He's a liar, a cheater, and an all-around garbage human being, which means that his being here is pretty on-brand for him. But you, Mom, I expected better from you."

"Harley, I just want what's best for you," Valerie crooned.

That hit home. "And why exactly is this waste of space what's best for Harley?" I demanded, grabbing two of the three wine glasses on the counter, handing one to Harley and keeping the other in my hand. I didn't even like wine much, but the idea that I was taking it from Connor made the childish part of me very satisfied.

Connor sniffed in my direction. "I can provide for her. I can get her a job in my family's company."

"I don't want a job at your family's company, ass hat," Harley snapped.

"Harley," Valerie interrupted. "It's a good offer. There's potential for you to move up the corporate ladder like you've always wanted."

Harley looked like she was about to burst a blood vessel. I rubbed small circles into her back, which Connor took notice of and glared at. "Valerie," I began, trying to modulate my own temper. "As pissed as I am that you're trying to sell my girlfriend down the river right in front of me, I'm more concerned about the lies you've been led to believe. For starters, where did you get the idea that Connor can actually get Harley a job in the Monterey hotel chain?"

Valerie cast a glance at Connor. I nodded sadly. "That's what I thought. Valerie, Connor doesn't have any sway over hiring decisions at the Monterey hotel chain."

Valerie shook her head while Connor looked like he wanted to stab me with the wine bottle. "But he got her the internship there before..."

Harley scoffed. "Is that what he told you? Mom, I got the internship there on my own. Connor was working as an intern too, but he didn't even know I was getting brought on until I ran into him by happenstance."

"And Connor was fired from his internship at the Monterey Hotel group for coercing his female coworkers into doing sexual favors by throwing around his family connections and threatening their jobs."

Harley and Valerie both eyeballed me. That's right, I looked him up. The second I realized he was gunning for Harley I did a background check and a deep dive research on all things Connor Monterey. In fact, most of the days I spent holed up in my room doing research were spent looking into the life surrounding Harley Malone.

Valerie looked appalled. Connor looked pissed. But Harley looked disappointed in her mother.

"Harley, I'm so sorry," Valerie said. "Maggie mentioned that the inn was struggling but that you were booking more conference room reservations. Connor said it wasn't enough to keep you afloat and that you'd need something more secure."

Harley froze. "You told Connor what reservations I was securing for the conference rooms?"

Valerie looked confused. "Well, sure we talked about it."

Harley shook her head. "You have no idea what you've done. You could have sunk my business, do you realize that?" Harley turned towards me. "Can you take me home? These two deserve each other."

Chapter Fifteen

Bounty Hunting

Harley

The ride back to the inn was silent with Malcolm flashing me concerned looks out of the corner of his eye. I sighed and shifted in my seat.

"I think it's safe to call off the fake boyfriend thing. Clearly, it's not making much of a difference."

Malcolm drummed his fingers on the steering wheel. "Maybe we just need to try harder," he suggested. I raised an eyebrow at him.

"I would've thought you'd be jumping to get out of this arrangement."

He shrugged, but his fingers tightened against the steering wheel. "What are friends for? Besides, you're by far the best fake girlfriend I've ever had."

This managed to get a small smile out of me as we pulled into the inn's parking lot. "Can you just drop me over there?" I asked, pointing to the run-down carriage house. Malcolm turned the wheel and directed us to the other side of the parking lot. He put the car in park and unbuckled his seat belt. "You don't have to come," I said. "I can see you in a bit."

"Not a chance, Malone. I'm a researcher, remember? And this has all of my investigative bones tingling."

I shrugged and got out, making my way toward the abandoned structure with Malcolm on my heels. "Watch your step," I advised. "It's pretty run down."

I pushed open the front door that had been hidden behind dense vegetation and ivy. It protested with a whine as I shouldered it open. It had been a few months since I had been in there.

"Whoa, look at this place," Malcolm said, running his fingers over the old walls. I couldn't tell if his astonishment was good or bad, so I let it hang in the air as I wandered through the space. "So, tell me, Harley. What's your plan in here?"

I turned back towards him, surprised. He shrugged. "A master renovator like you wouldn't have bought this property without having plans for the carriage house. I bet you see potential everywhere in here."

I smiled. He really understood. "This is what sold me on the property, honestly." His eyebrows winged up. I ran my hand over the old wooden door frame. "I know it doesn't look like much. But when I was looking at the inn, I was looking at what I could build for other people. This building, this was just for me. I never intended to live in one of the rooms, I wanted my own space like this, close enough to manage everything, far enough to take a breath if I needed it. But I've been so focused, financially and mentally, on getting the inn up and running that I haven't been able to make this place what I want."

"And what do you want in here?" He asked, brushing a bit of dirt from his glasses, leaving them endearingly askew.

I pointed towards the corner to our left. "I want a kitchen right there, with big windows facing the fields so I can see my future dogs play."

"Dogs? Not kids?"

I shrugged. "It's easier to have dogs when you're single. I never wanted to base my future around some imaginary person. I've found it makes people rush into relationships they have no business being in."

He nodded, thinking this over. "So, dogs in the field, kitchen in the corner. What else?"

I spent the next hour spinning around the building, showing Malcolm where my fireplace would go for cold Maryland winter nights, where my living room would go, complete with bookcases and paintings along the walls, where my bedroom would go, complete with my ensuite bathroom that would be the stuff of fantasies. Where the other bedrooms would go if I decided to have children, or where my future dogs could romp around.

Through it all, Malcolm stayed rapt in attention. It was like he could picture everything too. He would even throw in comments about crown molding and kitchen islands as we walked around the space. The hardest part? I could picture Malcolm there as easily as I could picture cabinets and kitchen sinks. I could see him running his fingers through his hair at a desk in the living room as he puzzled out the history of a town. I could see him joking with my cousin and sister as he grabbed my dad a beer.

Malcolm fit here. But just because I could imagine something didn't make it real. And I was going to have to put distance between us if I wanted to survive when he left. Even as a friend, it was getting harder to imagine letting him go.

When we returned to the inn, Malcolm gathered some notebooks and his laptop and left to scope out resources in the library to prepare questions for the psychic sisters at the séance. This left me scoping out the back field and surrounding forest of my property to figure out how in the heck I was going to pull off a haunted trail walk here.

I had tried, in vain, to get different community events hosted at my humble inn, but Connor had made sure to find ways to shut them all down. Now, as I was handed an event on a silver platter, I was realizing that, of course, the city council would stick me with an astronomically expensive event.

I was going to need hay bales for the children's maze, costumes, actors, and different family friendly activities if it was going to be anything like the haunted trail that the apple orchard put on every year. Maybe I could see if city council could give me a budget to work with? Penny might donate some old costumes, and I could get local high schoolers in the theatre department to volunteer if it looked good on college applications. But everything else? That was going to be difficult. Not to mention I might need to ask Oliver and my dad to have someone on-site every night so stupid teenagers don't try to burn down the woods.

As I was wandering through the fields and doing mental calculations, an older man with a rounded pudge in the middle called to me from just outside the inn. Stepping over my small pumpkins, I waved and made my way over to him.

"Hi there," I said. "I'm Harley, how can I help you?"

The man, an older gentleman a little older than my father, with greased-back silver hair shot out a hand with the enthusiasm of a used car salesman. I shook his limp hand in my own.

"Pleased to meet you. My name is Richard," he said, pumping my hand twice and then dropping it. "I'm actually hoping you could help me locate someone."

I tried to remain relaxed as every fiber of my being went on high alert. I tried to laugh but it came out hoarse. "I think you might be asking the wrong person. My dad is the police officer, not me."

For some reason throwing out my relation to law enforcement made me feel the slightest bit safer around him. He didn't look physically imposing, but the look in his eye was that of a fox looking for an entrance to a hen house.

He chuckled humorlessly. "Oh, I don't imagine you need to be qualified in bounty hunting, Miss. But I'm looking for a boy whom I'm told has been staying at your establishment."

I tried to look at disappointed as possible. "I'm sorry to say Richard, but I can't give out information on any guests, past or present. I'm sure you understand. Confidentiality laws and all that."

He nodded and looked at the sky past me. "This is a nice place you have here."

I wasn't sure what it was about the way he said it that made it sound less like an observation and more like a threat.

"Thank you," I said. "If you'd like to leave your full name and contact information, as well as the person you're looking for, I could leave a note for a patron if they are staying here. That's about the best I can do, I'm afraid."

He nodded sagely, then got a dangerous spark in his eye. "Well, how about you tell Malcolm Jones that Richard stopped by for a visit. He has my number when he decides to get ahold of me."

Ice ran through my veins. How did Malcolm know a guy like this? Richard gave off old-school mobster vibes and I found myself making sure there were no weapons that could kneecap me as he walked back toward his car. I watched him pull away and let out a shaky breath.

Malcolm Jones, what kind of trouble are you in?

Chapter Sixteen

Business Men

Malcolm

W hen I got back to the inn, I found Harley sitting on the steps in her pajamas. It was just past dinner time and I still had one of Harley's sandwiches in the mini-fridge in my room.

I grinned at her, and she smiled back warily. Something about her expression put me on edge.

"Hey friend," I said with a smile.

"Hey," she returned. As I advanced up the steps, Harley extended a white note between her fingers. It had been handled so much the edges had started to fray. "You had a caller while you were away." She watched me as I unfolded the note, as if watching for a reaction.

When I unfolded the paper, the words *Richard* and *locate* swam in front of my eyes. My gaze met hers.

"This guy called here?"

She shook her head. "No, he came for a visit." I felt ice in the pit of my stomach. Richard must be desperate if he's resorting to house calls.

"What did you tell him?"

"I told him that I couldn't legally divulge any person past or present who uses my inn's facilities. Or something like that. I protected your privacy, but he seemed to already know you were here. He was kind of intimidating."

I nodded. "Thank you for looking out for me."

She waited a beat before turning to me. "Is this another one of those things that isn't my business? Because as your friend, I'm concerned for you. As an innkeeper, I'm concerned for me."

I felt my expression darken. "Did he say something to you?" If Richard did anything to her while I was away, I would drive up to New York and bloody my fist in front of an entire borough's worth of witnesses.

Harley threw her hands up. "Not in so many words. It was weird. It was like he was paying me a compliment with his words and issuing a threat with his eyes. I'm probably being paranoid or something, but something about this guy was off."

I leaned forward and put my hand on her shoulder. It was difficult being this close in proximity without touching her and watching her big eyes as they recounted her fears made me want to chase away any threats and protect her like a gladiator.

"You don't have anything to be concerned about. He's a friend of my dad's, and I've been dodging his calls." I assured her. "I'll call him and take care of it. I'm sorry if it took you by surprise."

More importantly, Richard was going to be sorry he took her by surprise. I know the guy's M.O. He's the guy who looks you in the eye and smiles while he explains how he could rip your world apart. He's a combination of a shark and a bottom feeder. Guys like him made me sick, and I thought I had seen the last of him the last time I was in New York.

Harley searched my eyes for a moment before nodding. "Okay," she said. "I'm gonna head to bed. Do you need anything for the night?"

By "heading to bed" I knew Harley was planning on binge-watching home renovation shows and eating microwave popcorn in bed. When she asked if I needed anything, so many things raced through my mind, but I tried to be a good boy and shook my head. "I'm okay. Have a good night, Harley."

I slept like garbage that night as I thought of what I needed to do. I didn't want Richard coming around Burnt Creek, spreading his depravity like a cancer. I also needed to get the filming permits and schedules sorted with the town for when the crew came up. It was after breakfast when I made my way down to the town hall.

Burnt Creek Town Hall was a nice building of newer construction, although apparently, they dealt with their fair share of vandals. As I pulled into the parking lot, I saw a crotchety old man scrubbing away red spray paint on the sign that declared it 'Burnt Creek Clown Fall'. I docked points for lack of originality, but if that's the worst crime a kid could get into here, more power to them.

The door didn't have posted hours, just a regular "open" and "closed" sign, along with a handwritten note in permanent marker and terrible handwriting that proclaimed a city council meeting the following Monday. I pulled open the door and breathed in the stale air-conditioned room. The room was large enough with the standard bland linoleum and plastic chairs that everyone's seen in the DMV. On a raised platform, none other than Connor sat alone with his shiny brown shoes kicked up on the large semi-circle desk the council members shared at the front of the room.

At the sound of my approaching footsteps, Connor turned his head and sneered. "What do you want?"

"Ah, Councilman Monterey, such a pleasure to talk with a man on the town council."

"Still haven't stated what you want, Marty."

"It's Malcolm, but I guess that doesn't matter to you. Listen, my crew was hoping to film at a few locations around town, and I need to check with the town council if it was okay that we do so. I didn't see anything on the website, so I figured I'd ask in person."

Connor pulled his legs down and leaned forward on his desk with his fingers together. "Interesting, you need something from me."

"Nope. I need permission from the town."

"And I represent the town," he said, with what he probably assumed was a dangerous glint in his eye.

"Connor, man, I'm going to assume you didn't learn any life lessons in the past about trying to leverage your position to get what you want, so I'm going to spell it out for you. I just need to know if there's a permit or anything that our YouTube channel needs to fill out and supply to the city council. The only job you have here is to give me information."

"Well, there isn't a permit but there is a pretty hefty fee."

I narrowed my eyes at him. "Is there?"

Connor nodded slowly. "Filming rights are big business, you know. A town can't be too careful. We charge five thousand dollars per filming location."

"And who would I write the check to?"

A flicker of surprise crossed Connor's face as I called his bluff. "Just address it to Burnt Creek and the town can write you a receipt."

I waited a beat. "Are you sure about that fee, Councilman?"

Connor nodded enthusiastically. I scoffed. Amateur.

"I'll see what I can do," I said, watching Conner smile like a cat that played with the canary before eating it. What an idiot. Didn't he know how easily I could verify stuff like this? I decided to spend my day at the library getting things sorted with this new mess when I received a call on my phone.

DAD'S LAWYER – DO NOT ANSWER.

I accepted the call.

"What do you want, Richard?" I snapped.

"Malcolm, my boy, about time you took my call," Richard's booming voice filled my ear. "I was beginning to think you were avoiding me."

"What gave you that idea?" I asked sarcastically.

"Now that's no way to talk to the man who has your daddy's future in his hands, now is it?"

I gripped the phone harder than I probably should have. "His future was sealed the moment he made the choices he made. I don't owe him, or you, anything. And if I find out that you come around Harley or anyone else in this town, I'll call up my old contacts and make sure they start peeking into your extracurriculars."

The line went silent for a moment before Richard's cold voice filled the line. "Don't go making accusations you can't back up, Jones. That'll put you in a bad spot."

If I had two fucks to give, I would be nervous, but as it was, he was already on my shit list. "Richard, your business is with my father. For both of our sakes, let's keep it that way."

I hung up the phone and tossed it in the car before heading to address the other situation I've now found myself in.

Chapter Seventeen

Cloaks and Candles

Harley

After a long week of conversations on how to approach the psychic sisters, the night of the séance was upon us. Penny Wayward had told me over text that the sisters had purchased some interesting outfits for the séance and insisted that I get pictures of them in action. Dorothy O'Neil had insisted on an eight p.m. meeting time, stating that the dead preferred a darkened ambiance when they communed.

We drove to The Three Sisters' Psychic Services office in my newly fixed-up car which Jed proudly showed me purred like a kitten now. When I tried to pay for the repairs with the last few pennies in my dwindling account, Jed bashfully said the balance had already been taken care of. Malcolm was going to have a lot of explaining to do after tonight was done.

We arrived at ten minutes to eight for the séance at the Three Sisters' Psychic Services "office" which was really the sisters' old Victorian home. The front door was unlocked, the lights were off, and our calls out to the O'Neil sisters went unanswered. Malcolm and I exchanged nervous glances as I led him to the room where the sisters normally performed their psychic services and gasped out loud.

The room was lacking the O'Neil sisters but was alight with the flames of nearly a hundred candles. There was a table with five chairs where they frequently did tarot readings, but tonight it held something orb shaped beneath a black cloth in the center.

Although the room was empty, I could hear a deep humming from outside the room.

"Ms. O'Neil?" I called to the other room, realizing that any one of them could respond and it would still make me feel less creeped out. There was a doorway on the other side of the room leading to the main house but walking through the maze of candles seemed like a feat James Bond would be more comfortable with. If I couldn't even paint my own toenails, there was no way I could flex myself around open flames.

"What are the chances that this old building has a sprinkler system?" Malcolm said out of the side of his mouth.

"Pretty unlikely," I said, still searching for the source of the humming.

"We're totally going to die here," he said, both matter-of-fact and resigned.

"The next-door neighbor is a volunteer firefighter and he makes sure they at least have smoke alarms and a fire extinguisher in the kitchen," I whispered back.

From a doorway across the room, three short figures in long black hooded cloaks emerged. Their faces were shrouded by the low hoods, and each figure held yet another candle as they hummed deeply. In any other scenario, it would have been ominous and perhaps creepy, but the figures had to lift the bottom hems of the robe with one hand while holding the candle with the other, to make sure they didn't light themselves on fire from the candles on the floor, thus exposing two sets of white orthopedic sneakers and one pair of pink bunny slippers from beneath the cultist costumes.

"Hey, Ms. O'Neils," Malcolm said. I didn't have to look at him to tell that he was swallowing a chuckle.

"Good evening," the O'Neil sister in the front said, her voice pitched down an octave. I couldn't tell which sister it was, but when she approached the table, she sat the candle down, bobbing it and nearly dropping it before Malcolm reached out to steady it. He had to reach around a covered orb on the table, likely a crystal ball they got off of the internet.

"Thank you, Malcolm. I can't see a damned thing with this blasted hood on," she said, pulling it off her head, exposing Dorothy O'Neil. She shot a glare at the sister in the back and settled herself in her chair. The other O'Neil sisters and I sat around the table, while Malcolm made sure all the candles were sitting upright on the table and not trying to burn down the whole building, before taking his place.

The cloaked sister who came in last tipped her head almost all the way back to look at Dorothy, and seeing that Dorothy's hood was down, she let out an exasperated huff before pulling her own hood down. Mabel O'Neil, wearer of the pink bunny slippers, now wore a scowl directed at her older sister. "Why did you take your hood down?"

"I couldn't see a damn thing! I was liable to trip and light myself on fire!"

"Well, if you wouldn't have insisted on having enough candles to host Farmer Warren's birthday cake, you wouldn't have to worry about a fire!" Mabel shot back.

"I'm confused," Bertha O'Neil said, her face still shrouded in her cloak. "Are the hoods off or on? Because mine's kind of itchy."

Mabel rolled her eyes. "I told you to wash it before you wore it."

Bertha delicately pulled her hood down. "It's not underwear. I'm wearing stuff underneath it! Why would I wash it first?"

Dorothy looked suddenly sheepish. "You're wearing stuff underneath yours? Oh shit, Mabel are you dressed under your robe?"

"Don't be ridiculous, of course I am! We're going to watch the football game at the bar after this. You said you wanted wings."

Dorothy looked around the room. "Well, why the heck didn't anyone tell me we were going somewhere after this? I would've put on some damned clothes!"

Malcolm and I watched as the O'Neil sisters bounced conversation around like a tennis match, each of us trying not to acknowledge that Dorothy wasn't wearing anything but a birthday suit beneath her robe.

"Um, thank you for hosting this séance," Malcolm said, suddenly looking as if he realized what a terrible idea all of this was.

The older women seemed to remember that Malcolm and I were in the room, and quickly adopted more somber tones.

"Of course," Mabel said, eyes closed. "It is our sworn duty to commune with those who are no longer on this plane."

"Indeed," Bertha added. "And because you're already here, afterward we can do a tarot reading for only fifteen dollars."

Malcolm grinned. "Bertha, you're a shark."

Bertha beamed back at him. I had an inkling that Malcolm had an admirer in this little old lady.

"Shall we begin?" Dorothy asked.

"Right," Malcolm started, rubbing his hands together, realizing this is the moment that could make or break the séance. "We would like to commune with the ghosts of Jimmy Carpenter, Bob Walker, and Pete Grant."

The three sisters went quiet before glaring at each other.

"Why do you want to commune with those three gentlemen?" Dorothy asked sharply.

"We are trying to understand more about what led up to their deaths, to see if they might be haunting any areas of the town," Malcolm said somberly.

"And to help them cross over," I added quickly.

"Oh, yes, and that," Malcolm said with a nod. Sensing the doubt and upcoming protests from the women scorned by the deceased, Malcolm quickly added, "and any assistance the Three Sisters' Psychic Services provides would be mentioned on our popular YouTube channel, which would mean a lot of new customers for you."

"Would it?" Bertha asked, her eyes sparkling.

"It would," I added. "Not that you would be swayed by such earthly possessions."

Mabel quickly perked up. "Of course not," she insisted. "But if it means that we could help more people—"

"—and souls—" Dorothy added helpfully.

"—and souls. We would be happy to assist you."

"Wonderful," Malcolm said. "So, you're the experts here. How does this work?"

Dorothy quickly straightened. "Everyone grab hands," she commanded, extending her hands to Malcolm on her left and Bertha on her right. Mabel on my left quickly grabbed my hand with her sweaty wrinkly one, and Malcolm shyly cast a look in my direction before gently threading his fingers through mine. My heart rate picked up and I hoped my hands wouldn't get as sweaty as Mabel's.

Dorothy released Bertha's hand just long enough to pull the black cloth off of the orb on top of the table, exposing an upturned mirrored disco ball that must have come straight out of the eighties. The mirrors reflected the light of the hundred candles and sprinkled white dots all over the room, turning the somber atmosphere into something more like a prom.

"Is that a disco ball?" Malcolm asked, disbelief frozen on his face.

Dorothy straightened. "As it turns out, the gentlemen you seek loved to disco."

"Also," Bertha chimed in quietly, "we couldn't find a crystal ball on such short notice."

"I see," Malcolm said, struggling to school his face into a neutral expression. "Please, continue."

"Close your eyes," Dorothy commanded again, squeezing hers shut, only to pinch open one when she thought no one was watching. I fought a smile as I closed my eyes, still seeing little beads of light from the disco ball on the table through my eyelids. After a beat of quiet, we all nearly jumped out of our skin when Dorothy began shouting in a low baritone.

"OH, SPIRITS FROM THE GREAT BEYOND!" she shouted.

"Jesus, Mary and Joseph, do you have to scream in my ear?" Bertha asked, jumping to the side. Dorothy sighed heavily, as if it was a terrible inconvenience to speak at a normal level.

"I want to make sure they can hear me," she said as if explaining something to a toddler.

"They're dead, not deaf!" Mabel said from across the table.

"Ugh, fine! Now if I might continue!" Dorothy shot at her sisters with an accompanying glare. They nodded and promptly closed their eyes.

"Oh, spirits from the great beyond! We call to you on this dark night to request information from three of your...residents."

Malcolm squeezed my hand, and I wasn't sure if I was imagining how he was leaning his shoulder against mine.

"Okay," Dorothy said somberly. "I think we have reached the other side. What would you like to know?"

Malcolm shifted in his seat. "How long were these three men in town?"

"Oh that's easy," Bertha said in her normal voice. "They were here about three months. They stayed with us here in the house."

A stomp sounded from under the table and Bertha squeaked before glaring daggers at Mabel. Mabel pointedly looked at her. "You mean, the *spirits told you.*"

"Oh, right," Bertha cleared her throat. "The spirits reminded me. About all that."

Malcolm glanced at my chest, which made me flush, until I remembered that I had the recorder tucked in the front pocket of my shirt. The O'Neil sisters were clear about not taking notes so we could 'focus on the spirits'. I straightened my posture to lean my chest in closer to the conversation, and I might have imagined Malcolm's expression darken as his eyes flicked between my chest and my face and back down again.

"What do the spirits say about their disappearance?" I asked.

Mabel cleared her throat. "The spirits are telling me that they were last seen flirting with Dorothy at the hardware store." Mabel's voice started somber, but it was hard to ignore the bite that came toward the end.

Dorothy snorted. "The spirits are telling *me* that they were headed to Bertha at the ice cream shop when they were last seen by those of this earthly realm. Besides, Jimmy was the only one at the hardware store."

Bertha let out an indignant squeak. "The spirits are shouting at *me* that they never made it to visit me at the ice cream shop. The voices from the *other side* are telling me that they probably went to visit Mabel at the rail station they were all building together."

"They did no such thing!" Mabel snapped, her eyes open and fingers pointed at her sister. All the sisters had released their hands, leaving Malcolm and I the only ones holding hands. I squeezed his hand and went to let it go, but he tangled his fingers in mine and squeezed as he kept us together. Mabel continued her rant. "The spirits know that the boys never brought any materials back to the station, and they left me to paint walls all by myself."

"Well, you'll have to forgive them, Mabel," Dorothy said. "They were probably dead already."

Mabel sighed, devoid of fight. "Yeah, probably. It was such a shame. That Jimmy sure had a nice ass."

The other two sisters nodded in agreement.

Malcolm cocked his head to the side. "What did Jimmy buy at the hardware store?"

Dorothy scrunched her eyebrows. "I don't remember."

Bertha perked up. "Dorothy, you should consult the crystal ball—"

"—Disco ball—" Mabel interrupted.

"—disco ball to see if the spirits remember."

I glanced at Malcolm out of the corner of my eye where I could see him biting the inside of his cheek to prevent from saying something.

Dorothy reached out and placed both hands on the mirrored surface of the disco ball. "OH SPIRITS!" she shouted, causing us all to jump again.

"Oh hell, Dorothy! Just ask in your normal voice!" Mabel snapped. Dorothy looked sheepish.

"Right, sorry," she said. "Oh spirits, what was Jimmy buying at the hardware store? I can only remember Jimmy's butt from that particular interaction."

I fought to not roll my eyes. Dorothy roamed her hands over the surface of the disco ball. "I think it was...a shovel...some rope...and...oh shit!" she called out. She lifted her hand from the disco ball. "I think one of the stupid mirrors cut me!"

"Jimmy always was kind of an asshole," Bertha said sympathetically.

"I think that's all of the questions I had for the other side," Malcolm said, trying to cover up his laughter.

"Wait," Mabel said suddenly, grasping at her chest before peeking an eye over at me and Malcolm. "The spirits are overtaking me! The other side has something it wants to say to you two."

"Oh, that's right!" Dorothy said, her eyes wide as she tried to dip her hand discreetly beneath the table, where she was clearly trying to grab at something.

"The other side wants to tell you two that you are both facing danger, and the only way you'll get through it is by being together," Mabel said.

"And by 'being together,' the spirits mean dating," Bertha said with a nod.

"Is that right?" Malcolm asked with a look at me. My eyes were wide at the three women. Were they really trying to set me up with Malcolm at a séance?

"You know," I said with a polite smile. "We really appreciate your input—"

"Not *our* input, dear," Mabel said, suddenly free from being overtaken. She adopted a wistful voice. "The *other side*."

"Right, of course, the other side," I said with a dismissive wave.

Dorothy suddenly popped up from nearly beneath the table and stared at Malcolm intently. "You must take this warning seriously, and take Harley out to dinner—"

"—or brunch—" Bertha added helpfully.

"—or the spirits will be very disappointed!" Dorothy finished gravely, and with a hard pull of her hand, something that resembled a sheet attached to a string rose up from the ground on the other side of the room. As a chorus of overly exaggerated gasps echoed between the sisters, along with a choir of "ooh, the spirits!" Dorothy pulled both her hands to her cheeks in a show of surprise, but in doing so, she let go of the string holding up her fake spirit, which promptly dropped to the ground right on top of a mass of lit candles.

"Oh shit," Malcolm said. "Call the fire department." We both quickly pushed away from the table, Malcolm grabbing his jacket from the back of his chair to smother the flames, and me running to the kitchen for the fire extinguisher beneath the sink.

As I shot the foam from the extinguisher, the smoke alarm started screaming from another room and the three sisters were scrambling over each other to stand on the dining chairs as if being taller would prevent the fire from reaching them, Dorothy inadvertently flashing the whole room as her cloak opened. I made a mental note to go over fire safety with the sisters when we weren't in the midst of an actual fire.

"Dorothy, call 911!" Mabel shouted over the noise.

"I didn't put on clothes, what makes you think I remembered a cell phone?" she shouted back.

The fire was out in less than a minute with our combined efforts, and we spent another ten minutes blowing out the remaining ninety candles around the sweltering room as the sirens and lights from the window alerted us to the arrival of the fire department.

"Guess Tommy next door called the fire department." Dorothy sighed.

"He's a good boy," Bertha said. "We should take him some cookies."

The O'Neil sisters glanced out the window at the red and blue lights outside.

"Oh! The hot firemen are here!" Mabel said, clapping her hands together. "Dorothy, quick, take my clothes! I want to wear my birthday suit when they rescue us."

Dorothy swatted at Mabel's grasping hands. "Hands off, you horn dog!"

"Ladies, I think we can just walk out," Malcolm said, holding out a hand toward them. Mabel deflated and grabbed his hand while we helped them down and out to the front yard.

Malcolm and I sat on the grass in the glow of the firetruck lights as we answered questions about the fire, played the fire chief our recording from the séance, and passed a bottle of water back and forth.

My dad pulled up in his police cruiser, with Gus the goose riding shotgun. I heard my dad order Gus to stay, just in case Gus suddenly sprouted opposable thumbs and decided to commandeer the vehicle.

"Well," my father began with a sigh, hands on his hips, watching the scene unfold with that ridiculous toothpick in his mouth. "Which one of you tried to light the old ladies on fire?"

Chapter Eighteen

Ashes, Ashes

Malcolm

I was finally able to get Harley and myself back to the inn around midnight. Harley offered to have the O'Neil sisters stay with us at the inn for free, given that the séance was our idea, but the firefighters declared it was safe for them to stay at their residence so long as they forfeited all the candles in the house.

The flashing lights of the fire truck and unused ambulance faded into the background as we twisted and turned the car down the town streets back toward the inn. Despite having no other guests, we kept quiet as we entered and climbed the stairs. I kept my hand at the small of her back because after the fear of tonight, not touching her was not an option.

When we were at the O'Neil sisters' house and the flames began, my mind went blank with every thought except one: *not her*.

Of course, the three old women climbing on top of the table were in the back of my mind, mostly because they kept chatting away as if it was a normal evening and because one was nearly naked. But I knew as soon as I saw the sheet light on fire that I would have thrown myself onto the flames if it meant protecting Harley.

And she didn't even need protecting.

I didn't blame her when she ran from the room, but when she came back brandishing the fire extinguisher, she might as well have been Rambo. We took out the fire, and the smaller candles, as a team. It was moments like this that made it hard to remember that we were just friends, and friends were all we could ever be.

My hand on her back as we walked up the stairs was just my way of feeling that she was real. That she was still *here*. And she didn't shy away from it, almost as if she needed to feel me, too.

As I followed her down the hall to the door of her room, I thought that maybe the O'Neil sisters were right. Or their "spirits" were right. I should take her out to dinner. Just the two of us, away from the inn, where she might view me as just a guest. Away from naked old ladies and sisters and parents and ex-boyfriends and guard geese that might stand in our way.

She turned toward me, her hair still smelling like flowers and ashes. It made me think of the old nursery rhyme: *ashes, ashes, we all fall down*.

"So," she said, leaning back against her door with a tired smile. "Got any more friend adventures planned?"

I laughed. "Ready to jump back into the fray already?"

She shrugged, one corner of her lips lifting. "I mean, you've gotta admit, there's never a dull moment with our outings."

"Very true. In fact, I can't think of any other friend outings since I've become an adult where both the police *and* parents were called."

"Well, it helps when the parents are the police," she laughed.

"At least your dad didn't release Gus on me this time."

"Nah, too many witnesses."

I brushed a lock of hair behind her ear and the energy and adrenaline of the night felt electric around us. Harley looked up at me, her green eyes held me captive. For a moment, she looked...vulnerable. I saw her strength and her courage tonight. I saw her snarky exterior as she joked with the crowd around the fire. But in this moment, with me, she didn't have to be strong.

I felt my voice drop as I stared at her. "I'm glad you were with me tonight, Harley."

She swallowed. "I'm glad you wanted me with you."

I tilted my head to the side. For some reason that felt like a more loaded statement than she was trying to make it sound. I wondered who made her feel unwanted.

"There's no one I would have wanted more," I answered honestly.

Her eyes locked with mine, and I could feel one of her walls dropping with that simple admission.

Her hand slowly touched my chest. More electricity sparked, and I knew she could feel my heartbeat ready to burst out of my ribcage. Her eyes widened, seeing that I was as affected as she was.

My hand cupped her face, and her eyes dropped to my lips. I wet my lips and moved in closer, giving her time to back away if this wasn't what she wanted. But her hand on my chest snaked up to my neck, pulling me the rest of the way to her lips.

When we connected, her soft lips barely a whisper against mine, I could feel every ounce of blood in my veins screaming '*her, she's the one.*' We breathed in together, and she pushed harder against my mouth, our bodies aligning like they were cut from the same mold. Her hips pressed against mine, and it took everything in me not to open the door to her suite and push us farther. I opened my mouth instead, and our tongues wove together like they were speaking the same language. She tasted like honey and chai and ashes.

Ashes, ashes, we all fall down.

And in that moment, I fell for her. Maybe it was the anticipation, the waiting, the *wanting*, but I've never had a better kiss in my life. It was electric.

When we finally pulled away, Harley's brows were furrowed in what I assumed was my expression as well. I just wasn't sure if it was for the same reason. Had it ever felt like this before? I had known her for two weeks. That wasn't long enough to feel like this. *Was it?*

I ran my thumb over her bottom lip. It didn't feel like magic, but somehow it was. She was magic. The kind of magic I could spend forever with. The kind of magic I wanted to come home to.

That thought stilled my hand.

I couldn't come home to her. She lived here. I lived in New York. Even if I *did* live here, I traveled constantly for work with Ben. Could I really ask her to wait for me? For days? Weeks?

How long until she wouldn't want that anymore?

She belonged here, my innkeeper. And I didn't. New York held responsibilities I didn't want to face yet, but I wouldn't ask her to wait around for me, even if that meant that she found someone else. Someone else who would come home to her.

My eyes dropped, and I stepped backward, away from her warmth, away from the possibilities of us.

"Malcolm?" she asked, taking in my expression.

"I'm sorry," I said, not meeting her eyes. "That was a—"

"Don't say it," she said, firmly. When my eyes met hers again, there was a fire in them, but there was also hurt. She knew what I was going to say, and she didn't want to be thought of as a mistake. But I knew before I kissed her that it would make me want a forever that I had no right to.

"Good night, Mr. Jones," she croaked out.

She turned toward her door quickly, but not before I saw her eyes brimming with tears. My gut churned with the knowledge that I was the one who put those tears there. She gave me her vulnerability, and in return, I gave her pain.

And now we were back to me being Mr. Jones. *Fuck.*

I reached for her, but she had already slipped into her room. I had to tell myself that it was better this way. It would hurt a lot more if she fell as hard for me as I had fallen for her, only to find out that it couldn't work. But something in my chest said in saving her I was dooming us both.

I walked back to my room, my feet feeling like lead. As I stared up at the ceiling, I hoped for sleep that never came.

Chapter Nineteen

Nutmeg Nightmare

Harley

Malcolm thought the kiss was a mistake. That we were a mistake. That *I* was a mistake.

But that kiss didn't feel like a mistake to me. It felt like coming home and going on an adventure all at once. It felt special. It certainly never felt like that with Connor.

I couldn't help the tears that spilled over when I entered my room, hoping that he didn't see them before I turned around. He didn't deserve to see my tears.

My sadness morphed into something more fierce. I kicked my shoes off and threw them into my closet. I turned putting on my pajamas into an exercise of anger.

I had given him an out. I told him he was just a guest and *he* pushed for us to be more. For us to be friends. He had leaned in. He had kissed me.

Then he said it was a mistake.

I shook my head. I was so stupid to think that he would ever want something more with me. Sure, he was the one who said the words about wanting to be friends, spending night after night watching movies and talking late into the evening. And he was the one who leaned in for a kiss tonight. But I was the idiot who trusted him, who kissed him back. I lay on my bed, staring at the ceiling, my traitorous mind wondering what it would feel like to have him lying here with me if the night had gone differently.

But no. He thought the kiss was a mistake, and I thought that falling for him was a mistake. And that's what really happened. I fell for him...like an idiot. And he broke my heart, because that's what men do.

The next day, Malcolm avoided me, not coming down for breakfast, not stopping by the front desk, and he even went so far as to wait for when I went to the bathroom before sneaking out the front door.

Quite honestly, it was a waste of energy on his part. I had no intention of acting like he was anything more than a normal guest. If anything, he did us both a favor. Did I really want to be with a ghost hunter? Nope. I wanted to be by myself.

I spent the day looking into getting the inn a better social media presence and promoting coupons and package deals. I even got notified of two new reservations for a few months down the line from those promotions.

When Monday rolled around, Malcolm was still avoiding me. Before the séance fiasco, we had talked about going to the city council meeting together, me to talk about finding someone else to host the Haunted Trail and Malcolm to talk to the city about acquiring the proper permits for filming in the town. But when five thirty came, his car was gone from the parking lot, so I left alone.

Maggie was manning the front desk when I left, and I made sure not to answer her questioning gaze. Her puzzled stare was my kryptonite, and it usually made me spill my secrets like crazy. But I didn't want to go to the city council meeting with red-rimmed eyes, so I kept my words to a minimum when I left the inn.

The town hall doubled as a reception hall in the summers, so it was one of the nicer and newer buildings in Burnt Creek. There were more than a dozen cars in the parking lot, mostly belonging to the city council members, but there were also some from the citizens bringing questions and complaints, and the normal attendees who brought snacks and provided commentary on the city council meetings.

I hated city council meetings. I tried to avoid coming to them because Connor was a city council member and when I attended, he alternated between flirting shamelessly at me and making not-so-subtle digs at my competence of running a business.

I found a seat next to Avery, the front desk clerk at the police station. Her strawberry blonde hair was pulled back into a ponytail, and her lips were painted a bright, flirtatious red. She passed me her popcorn bag.

"Anything exciting yet?" I asked.

"No, but it's Monday, the bars are empty, and my so-called boyfriend won't answer my texts, so this is the busiest place in town right now." Avery sat a piece of popcorn on her extended tongue and slowly drew it in.

"Well, if you're on the prowl for a different boyfriend, I hope you're willing to scrape the bottom of the barrel because Connor is the only single guy here our age.

She crinkled her nose as we both cast our gazes at the pompously overdressed councilman. "Ew. No. Sadly, I'm the kind of girl who will wait until the relationship is fully dead, then spend another three weeks insisting I can resurrect it. So, let's focus on you, my single friend. It looks like that Malcolm fella Miranda called about is here. Word on the street is you're dating him."

I felt my innards twist as I caught myself looking around for him. I spotted the back of his head two rows down and I lowered my voice. "Nope, not dating him. He was kind enough to accompany me to a family dinner to fend off Connor, but that's as far as things went."

Avery gave me the side-eye and dropped her voice. "So, you're telling me you don't have feelings for him."

My gut churned tighter. "He's a temporary guest," I said, deflecting the question. "And he doesn't strike me as the type to be emotionally available."

Avery snorted. "Well, you don't need emotionally available. You need physically able. Temporary could suit you just fine." Avery paused, eyeing me again, before quickly amending, "Or I could set him up with my cousin. Unless you want him to be yours. I mean, is he yours?"

My stomach dropped all the way to the floor because Avery was asking for permission that wasn't mine to give. And while it would kill me to see Malcolm with her cousin, or with anyone for that matter, I wasn't going to hold anyone back because I went and caught feelings.

"No, Avery," I said quietly. "He's not mine."

The mayor stood, directing us to the flag behind him and we recited the pledge of allegiance. As we were standing, Jaynie snuck in and sat down on my other side, a bag from Trick or Treat in her hand. When we are all seated, the council members, consisting of Dorothy O'Neil, Connor the Dickbag, and a few others sat next to the mayor behind a U-shaped desk facing the collection of chairs we were all sitting in.

"Did I miss anything?" Jaynie asked, digging into her bag and distributing blueberry scones to me and Avery.

"Nope," Avery said, tilting the popcorn to Jaynie. "But it looks like we have a full house tonight so anything can happen."

"Awesome, I was bored at home."

Phillis, the robust secretary who consistently wore too much make-up, began reciting items on the agenda that had been removed before turning her attention to the mayor. Mayor Harding, a tired-looking bald man, who looks more at home on his fishing boat than he does behind the desk reading off notes wearing his wife's purple reading glasses, began the agenda by issuing a proclamation.

"All right. Based on popular opinion," his eyes cut to Phillis, and he grumbled "and a fair bit of nagging," Phillis shot the mayor a look, and Dorothy gave a victorious smile. "December second will be known now as 'Spare the Goose' day after our esteemed police mascot." There was a fair amount of clapping, myself included, and Mayor Harding motioned with his hands for quiet.

"Now it's time for oral presentations," the mayor began.

"Whore speculations?" Benny Goodfellow asked loudly, leaning forward on his cane.

"No," Reynold Sapenski shouted, his hearing aid out as well. "He said 'moral abominations.'" Reynold then mumbled loud enough for all of us to hear, "Dumbass."

Mayor Harding brushed a frustrated hand down his face. "Oral presentations!" he corrected the men loudly into the microphone, which squealed at his outburst. "The community can address the council at the podium. We'll start with those already signed up on our list, and then we'll move to any new requests."

Mayor Harding motioned to Phillis, who read off the list for Sullivan Schnieder to make his request.

"Hmph," Jaynie snorted beside me. "Old Snivelling Schnieder is retiring in two months and he still can't go to a single city council meeting without trying to knock me outta business."

Sullivan Schnider was a bitter man, narrow of face and nose with his lips in a permanent sneer. His business, Thanks By Giving Flowers, had been at war with Trick or Treat since Jaynie moved in nine years ago. Every month he would approach the city council with a myriad of complaints, from Trick or Treat "smelling too loudly" and making it where his patrons couldn't enjoy the scent of his flowers, to Jaynie's customers purposefully parking in front of his half of the building, costing him valuable shoppers. Mayor Harding did his best to settle his disputes where he could, but the rest of the time, he simply gave a gentle 'suck it up' speech and moved on.

Sullivan approached the podium, his sneer already evident and Mayor Harding sank his face in his hands as the secretary wrote the minutes.

"Thank you, city council," Sullivan said, in a nasally voice. "As many of you know, I own Thanks By Giving Flowers, which shares a building with Trick or Treat Bakery."

"Here we go," Jaynie said, grabbing some of Avery's popcorn with a chuckle. I pulled my gaze from the back of Malcolm's head where it kept drifting despite my best efforts.

"It has come to my attention after a rather violent sneezing attack by one of my customers that Trick or Treat has been using entirely too much nutmeg in their baked goods." Sullivan took this moment to look at Jaynie with a narrowed leer. "It's everywhere! The apple pies, the pumpkin pies, all the pies have a copious amount of nutmeg, and it's in the air all around us! I will not stand by as our beautiful town and businesses are overrun by this nutmeg nightmare!"

"Oh, he's really fired up today," I noted.

"Yeah, but he's barking up the wrong tree," Avery said, nodding toward the mayor as she shoved a bite of blueberry scone in her mouth. "I have it on good authority that the mayor loves Jaynie's apple pie more than his wife's or his mother's. He'll put the kibosh on this complaint quickly."

Jaynie grabbed another handful of popcorn from Avery as Mayor Harding lowered his hand from his face and glared at Sullivan.

"Sullivan, if I have told you once, I have told you twenty times. The city council cannot and will not force any bakery or restaurant to change their menu or edit their recipes. And I happen to know that Mrs. Wilkenson was the one who had a "violent sneezing attack" in your shop and I also know that Mrs. Wilkenson is allergic to flowers. She was only there because you refuse to take orders over the phone, so if anybody is to blame for your customer's allergic situation, it's you."

Sullivan bunched his face up and stomped back to his seat. He'd be back the next month with a new complaint.

"Next up, Malcolm Jones," Phillis read.

Malcolm stood two rows in front of us, and I tried not to sink into my seat. His broad shoulders were back with a confident air around him as he approached the podium. I tried to forget the feeling of my hands in his hair as we kissed. Malcolm passed around a few stapled sheets of paper to the council members. He adjusted the microphone, and I could see his charming smile from the side of his face.

"Council members, thank you so much for giving me your time today. My name is Malcolm Jones and I'm the lead researcher for *Spirits, Seekers, and Skeptics*, a YouTube film crew that investigates the histories and locations for possible paranormal activity. Now, whether or not you believe in the paranormal, I think we can all agree that when a popular YouTube channel boasting over nine million subscribers films in a location, that location brings in a lot more tourism. In fact, on your first page, you'll find not only our channel's current subscriber count, but also the locations we've done episodes at in recent years and the level of tourism growth following our air date.

"All this is to say, it would be incredibly beneficial for the town of Burnt Creek to be featured on our channel. Yet, it has recently been brought to my attention by one of your council members when I properly notified the town of our intentions, Mr. Mayor, that in order for us to be allowed to film on property belonging to Burnt Creek, we would need to purchase a five-thousand-dollar permit to film here."

Mumbles went out around the audience as the mayor's eyebrows quirked slightly.

"You can imagine my surprise," Malcolm continued, "when I combed through the city ordinances and bylaws and found no mention of film permits or their five-thousand-dollar price tag. So I thought I would go right to the source because it would be a shame if the level of tourism growth you see on those papers is denied to Burnt Creek because of a simple misunderstanding."

I had never seen Malcolm like this, so commanding. He could have been a lawyer. I had to admit it got me feeling a little hot between my legs. There's nothing as sexy as a confident man, and Malcolm exuded confidence standing behind that podium.

It took less than a minute of the mayor looking around at the council members to find the responsible party.

"Mr. Monterey," the mayor looked to Connor, who was suddenly quite interested in the paperwork in front of him as he shifted in his seat. Based on the smug grin I could see from the side of Malcolm's face, I could guess who gave him the information on the permit. "Are there any laws, bylaws, or ordinances pertaining to filming rights in Burnt Creek?"

Connor's face lit red, and he shuffled some papers in front of him. "At the moment, sir, I can't think of any, although I feel it would benefit the town for us to introduce such a permit."

"I see," the mayor said, his face locked in stone. "Well, given the amount of time you've spent on city council, I'm sure you're aware that such a change would need to be submitted and voted on. It's not a decision that we make unilaterally."

"Damn," Jaynie said, "the mayor is on fire tonight."

"One of the O'Neil sisters had a psychic vision in the dairy aisle yesterday that his mother-in-law is staying with him and his wife for the next two weeks," Avery said. "Apparently, she's a real peach."

Mayor Harding addressed the rest of the council members. "For the sake of a fair decision, I will open it to a vote among the council members. For those in favor of allowing this YouTube Channel to film here, without paying for a permit, say 'aye.'"

All but Connor agreed, and he said 'nay' for the record next. The decision passed for the YouTube channel to film, and as Malcolm turned to walk back to his seat, his eyes danced with pleasure that only broke when his eyes met mine.

"Next up," Phillis announced, "Harley Malone."

I stood and shuffled down the chairs to the podium, where I moved the microphone down to my level. I could feel Malcolm's eyes on my back, but I focused on the task ahead.

"How can we help you, Miss Malone?" Mayor Harding asked, his eyes softer. The mayor has known me since I was walking around in diapers and he and his wife used to sneak me candies at community functions when I would accompany my dad.

"Well, I was recently asked—"

"Sorry, could you speak up?" Connor asked into his microphone. I shot him a glare, knowing full well everyone could hear me fine.

"I was recently asked," I said with more force, "to host this year's Haunted Trail at my inn's property. For many years, the trail has been hosted by Joe's Apple Orchard, but he recently stopped because a group of teenagers nearly burnt down his orchard last year. And although I am appreciative of the opportunity, given the rejections I've received in the past to host community events, I don't want to host the Haunted Trail on my property."

"But Harley, this is so important to the town," Dorothy said.

"And the town can still host it, on the town's property," I said, trying to maintain a smile through gritted teeth.

"But there's nowhere else in town with enough parking and lot space for a proper Haunted Trail," she insisted.

Connor sneered behind his microphone. "I can understand your resistance, Harley. It's a lot of responsibility, and it's normal to feel like you're not up to the challenge. I can offer my help, since you're feeling overwhelmed."

I ground my teeth, fighting the familiar feeling of hopelessness. "I'm not overwhelmed, Connor. And it has nothing to do with feeling up to the challenge."

"So what's the hesitation, Miss Malone?" the mayor asked.

"Will the city council be allotting funds for the Haunted Trail?" I asked.

"We really don't have any room in the budget for that. Joe always paid for the materials that went into the Haunted Trail," the mayor said.

"Yes," I said, trying to rein in my annoyance. "But Joe also made a killing off of his apple cider, apple pies, and all his other goods from the orchard. I doubt the Haunted Trail is going to bring in enough business to my inn to offset those costs, not to mention the work you expect me to put in."

"Well, I'm sure you can come up with something to sell," Phillis said.

"Sure." My hands gripped the podium. "I can sell tickets."

"Tickets?" Connor asked. "Tickets to what?"

"Tickets to the Haunted Trail."

The council members gasped. "You can't do that. It's a community event!" Dorothy said.

"It isn't a community event unless the community pays for it or hosts it. If you want me to host it, those are my terms. I get to charge admission. If I'm risking damage to my property and purchasing all of the necessary materials, I'm getting compensated."

"I don't know why you even bothered asking her," Connor said. "It's not like she's even going to pull it off in time. Besides Maggie to help her, she's going to try putting it together alone."

I could feel my shoulders caving in. Was he right? I couldn't pull this off. Maggie really was the only help I would have around the inn and she'd be manning the front desk most of the time. I would be doing this alone.

"No, she's not," a voice from behind me said. My heart started racing as I turned around and saw Malcolm standing, calmly looking at the city council members. "I will be helping her, along with my crew."

Chapter Twenty

Working with Tools

Malcolm

*W*hy *am I standing? Sit down, man, this isn't your fight.*

"Sorry," Smarmy Connor said into the microphone. *God, this guy was such an asshole.* "Am I to understand you're volunteering for our community's Haunted Trail?"

"No," I said, calmly. "I'm volunteering for *Harley's* Haunted Trail. As Miss Malone already pointed out, if the community isn't funding it, then the community doesn't own it. So I will be helping her in whatever capacity necessary to ensure the Haunted Trail goes off without a hitch. And I'm also volunteering the help of my crew. We will be available to her to set up decorations, distribute advertising, even selling tickets."

Connor's mouth formed a tight line. The mayor eyed me for a moment, flicking his eyes between myself and Harley before smirking. "Well, it looks like you have everything under control then, Miss Malone. I look forward to seeing what you and Mr. Jones put together."

Harley smiled tightly before giving a short nod and walking back to her seat. I avoided her eyes, still watching the council members. I shouldn't have said anything, but I couldn't sit by while Connor berated her in the presence of the rest of the city council members. And I saw the way she looked when he pointed out that besides Maggie, she was alone. That wasn't even fair. She had family here. She could have asked them for help. Hell, her dad would have probably gotten the whole police force involved if it meant helping Harley. But none of that mattered because when Connor started shaming her, she crumpled right in front of my eyes. Is this what it was like when they were dating? Him stomping out her flame until she was a shell of herself?

But isn't that what I did? I kissed her, and then I pushed her away. I could still feel her on my lips. That kiss that shifted my world. I've avoided her like the plague, taking the coward's way out. But all I could think about whenever I pictured being near her was pushing her up against the wall and claiming those lips again.

I hurt her. I could hear it when she was talking behind me at the city council meeting. She kept her voice low so I wouldn't hear, but sound carries in a place like that. She denied us dating, but it didn't escape my attention that she didn't answer the question about having feelings for me. Did that mean that she still had feelings for me? Or did it mean that it wasn't worth her time to answer?

I wasn't even supposed to care. She was right; I was temporary. And she deserved more than temporary.

But despite trying to avoid her, I had just told the whole town that I would be putting the trail together with her, essentially throwing myself in her path.

As the city council meeting wrapped up and everyone stood and started to exit, I turned around toward the three women behind me. "Harley," I said, and her eyes turned to me in surprise before darting away again. *God, I miss her just looking at me.* "When the crew gets to town, let us know whatever you need, and we'll help you get it together."

"Thank you," she said quietly. Jaynie from the bakery and Avery from the police station glanced between Harley and me like they were watching a daytime soap opera. Avery was even eating popcorn.

Where the hell had she gotten that?

I tried to exit the row of chairs just as Dorothy O'Neil came up behind me and tapped me on the shoulder.

"Dorothy, hi," I said, noticing Harley try to escape with Avery and Jaynie, but Dorothy called her out as her friends escaped.

"Hello, Harley, Malcolm," her frown was severe, contrasting her matching bright yellow tunic shirt, linen pants, and shawl. Harley freezes for a moment before facing Dorothy and me. "The spirits are unhappy with you two."

Harley sighed. "Well, my horoscope said I would disappoint someone but to forgive myself, so I expected this and have already loved myself through it."

I couldn't help myself, I snorted in laughter but tried to turn it into a cough. From the look Dorothy sent my way, I wasn't as successful as I thought. How could I forget Harley's quick wit in just a matter of days? I missed her so damn much.

"We told you the spirits would be very upset if the two of you didn't have a date, and here you are, not dating."

My mouth gaped open. I had to think quick on my feet. I had a feeling saying what I really wanted, that it wasn't any of her fucking business if we were dating or not, wouldn't go over well. "Dorothy, after your spirits said we should date, the room lit on fire. It's hard to take that as a good omen."

"Yeah," Harley agreed. "The spirits said we would be in danger and the only way through it was together. Then we were in danger from the fire, and we made it out by putting out the fire together. It seemed the...prophecy...or whatever was fulfilled. So, we should be free from having to date based on the spirit world opinion."

I don't know why it felt so annoying that Harley was defending why we shouldn't be dating, but it got under my skin. Why did she make it sound like dating me would be a chore? I mean, I wasn't the world's best catch, but I would have treated her right. I would have taken her out on a picnic down to Burnt Creek to see the changing leaves reflect over the water, just like she said when she told me the history of the town. I would have packed her pastries from Trick or Treat because they're the way to her heart and iced pumpkin spiced lattes because even though she thinks it's cliché, it's still her favorite.

I probably would have kissed her. A lot.

"The spirits still want you to date. The spirits are still unhappy, and there will be grave consequences should you not listen to the spirits." Her voice took on the same ominous tone as the night of the séance.

"Did you line this building with candles?" I deadpan. "I swear to the spirits, Dorothy, if you and your sisters burn us all alive in here to prove something is coming from the spirits, I'm haunting you from the grave."

"Did you bring candles?" Harley asked, her eyes wide in fear. Dorothy's eyes darted to the side before quickly pulling out her phone and typing rapidly before slipping it back in her pocket.

"...no," Dorothy said slowly as her phone starting dinging loudly in response to the text she must have sent out.

Harley put a hand to her forehead. "Dorothy, you should listen to Malcolm. He has the most experience with hauntings, I bet he'd be a very efficient ghost when he torments you and your sisters."

Dorothy's eyes open wide. "Nope, everything's fine. However, I have something unrelated and rather urgent I need to attend to."

As Dorothy scuttled away toward the main exit, I blew out a breath. "Does this building have a sprinkler system?"

Harley chuckled. "Yeah, it'll piss the mayor off to have to use it, but we should make it out alive even if we're a little damp."

"Well, that's a relief," I said with a grin. For a moment, we smiled at each other, and we were back to the easy way we were before when we were just Malcolm and Harley. But when my eyes flicked back down to her gorgeous lips and back up to her eyes, her eyes darted away, and I could see her walls coming back up. Part of me wanted to climb each of those walls until I was behind her defenses where I belonged. But another part of me, the part of me that wanted to protect her heart more than I wanted to appease my own, allowed the distance without pushing.

"Um, Phillis over there used to run the library," she said, nodding to the lady who read the minutes during the meeting. Her face was covered in makeup that looked more like it belonged on a stage and she was talking with the mayor who nodded tiredly. "She might be able to help you see if there's any old local newspapers somewhere."

Excitement drummed in my chest as I turned to see where I can find an opening to talk to her, but when I turned back to talk to Harley, she was already almost to the doors.

"Harley," I called out. She turned slightly, and I could see the sadness on her face. It reminded me of the night we kissed. "Thank you."

She nodded and walked away. I know I made the logical decision by not allowing anything more to happen between us, but I didn't realize how good of a friend she had become in such a short amount of time since I've started staying at the inn. Not only did I lose the person who could kiss me like no one else, I also lost the person who could joke about anything and hold me accountable for being a jerk.

But this aching in my chest was proof that I needed to cut it off now before this pain got any worse.

I made my way over to Phillis, who was now standing alone, rummaging through her purse.

"Hi, Phillis?" I would've liked to have used her last name to show more respect, but Harley never gave it, and I was running into a time crunch.

"Ah, Mr. Jones," she sang. I had a feeling she was one of those women who was intensely into the theatre. "To what do I owe the pleasure?"

"I was doing some research on the town, and I've found that there's unfortunately no newspaper here anymore. I looked at the old offices the newspaper was housed in and there aren't any old copies of the newspapers from before. Someone mentioned you used to run the library here in town. I didn't know if you knew of any copies of the old newspapers or anything digital?"

"Oh, I'm sorry to say I don't. Not physical copies and certainly not digital ones. The computers in the library are still from the dinosaur age, or at least from when I was still there," she said with a chuckle.

"Do you know anywhere in town that might have any old copies?"

"Just snippets here and there around town where people framed them for their businesses. But unless the stories meant an awful lot to folks, they threw the papers away. There wasn't much of a paper anyway, sorry to say."

My stomach sank. Having the scanned newspapers factored into the animations of our episodes and were some of the viewer's favorite parts. "I understand. Thank you for your time."

"No, thank you, young man. I've been waiting for ages to see someone call out Mr. Monterey on his unethical and slimy practices for a while now. I haven't seen that much justice served to him since Harley dumped him right on his rear end."

I debated on if I should ask more. Eventually, the words just tumbled out of me. "Has he always talked to her like that? Condescending and passive-aggressive?"

She nodded sadly. "We all saw it, but she was blind to it for a long time. We were all so proud of her for opening that inn, but he kept saying things to her that made her doubt her decisions and belittling her confidence. It took her twice as long as it should have to open that inn with his shoddy business advice. I always suspected he was trying to stop her from starting up her inn so she would come work with him again at his family's hotels."

My eyebrows raised. "Do you think he'd actually have the pull for that?"

She shrugged her shoulders. "Tough to say, his mother is pretty tight-lipped about their actual relationship with the Montereys. I know that Harley interned at the Monterey Hotel Group, got in all on her own merit, but he would always make her feel like she owed him something for working there. He's such a tool."

Despite my anger at Connor, I snorted at hearing her call him a tool. Now I understood why it had taken so much convincing to make Harley believe in her theatre room and the options for the inn. He must have done a real number on her self-confidence. It made me realize how far she really must have come in those two years to be able to stand up to him in front of the whole town. She might not have needed my saving tonight, but I'm really glad I gave it.

But this was one more reason why she needed me to keep my distance. I couldn't be another guy who got close to her just to let her down.

Chapter Twenty-One

Kissed, Dissed, and Ghosted

Harley

It had been three days since Malcolm stood up for me against Connor at the town council meeting. Three days since he said he'd help me with the Haunted Trail. Three days since I've seen or talked to him. Every morning I think he's going to come down for breakfast, but he's gone before I wake up and doesn't come in until after I go to sleep. For all I know, he's choked on the sandwiches I supplied him and now he's just a corpse, rotting away up there.

Well, that's not true. I might have quietly pushed my ear up to his door to make sure I could hear the clicking of his keyboard or him humming while he put visuals together.

I knew he was purposefully avoiding me, and it was the most childish thing I had ever seen. If I would have known that he was going to ghost me after making that grand declaration in front of my ex and the entire town, I would have just shoved the Haunted Trail off onto someone else.

I couldn't even talk to Maggie because she was gone with Avery to Vermont for their annual trip for Oktoberfest. I've talked to Jaynie, mostly because she called the second morning in a row that Malcolm went to her bakery for breakfast instead of staying here. In a move of solidarity, Jaynie told me how she gave him her signature "you fool" look that she usually reserves for men and rowdy teenagers.

With Maggie gone, I was also faced head on with the growing pile of late bills and final notices that she'd been organizing out of my eyesight. As much as the sight of my debt put a sinking feeling in my stomach, I was buoyed by the reminder once again that Maggie was putting in some real effort around the inn, more than what a normal employee would give.

I was pulled from my pondering, or more accurately, my sulking when the front door opened and a gorgeous man walked into the lobby. Dark, thick hair that swept back away from his forehead pulled my attention to his strong brows and sharp brown eyes. I was mad at myself that my stomach didn't flip at the sight of him. Not like it did with Malcolm. The handsome man held a phone to his ear as he scanned the desk, breaking into a dazzling smile when his eyes landed on me.

Where did these magnificent men come from? Was there a wormhole spitting them out just outside of town? Was that how wormholes worked?

"Yeah, yeah I just got here," the stunner of a stranger said into his phone, giving me a wink that sadly didn't put my heart into flutter territory. "I'll talk to her and figure it out."

Was he talking about me? He made a noise into the phone and tucked it into his pocket as he approached the desk.

"Hi there," he said, flashing me another dazzling white smile. I bet he got a lot of ladies with a smile like that. "My name's Davis. I'm part of the Spirits crew."

"Oh, yeah," I said, turning to grab an old iron key from the case behind me. "I'm Harley. I thought you all weren't coming until to-morrow."

"We're not. I just had some time and wanted to come early to scope out the space for the audio equipment. I run the recordings and microphones for the channel. I mean, if that's no problem."

"No problem at all," I said as he took the key from my hand a little slower than necessary. He was really good at this. "Why don't I show you around the inn?"

"No need," a voice came from beside me, making me jump. "I can do it." Malcolm turned the corner and enveloped Davis in a hug. My stomach flipped at the sight of him, followed quickly by a rush of anger.

This guy kissed me, dismissed me, ghosted me, then ran to my rescue at a city council meeting just to fall off the map again. And yeah, I could've thought he was dead because I hadn't seen him in days, but really, I was more surprised he lived this long at all if this was how he treated women.

It also made me irritable to have him and Davis next to each other. Having two male specimens of such attractiveness should be against the laws of nature.

"Hey man, how have you been?" Malcolm asked, giving Davis a slap on the back as if he hadn't a care in the world. Irritation simmered at the base of my spine. I wanted to feel like I didn't have a care in the world. But if he could act like that, then so could I.

"Good, good. I thought I'd come by a day early in case you alienated our gracious host," Davis said with a laugh. When Malcolm and I looked away from each other, Davis' laughter abruptly died. "Oh, shit."

"It's fine," I said with an overly casual wave, purposefully avoiding looking at Malcolm. "I'm excited to have you guys here. Is there any equipment you need help bringing inside?"

"That's kind of you, but I'd never ask a pretty girl to carry my bags." Davis certainly had a way with that smile of his. I swear I could hear every woman's heart breaking for five square miles. "But if you're around in a bit, I'd love someone to show me the sights."

Malcolm glared at Davis. "Watch it," he growled under his breath.

"Ignore him," I said cheerily. "I'd love to. Let me know when Mr. Jones finishes the tour, and I can take you to go see the town."

I could feel Malcolm's eyes on me the moment I called him "Mr. Jones" again, but I kept my eyes on Davis. At least this attractive man seemed to think I was worth his time. The only bummer was that his gaze didn't send my blood thrumming through my veins, but maybe that came with time.

"Thank you, Harley," he said, knocking his knuckles on the desk with a boyish grin. "I'll see you in a bit."

"Can't wait," I said, doubling down on my most welcoming smile.

Malcolm grabbed a fist-full of Davis' shirt and pulled him back out the front door, the glare still frozen on his face. Davis happily went, not at all concerned about the anger coming off Malcolm. As the door closed behind him, I could see Malcolm stepping in front of the glass front door with his arms crossed in front of him, facing Davis.

"Off limits," he said firmly, his voice muffled slightly by the barrier of the door.

"Oh, come on!" Davis said, throwing his head back. "You're clearly not doing a great job of things, and that girl is way too pretty to be waiting around for the likes of you to get your head out of your ass."

My cheeks flushed at the compliment I clearly wasn't supposed to hear.

Malcolm shook his head, maintaining his stance. "Davis, it's not happening. You don't know the full story, and you don't need to know. But she is off limits."

"You saying she's yours?"

"If it gets you to keep your paws off her, then yeah. She's mine."

I couldn't decide if I liked the idea of Malcolm staking his claim and showing his jealous ways or if it pissed me off. Either way, a jolt ran through me at his words.

She's mine.

This was the same guy who kissed me, then treated me like a stranger. Just then, Maggie came around the corner and put her bag loudly on the counter. "What are you—"

"Shh!" I slapped my hand over her mouth and dragged her down behind the desk. The voices stopped outside as Maggie looked at me with wide eyes. When I peeked my eyes up above the desk, the two men were gone. I let go of Maggie's face and stood up.

"What the hell?" she demanded. "I think you smudged my lip-stick."

I looked over her face. "Nope, you're good. What are you doing here?"

"I just got back from my trip and remembered I left my laptop here. What are *you* doing?"

She propped a hand on her hip, sporting her classic Blue Rover Band charm bracelet, and waited as I tried to make myself appear natural in the chair behind the desk, but even I had to admit that I looked like an awkwardly staged mannequin. It took a moment before I huffed out a frustrated breath. "Malcolm's friend, Davis, from the YouTube show, just came in and started flirting with me and Malcolm went all neanderthal on him with the 'off-limits' and 'She's mine.'"

"Whoa, really?"

"Yeah, but I wasn't supposed to hear that part of the conversation. They were on the other side of the front door, and we both know that doesn't block sound for shit," I whispered loudly to prove my point.

"Huh," Maggie said. "But Jaynie texted Avery who told me that Malcolm's been avoiding you."

I sat in the chair and studied my shoes. Damn small towns. "Harley," Maggie prodded, checking to make sure the guys still weren't near the door. "What aren't you telling me?"

"We may have kissed, just a little."

"Whoa, when was this?" Maggie asked, pulling a stool from beneath the desk and sinking into it.

"A week ago. Ugh, and it was incredible, and I thought things were really going places but then he just dropped off the face of the Earth. When he was near me, he treated me like a stranger, the rest of the time he's been completely avoiding me. Now someone else is interested, and he's suddenly acting like he has a right to lay a claim to me like a toy on the playground?"

"Wait a second," Maggie said, crossing her arms in front of her chest. "You kissed him a week ago, and this is the first I'm hearing about it? I mean, I knew something happened between you two, but I thought it was just an argument or something."

"No, we kissed, and then he said he was sorry, and tried to say it was a mistake. Then he avoided me like the plague."

"Wow, that's a dick move."

"Yep," I agreed, running my hands through my hair in frustration.

The front door opened again, and the two guys came back inside. Davis was carrying two silver cases and Malcolm trailed behind him with two bags hung over his shoulders. As Davis walked by, he wiggled his eyebrows conspiratorially at me before walking upstairs. Malcolm had his lips in a thin line with his brow furrowed as if he was presented with a particularly difficult math problem.

They disappeared around the corner and Maggie turned to me, adjusting her horn-rimmed glasses that were bright green today. "Don't take this the wrong way because I'm fully on Team Harley, but is there a factory somewhere creating perfect male specimens? Because they certainly don't make them like that around here."

"God, right?" I snorted. "It's like a model convention. People shouldn't be allowed to be that beautiful."

Half an hour passed with Maggie filling me in on the highlights of her trip, when we heard steps coming down the stairs. Davis turned the corner and approached me, handing me back the room key. "Sorry Harley, I'm gonna have to take a raincheck on the sightseeing."

I gave him a half smile and a raised eyebrow. "Uh huh."

"I'll see you tomorrow for check-in," he said before heading out the door.

I sighed to Maggie, watching Davis walk out the door. "I guess the neanderthal routine worked on Davis."

Before Maggie could respond, we heard Malcolm's footsteps on the stairs. A moment later, he turned the corner and locked eyes with me. "We need to talk."

Chapter Twenty-Two

All the Relationship Vibes

Malcolm

I nodded my head toward the stairs and Harley's eyes went wide. "Now? Malcolm, I have to close up."

"Maggie?" I asked her sister, hands on my hips. Sure, I was coming off as slightly crazy and more than a touch domineering but seeing the way she smiled at Davis when she would only ignore my existence, made me want to disintegrate one of my best friends into dust.

"I can close up," Maggie said, grabbing Harley's shoulders and steering her around the desk toward me. This also earned Maggie a slot on my annual Christmas card list.

"Traitor," Harley hissed at her.

"I'm sure you'll thank me later," Maggie whispered back, both in clear hearing distance of me. She then pointed a dangerous smile at me. "Don't make me regret this."

"Yes, ma'am," I said with a nod, then grabbed Harley's hand and pulled her toward the stairs. It took a few seconds for her to get her wits about her and yank her hand from mine.

"What is going on with you, Malcolm?" she demanded as she reluctantly followed me to my room. When I didn't answer and just held the door open for her, she rolled her eyes and walked through, the proximity forcing her to brush against me. And yeah, I did that on purpose. And I didn't miss the way her nostrils flared and her eyes sank shut as she smelled my shirt.

The added effect was our two scents together combined and made the sweetest perfume that made me slightly dizzy for the effect it had on me. *God, I missed her.*

I closed the door behind me and indicated for Harley to sit on the bed. She raised an eyebrow and instead chose to sit on the settee by the window, just to be contrary. Although, if I was being honest there was an immediate awareness of her being in my room, near my bed, that had every fantasy I had of her flooding my brain. I had to immediately tamp down those thoughts.

For the first time since the city council meeting, Harley was actually looking at me. Actually looking at me. Admittedly, it wasn't my best look. My hair was probably standing in a million directions from where I had run my hands through it and the bags under my eyes could have counted as checked luggage on most airlines.

I started pacing in front of her, casting nervous glances her way. This was the first time in days that she had seen me and being close enough to touch her was making my heart hurt.

"Malcolm," she said quietly, extending a hand in my direction that she promptly placed back in her lap, then looked back down at her feet. I stopped pacing and looked at her. "You wanted to talk, so talk."

I moved slowly now, with purpose, as if approaching a deer in the wild. I needed her to listen, to understand. I couldn't stay away from her any longer, and I couldn't stand the idea of breaking her either. I walked until we were toe-to-toe and sank into a crouch in front of her. Looking at her face, I took a gamble and gently placed my hands on her knees. My hands zinged with electricity at touching her again, even through a layer of fabric, and she blinked quickly to keep her eyes from tearing up. Knowing I was the reason for those tears was like a knife to my chest.

I lifted one of my hands and tucked it beneath her chin, as if asking her to look at me. It reminded me of our kiss, bringing a fresh wave of misery. When her gaze met mine, I saw the same misery I've been feeling reflected back at me through the sheen of water.

"Harley," I said, her name like a prayer on my lips. "I'm so sorry."

"Sorry for what, exactly?" she asked softly, her lips barely moving. "Sorry for disappearing, or sorry for kissing me in the first place?"

I closed my eyes, I didn't want to see that pain I had put her through and shook my head. "I'm not sorry for the kiss. Never sorry for that. And I shouldn't have said that it was a mistake. It wasn't a mistake."

"Then why?" she asked. I knew what she was asking. *Why did you push me away? Why did you disappear? Why haven't you kissed me again?*

I sighed. "I'm sorry for not talking to you afterwards. I didn't mean to kiss you, it just happened."

"That's what every girl wants to hear," she mumbled, turning to look away. I gently gripped her chin and brought it back to me. Her face looked so small, so delicate in my hands.

"I wasn't finished, Harley," I said, staring into her eyes. "It happened because I can't control myself around you. And you deserve more than some guy blowing into town, only to break your heart when he leaves. I travel so much doing this job with Ben. It's not a life that lends itself well to relationships or families, and you're a relationship and family kind of girl."

"And you're not the relationship kind of guy?" she asked, with a nod.

I hesitated, making sure I was explaining things correctly. I didn't want her thinking I was the guy to turn up and kiss women under the guise that he wasn't a relationship kind of guy. "I am a relationship kind of guy. I'm the kind of guy that would fall really, really hard for you if I let myself, which wouldn't be fair to either of us when I leave.

And...fuck, Harley, I miss you. I miss hanging out with you and sharing late-night conversations. I even miss your god-awful popcorn."

"Hey! My popcorn is amazing!"

"You put ranch powder on it. You're basically a heathen." She grinned at me, and for a moment it felt like us again. Before I broke us.

Her smile faded as she nodded to herself. "So, it's not that you don't want to be with me, but you don't think you can."

I sighed. "Basically."

She took a moment to think it over, rubbing the velvet fabric of the chair under her fingertips. "I'm annoyed that this time was wasted when you should have just said all this to begin with. Getting the disappearing act from you sucked. Even if we were just friends, friends don't ghost friends. But I realized that as much as this kind of sucks for me, my heart is breaking for you. I mean, can I ask, what does this mean for your future?"

My eyebrows furrowed. "What do you mean?"

"Putting aside how mad I've been at you, I'm asking this as a friend, as someone who cares about you, not as someone who expects anything from you," she clarified. "What you just described sounds like a really lonely life. Is that something you're happy with? Are you planning on not settling down ever? I'm not even talking about me. I know that I'm not the girl for you, and that's okay—"

"What do you mean, you know you're not the girl for me?" I felt almost angry at this declaration, which was even more confusing.

Harley sighed. "Malcolm, it's pretty obvious to me that you're the guy who will make anything work if he wants it badly enough, and the fact that you're shutting this down before anything goes further tells me that you don't want us all that much. I'm not saying that to offend you. I'm saying that to put things in perspective for both of us. It's good we aren't getting involved in something that we aren't willing to put the work into. The point is that you strike me as the type of guy who's going to want that one day, the house, the wife, the kids. And one day you're going to want to find her, whoever she is, and then what?"

My eyes narrowed as I looked past her shoulder, thinking. She sat quietly, allowing me to process. I liked that about her. She knew when to let me be in my own head.

"I don't think I have an answer to that," I admitted slowly. "I haven't allowed myself to think that far ahead in a long time. And there's more to it than what I've told you. I have decisions waiting for me in New York, decisions that I don't feel ready to make yet."

"The lawyers who were calling you that day?" She asked quietly, not sure if I was still angry from the last time she asked about it. I hated that I put that kind of doubt in her.

"Yeah, they're putting the pressure on me to make some pretty major decisions that would impact a lot of people. I've been just trying to live my life while I figure out what to do and you, Harley, I was not expecting you. You were the best possible thing to happen to me at the worst possible time."

I tucked a piece of hair behind her ear, so gently I could barely feel it. I could feel the heat swirling in my stomach as her gaze darkened. My eyes flicked to her lips and without realizing what I was doing, I ran my tongue over my bottom lip. I was suddenly very aware of the space between every inch of our skin. An inch apart at the elbows, a breath apart at our hands.

"Malcolm," she said, breathier than she probably anticipated, but my jaw clenched when I heard it. "If I accept your apology for you avoiding me for a week, can we go back to how it was before? Even if it's as your friend? I've missed you, too."

I paused for a moment and shook my head. "I don't know if I can go back to being just friends with you, Harley. That kiss rocked my world, and every time I'm with you, I want to do it again."

She took a shallow breath. "Does that mean you want to kiss me now?"

"More than anything."

"Then kiss me," she demanded. I hesitated, holding on to the last strain of self-control I had in me. "Malcolm, can I be honest with you?"

I cupped my hand around her cheek. "Always."

"Okay then." I steeled myself for what was about to come out of her mouth, but I think between the two of us, she was the brave one. Harley took a deep breath. "I like you a lot. I think you know that. I like kissing you a lot. I think you know that, too. And I get that you're not going to be around here forever. That's unavoidable. Your job demands it. But what if we could be together even knowing there's an expiration date? I mean, we still have two weeks together. Are we really going to waste it avoiding what we both want? Avoiding each other?"

She sat with bated breath as I processed what she was proposing, and when I understood, my eyebrows parted, and my eyes went wide.

"So, let me get this straight, you want to date...for two weeks...knowing I'm leaving?" I asked in disbelief.

She placed her hand on the back of my neck, not putting pressure, just enough to show intention. "I want whatever part of you I can get. I don't want to look back and wonder what it would have been like to be with you. So yes, that's exactly what I'm proposing," she said, shoulders squared in confidence. She's so damn pretty and when she squares her shoulders like that, her chest pops out, revealing the curves of her breasts. I forced myself to look up at her eyes instead.

"This could end in disaster," I warned, already leaning into her.

"At least it's a disaster we chose together," she agreed, leaning in even closer to me. Our lips brushed and for a moment my brain melted. But something Davis said jumped into my psyche. If I wanted her, I needed to be clear with my intentions.

"Wait, Harley. I want rules."

Harley pulled away from me a little. "Rules? Like what? I don't call you when it's over? No staying the night? Don't feed you after midnight?"

"No, Harley, I don't want us to be like that. I don't want some...some fuck buddy. I don't want to just use you for your body, although I can't tell you how much I want you right now." Her cheeks flushed at my admission, and it made me wonder what other part of her lit up when she blushed.

"Not fuck buddies," she agreed, running her hand through my hair in a very distracting way. "Rule number one, we'd be in an exclusive relationship until you go back home to New York or wherever it is that the Spirits Channel goes. We get all the relationship vibes. I'm talking handholding, neck kissing, epic cuddles."

Images flashed through my mind of us doing those things, holding her hand, pressing her body against mine after a long night, kissing her just because I felt like it. My heart thudded in my chest in excitement and the tightness in my pants showed me that my dick agreed. Although her proposal was sassy and full of life, it was growing increasingly apparent that she was nervous about this idea, too. I couldn't tell if it was the idea she was worried about or my reaction to the idea, and as much as I didn't want to put myself in a position to fall for her, I realized it probably had already happened.

I grinned at her. "I should warn you, I'm a pretty impressive cuddler. You might not be able to handle all my cuddles."

She laughed, some of the tension easing from her body. "I think I'll take my chances."

And this beautiful woman pulled on the back of my neck just enough to tell me she was ready, she wanted this, though her eyes showed me how nervous she was. We never made it to rule number two. I submitted, pulling her closer, claiming those lips that I hadn't been able to get out of my head. They were just as soft as I remembered and I stood her up so I could deepen the kiss, pulling our bodies together as one.

She popped up on her tiptoes, using my hips as balance and it was the cutest thing I think I'd ever experienced. I held onto her lower back, keeping her pressed against me, and I slowly slid my hand to the curve of her ass, testing the limits of how far she'd let this go.

Because I wanted her.

I wanted her in every way I could have her. And if she wanted us to be in an exclusive relationship for two weeks, I was praying that sex was involved because I'd thought of little else since we'd been apart.

As my hand slid lower, she pressed her hips closer into me, enjoying every second of this. She flexed her hands that were on my hips, and she slowly dipped them beneath my shirt, feeling the planes of my stomach. I'm not ashamed to admit that I might have flexed a little bit when she touched me, and from the sounds of her moans, she appreciated the work I've done to keep myself in shape.

Our kisses were slow but needy. We couldn't get close enough. She lifted my shirt a little higher and I paused our kisses just long enough to pull my shirt off and out of the way. She stared for a moment at my exposed chest, giving the same look she gave me that night I first came out of my room with my shirt off to investigate the disturbing sounds of the elderly guests getting it on. Her eyes filled with pure desire. She came back to me, connecting our mouths in a desperate passion as she ran her hands over my stomach, my chest, my shoulders. Everywhere our skin connected was electric and I wanted more.

"Do you want this?" I asked, breathing heavily as I toyed with the bottom of her shirt, barely lifting it up her back. I didn't want to stop, but I had to know that we were on the same page before I started something she wasn't ready for. She lifted her shirt off, exposing a black lace bra that held her perfectly round breasts and made my mouth water.

"Yes, I want this," she said, her voice breathy in the way that I loved. "I want you, Malcolm."

"Fuck, yes," I groaned out. I spun us around and backed her toward my bed, laying her down and running my lips down her neck. Sliding one hand behind her back, I made quick work of undoing her bra and slid it down her arms, exposing two beautiful pale orbs with rosy pink nipples. This woman was going to be the death of me. None of my fantasies could live up to the moment I saw Harley actually laid out on my bed.

"God, Harley, you're so beautiful." I lowered my head to suck one breast into my mouth while my other hand cupped her other breast, full and plump, fitting perfectly in my palms. I flicked my tongue against her hard nipple while my hand squeezed the other one gently. She let out the sweetest, most erotic gasp.

I switched sides and I felt her eager hand at the back of my head, holding me against her. Her hips flexed, desperate to get traction. I released her other breast and slid my hand down to the button on her jeans and popped it open, ready to give her some relief. Harley lifted her hips and helped me shimmy the jeans off, exposing a pair of white bikini underwear with tacos on them. I chuckled to myself, and she lifted her head up to look at me.

"What's so funny?" she asked.

"I like your underwear," I admitted, kissing her again while I looped my finger in the top band and slowly pulled them down, exposing her gorgeous pink flesh. Once her clothes laid in a heap at my feet, I slid a finger down her slit and moaned against her.

"God, baby, you're so wet." I swirled my finger inside her and slowly slid back up until I found her clit. I circled my finger around her sensitive nub, causing her to buck her hips.

"Malcolm," she moaned.

"Baby, I want to taste you. Please let me taste you," I wasn't above begging if it meant I got to put my mouth on her. I was praying she wasn't one of those girls who was embarrassed or ashamed about allowing someone to cherish them. Instead of answering, she opened her legs wider, encouraging me to keep going, and it was the single hottest thing I've ever experienced.

I lowered my mouth down her body, licking and teasing her nipples along the way until I made it down to her pretty pink slit, careful not to smudge my glasses. I wanted to see everything. At our connection, Harley moaned so sweetly, her hips bucking against me. I loved how responsive she was. Each moan caused a twitch of my hardened cock that was pressed against the inside zipper of my jeans. I held her legs open with my elbows, her hips down with my hands, and I worshipped her. I alternated positions and tempos, studying her body like a scholar to find what she liked. When I got into a rhythm she responded to and her moans grew louder, I slid a finger inside her and curled it in a 'come hither' gesture.

"Oh, my god, Malcolm," she breathed out. "Malcolm, I'm going to—"

Her body shuddered as she came against my mouth. I felt like an Olympian who crossed the finish line with his arms in the air, declaring victory. Feeling Harley shiver beneath me gave me a high like no other. I licked her over and over, lapping up her juices as she trembled from her orgasm until she collapsed in exhaustion. And we were only getting started.

Chapter Twenty-Three

Intertwined

Harley

Malcolm rubbed his hands on the inside of my thighs as I relaxed my muscles again and we locked eyes while he was still between my legs. "Oh, my god, Malcolm. I have no words."

He grinned up at me, licking his lips, with my sweetness still on his stubble and crawled up to kiss me. I didn't shy away, instead kissing him back full force, showing my appreciation.

"Pants off, Malcolm. I need you," I said between kisses. I didn't have to tell him twice. His erection pressed so hard against the inside of his jeans that it must have been painful. He made quick work of popping open his jeans and sliding them and his boxer briefs down his legs. When his cock sprang free, my mouth fell open. It had been an admittedly long time since I had even seen a penis, let alone one primed and ready to go, but I worried Malcolm's thick member would be painful. Sensing my hesitation, Malcolm slid his hand up my body until he cradled my cheek.

"Don't worry, baby. We'll go slow, I'll take care of you. Do you trust me?"

I nodded. I did trust him. I trusted him to take care of me. He knew he was a larger guy. He had length, but he was also thicker. He pulled open the drawer on the bedside table and grabbed a condom, sitting it on the bed as he nestled himself beside me.

He kissed me, and I felt my body tense as he pressed his length against me. He moved his hand between my legs. "Relax for me, Harley."

I relaxed enough to let my legs fall open, and he gently swirled his finger around my sensitive spot. I groaned against his mouth and moved my hips along with his finger. Gathering the juices from my orgasm, he slid one finger inside me.

"Fuck, baby you're so tight."

"It's been a while," I admitted sheepishly. He pumped his finger in and out of me, waiting until I relaxed again, then he slid another finger in. Once he put the third finger in, making sure I wasn't too uncomfortable, he pulled his hand away and positioned his cock at my entrance. I could tell it was taking everything he had not to push himself inside me too fast. His dick twitched in anticipation, and I could feel the sweat on his skin from holding back.

He kissed me again as he slid, ever so slightly inside me. "I need you to relax, baby. Breathe. We're gonna go slowly."

I nodded, kissing him again as he pulled out again and pumped in just a little more. He felt so warm and tight against me, he was nearly shaking with the need to push himself inside of me. He rocked back and forth, slowly giving me more each time.

"I can take more, Malcolm," I said. "I need more."

He pumped a little further inside this time, and I gasped, feeling fuller than I had ever felt. He froze, searching my face for pain, but continued when I nodded at him. He withdrew farther and pumped harder, seating himself nearly all the way.

"Oh, God, Malcolm. You feel so good. Keep going."

He didn't respond, he just focused on pumping while watching my tolerance. His hands gripped the pillows behind me as he thrusted all the way in, his balls gently slapping against me as I moaned. He gritted his teeth, trying hard not to lose control.

"Do you feel okay, baby?" he gritted out. "I gotta know I'm not hurting you."

"I'm good, Malcolm, give me more. I need you to move. I want you so bad."

He moaned at my words and started pumping harder, my hips matching his rhythm and my moans turning into loud gasps of his name. I took a deep breath as his hips shifted angles. "You really know how to impress a woman," I said breathlessly.

"I had to make up for my first impressions," he said, wearing a satisfied smirk.

He moved faster, dropped his forehead to mine. We were in sync, connected beyond anything I'd ever felt before. The sound of his name on my lips had him losing control as he rocked furiously into me, my nails digging into his back with need.

All at once, a rush of euphoria traveled through me, curling my toes and fingers as I came against him. I shouted his name and clenched around his cock as I came undone. My release encouraged his as the euphoria overtook him, arms and legs shaking as shot after shot of his come drained from him. Nothing could have prepared me for how gorgeous Malcolm Jones was when he was coming undone inside me.

He fell against me, our foreheads touching as we breathed together. Our skin was coated in a fine layer of sweat, his chest pressed against my breasts and when he looked down at me, our eyes connected with him still inside me. A look of...something passed over his face and he touched my cheek like he was memorizing every freckle.

Malcolm got up only long enough to dispose of the condom before climbing back into bed, flipping the covers over us, and wrapping me in his body until we could feel each other's heartbeats. Neither of us said anything, and I realized things would never be the same for me. The connection was something I could never replicate. Our spirits intertwined, feeling like I was truly a part of him. Being skin to skin like that as we curled together was almost as intimate as the sex itself, and I had never wanted to be as close with anyone as he was with me.

He lay awake beside me, and I could feel him brushing my hair back as I sank into a restful sleep.

Chapter Twenty-Four

Rockstars and Recordings

Malcolm

Waking up with Harley's feet tangled with mine, her scent in my sheets and hair strewn across the pillow was the sweetest form of heaven I've ever experienced. She was delicate in sleep, a break from the spitfire that I knew her to be when she was awake. My hands acted on their own accord as they reached to brush her hair from her face. I had done the same the night before, running my fingers through her hair until I heard the even breathing coming from her lips. Once I knew she was fast asleep, I allowed myself the luxury of falling asleep next to my girl.

This, right here. This was what forever should feel like. Harley's body inches from mine, a soft rose on her lips from late-night kissing. I knew there was no way I could go back to the way my life was before Harley. We connected the night before in a way I had never thought possible. And I knew she felt it too.

Her phone on the bedside table started a soft alarm that threatened to grow, and I reached over and turned it off. I wasn't going to let an alarm wake my girl up. Yeah, *my girl*. I grabbed my glasses from the bedside table and put them on before turning back to Harley. Scooting closer, I lowered my forehead to hers and nuzzled her nose. She let out an adorable little moan and reached out with her delicate hand to stroke my chest.

Something about this woman just made me feel like a man. I wanted to protect her from the world. I settled for wrapping my arms around her waist and pulling her bare body toward me. Her eyes fluttered open.

"Good morning," she said with a smile.

"Morning," I said with a smile. I ran another hand through her hair. I couldn't keep my hands off her.

"So last night happened," she said with a smile, then looked down at our bodies pushed together, obviously feeling the effect she had on me. "Based on *that*, I'm assuming you want it to happen again?"

My smile nearly broke my face as I slid my stiff length against her. "I want you as much as I can have you," I said, honestly. I nuzzled my nose into her hair, breathing in the smell of her shampoo, before brushing my lips against hers. She kissed me back, taking it from a pace of gentle caresses to demanding need. Her arms wrapped around my neck, rubbing her fingers against the scratches she no doubt left on my back last night. Her legs wrapped around my waist, pulling us closer together, asking for more with each thrust of her hips.

I slid my hands between her legs and felt her warm wetness. "Shit, Harley, you're really ready."

"I want you, Malcolm," she whispered against my mouth. "Don't make me wait."

I rubbed the head of my cock against her entrance, coating it in her juices. *God, I could drown in her.*

"Fuck, baby, condom," I said, pulling back. I never forgot a condom, but this woman could make me forget my own name. I pulled a condom from the side table. Davis, for as big of an asshole as he was for flirting with Harley, still made sure I was stocked up on condoms before he left for the night. I wasn't expecting to need them, but he's the boy scout of sexual encounters, always prepared.

Harley kissed my neck and ran her hands down my back as I ripped the wrapper open with my teeth and slid it on.

"Now, Malcolm," she demanded, pulling my hips toward her. "Don't hold back. I need you."

I locked my lips to hers as I grabbed my length and lined it up with her opening. In one solid thrust, I slammed into her, bringing a moan from her lips around my kiss. Grabbing onto her hips with a grip that could bruise, I pulled out slowly, reveling in the feel of her before slamming in again. Harley wove her fingers through my hair and tugged, giving a delicious bite of pain as she demanded more with her hips.

Obliging her, I took off at a frantic pace. This wasn't the slow lovemaking from the night before. This was carnal. Her hips rocked against me, grinding her clit against my pubic bone, and when I felt like I was close enough to burst, I paused, flipping onto my back and dragging her on top of me. She sat, straddling my hips with my cock inside her as she began to ride me. I reached out and rubbed her clit with my thumb as she ground and lifted against my cock, throwing her head back in ecstasy, her long hair tickling my thighs.

Watching Harley on top of me, her round tits bouncing with each thrust would forever be burned into my memory. Harley's hand sat on my chest, keeping her balance and occasionally digging her nails into my chest when she was particularly taken. And when her body clenched, she called out my name again, and I followed right behind her, grabbing her hips and bucking savagely against her, feeling my balls slap against her ass, freezing as my muscles locked and I came inside of her again.

This time, she fell against me, curling into my arms as I softened and slid out of her. I kissed her forehead, her hair, her nose, her lips, every piece of her I could. "You're amazing, Harley. I'm so happy I'm with you."

She glanced up at me, taking her finger and sliding my glasses a little further up on my nose. "I'm really happy I'm with you too. You make me happy."

And damn, if that didn't warm my heart. Her eyes tilted down as her finger ran circles on my chest. "Just don't ghost me again, okay?"

I could hear the vulnerability in her voice as she glanced away. I pulled her close to me and kissed the top of her head. "I won't, I promise."

We laid like that for a while, wrapped in each other's arms, until I got a text on my phone from Davis saying that he would be at the inn soon. We showered, which led to an extra half hour of time together. Not that either of us were complaining, just doing our part for the environment.

When we finally made our way downstairs, Harley's hair combed back into a basic ponytail from the shower because apparently, I took all of the time she would have spent drying and styling her hair, but I don't think she was really protesting, we found Maggie already sitting behind the desk. She had organized stacks of papers waiting, along with keys for the rooms set aside.

Maggie gave us a wry grin as she held a cup of coffee up to her lips. "You're up late."

Harley grabbed the cup from Maggie's hands and took a swig of the coffee. "I figured the employee of the month could handle things for a bit."

"Damn straight," Maggie said, pulling forward a trophy with a small baseball player on top. She had taped a doll-sized electric guitar to the bat, making it look like the figure on the trophy was about to smash the guitar in a post-rock haze. Maggie turned and looked Harley dead in the eye. "I'm a rockstar."

We were in the dining room eating pastries and drinking coffee when Davis stormed in, a black blazer with the sleeves rolled up blowing behind him, a laptop in his hands, and a huge smile on his face.

"Hey Davis, I didn't realize you were—" I began.

"Malcolm, you're never going to believe this!" he interrupted. Davis' eyes were alight with the thrill of discovery. Harley and Maggie exchanged looks while I raised an eyebrow at Davis. "I came in early and I didn't see you guys, so I went upstairs to get some audio stuff set up early, and I realized I accidentally left one of the recorders going all night!"

My hand froze as I was bringing coffee to my lips. I willed myself not to glance at Harley. "Oh?"

"Yeah," he said, waving me off. "I was doing some tests on the equipment to make sure I had all of the settings right yesterday. Anyways, I figured I would check out the audio to get a feel for what we could expect for the Halloween episode, and check out what I found!"

Davis sat the computer on the dining table between the scones and spare cups for coffee and scrolled through the audio files, clicking until we saw a spike where the microphone picked up activity.

"I found evidence of a haunting!" He glanced between all three of us, making sure we were all watching before pressing play. We all three leaned closer as the sound of ambient noise filtered through the speakers. As the spike in the audio program came up, we heard a very distinct woman's voice breathing a name.

"Malcolm," Harley's voice from last night breathed loudly, catching in the microphone. My eyes widened and a grin fought its way toward my lips. Remembering that moment threatened to make me hard all over again. Davis, in his excitement, played it twice more before Harley slammed his laptop shut.

Davis looked confused as he glanced around the table. Harley's face was bright red, her hand covering her face. Maggie's lips were curled into a smug grin as she kicked her feet up on one of the dining chairs, chewing on a muffin.

"Malcolm, man, I know this isn't your thing, but you've gotta admit, this could really be something," he said, still glancing around in confusion. "We've got real evidence of a haunting here!"

"I don't know, Davis," I said, smiling behind my coffee mug as I locked eyes with Harley. "I think this could turn me into a believer."

Chapter Twenty-Five

Off-Limits

Harley

After a lot of back and forth over whether or not to tell Davis that what he heard was not, in fact, evidence of a haunting, much to my mortification, Malcolm pulled Davis aside before the rest of the crew got there and told him to delete it. I wasn't around for that conversation, but based on the way Davis' eyebrows wiggled at me when he came in from outside, I think he understood what the source of the sounds on the tape were.

Today was the day the rest of the ghost hunting team arrived, and Maggie and I had prepped in advance. Their stay had to be perfect, or I risked losing the inn forever, along with any future shot of owning my own business. This led to me checking each of the rooms three times before Malcolm intervened.

"Harley, you've seen our video, you know they're just normal people. Quit panicking."

My eyes went wide, and I quickly looked at the pillow I had been adjusting for the last ten minutes. Malcolm dipped his head down to look at me and grinned. "Harley?"

I sighed and winced. "About that," I started. Malcolm howled in laughter.

"What is so funny?" I demanded.

Malcolm finally stifled his chuckles. "I'm not saying this to be an asshole," he said, hand to his heart like he was reciting the pledge of allegiance. "But do you know how much fan mail we get from random girls, and the one girl I actually want has never seen my show?" He laughed harder.

I found myself chuckling too. "You're not mad?"

"Mad?" he asked, still laughing. "No, baby, I'm not mad. I'm surprised you'd be cool with us filming here without having ever seen the show though."

I shrugged. "Maggie vouched for you guys, and I trust her. Plus, there wasn't much to lose."

An hour later, three large black vans pulled into the parking lot. A few men and women got out and stretched. Maggie was in the kitchen, and I called to her that the crew had arrived. She straightened her glasses—red today—and headed out to sit behind the welcome desk.

As the men and women filtered in, all chatting amongst themselves, they moved out of the way as a guy of medium height with dark hair and thick eyebrows meandered up to the counter. As his eyes met Maggie's, both of their bodies stilled.

"Hi, Ben," Maggie said quietly, a small, wistful smile playing on her lips.

"Maggie?" Ben asked, shock in his voice. I tried to remind myself that the last time Maggie had seen Ben was at Archie's funeral three years ago, and Maggie looked a lot different then. She was still her natural blonde, but she had tried to fit in with a different crowd, straightening her curls, wearing dark eyeliner and contacts, dark clothes, and a myriad of bracelets had lined her wrists. But this Maggie was more like a punk pinup girl, her natural curls bouncing freely around her face, bright red lips, still the same high tops on her feet, and her signature horn-rimmed glasses.

I stared at the two of them, surprised at the level of tension surrounding them. The front door of the inn opened again, and Davis walked in. When he saw Ben frozen in front of the desk, Davis walked up, only to skirt around Ben and extend a hand toward Maggie.

"Hi, I'm Davis," he started smoothly, engaging in his charming smile. "We met earlier but I didn't get your—"

"Off limits," Ben said firmly, his eyes never leaving Maggie. A pink blush ran up Maggie's cheeks as Davis tilted his head back in exasperation.

"Seriously? Between you and Malcolm, I'm starting to think you all want me to become a monk."

"Poor Davis," one of the women teased with a roll of her eyes. She had the same dark hair as Davis, and the same stark brown eyes, wearing sensible jeans and boots. "You'll just have to keep it in your pants for a night or expand your hunting ground. For a manwhore, you're kind of lazy about it."

"Shut it, Darla," Davis replied.

Malcolm leaned in to whisper in my ear. "Darla is Davis' sister. The two of them got into ghost hunting when Darla was featured on TV for having experienced paranormal encounters as a kid. When they were kids, Davis was the only one who believed her, so they're pretty close."

I grinned. "Seems like it."

Malcolm's hands rested on my hips, and he kept his body pressed against my back as he prepared to run commentary on the rest of the crew in the lobby. Ever since last night, it's like he couldn't stand not touching me, and I loved it. He was really taking this two-week relationship thing seriously, and it made me wonder how I was ever going to let go at the end of the two weeks. But that was a problem for future Harley. Present Harley was really just pleased as punch to have Malcolm's hands on me.

Another woman, this one with shoulder-length turquoise hair and a floral dress dropped a large bag on the floor. "That's Zoey," Malcolm whispered in my ear, tickling my skin with his breath. "She does the filming and editing along with Cameron, who's over in the corner texting on his phone."

I looked to where Malcolm nodded to see a lumberjack-looking man in the corner with a styled beard, wearing a blue flannel shirt rolled up to his elbows exposing two sleeve tattoos and wearing dark wash jeans.

"Hey, Ben, are you gonna check us in or check out your lady love all day?" Zoey asked, rubbing her sore shoulders.

"I like her," I decided.

A blush rose up in Ben's cheeks, but he kept his eyes trained on Maggie. "It's really good to see you, Mags."

"You too, Ben." She shook her head as though trying to clear her mind. "Here, let's get you guys checked in and Harley and I can help you with your bags."

Giving Malcolm's hands a squeeze where they rested on my hips, reluctant to move away from Malcolm's warmth, I moved behind the desk and began dishing out keys while Maggie worked with Ben to sign all of the paperwork on payment. Malcolm and I guided the crew upstairs, while Malcolm helped carry the bags, insisting that I didn't need to carry anything. When his back was turned, Darla handed me a lightweight case with a wink, and I smiled gratefully. Malcolm guided Davis, Cameron, and Ben down one hall, and I showed Darla and Zoey to their rooms closer to mine.

When I opened the door to Darla's room, I sat down the case she gave me and turned to find Darla and Zoey blocking the door with matching smirks on their faces.

"So, what's the deal with you and Malcolm?" Darla asked, flipping her dark hair over her shoulder. I could feel the heat rising in my cheeks. I scanned her face for any hint of malice but only found curiosity. It had never occurred to me that Malcolm might have had a past with another girl on the team.

"What do you mean?"

"Oh, come on," Zoey chimed in with a roll of her eyes. She walked over to the bed and bounced down on it. "We all saw the way he was holding you like you were the holy grail."

"Is that not normal for him?" I asked, hating how insecure my voice was as I absently rubbed my finger against the top of the desk.

Darla snorted. "Um, no, that's not normal for Malcolm. We've been doing this show full-time for three years now, and I don't think I've ever even seen him with a woman. Much less as attached as he seemed with you."

I felt my stomach flip just as Malcolm came up to the doorway.

"All right, ladies, I'm going to steal Harley. Mostly because I don't want you both hounding her with questions."

I shrugged with a smile. "Who's to say I'm not hounding them with questions?"

"Ooh, I like her," Zoey crooned. Darla gave a smirk.

His eyes went wide, clearly not having thought about that. "Neither option is good," he decided. Looking toward his colleagues, Malcolm announced, "Meeting in thirty minutes to go over scheduling and research. Harley, can the crew meet up in the living room?"

"Yeah, go for it. Maggie and I need to prep for breakfast in the morning, so we'll be in the kitchen if you guys need anything. Did you get a list of allergies from the guys?"

Malcolm shook his head. "None of the crew is allergic to anything, but if you ask them, Cameron will say he's allergic to cherries because he doesn't like the taste, and Zoey will say she's allergic to green olives because she feels like they stare at her while she's eating."

Zoey threw a pillow at the door. "Some things are sacred, Malcolm!"

I smiled. "To be fair, green olives are really creepy, especially when the red pimento pits are in them."

"Thank you," Zoey said, indicating toward me.

"So, no cherries and no olives," I confirmed. "Got it. Maggie and I will do a spread so there are some options for everyone."

I followed Malcolm out of the room, holding his hand as he guided me downstairs to the empty dining room where he promptly spun me against the wall and kissed me hard. I kissed him back, smiling against his lips.

"Did you miss me?" I asked with a giggle.

"Absolutely," he said, holding my hips against the wall. "I don't know how I'm going to get any work done when your lips are taunting me like this."

To prove his point, he lowered his lips to mine again.

"The girls were asking what was going on with us," I said, as Malcolm moved his kisses down to my neck. "I tried to play it off, but it's not like you're subtle about us."

He stopped for a moment, looking at me. "Do you want me to be subtle? Because I gotta be honest, if I only get you for two weeks, I don't want to hide this. I want to have every moment I can with you."

"So, you don't mind if your friends know?" I asked, surprised.

"Not at all. I mean, as long as you don't mind. They'll be nosy and ask questions, but as far as I'm concerned, we're together. In fact, rule number two: even if this thing between us has an expiration date, you still matter to me. I'm not going to hide you. Okay?"

I smiled wide and nodded. "Okay."

"Now, we've got about twenty minutes before I have to be a responsible member of the team, which means that's twenty minutes I get to spend with you," he said, his voice low and sultry.

Malcolm moved his hands from my hips to grasp my hands, pulling them up above my head and pinning them in place with one of his large hands. His other hand slid down my arms until it cupped my breast and squeezed gently while his leg slid in between my thighs.

Malcolm kissed me, delicately slipping his tongue in my mouth while he rocked his thigh between mine, putting the perfect amount of pressure against the apex of my thighs. I moaned against his mouth as quietly as I could, loving the feeling as he slid his hand beneath my shirt to grab my breast beneath my bra.

I dipped my hips to grind against his thigh, not caring that I was dry humping Malcolm's leg like an animal in heat. I needed relief from the building tension between my legs. He tweaked my nipple as he nipped at my bottom lip. "Does that feel good, Harley?" he whispered low. I was only able to whine in acknowledgment as I bucked against his thigh again.

"I need more," I complained. He tightened his grip on my hands above my head and pushed his lips against my ear. "Okay, but I need you to be quiet, yeah?"

I nodded frantically. Malcolm checked over his shoulder toward the door before removing his hand from my nipple and moving it down to unsnap the button of my jeans. I leaned into him as he slid his hand beneath my panties and dipped his finger into my entrance. He pumped a couple of times before pulling out and swirling his finger around my clit.

The building friction against my clit was getting to be too much, and he swallowed my impending moan with a kiss. He broke the kiss and whispered against my ear again. "Good girl. I want you to ride my hand like you rode my cock this morning."

Holy hell. I pumped my hips forward, grinding against him like I did when I was on top of him, and he kept his mouth near my ear, licking and nibbling on my earlobe.

In a flash, I was coming, wrapping my leg around his hip as wave after wave of satisfaction flooded through me. Malcolm kissed me hard to quiet my moans and held me up as my legs gave out, both of us breathing heavily. He pulled his hand out of my pants and buttoned me back up.

I started giggling uncontrollably after I caught my breath. "We just did that in my dining room, with all of your coworkers upstairs."

He started laughing softly, his forehead against mine. "I told you, Harley, I can't help myself around you. I'm addicted." He lowered a kiss to my lips and gently stood me upright, making sure I could manage on my own. Then he adjusted his visibly hard cock in his jeans. I winced as I looked at it. "Is there anything I can do to help you with...that?"

He chuckled and shook his head. "Not a chance, I'm saving that for tonight."

My eyes went wide. "How is that going to work with everybody here? We can't exactly go at it like rabbits where everyone can hear us. I didn't even think of that."

He shrugged. "We'll figure it out. In the meantime, I'm going to have to cover this up as much as I can and hope no one notices the raging hard-ons I get around you."

I chuckled and slid my hand along his length that was pushing against his jeans. He leaned in for a moment to my touch before jumping away. "Behave yourself, woman."

"Never," I answered with a saucy wink before sauntering out of the kitchen to check in with Maggie about which recipes we wanted to put together for the morning.

Chapter Twenty-Six

The Crew Inquisition

Malcolm

I adjusted myself in my pants one more time as I struggled to slow my heart rate back down. That woman was going to be the death of me. Watching her interact with Ben and my crew so seamlessly when they arrived made me see how easily she could fit into my world. And when she let me hold her hand in front of Darla and Zoey, showing them that she's mine, I felt a primal urge come over me. I want the whole world to know that she belongs with me.

As I walked into the living room, Ben already had the file I gave him earlier spread out on the coffee table but was ignoring it in favor of folding his arms together, clearly waiting for me to say something. Davis, now freshly showered and wearing another blazer and a knowing smirk directed at me, sat in a navy blue armchair with a yellow legal pad and pen, ready to take notes. Darla and Zoey sat on the loveseat whispering to each other, Zoey with her iPad decorated in floral prints that matched her blue hair and Darla with her plain laptop, all synced up with each other.

I sat down next to Ben, painfully aware of how my four friends were eyeing me. I tried to pretend I didn't see them, instead shuffling some of the papers I brought in with me. Except that I had already organized the papers, so I was really just moving them an inch or two to the left or right. I cleared my throat just as Cameron sauntered in, sleeves rolled up exposing his tattoos, and standing in front of us with his hands on his hips. If someone didn't know Cameron, he could look intimidating as hell with his linebacker build, lumberjack beard, and motorcycle club haircut, but we all knew he was the most lovesick puppy out of all of us.

"Well?" he demanded. "Did anyone ask him what's going on with him and the girl?"

I sighed. Of course, he wasn't even going to ask me.

Zoey smiled at me, as she too decided to circumvent the main guy in the room with answers. "Not yet," she told him, tucking a strand of blue hair behind her ear. "I figured we should wait for you, so we didn't have to repeat ourselves. You know how needy you get for the details."

"Damn straight," he said, bobbing his head so far that his beard touched his chest. "The details are what matters, guys." Cameron waited a beat, now staring directly at me, and I noticed the rest of the crew was doing the same. "So," he demanded. "Out with it."

I nodded slowly, knowing I couldn't avoid it but was suddenly averse to telling them. Once it was out, really out, it wouldn't be Harley's and mine anymore. "Harley and I are together."

A chorus of outbursts erupted from all sides, ranging from congratulating me to asking how it happened to how serious it is. I raised my hands to quiet them, already knowing this was going to be more complicated the more I went into the details. As they waited for me to continue, I rubbed the back of my neck.

"Oh, no," Darla said, looking suddenly crestfallen. "I really liked her, what did you do?"

"Why do you assume I did something wrong?" I asked defensively.

"Because," Davis pointed his pen at me as he slouched in his armchair, wearing an almost identical expression as his sister. "You always rub the back of your neck when you're afraid to tell us something. The only reason you'd be afraid to tell us something is because you did something really stupid. I already know you tried to stay away from her and look how that turned out. Oh, shit, is she pregnant?"

"What? No!" I exclaimed, all at once surprised and annoyed that a surprise child of mine would elicit that reaction.

Darla interjected, "Davis, use your head, he's only been here two weeks. That's not nearly enough time to figure out if she's pregnant."

Davis nodded in agreement, rubbing a hand over his clean-shaven chin. I buried my head in my hands.

"Let the man speak," Cameron said, as if he hadn't started the inquisition in the first place.

I sighed and figured I should just come right out with it. "Harley and I agreed to see each other while I'm here, and when I leave, we call it quits. It's a relationship with a predetermined expiration date."

Silence engulfed the room. Darla was the first one to break the silence.

"Malcolm, that might be the dumbest thing I've ever heard." Darla was never one to mince words, and her take-no-prisoners personality made this especially cutting.

"Yeah, man, what are you thinking?" Davis asked. "That sounds like something I would do."

"No, it's not," I countered, my frustration rising. "You would find a girl to sleep with temporarily, that's not what this is."

"So, you aren't sleeping with her?" Davis asked, his brows furrowed in frustration. "You called 'Off-limits' on a girl you aren't sleeping with?"

"Well, yeah, we are," I said hesitantly. I was not the kind of guy to kiss and tell, but this was too important to not clarify. "But it's not just that. We're actually together. Like, dates and exclusivity. Relationship stuff. It's not at all like what you do."

Zoey shook her head and looked at me with something akin to pity. "Malcolm, do you like this girl?"

"Yeah, I do," I said, running a hand down my face.

"But like, how much?" She asked softly. "Because I saw the way you were looking at her. You were looking at her like she's a forever kind of girl, and she was looking at you the same."

My stomach flipped and I couldn't stop the grin from coming over my lips. They noticed her looking at me that way? What else had they noticed?

"Oh, look at that smile," Cameron said, waving a hand at me before sinking to the floor beside Davis's chair. "He's a total goner."

"So why are you already planning on ending it?" Darla asked. The rest of them looked at me.

I rubbed the back of my neck again, only pulling away when I remembered that it was my tell.

"It's just not sustainable," I said quietly, looking toward the kitchen. Harley and I had already agreed to this, but for some reason, I found myself not wanting her to overhear me say it. After last night, I didn't even want to be saying it. "I mean, she lives here. My home base is in New York. We travel constantly for the channel and I'm usually in a location for even longer gathering the research and filming rights that we need. It's not a way to have a relationship." I shook my head at myself. "Anyway, this is crazy. We've known each other for two weeks. I mean, we shouldn't even be having this conversation."

I winced as I heard the words come out of my mouth. They weren't untrue, Harley and I had only known each other for two weeks. But somehow I felt closer to her in those two weeks than I had felt in any past relationship. An uncomfortable silence settled over the room as the rest of the crew considered this.

"That's it," Ben said, voicing his opinion for the first time. "I call bullshit."

I looked at him in shock. "What?"

"I. Call. Bullshit," he repeated slowly. "You want to come up with excuses to not give this a real shot? Fine. But don't use the channel as your excuse. Our channel doesn't belong to some big corporation. The people in control of it are you and me, and the only people we take into consideration are the people in this room. That means if something needs to change to meet our needs, we do it. So, stop coming up with bullshit justifications to not be with this girl. Your home base is in New York? Move. People move all the time. I mean, for fuck's sake Malcolm, you don't even like New York anymore. You want to spend more time with your girl? We find more places locally, so we travel less. And as for knowing Harley for only two weeks? Every person in this room knows you, Malcolm. If you know that Harley is it for you, then it doesn't matter if it's been two weeks or two years. When you know, you know."

I sat in stunned silence. In all the years Ben and I have been running this channel, we've never talked about changing anything. And he's certainly never been so frank with me about my dating life. The only thing I'm not surprised about is Ben calling bullshit when he sees it.

"So," Cameron said, folding his tattooed arms in front of his chest now. "The question now is, is she your girl? Because if she is, you need to figure out a way to woo her."

Davis snorted. "Woo her?"

"Yes, Davis," Cameron said with a frustrated huff, "fucking woo her. Make sure she's wooed."

"Can we please stop saying 'woo?'" Ben asked. "But Cameron's right, she needs to know you're serious about her. If she's it for you, you need to pull out all the stops. Lock it down."

"Yeah," Darla said lazily, drumming her black fingernails on her cheek. "Really romance her. Now, if you're all done painting your nails and braiding each other's hair, I'd really love to get to figuring out this schedule for the next two weeks so I can catch some sleep. It was a long drive."

Cameron pointed a finger at Darla. "Darla, it's important for men to talk about their feelings. We will not stand by and let toxic masculinity run rampant while our fellow dude suffers."

Darla sighed, "You're right, I'm sorry. You can put the TED talk on hold. I'm just really tired."

I nodded, then grimaced. "We also need to factor in some time to help Harley with the Haunted Trail. I volunteered all of us to help with it, I had to throw down the gauntlet in front of Harley's ex-boyfriend at a city council meeting."

I smiled apologetically at the blank stares coming my way.

Ben sighed heavily. "All right then, let's open up the schedules, guys."

"Hey, wait a second," Davis said, glaring at Ben. "Is nobody going to talk about the fact that you called 'Off-limits' on Maggie?"

Darla groaned and shut the lid of her laptop.

"No shit?" Cameron asked, scrambling to his feet and assuming his hands-on-hips stance again. "When did this happen?"

"When your face was buried in your phone," Zoey mumbled.

"I was texting my mom, Zo," Cameron said with a roll of his eyes. "Y'all know how she gets when we get to a new location. And if you want to see any of her zucchini bread ever again, you won't poke fun at her checking in on her grown son."

Everyone in the room quickly backed off. Mama D's zucchini bread was sacred.

"So, what's the story with you two?" I asked, happy to get the attention off me while I figured out what I wanted to do about Harley.

Ben shrugged, trying to look nonchalant, but I could see the jitters in his thumbs. "She used to date Archie. They were dating when he passed away."

I nodded slowly. "Yeah, so that's the story with her and Archie. What's the story with her and you?"

Ben's hands clenched. "There isn't a story with us. She was Archie's. She's his. She looks good now, happy. And I'm happy for her. But I'm certainly not going to come around trying to replace my dead brother for her."

"Damn, dude, that's kind of harsh," Davis said from the chair, wincing.

"Yeah," Zoey said, her eyebrows furrowed in a rare show of anger. "Just because she was with Archie doesn't mean she's looking for someone to replace him. It's hard being the girl who lost a boyfriend. Everyone puts a shrine around us and acts like we aren't allowed to love anyone else or else it's disrespecting their memory or something. She doesn't belong to Archie, Ben. He can't call dibs from the grave."

Darla placed her hand over Zoey's fist that she probably didn't realize she had formed and gave it a supportive squeeze. Zoey joined the team about six months after her live-in boyfriend passed away. We met when she emailed us asking us to investigate her house for paranormal signs and after Ben found some evidence in the recordings, Zoey decided to sell the house to help her move on. That job was the only time on this channel I seriously let myself consider the possibility of something more out there. Soon after, Zoey was quitting her job as a wedding videographer and called us asking for a job.

Ben clenched his hands again and pulled at the papers on the table. "Let's focus on getting the schedule down. We've all got a long two weeks ahead of us for the Halloween special. Malcolm, can you go over the research you've found on the inn? Let's start there."

Chapter Twenty-Seven

Foot Licker

Harley

As the crew worked in the living room on whatever it was that ghost hunters worked on, I was elbow-deep in my fridge trying to figure out what to feed everyone for breakfast the next morning.

"So, I'm thinking we should do two types of muffins, pancakes, and sausage," I said, looking in the fridge for ingredients.

"I'm thinking we should talk about whatever is happening between you and Malcolm," Maggie said, leaning against the counter. "Yesterday you two weren't even speaking and today you can't keep your hands off of each other."

I nodded, a blush rising in my cheeks. "We talked last night. He's been trying to keep his distance after the kiss because he knows he's leaving and didn't want us getting attached just to wind up with broken hearts."

"So, what changed?" Maggie asked. "Is he staying?"

I sighed and shook my head. "No, but I told him that didn't matter. I told him I wanted him for however long I can have him, and that when he leaves, it's going to hurt but it's going to hurt whether or not we pushed things further. I'd rather have the memories, you know?"

Maggie looked at me like I grew a second head. "Let me get this straight, he tried to protect you from getting hurt, and instead you talked him into some whirlwind romance that's going to end cata-strophically, leaving both of you completely wrecked?"

"Maggie, it's not like that. We both decided that when he leaves, we split. There's nothing catastrophic about it," I lied. No matter how much I willed myself to believe it, too, after the night before there was no way I was going to get over him.

"Harley, I've seen you with guys before. I saw you with your high school boyfriends, with your college crushes, and unfortunately, I've seen you with Connor. I have never seen you look at someone the way you looked at Malcolm today. And I've never seen anyone look at you the way he did."

"How did he look at me?" I asked, my voice quiet, afraid to know the answer.

"Like he'd rather stop breathing than let you go."

I gripped the counter as tears pricked behind my eyes. "I can't ask him to stay. We haven't even known each other for a month."

"Harley, does he make you happy?"

I nodded as a tear traveled down my cheek. "So happy."

Maggie sighed, resigned. "Then, I guess enjoy your time with him. And when he leaves to go home, if things are still going well, then find a way to be with him. People do long distance relationships. It's possible. He travels a lot, so I'm sure his travels would bring him through Maryland at one point or another." Maggie wrapped her arms around me in an uncharacteristic show of affection. "I just don't want to see you orchestrate your own heartbreak." As she released me from the hug, Maggie leaned against the counter. "So, is he good in bed?"

I choked on my breath. "Maggie!"

She wiggled her shoulders. "Come on, dish. I knew even before the recording from the way you two were hanging all over each other this morning that you two did the horizontal boogie."

"Okay, grandma," I said with a snort. I tilted my head back and forth as a blush spread across my cheeks. "Yeah, last night was...amazing."

"I knew it!" She said, slapping at my arm. "Did you get any use from Wilma Rainer's sexy toy gift bag? Tell me everything! Is he big? Is he kinky? Ooh, I bet he has a weird fetish because he's a ghost hunter, you know? Did he pull out some weird moves? Did he lick your feet? Ooh, he totally looks like a foot licker!"

"Whoa, Maggie, slow down! Malcolm is not a foot licker!"

"Have you asked him?" Maggie asked, her eyes serious behind her glasses. "Sometimes guys don't come right out and say it. Sometimes you've gotta ask them."

"How would that even come up in conversation?"

"Who says it needs to come up on conversation? You just ask him!"

"What, just out of the blue say 'Hey, Malcolm, do you like to lick feet?'" I ask with a roll of my eyes.

"Can't say I've ever tried it," Malcolm's voice came from behind me, causing me to shriek and jump. Maggie busted out laughing as I tried to collect my breath.

"Malcolm Jones, don't sneak up on me like that!" I yelled at him as my hand covered my racing heart. He circled his arms around my waist from behind and rocked me back and forth, chuckling as I caught my breath. He kissed my temple. "Sorry, Babe, I couldn't resist."

"Babe, is it?" I asked, raising my eyebrows at him.

"Damn straight," he said with another kiss to my temple. "I'm whipping out all of the pet names. Babe, honey, sweetie, snookums, the whole nine yards."

I rolled my eyes. "What are you doing in here, snookums? I thought you guys were in a meeting."

"Yeah, I came to grab some water," he said, giving me a squeeze and then releasing me to grab a bottle of water out of the fridge. "Carry on with your girl talk." Malcolm backed out of the door with a wink in our direction.

Maggie locked eyes with me as I smiled so wide my cheeks hurt. "Girl, you're in trouble."

"Deep trouble," I agreed. "Speaking of trouble, what was going on with you and Ben?"

Maggie shifted her eyes to the side as she shrugged. "I don't know what you're talking about. So, you were thinking muffins? Maybe we can do our lemon poppyseed and our apple strudel muffins."

"Mags, you're avoiding."

"Ugh," she tipped her head back. When she finally spoke again, her voice was barely a whisper. "Ben thinks Archie and I dated."

My eyes widened. "What?"

Maggie nodded. "He and his whole family. In fact, they think we were dating when Archie died. And Ben...God, Ben has always been this untouchable guy. And he was always so nice to me. At the funeral, even though he was devastated, he made sure to hug me and tell me I'd always be part of the family. And I felt so fucking guilty, Harley. But I couldn't tell them the truth."

I nodded slowly. "So, he still thinks—"

"—that Archie and I were in love." Maggie buried her face in her hands. "So, all I will ever be to Ben is the girl whose heart broke when his brother died. And it did, but not in the way he thinks."

"Wow, that's..." I took a beat to process, not knowing what to say. "Maggie I'm sorry."

She nodded, blinking quickly. We hadn't talked about Archie in a while, but I knew she still thinks of him. Archie was the closest person she had to a brother, and when he died, Maggie's world shifted on its axis.

"But you've been watching Ben for a while, haven't you? I bet you've seen every one of his videos on YouTube."

She laughed. "Yeah, I have. God, I'm pathetic."

"You're not pathetic, Mags," I argue. "It's not like you're crushing on a guy who doesn't know you exist. You hadn't seen Ben in three years and when you asked him to come here, he dropped everything and came. He didn't even know if there was anything of consequence here and he still sent Malcolm. I mean, the guy booked our entire inn for two whole weeks just because you said we were struggling! That doesn't seem like something someone would do out of pity."

Maggie shook her head. "I don't want to get my hopes up," she quietly admitted. "It was really good to see him though."

Sensing that Maggie needed some time, and in need of my own time to process things with Malcolm, Maggie and I started pulling out the butter to soften at room temperature and making sure we had all the ingredients for the morning. We worked in tandem, prepping dough for the morning pastries and making grocery lists for the rest of the week, all the while in our own heads, fighting thoughts we didn't want to voice aloud. When we were finished, Maggie grabbed her purse and coat from behind the front desk and waved goodnight before heading out the door.

A few minutes after the front door shut, I heard footsteps on the stairs as Malcolm made his way to the entryway.

"Do you have any plans tonight?" he asked, rubbing the back of his neck.

I grinned. "Is this one of those cliché 'come here often' phrases or are you actually asking me?"

He chuckled. "I'm actually asking you." I tilted my head to the side as I saw him drum his fingers against his pockets before pulling his hands behind his back. Was it possible that Malcolm Jones was *nervous*?

"I was thinking about making myself something for dinner but didn't have anything concrete."

"Good, because I would like to ask you out on our first official date," he said, rocking back and forth on his feet with a grin on his face.

My grin stretched to a surprised smile. "And what would this date entail?"

"It's a surprise, but all I can tell you is to dress warmly."

"Will there be food involved?"

"Abso-freakin-lutely," he said. "I gotta feed my girl."

My smile was so large it was hurting my cheeks, but I couldn't help but smile at how natural it felt to have Malcolm call me his girl. "How long do I have to get ready?"

"Can you make it in thirty minutes?" he asked hesitantly.

"As long as I don't need to bring anything special, I can make it in twenty."

"All right, I'll meet you down here, pretty lady."

Malcolm spun on his heel and walked toward the living room with a new swagger in his step that was downright adorable.

Chapter Twenty-Eight

Do Not Answer

Malcolm

I got the keys to Davis's pickup truck and the GPS directed me toward the For-Rest in Peace Campground. Harley sat buckled up in the front seat, and I'd be lying if I said my hands weren't sweaty. I still don't know what's going to happen after our two weeks are up, but Cameron was right, Harley deserved to be wooed.

We swung by Creepy Crust Pizzaria on the way, and Harley raised her eyebrows at me when I pulled the pizza box into the cab, but I offered her a grin and said nothing about the surprise. Davis had lent me his blowup mattress and sleeping bags with a knowing look that I ignored, and I grabbed some pillows and champagne from the Inn.

I pulled down the road to the campground and Harley gaped out the window. "Is this the campground? I haven't been here since I was a kid!"

"Yeah, it is. Davis told me about it, he said he came to this one a few years ago."

"I'm glad you told me to wear warm clothes," she said, her excitement palpable.

I park for a moment at the entrance to get us checked in and buy a bundle of firewood. Then I loaded it in the back of the truck and hopped back in. I pulled us into the secluded site that backed along Burnt Creek, the namesake of the town. When I parked, Harley stepped out of the truck and took in the fire pit and creek.

"We're spending the night under the stars. No tent, but I've got a blow-up mattress for the back of the truck." I said, trying to gauge her reaction. When she said nothing, I nervously busied myself grabbing the gear from the back to start setting up. Davis warned me that it takes a while for the mattress to inflate, so while the air was getting pumped in by the automatic air machine, I started building the fire. While I stacked the logs, Harley grabbed some sticks and twigs, placing them in a pile beneath the larger logs. I liked that she didn't mind getting her hands dirty. I could tell when I saw her in the pumpkin patch that she wasn't the kind of girl to be afraid of a little dirt.

The mattress finished filling with air and the fire was in full force when I backed the truck a little closer to the fire. Harley made the bed up and sat next to me on the tailgate, her smile brilliant, the fire just close enough to warm our feet. I tucked a blanket around our legs, forcing us in closer proximity. Harley didn't seem to mind, snuggling in closer to me. I pulled the pizza from behind us and landed it on our laps.

"Ah, my hero," Harley said with a smile.

"Only the best for my lady," I said. With my roots in New York, I've been to five-star restaurants with celebrity chefs, but nothing compared to eating cheap pizza out the box on a tailgate with Harley.

It surprised me how remarkably easy it was with her. Watching Harley in the glow of the firelight was like watching something ethereal. I couldn't help scanning over her face, her throat, her collarbone. I remember my mouth over all of those parts of her, tasting her sweet skin.

"Harley," I said, noticing how she swallowed at my saying her name.

"Mm hmm?"

"I've been trying to be a perfect gentleman here, but I should let you know that I'm trying hard not to ravish you under the stars."

Harley cocked an eyebrow in my direction. "Why on earth would you go through such an effort to resist? By all means, Malcolm Jones, ravish away."

I shut the pizza box and pushed it to the side as I captured her mouth on mine.

I pulled her up to the blow-up mattress, grinning as it dipped, forcing her in closer to me. I felt myself growing hard behind the zippers of my jeans, but I wanted her to feel good first. I unbuttoned her pants and slid them down her legs. I wanted to take off her shirt, but it was starting to get just the slightest bit chilly, and I didn't want the cold to take away this moment. She climbed on top of me, her hair long enough to tickle my hands that rested just above her bare ass.

"Ow!" she said, lurching back. I froze.

"What? What's wrong?"

"Something just bit me!"

"Where?" I asked, looking her over.

"On my butt!" she said, looking over her shoulder. "Friggin' mosquitos."

I apparently didn't think this through. But I'm a firm believer in making lemonade out of lemons, so I flipped her around on all fours, twisting her so her ass was in the air and her breasts were pushed into the mattress.

"Here's how this is going to go, baby," I said, leaning over her to whisper in her ear. I could feel her shiver beneath me. "You're going to keep this perfect ass in the air, and I'm going to tease you over and over until you come. Then I'm going to slide into you and take you hard until you come again. And if a mosquito dares to land on your perfect ass while I ravage you, I'll just spank it away."

I nipped at her earlobe, and she let out a surprised pant. I had never been this guy before Harley. Sex was always fine, good even, but I never felt this level of desire before I met her. I tangled my hand in her hair and kissed her cheek before standing up on my knees. Harley pressed herself against me, begging for this newfound assertiveness to be put to the test. Seeing Harley's pale round globes up in the air, waiting for me to do whatever I wanted, made me feel powerful, and at the same time protective. She was giving herself to me, and nobody else could have this.

I dragged my fingers lazily through her slit, feeling her swollen clit and moving further down. She was so wet for me. I dragged her juices against her backside, rubbed, and gently slapped her ass. Harley's gasp was instantaneous, and she wiggled her ass at me to do it again.

My girl likes to be spanked.

I wouldn't pretend I didn't love it too, and if this was what she liked, I was going to give it to her. But first, I wanted to tease her. I rubbed my hand over the spot I had just spanked, then moved lower, cupping her slick folds and before diving in with my fingers. Harley's breathing hitched and she started to moan.

"Malcolm," she rasped, spreading her legs wider.

"That's it, baby, spread your legs for me. Let me in."

I leaned over her, giving me more balance to thrust my fingers inside her while I rocked the hilt of my hand against her clit, giving her the sweet friction I knew she so desperately needed. With a few more pumps of my hand, she was clenching around my fingers with a groan.

I couldn't wait any longer. I pulled a condom from my pocket, unbuckled my pants, and sheathed myself. I needed to be inside her. I pumped myself to relieve some tension only to feel it come flooding back in when I lined myself up with her slit.

"Do you want me, baby?" I asked, my tip dancing at her entrance.

She whimpered in response. I lined my left hand up to her backside and gave a swift but gentle smack. She bucked against me, her slit coating my dick in her juices.

"Harder," she rasped. I rubbed my hand against where I just smacked. I hesitated, wanting to make sure I didn't hurt her. "You aren't going to hurt me," she said quickly as if reading my mind. "I'm not made of glass."

I nodded, then slapped her ass harder.

"Yes," she hissed, pushing herself back toward my throbbing dick. "Please, Malcolm, I need you."

Not giving even another moment's hesitation, I slid myself inside her to the hilt. She rocked back against me, but I grabbed her hips to still her. If she kept rocking like that, I was going to come before she got even an ounce of pleasure.

"Baby," I growled in warning, "wait your turn."

"I need you to move," she complained. I could still feel her shaking around me. I slowed my breathing for a second to get control of myself. Then I took off. I slammed her hips back into me, again and again. Her soft gasps at every connection made me harder and faster and when I reached my hand around her, rubbing the top of her folds, she fell apart around me, milking me until I reared my head back in ecstasy with a roar.

We stayed like that for a moment before I pulled out of her, tied off the condom, and slid Harley under the sleeping bag. I checked to make sure the fire was out and put the food in the truck before crawling in next to her. I tucked her into my side, and she rested her head on my chest. The sky was clear, and we could see every smattering of stars perfectly.

Harley sighed contentedly, and I realized that this is what I wanted. I wanted someone I could lay with without having to say anything, just both of us enjoying the moment. Why the hell was I planning on giving that up in two weeks?

My phone rang in my pocket, and I pulled it out to silence it. The caller ID read "DAD'S LAWYERS—DO NOT ANSWER". I sighed and put my phone away. Harley tensed beside me and I knew she saw the screen.

"I know you're dying to ask," I said, trying to grin my way through this conversation.

Harley shook her head. "The last time we talked about it, it didn't go well."

It killed me that I treated her so poorly that she was afraid to talk about something with me. It wasn't something that I really wanted to talk about, especially not with a two-week fling. But even that description made me inwardly flinch. Harley wasn't just a fling, she was so much more. And if there was anyone that I should talk to about this, it was her.

"My dad is in prison," I said suddenly. Harley's eyes widened in surprise, but I knew I was going to drop an even bigger ball. "And I put him there."

If there was a sound I could associate with that moment, it would have been a record scratch. Everything stopped. The trees seemed to stop moving, the crickets seemed to quiet down, even the creek next to the campsite seemed to slow as it waited for me to continue. Harley turned her head fully to face me and blinked slowly as she was absorbing this information.

"You're going to need to elaborate," she eventually decided. I nodded, unsure of how to have this conversation. I hadn't spoken about it in years.

"My father owns a newspaper conglomerate in New York City. My entire childhood was focused on me taking it over one day, but I didn't want to get there through nepotism. I know how everyone looks at the guy who was just handed a company, there's no respect there. I decided to go to school for journalism with a minor in business and worked my way up. I started as a beat reporter for one of the smaller newspapers, writing articles here and there. Eventually, I worked my way up to having a steady column and so on and so forth. After a few grueling years, I finally worked my way up to Editor in Chief for one of the papers."

I took a pause, remembering the offices I used to work at. The phones were always ringing, people were always rushing around to make sure the layout was working, and the graphics were on point for advertisers. It was energizing and exhausting all at once.

"One day, one of my lead investigative reporters came to me with a big story. She had found a network of crime among the higher-ups in the city, from money laundering to blackmail. It was big, and it was an great opportunity to put some of our smaller newspapers on the map. I was excited, so I told my dad about it over dinner. He immediately shut it down."

Harley's eyebrows furrowed. "Why would he do that?"

"I didn't know at the time, I thought it was strange. But I started working with the investigative reporter, Meghan was her name, to figure out how far the network went. We were working on it about two weeks before my father's name came out on the list."

Harley gasped. "He was involved?"

I nodded. "He was using the newspaper advertising funds as a way to launder money for dirty politicians. I finally understood why he was so adamant about shutting down the story."

"What did you do?"

I shrugged, thinking back on that time. "At that point, dad was watching what we were printing really closely, so we couldn't print through our own paper. Meghan and I decided that she would quit and go to a competitor. We timed it right so that when the story hit the printers with Meghan, I would go to the feds and give them copies of everything to use as evidence. I was honest with them, I made sure they knew that my father was on the list. I was there the day they arrested him."

Harley was quiet for a moment. "Did he know that you were behind it?"

"I made sure he knew. My whole childhood, he preached about ethics and standing up for what was right, even when it was hard. I don't know when he decided that money was worth more than integrity, but I wanted to make sure that I wouldn't become him."

"That was really brave of you," Harley said quietly.

I shook my head again. "Honestly, Meghan was the brave one."

"How do you mean?"

"She had a family, a husband, two kids. And she was the one who uncovered everything. After the story broke, there was a lot of talk of whether her and her family would go into witness protection."

"That's...wow, you're right, she was really brave," Harley stared at the fire again. "So why are his lawyers calling you? I thought this happened a few years ago?"

I nodded. "It did, but the thing is, dad's been trying to get out of prison since he got in. His legal team is expensive, and he's run out of money. He wants to sell the newspaper business to get more liquid capital. Sometime after I became the Editor in Chief, but before all of this happened, Dad ran into some money problems and asked me to buy into the business. I had some money saved up, so I did, but discreetly. He didn't want any of the employees jumping ship thinking the business was in trouble. But now that means that he needs my signatures to sell the business, because it's mine too."

"So why are you dodging his lawyer's calls?"

I shrugged. "Because I don't want him to have the money from the sale. And I don't want to buy it from him, which was the other option. I don't want him to find a way out of prison when he so obviously deserves to be there. I don't want all of the employees of the newspapers to be at risk of someone buying the company and cleaning house." He sighed, running a hand over his head. "But I also don't want to be associated with that legacy anymore. I'm torn. And I certainly don't need the money for anything. I've always been good with my money, and I invested into the ghost hunting business with Ben, which is going well. I'm set, but Dad's lawyers keep calling me, reminding me of the countdown. I told them I don't want to sell, but Dad has a parole hearing to get him out on early release, and his lawyers won't represent him without getting paid. The family lawyer won't take no for an answer."

I waited with bated breath to see Harley's reaction. Would she think I was a monster for refusing my own father his freedom? For putting him in prison in the first place? Finally, Harley nestled in closer.

"I'm glad you told me," she said.

"Me, too," I admitted, breathing a sigh of relief she hadn't pushed me away. *Me, too.*

Chapter Twenty-Nine

No Commitments

Harley

Lying with Malcolm in the back of the truck beneath the stars should have filled me with peace, but my mind was reeling. I had never thought that Malcolm joined the ghost hunting team as a way to escape. He exposed his own father.

"How long has it been since you've been back there?" I asked.

"To New York or to the newspaper?"

"Both," I said. "Either."

"I go back to my apartment in New York once a month or so."

"And the newspaper? Or to see your parents?"

Malcolm was silent for a bit. "I left the day after my father was arrested. I haven't been back since." He glanced down at me. "Lately, I've been wondering if I'll ever go back."

"You don't want to take over the company?"

He shook his head. "Even though I own part of it, it never felt like mine. I mean, I suppose I could make it mine, but honestly I feel like so many people there look at me and only see my father. It never used to bother me until I found out he was a crook. That's not something I want to be associated with."

I nodded and cuddled closer to him. The fire was dimming, but our main heat was each other anyways. The sleeping bag was doing its job wrapped around us. Our feet danced with each other in our socks. This felt like perfection.

"Can I ask you something?" he asked quietly. "You know, since we're baring our souls."

I chuckled a little. "I suppose."

"What happened with you and Connor?"

I wasn't expecting the question, although I should have. I blew out a breath. "I dated Connor in high school. He was on the football team and I was a marching band geek. I considered myself lucky that he ever spared me a passing glance."

"Marching band geek, huh? What instrument?"

"Clarinet," I said proudly.

"I can see it," he said with a laugh. "Continue."

I rolled my eyes. "Anyways, Connor asked me out when he was a senior and I was a junior. I was convinced I was the luckiest girl in the world. We dated for seven months before he went off to college, and I never heard from him again. He never even had the guts to break up with me. One day he was just gone, no calls, no texts. I saw on his social media accounts that he was sleeping around with a bunch of different college girls. I was, of course, devastated. He was my first everything."

I let myself remember those days. The awkward high school me, crying into her pillow over a boy who wasn't worth her time.

"But you two got back together?" Malcolm asked, not judging, just curious.

I nodded. "A few years later. I went to a different university. I was studying hospitality and tourism management, I knew even then that I wanted to run my own bed and breakfast. I had an internship at the Monterey hotel group. I had completely forgotten that the Montereys were Connor's extended family. Some distant cousins or something. Anyway, he was there.

"I was so nervous to start there, in a place so intimidating, that it was a relief to see a familiar face. He flirted with me, told me how good it was to see me after all those years. I chalked the high school break up and cheating to immaturity. I figured we were just kids then; I shouldn't hold it against him. So, we dated again. We were together for five months when Maggie told me that he tried to sleep with her."

"God, what a dick."

I sighed. "Yeah, it was frustrating. My mom thought we were going to get married and give her grandbabies."

"Did you think that?"

I paused for a moment and shook my head. "No. I didn't love him. When we were in high school I thought I had loved him in the moment, but when we reconnected I knew it wasn't love. It was...familiar...if that makes sense. But I would have broken up with him eventually even if he hadn't pulled that thing with Maggie. I hated the way he made me feel about myself. He would always tear me down with these snide comments about how I was too inexperienced or didn't know the trade well enough to start my own bed and breakfast. There are days lately when I'm starting to think that he's right."

I sighed, not wanting to admit this to Malcolm or to myself. "If it wasn't for Maggie reaching out to Ben, I'm not really sure what we would have done. I spent a lot of money on the restoration of the inn, making sure everything was perfect. But Maggie says I lack confidence. I had so many ideas for ways that I could generate money and now they seem like childish fantasies."

"Like what?" Malcolm asked.

"Weddings, family reunions, corporate retreats. I had so many dreams for my little bed and breakfast."

"Why didn't you act on any of them? That sounds like a perfect fit for the inn."

I shrugged under Malcolm's arm. "Because I brought them up to Connor, and he would bring up all of the reasons it would never work.

Then he would chastise me for not thinking of those things sooner and use it as a reason why I wasn't ready to open my own place. I mean, his family owned one of the biggest hotel chains in the country, so he would know what he's talking about, right?"

"His family owns those hotels, not him. He didn't make any decisions or pour any blood, sweat, or tears into making the hotels a reality. I think you may have given him too much power."

I sighed. I know that I did, but hearing it from Malcolm made it more real.

"I'm building myself back up. But I don't think my self-esteem could take the hit of losing my inn. I worked so hard for it."

"Well, hopefully, the show gets you some good exposure."

I took a breath and, glancing at him out of the corner of my eye, I gambled saying what I'd been thinking since we started the night. "Maybe one day the show will bring you back down this way. I hope you know that after our two weeks are up, you're always welcome to come back and visit the inn."

Malcolm's body stilled, and I wondered if I stepped out of line. My heart fluttered nervously in my chest. We had promised each other the two weeks, no commitments afterwards. I didn't want him to think I was clingy.

"What if..." he said slowly. "What if I didn't have to come back?"

My heart sank like a stone. I started to shift away from him, but he held me close.

"I mean, what if I didn't leave?"

I looked up at him, my eyes wide. "Do you mean that?"

"Would it freak you out if I did?"

I shook my head. "Would it freak you out if I wanted you to stay?" I asked. "I know we haven't known each other for long. It's a big ask."

Malcolm smiled down at me. "There's a lot to figure out, but if there was anyone worth staying for, it's you."

My body tingled from head to toe. Would Malcolm really stay for me? Build a life with me?

We stayed up a while longer, Malcolm pointing out different constellations in the October sky and me making up different names and backstories for them. We laughed through the night, finally falling asleep curled into one another. Even with the mosquitos and October chill, I couldn't remember a more perfect night.

Chapter Thirty

Feast and Filming

Malcolm

H arley and I left the campground early, feeling tired but satisfied. The air mattress had deflated in the middle of the night, forcing the two of us toward the center, toward each other. That was fine with me, I wanted as little distance as possible from this girl. Her hair was a mess, and loose tendrils fell around her face from the messy bun she put it in the night before, but I had never seen a woman look more beautiful. We knew each other's secrets now, and we were still here. This didn't feel like a whirlwind romance. This felt like forever. It felt right.

I knew I needed to make a decision, and not just with Harley. I couldn't keep dodging calls from my father's lawyers, and I couldn't keep hiding behind the YouTube channel as a reason to hold off on making a decision. And I'd stupidly told Harley that I would stay for her. I wanted to, God how I wanted to. But I shouldn't be making promises that I wasn't sure I could keep. And maybe it was crazy, but she wanted me to stay. And now, looking at Harley, I'm seeing a future that I thought was years away, right at my fingertips.

There's no way to make everyone happy, but maybe if I can make myself happy that could be enough. And Harley makes me happy.

When we arrived back at the inn, sneaking in to make sure we didn't wake anyone, Harley and I jumped into the shower together in the bathroom attached to her room. Maggie was quieter than usual when

Harley and I got into the kitchen. There was coffee already in the pot and a cup of coffee half drank in front of a very tired-looking Maggie.

"Morning, Maggie," I said. She glared at me and grunted in response. I wasn't sure how to take that, so I grabbed two cups of coffee, sliding one to Harley, before rolling up my sleeves. "All right ladies, how can I help?"

Harley took an appreciative swallow of her coffee and groaned. It was nice to know I was good at making her groan outside of the bedroom, too. Maggie eyed me suspiciously through puffy eyes and pointed at a large carton of eggs on the counter.

"Can you crack eggs, Casanova?" she asked. I snorted at the nickname.

"Yes, I can crack eggs. How many do you want?" I asked. Maggie proceeded to pull down several bowls with different number of eggs needed in each and I got to work. Harley and Maggie moved together in the kitchen in a practiced dance, both managing to be right on top of each other without ever getting in the other's way. It reminded me of how Ben and I used to be as teenagers when I would practically live at his house during the summers. Only we were making pizza rolls and hot pockets, not enough healthy breakfast foods to feed eight adults.

The bowls of eggs that sat in front of me were taken away to mix in other ingredients. Some became a quiche, some became muffins, others were taken to the stovetop to become scrambled eggs.

As Harley and Maggie made the breakfast they had planned out the night before, I overheard some noises coming from the other side of the kitchen door as someone had come downstairs.

"Oh, shoot," Harley said, wiping her hands on her apron that looked so adorable on her. "Maggie can you go set the table? I think someone's already up."

Maggie's eyes went wide and she started shaking her head. "Harley, I don't want to run into—" Her voice broke off as her eyes cut to me. I wisely looked down at the countertop I was wiping down, choosing to work on an imaginary tough spot.

From the corner of my eye, I could see Harley wasn't sure what Maggie was talking about, but if my conversation the day before with the crew was any indication, I would guess Maggie was avoiding Ben. After Maggie did such a solid for me with Harley, I wasn't about to put her in an uncomfortable situation.

"You know," I said, rubbing the back of my neck. "Maggie looks pretty busy. How about I grab some stuff and get whoever is awake started with some coffee?"

Harley melted and looked at me like I hung the moon. Maggie looked at me with her own brand of early-morning, puffy-eyed appreciation. I grabbed the mugs from the cupboard and the pot of coffee freshly brewed and headed into the dining room.

On the other side of the room, Ben was sitting at the far side of the table, a laptop sitting in front of him and his hair a mess.

"Hey man, you look like shit," I said with a grin. He turned his bleary eyes my way and I guessed that whatever sleepless torment Maggie was going through, Ben was on the receiving end of it as well.

"Can I fire you?" he asked wearily.

"Sure," I lied. I put the pot of coffee in front of him.

Ben eyed the pot of coffee. "You're hired again," he said and got to work pouring it into a mug.

"Glad to hear it," I said. "So you wanna tell me what's got you on the ropes? I haven't seen you this sleep deprived since you were working on the startup."

Ben cut his eyes to the kitchen where we could hear the clattering of pots and pans on the countertop. "Is Maggie in there?" he asked, dropping his voice low.

I looked over at the door as if I could see through it. I nodded to him and he sagged in his seat.

"Why is that a problem?" I asked. "I know you like her. I don't blame you either. Maggie is awesome. She has a wicked sense of humor and she really helped me out with Harley."

Ben groaned. "I really wish you hated her."

I leaned back. "Why?"

Ben pinched the bridge of his nose. "Because I know she's awesome. She's always been awesome and she's always belonged to someone else. I need her to not be awesome. I need her to be terrible. I need her to have bad breath, or be really into politics, or hate the Blue Rovers."

I winced, remembering Maggie's bracelet. "I'm pretty sure the Blue Rovers are her favorite band."

"Fuck me," he groaned.

Zoey and Cameron came down and sat at the table. Cameron was mooning over Zoey like normal and Zoey was completely oblivious, pulling her blue hair into a topknot.

"I'm just saying tattoos can be dangerous, Zo," Cameron said, his eyebrows creased in the same expression that frequently comes over his face where Zoey was concerned. "You have to find the right person and the right shop. Plus, it's hard finding the person who can give you exactly what you want."

Zoey sighed in exasperation. "Cam, I know this already. If you're that concerned about it, come with me. You've had plenty of tattoos, you can check out every artist."

Cameron paused in exasperation. "Zoey, it's going to hurt. Like a lot," he said, his eyebrows pulling in concern again.

"Then you can be there to hold my hand," she said, patting his arm. I don't know how it was possible that she missed the blush that crept up his face. "It's happening, Cam. Deal with it."

Zoey turned her attention to us. "Good morning, gentlemen." She eyed the coffee that sat on the table and turned to me. "Do you think Harley has any tea?"

I shrugged. "Probably, she's just in there if you want to check."

"Awesome," she said, walking over to the door to the kitchen and swinging it open. I didn't miss how Ben looked through the gap in the door and then, seeing Maggie, immediately shifted his gaze toward the salt and pepper shakers on the table as if he had been searching for them his whole life. I can't remember the last time my best friend was a mess over a girl. High school, maybe?

Darla and Davis came in just as Harley and Maggie were bringing in the trays of food to the buffet table off to the side. I hopped out of my seat, grabbing a pan from the kitchen and the silverware holder before placing them where Harley directed me to. Zoey was sitting next to Cameron and Ben, sipping hot tea from a mug as everyone else loaded food onto plates and settled in for breakfast.

Harley opened the conversation easily like the hospitable innkeeper she was by asking the crew where they were going to film first. This led to conversations about the filming process and how Ben and I chose our assignments. She leaned in and was engaged, listening to the conversation with rapt attention and making everyone in the room feel like they were the most interesting person alive. She easily swapped jokes with Davis and Darla, food and recipe reviews with Zoey and Cameron, and somehow even managed to get Maggie and Ben away from their awkward sidelong glances at each other and involved in the conversation.

And through it all, Harley looked *happy*. Being surrounded by family and friends, even people that she had only met the day before, Harley was in her element and practically glowing. It made me think about what it would be like when Harley had a family of her own. Would she listen to a toddler's ramblings with rapt attention? Would she laugh at a six-year-old's fart jokes even if it was the seventh time that day she had heard it? Would she pull a broody teenager out of their own angst and get them involved with the rest of the family?

Would I be there when she did?

That was the thought that stuck with me throughout breakfast and during clean up. Harley waved me off when I offered to help, instead insisting that she needed time to corner Maggie into some girl talk.

After breakfast, we buckled down to get ready for filming. Harley's inn was going to be the first place we filmed, making sure to film at night for the added effect our viewers loved. I showed Zoey and Cameron the living room wall of newspaper clippings and other areas of the inn where they got some B-roll. I helped Davis and Darla get the audio equipment set up in one of the bedrooms to record the monologue of the inn's history for the first episode. Darla does the narration for our episodes because her voice sounds like a mix between an NPR talk show host and a creepy tour guide. It brings the right amount of professionalism and unsettlement to the show.

We kept the audio set up in the bedroom so it would be ready for announcing things that happened when we investigated the inn.

"So we're filming in the living room and the basement, right?" Darla asked, her notepad in hand. Darla often appeared on camera, in equal parts delight for our male viewers who liked to look at pretty girls and the female viewers who wanted representation on screen. We liked having her on because she was damned good at finding the best places to film. Darla had a sixth sense of when things might go awry and always managed to get it on film.

I nodded in the affirmative. "Yeah, and I was thinking upstairs, too." Davis said. Darla paused for a moment, looking upstairs with a faraway look in her eye.

"There's nothing up there," she stated finally. Davis nodded and went upstairs to grab his sound equipment and bring it back down to where she directed. We learned a long time ago not to question Darla's decisions on this kind of thing.

Chapter Thirty-One

The Old Distillery

Harley

As the crew set up cameras and sound equipment in various parts of the house in preparation for filming that night, I largely tried to stay out of the way while also being available for questions on if they could move furniture for the best filming shot or making lunch for everyone. Maggie quietly left to go back to Dad's house to work on some decorations planned for the Haunted Trail, and I didn't miss how Ben's eyes tracked her movements as she left.

As night rolled around, I made myself scarce as the crew started filming in the living and dining room, what used to be the tavern at the inn. They spent roughly an hour there before Darla declared that they wouldn't find anything there tonight, and they moved down to the basement.

I didn't go to the basement if I could help it, despite my drunken jokes with Malcolm about there being too many stairs. It was just creepy down there. The realtor told me that in the late 1800's that the basement was used as the kitchen for the tavern, as evidenced by the large hearth and fireplace there, along with a smattering of old cast iron pots still left there when the inn was abandoned. But for me, I never felt completely alone when I was there.

The crew was in the basement for over an hour doing visual checks with the dark interior now that the light had faded from the windows.

I hid in the kitchen under the guise of preparing for the next morning's breakfast.

"Hey, Harley?" Ben called from the basement. I hesitated and walked down the old steps.

As I descended into the common area of the basement, I was acutely aware of the cameras pointed at me. I realized they must have been in the middle of filming an episode, not just testing equipment anymore.

"What's up?" I asked, forcing myself to focus on Ben and Malcolm.

Ben waved me over to him and showed me a device in his hand. "Do you know what this is?" he asked me.

"No clue."

He nodded. "This is a thermal imaging camera. It can tell us if something abnormal is happening with the temperatures in the room. Cold spots, drafts, stuff like that. We use it to locate evidence of the paranormal."

I nodded. I had heard of stuff like this before. Ben held the camera, then pointed at the screen on his computer where it showed the thermal readouts in different bright colors.

Ben pointed the camera toward Malcolm, showing what he looked like in thermal color. I assumed it was for the camera that Cameron had pointed at the screen over Ben's shoulder.

"This is what a person looks like in thermal imaging. They're warm, so they show off colors of bright yellows and greens with hints of red, unless you have glasses like Malcolm, those show up blue." Ben moved the camera to point at a wall on the far side with a window at the top. "This is what an exterior wall looks like. See how there are lines that are a different color in the head signature in the walls?"

I nodded.

"The thermal camera is picking up the framing of the exterior walls. That's why those lines are so uniform."

Ben moved the camera again to face a wall with no windows to the left of Malcolm. "What do you see here?"

I looked at the screen and tilted my head. "Um, I see no lines."

Ben nodded his approval. "Do you know why that is?"

I shook my head, feeling like a kid in class who should know the answer but didn't do their homework. Ben was radiating excitement. "That's because this isn't an exterior wall."

I furrowed my eyebrows, looking at the wall. I ignored the cameras recording me and walked over to the wall. I felt the wood against my hand. It was kind of cold, like there was cool air coming from the other side. I felt Malcolm and Ben walk up beside me, and I ignored the microphone boom that was above my head. I knew Davis had it up because I wasn't wearing a microphone. They were the masters of adapting on the fly.

Malcolm knocked on the wall a few times, but because it was all wood, it was difficult to determine if it was hollow or not.

"Would it be too much to ask for us to pry open some of these boards?" Malcolm asked, his face trying to mask the glee matching Ben's face. Malcolm may not believe in ghosts, but I could see how much he loved this, the thrill of the mystery.

I shrugged. "Go for it, just be careful, I don't know if there are any wires behind here."

"The thermal imaging didn't pick up any live wires," Ben said, pointing at the screen. Darla came over and handed a crowbar to Ben and a flashlight to me. Malcolm and I backed up as Ben put the crowbar between two boards and pulled. Instead of the board coming free, a whole section of the wall shook as one. Malcolm and I looked at each other. My heart trilled in my chest. I was catching the mystery bug too.

Ben furrowed his head in concentration and shifted his weight behind the crowbar. "It feels like this part of the wall moves together."

He started shifting his body front to back and we heard the loud squeak of rusty metal as the panel shifted out an inch toward us.

Malcolm called out, "Cameron, Zoey, are you getting this?"

"We got it, boss," Zoey said, capturing the scene from afar while Cameron got in closer.

When Ben shifted the panel again, another high-pitched squeal came from the secret door as it pulled forward further. Malcolm shimmied his fingers in the exposed crack and pulled with Ben.

I angled my flashlight toward Malcolm and Ben's fingers, allowing some light to infiltrate the now exposed crack in the secret door. When my eyes fell on the space behind the wall, I let out a scream, dropping my flashlight and backing away.

The other flashlights pointed my way as I wrapped my arms around myself.

"Harley, baby, what's wrong?" Malcolm asked, grabbing my arms. I pointed a finger in the direction of the crack.

"There's a body in there."

Malcolm looked back toward the dark opening in the wall and then back at me. "Harley, honey, I'm sure it's just a prop or a mannequin or—"

It's a body, Malcolm. An old one. It's a dead guy. Or girl. I don't know gender, I just know dead."

Malcolm rubbed his hands up and down my arms as Ben looked to Darla from behind the computer. She stepped forward, grabbing my flashlight off of the ground and shined it in the gap for a moment before turning to look at Ben and then Malcolm.

"Malcolm, she's right. There's a body."

"Oh, my god," I breathed out, tipping my head forward. Words poured out of me as my brain tried to catch up with the events. "There's a dead body in my inn. An old dead body. Oh, my god, do you think the realtor knew about this? The home inspector? Oh, I am so giving that guy a one-star on his Yelp review."

"Harley, baby, I need you to breathe," Malcolm said, stroking my back.

I nodded, faintly aware of Darla and Ben working together to pull the hidden door free. There was a flurry of camera activity as the door fully opened, exposing the mummified corpse sitting at a table with what looked to be an old distillery. The skin was darkened with age and pulled taut over his face. Old scraps of fabric hung off the thinned frame of his body.

"Nobody touches the scene, it's all evidence," Malcolm said over his shoulder.

"Oh, my god. I've got to call the police. Because there's a dead body in my inn."

"I'm already on it," Ben called over to us. "Malcolm, maybe you should get Harley upstairs."

I heard Ben on the phone with the police, and I allowed Malcolm to pull me upstairs.

Within ten minutes, two squad cars pulled up to the inn. Thankfully, dad didn't bring Gus with him this time. Oliver rode along with him, wearing his official uniform, while Tanya and Dennis, two other officers who have been around since badges were made of lead, rode in the other squad car.

Dad opened the front door, his signature toothpick sticking out the side of his mustache.

"Hi Dad," I said wearily.

"Pumpkin," he said with a perfunctory kiss to my forehead, while somehow managing to avoid spearing me with the toothpick. He turned to Malcolm, raising an eyebrow. "I'm getting a little tired of you calling the emergency line."

"Well, the next time there's an emergency, I'll just call for pizza," Malcolm smirked.

Chapter Thirty-Two

Mandate

Malcolm

The police finished up in the basement and took the body away sometime around five in the morning. Harley, despite her shock at having lived in the inn as long as she had with a dead body under the roof, still managed to make coffee for all of the officers and Maggie who had shown up after she realized that the call her dad was on was at the inn, which meant Harley was running on no sleep.

As morning broke, I told Maggie that she was welcome to sleep in my room as I'd be with Harley. She was resisting sleep after seeing the corpse in her basement, but I knew that she would regret not sleeping. That didn't mean I wouldn't be plastered to her side the whole time. As we fell into her bed, she curled her body around me, forming to me like a second skin. I wove my fingers in hers and quietly recited facts about various towns I had researched until her eyelids drooped closed.

I waited until I saw the slow and steady rise and fall of her chest before I allowed myself to fall asleep as well.

It was only four hours later when I felt Harley stir beside me. When we got downstairs, I found Darla sitting at the table with Jaynie. Darla was shoving her face full of pastries. When Jaynie looked up at Harley and me, her face melted into a knowing grin.

"Hey there, lovebirds," she said, pushing a cup towards Harley. "I made you a pumpkin spice latte."

Harley's shoulders, which had been bunched tight since we woke up, suddenly relaxed. "Thank you, Jaynie." She glanced down at the pastries. "You brought pastries?"

"Of course!" she said. "You didn't think I'd let you make breakfast after staying up all night, did you? Word's all over town about y'all finding a dead body in your basement. Mabel had a vision in the flower shop first thing this morning. It's been spreading like wildfire."

Harley buried her face in her hands. "Great. I'm ruined. Nobody is going to want to stay at a creepy old inn where corpses are turning up left and right."

"Corpses?" Jaynie asked. "You found more than one? Maybe you have an infestation of corpses. You know, I have a cousin in Louisiana that might have a recipe for an amulet that could help. I'm gonna need some mint leaves, though. And good news! It doubles as birth control."

I wasn't sure what kind of voodoo amulet birth control she was talking about, but I was pretty sure we were going to stick with condoms.

Darla was looking at us wide-eyed with a mouth full of croissants when Cameron came into the dining room.

"Oh, good, you're up," he said, snagging a cinnamon roll. Based on the crumbs on the front of his shirt, it wasn't his first. "The officers taped off the basement so we can't go down there, but I think we got everything we need from the scene while we were waiting for the cops to show up. They asked for a copy of our footage, but I got to keep the originals for the show because it's clear it isn't a fresh crime."

Harley groaned beside me at the mention of her inn now being a crime scene and put her head on the table.

"Harley, honey, it's going to be okay," I said, rubbing her back. "After this episode airs, the inn is going to have to add on more rooms to keep up with the demand."

Harley tilted her head to the side to look at me, clearly unconvinced. I rubbed her back and looked back at Darla. "Where are we filming tonight?"

"The cemetery if the weather holds out. Weather report says it's going to rain. I'm working on the script now for the teasers we're going to launch later this week and for the episode. We've already got enough raw footage to cut together for it."

I nodded. Harley might not have realized it, but finding a body in the basement might have been the best thing that's ever happened to her. I mean, probably not great for whoever used to occupy the corpse, but with our subscribers waiting for the next episode, paired with the Halloween special, Harley won't be hurting for customers any time soon.

"Well if you end up staying in, maybe you can make sure Harley finally sees some of our shows," I said, grinning from ear to ear as Darla swiveled her head toward Harley.

"Hold up," Darla said. "You've been just blindly letting us film here? Oh hell no. Fuck the weather, we're staying in tonight. Your theatre room gets wifi, right?"

Harley nodded hesitantly. Zoey pointed to Darla. "I'm on it. It's a pajama party night."

Jaynie left, regretfully stating she had to get up early for the opening shift tomorrow. Around five p.m., clad in an array of pajamas, Darla, Zoey, Maggie and Harley gathered in the theatre room to watch our shows, starting right from the beginning. I was hoping that Harley wouldn't judge us too harshly on the quality of video and audio. When we were first starting out, we really had no idea what we were doing, and it was a few episodes before we found Davis to help out.

Just as their pizza was about to be ordered, a text alert pinged on Harley and Maggie's phones. Harley pulled her phone out and blew out a breath.

"Oh boy," she said, passing the phone to Maggie.

"What's wrong?" I asked.

"Avery called a Mandate," Harley said.

"A...what?"

"A Mandate," Maggie repeated. "It's code for a breakup. Because a man is always involved, and it marks the date when she takes a sabbatical from dating."

"But her sabbaticals never last long," Harley admitted.

"I'll get the wine," Maggie said, heading toward the kitchen.

Darla was practically dancing in her slippers. "Invite her over! Add her to girls' night! I love the idea of an anti-man night!"

I fought the urge to cover the delicate member between my legs. As Harley was typing out her message, the front door of the inn opened. As we walked toward the door, I saw Davis coming down the stairs to greet a rather pissed-off looking Avery.

When Davis saw that a pretty girl was at the door, his stride slowed and he moved his shoulders in the way that showed off his gym membership. He tried to teach me how to walk like that once, but I didn't want to look like an asshole, so I wisely didn't copy him.

"Hi there," Davis said, extending his patented charming smile.

Avery looked at his smile with disdain. "Ugh, men," she sneered, and walked right past him.

Davis dramatically clapped a hand to his heart. "My pride is wounded, but my interest is piqued," he said, following Avery with his eyes where Darla and Zoey shuffled her out to the theatre room.

I shook my head at Davis. "Nuh uh, man. She's on a man-hating spree and that shit is contagious. We're heading to the bar for our own safety."

Harley came in to give me a kiss on the cheek. "Have fun, but not too much fun," she warned.

"Don't worry, Brandon's meeting us there," I said. Her eyebrows arched in surprise that I invited her cousin to go on a bar run with us, but she said nothing. Davis, Ben, Cameron, and I loaded up in one of the vans just as the rain started to pour. The weather prediction was right, this was going to be a nasty one. I was just glad we didn't set any equipment up during the day.

Chapter Thirty-Three

Self-Discovery

Harley

"So what happened?" I asked as I handed Avery a full glass of wine. Introductions had been made while Zoey and Darla moved the chairs and loveseats to sit in a semi-circle around the TV so we could all see each other. I was drinking red wine and wearing my favorite Halloween pajama set, covered in pumpkins and black cats. Maggie was sitting with her own glass of wine, sporting neon green frames on her glasses, a plain tee-shirt, and Blue Rovers Band leggings. Her legs were propped up on the side of the armchair she was sitting on. Darla, in an uncharacteristically pink matching pajama set and Zoey in workout shorts and a floral tank top sat on one of the loveseats, leaning toward Avery in rapt attention.

Avery, who arrived too early to get the note on pajamas was wearing the same outfit she wore to work at the police station, minus the button near her neck that had popped off when she was waving her arms around in fury.

"He told me he missed his freedom," Avery scoffed. "Do you know the last time I saw him was two weeks ago? The last time we texted was four days ago. We practically weren't even dating. He had plenty of freedom, the asshole." She took a large gulp of wine. "This is good wine."

"Thank you," I said. I decided not to point out she said the same thing the last time.

"So why do you think it didn't work out?" Zoey asked.

Avery tilted her head in thought. "I don't know," she admitted finally. "Honestly, I'm not sure it ever would have worked out. I have a habit of picking guys that are destined to be selfish pricks. When you make the same mistake this many times, you've gotta admit the common denominator is the likely cause."

"The common denominator being you?" Darla asked, swirling whisky in her glass. She wasn't much of a wine drinker. Avery nodded. "So what are you going to do about it?"

"I'm taking a—"

"Sabbatical from men," Maggie and I finished for her. Avery furrowed her brows in frustration.

"What?" she demanded. "It's a good plan."

"Avery," I started gently. "I'm not saying taking time away from dating isn't a good plan—"

"But we are saying that you never actually do it," Maggie said bluntly.

"Maggie," I hissed. She just shrugged at me. Avery's shoulders sagged and she took another large gulp of wine.

"No, she's right. I only take a break from guys until someone new is interested. I never really take the time to figure out who I am outside of a relationship. It just helps me feel like being out of a relationship is my choice."

"That's very self-aware," Zoey said sagely.

"Thank you, Zoey." Avery said, filling up her wine glass again.

"So," Darla said, draining her whisky. "What are you going to do about it?"

Avery paused for a moment. "I'm setting a time limit. I'm taking a year off." Wine almost came out of my nose at this, but Maggie actually spit out her wine at Avery's next words. "I swear on the lives of the Golden Girls."

"I thought they were all dead?" Darla whispered to Zoey.

"Too soon, Darla," Zoey said, shaking her head. "Too soon."

"The Golden Girls is what Avery calls her goldfish," I explained.

"They're named after the Golden Girls?" Zoey said. "That's so cute!"

"Well, there's four of them and they rotate out as they pass away, so they don't have individual names. But they're the perpetual Golden Girls." Avery said. "And I love them. And I'm doing this. I'm taking a year off of dating to engage in self-discovery."

"I'll order you a vibrator," Darla said, pulling out her phone. "That always helps me with self-discovery."

The pizza arrived not long after and Avery, now dressed in some of my pajamas, was cuddled up on the couches with the rest of us getting ready to watch the first episode of *Spirits, Seekers, and Skeptics.* I was low-key terrified that I was going to hate this show. This was Malcolm's job, and now that I know the other members of the team, how could I look them in the eye if I thought the show that they worked so hard on was stupid?

Darla navigated the screen to the channel page, which I had to admit looked really cool. It had a professional shot of all six of them like something you'd see on the History channel. Darla scrolled down to the first episode of season one and clicked 'play.' The show opened with a title sequence of flashes of different places the team must have investigated as Darla's voice, more sedate and creepy than I had ever heard it before, filtered through the speakers.

"On this episode of *Spirits, Seekers, and Skeptics,* paranormal investigators Ben and Malcolm are called to explore a ranch in upstate

New York where something has been spooking the horses at night. Will what they find have more than just the horses running?"

The screen changed to show night vision footage of horses in a barn jumping up on their hind legs in obvious distress. I listened as Darla went over the history of the ranch, including a supposed accidental death from a rider falling off a horse, and I watched, entranced, as Ben and Malcolm, brandishing various equipment explored and reported the strange sounds and readings throughout the night. When the episode was almost finished, however, Ben and Malcolm sat together in a room and shared their report.

"So is it paranormal? Or just normal?" Ben asked the camera, then turned to Malcolm. "At the time, I thought it might be paranormal, but you had other thoughts."

Malcolm nodded then motioned to a screen beside him. "Yeah, let's break it down though. What do we want to talk about first?" I watched in awe as the Malcolm on the screen, with his hair a little longer, and wearing different glasses, looked back through the footage and photographs and pointed out alternative reasons for the sounds the readings they got. Electrical interference from wireless devices, a tree too close to the barn that had recently been struck by lightning, making a previously undisturbed limb low enough to hit against the roof of the barn when the wind blew. The ultimate consensus was that there was no paranormal activity found on the ranch.

The girls all went to sleep, Avery bunking with Maggie in Malcolm's old room, but I stayed awake watching Malcolm's show. I watched through the episodes of them investigating Zoey's house after her boyfriend passed away. Oddly, I felt closer to the woman than I had before knowing that. She must have known that as I watched I would find out about how she came to be on the show. She was so strong.

I also, saw the episode in the dilapidated manor where Davis fell through the floor and had to get seven stitches.

Around one in the morning, I felt a kiss on my forehead. Malcolm nuzzled my nose with kiss from behind the couch.

"You're up late," he said with a grin. "Watching anything good?"

I chuckled. "Yeah it's this ghost hunting show, have you seen it? I thought it was going to be hilarious, but it turned out to be really good."

"You liked it?" he asked. It only occurred to me in this moment that Malcolm might actually be nervous about my reaction to his work on the show.

"I really did," I admitted. "I'm midway through season two already. Cameron was a good addition."

"Yeah, we thought so too." Malcolm came around the couch and grabbed my hand. "Ready for bed?"

"With you? Hell yes."

Chapter Thirty-Four

Dinner and a Show

Malcolm

The weather cleared for the next night's filming, leaving behind air cold enough for us to breathe fog. Maggie insisted we scout out the best formation of the Haunted Trail so that we could be prepared with distractions if we run into a stretch of the path that the people coming into the scenes saw the people coming out of them. I was also tasked with gathering and placing bales of hay to mark off the kid's trail. By the time Penny Wayworth came by to deliver the outdated costumes she had lying around for us to use, I was covered in scratches and sneezing like an allergic kid after snuggling with a dog.

In the afternoon, Harley, Maggie and I went around town posting flyers for the Haunted Trail, selling tickets, and visiting the high school to see if local theatre teens would be willing to be unpaid participants, while the rest of the crew scouted out the cemetery for filming purposes. I had volunteered to go, but Cameron said my general lack of filming knowledge would make me most productive on the sidelines and Davis said that my constant sneezing was going to annoy him even more if I was next to him on the sidelines. So I was basically told to stay the fuck away. Fine with me, it was cold outside.

By the time we met up with the crew at Witches' Brew, my sneezing was gone, the tickets were sold, and Harley made sure to kiss every scratch on my body.

"So, how'd it go?" I asked Ben.

"We ran into some...complications."

My eyebrows furrowed. "What kind of complications?"

He chuckled sardonically. "Oh, you'll see."

Harley's Aunt Shelly came by to visit while we were eating the last of our dinner. "So which one of you boys is the one about to make an honest woman out of my Harley?" Next to me, Harley choked on her drink.

"Aunt Shelly!"

Shelly gave a big belly laugh and smacked the back of her chair. "I'm just playing, kiddo. Brandon already told me all about how your frog prince has a two-week timeline before he goes back into his reptilian status and slips away again."

"Jesus, Aunt Shelly," Maggie grumbled.

"What?" Shelly asked. "I get it, a girl's gotta get her kicks somewhere in a small town. But I'm just saying, you let me know when the boy's gone because I've already got a man excited for a blind date next month."

"Aunt Shelly--" Harley called but Shelly had already skirted around three tables and was saying hello to a batch of regulars.

My stomach turned as I realized that the woman who was in my bed today already had a date set up for next month. Sure, it wasn't a date that she set up, but it was one that she was free to go on as soon as our two weeks was up. I didn't have a right to be royally pissed about it, but it didn't stop the burning in my chest.

I bought Harley's dinner and kissed her goodbye in the parking lot. Maggie was going to look at an apartment that wasn't above their father's garage, and Harley was going for moral support. Ben drove us to the cemetery in silence, but I didn't miss the glances the crew threw my way.

I distracted myself with the file in my lap outlining our plan of action for the night. Ben had already gotten in touch with Oliver to see exactly where the bodies were located when they were unearthed so we could get B-roll of the location during the day. We'd probably need to get more at dusk to give it the creepy effect that the viewers enjoyed. But as we drove closer to the cemetery, the empty streets started to clog up as a row of cars were pulled up to the fence surrounding the cemetery.

"Is there a funeral?" I asked, shuffling through my paperwork. I made sure to check with the local funeral home that no events were scheduled, same with the newspaper.

Ben chuckled beside me. "Nope, those lovely townsfolk are here to see us."

I whipped my head toward him. "You have got to be kidding me."

Cameron and Davis were laughing in the backseat when we pulled in. Before Ben even cut the engine, I jumped out of the van to find what felt like half the town in lawn chairs next to various graves, passing around beers and getting ready for the show. I swore under my breath.

I looked around to try to find someone reasonable to talk to about this and found Mayor Harding sitting in an old fold-up chair next to an older gravestone with his surname on it. He was dressed in a long flannel shirt and worn denim jeans.

"Mr. Mayor," I said, standing in front of him with my hands on my hips. Despite my power stance, he merely lifted a beer in salute.

"Afternoon, Mr. Jones. Nice weather we're finally having."

"I guess," I said, running my hands over my neck. "Can I ask what everyone is doing here?"

"We're all just visiting our long past relatives," he said, stroking a hand over the gravestone next to him. I glanced around, spying the other townsfolk.

"Oh, come on! Benny Goodfellow can't even read the name of the gravestone because it's from the eighteen hundreds." Benny, the old man who had been front row at the town council meeting incorrectly repeating the mayor's words, jolted in his lawn chair as fast as his arthritic knees could move and looked at the faded gravestone for probably the first time.

"We're old friends," he insisted, then clinked his beer against the headstone in a 'cheers' motion.

The crew was already unloading the equipment from the van in preparation for filming. I walked up to Ben. "You really think we can film with all these people here?" I asked.

He chuckled in his usual good-natured self. "I guess we'll see. Barring any unforeseen circumstances, you might just need to yell 'quiet on set' like they do in the movies."

I huffed out a breath. With the interruptions in the weather, we didn't have much wiggle room for the filming schedule. Just as I was thinking of how to manage the crowd, a head full of white hair popped out of a minivan with Three Sister's Psychic Services emblazoned on the sides.

"Aw, hell," I cursed and made my way over. As Dorothy O'Neil stood up, I got a glimpse of her outfit and immediately covered my eyes. "Dorothy, what the hell are you wearing?" I asked, still covering my eyes. But it was too late. My eyes were still seared with the visage of Dorothy O'Neil dressed in a see-through lace negligee from the sixties and a set of pearls.

I felt her rap me on the arm. "Language, young man! And for your information, we are dressed to be your lady in white."

Ladies in white? From the image burned in my mind, I could tell that the lingerie Dorothy was wearing had yellowed with age well past the point where someone could call it white. I felt the blood drain from my face when I registered another keyword that she used. "*We?*"

"Did he like the outfit?" Mabel called as she shuffled out of the van. My hand dropped to my hips in my power stance before I realized my mistake and caught an eyeful of Mabel O'Neil dressed in a bra and high-waisted underwear with a gray lace robe and tall white gogo boots. I swore again as I brought my hand up to my eyes, with earned me another sharp rap on the arm from Dorothy. "I told you it was lady in *gray*, not lady in white!"

"Miss O'Neils, we don't need ladies in white on the show," I said through clenched teeth, still not looking at them. "Or a lady in any color. We don't stage our shows."

"But look at all this talent you have at your fingertips!" Dorothy exclaimed.

"Hey Malcolm," I heard Cameron call from around the van. "Ben is asking for—Oh, shit, oh god, I—Ow!"

"Language, young man!"

"Sorry, ma'am." I heard Cameron call. "Um, might I ask why you um, lovely ladies are, uh, so...scantily clad?"

I snorted behind the hand covering my face. Hearing Cameron's reaction was almost worth having to see two of the three fake psychic sisters in various degrees of undress. Almost.

"We are your ladies in various colors," I heard another voice, which must have been Bertha, from inside the van. I knew better than to look this time, but by the groan I heard come from Cameron's way, he hadn't learned his lesson yet.

"I don't understand," Cameron said.

From the sound of it, Bertha had managed to extricate herself from the vehicle. "Well, you see, young man," Bertha huffed. "Dorothy thought the show was going to need a lady in white. Mabel swore that ghosts always looked like ladies in gray. And of course, I thought you hardworking gentlemen could use a lady in red."

I felt the blood rush back into my face. "I already tried explaining that we don't use actors on our show," I said in a strained voice.

"I'm gonna go get Zoey and Darla," Cameron decided. I breathed out a sigh of relief as I followed him through the crowd of lawn chairs and gravestones. In the short amount of time that I had been getting scarred for life by three little old ladies, our crew already had almost everything out of the van and set up.

"Zoey and Darla," Cameron called to them. "Your presence is needed over there by that van."

Zoey and Darla were talking to Avery who had set up her chair by a newer gravestone with fresh flowers on it. She raised a glass of wine my way and drained it.

I couldn't even guess where she had gotten wine at a cemetery. When it came to obtaining food in strange places, Avery seemed to have a gift.

Zoey and Darla got the O'Neil sisters shepherded back into their van. Oliver came around wearing his police uniform to convince the viewers that the visiting hours at the cemetery were over, unless they had special permission from the cemetarian. By this time, the sun had fallen away and we were left alone in the total darkness of the cemetery with the exception of the lights from our equipment.

Cameron filmed us with the larger camera while Zoey stood near the laptops, monitoring the feed from two other cameras we had placed at a distance to record us. Davis, annoyed that he wasn't the one who got to take Avery home, had miked up Darla, Ben, and me. He was now catching ambient noises and footfalls as we walked around asking questions to the air.

"Bob Walker?" Darla called to the tombstones as she slowly walked around the space. "We know that you were buried here in a shallow grave, but we don't know why. Does that make you angry?"

Ben held a device in his hand that lit up a made noise when it encountered electromagnetic fields but had been silent so far.

"How about you, Pete Grant?" Ben asked the surrounding area. "Are you upset because you're stuck here?"

I listened as the air around us reflected only the sounds of surrounding trees.

"How about you, Jimmy?" I asked the air. It always felt ridiculous doing this, but after finding a dead body yesterday, I somehow felt more in tune with the hocus pocus of the afterlife nonsense.

After I asked the air about Jimmy, the device in Ben's hand made a squealing noise as the lights showed a sharp spike.

"Did you guys see that?" Ben whispered. "Malcolm, talk to him again."

"Um, sure," I said, struggling to drum up conversational points. Something gave me the feeling Jimmy wasn't a what's-your-favorite-color type of conversationalist. "Jimmy, we know about the railroad scam you three were running. But we don't know how you got from there to here."

A sharp noise once again came from Ben's sound machine in his hand. Something about it caused the hairs on my arm to stand on end.

"Hey," Davis said, looking at his laptop. "I think there's something here."

We huddled around Davis's laptop while Cameron followed us on the camera. Davis pointed at the digital readings from the microphones hooked to each of us as well as the ambient sound microphones. "This one is Malcolm's microphone," he said, pointing to a cluster of scribbles on the recorded line. "This is where you talked to the potential spirit. But look here, right after you said that last thing, something came up on the ambient noise recorder."

"I heard the high-pitched squeal thing from Ben's recorder," I said, furrowing my brows. From the corner of my eye, I saw a cell phone light up on the table near Zoey. Zoey clicked the screen off quickly and shoved it in a bag nearby.

Davis shook his head. "This is different, it's lower. Listen to this."

He moved the marker to just where I was finishing my sentence.

"—there to here." The digital recording from my microphone said. Then a harsh static came over the speakers.

"...or..."

Darla's head whipped up sharply and her eyes narrowed. "Play that again."

Davis rewound and played again. Again, the harsh static overrode the ambient noise of our surroundings, and an ominous sound came through. "...or..."

"Does that say 'or'?" Ben asked, leaning in.

"No," Darla said, her eyes wide looking at us. "It says 'four.'"

A vibrating noise came from Zoey's area near the laptop and I glanced over as she pulled a different phone from a jacket hanging on the back of the chair. She frowned at it and clicked it off.

Davis moved the marker back once more and played it through with me speaking to the 'spirit'.

"Um, sure," my voice responded to something Ben had said. "Jimmy, we know about the railroad scam you three were running. But we don't know how you got from there to here."

"*Four,*" the ominous voice intoned. I could hear it more clearly now, but I didn't know what it meant. Darla, nearly shaking with understanding looked at Ben and I expectantly.

"You guys," she said, eyes begging us to understand. "You said 'the railroad scam *you three* were running.' The spirit is telling us there was a fourth member."

That declaration hung in the air for only a moment before it was broken by Zoey, standing in a ball cap by the laptops holding her phone. In the excitement between the rest of the crew, I hadn't noticed Zoey's phone vibrating. The light of the screen illuminated her face when she looked at me.   "Malcolm, something's happened to Harley."

Chapter Thirty-Five

Surprise Visitor

Harley

The large black van with the *Spirits, Seekers, and Skeptics* logo on the side whipped into the parking lot. The headlights scanned over the red paint that covered the door to my inn as I sat on the front steps.

The passenger door jerked open and Malcolm, dressed in dark clothing from filming at the cemetery, ran toward me.

"Harley, baby, what happened?" he asked, cradling my face in his hands. His eyes darted all over my face and body, as if ensuring nothing had harmed me. The concern on his face made my guilt flare to life.

"Malcolm, I'm fine, honest."

From behind my front door, I heard the booming voice of my father. "You sure as hell are not fine, Harley Quinn Malone!"

Malcolm's lip quirked and he kissed my forehead. "We're going to circle back to your middle name another time, because that's easily one of my favorite things about you now, but first I need to know what the hell is going on here."

I sighed heavily and leaned my forehead against his. "Somebody just painted something on the front door and Dad's all worked up about it."

Dad walked through the door and closed it behind him, giving a hard look at it before swiveling that gaze at me. "You're damn right I'm worked up about it! And you oughta be, too, young lady."

I could tell the moment Malcolm's eyes left me and traveled to my front door. His grip on my shoulders tightened and his body went rigid. I had tried to shrug it off when I found it, but now that the adrenaline of coming home and finding the desecration of my front door had worn off and I was safe in Malcolm's arms, I couldn't stop my body from releasing the stress of the night. Tears flooded my eyes and started leaking from the corners of my eyes down my cheeks. Malcolm kissed a few of the tears before pulling me into his embrace.

"It's all right, baby, I'm here," Malcolm said, almost to himself. "I'm here."

I could hear the doors of the van open and shut as the other members of the crew came to evaluate the scene.

"What the fuck?" Cameron asked. I pulled away from Malcolm long enough to see Cameron staring at the door, hands on his hips and a pissed-off expression on his face. Zoey came from behind him and looked around his massive body. She gasped and covered her mouth.

By the time Darla walked up and saw the door, her lips were pressed in a firm line. Her eyes took in the word "Leave" painted in red diagonally across my previously white door. The paint had dripped down the door, collecting in a puddle on the front porch like a pool of blood. "Sheriff, do you have everything you need from the scene?" she asked.

My dad looked at Darla appraisingly, then nodded. "Got the pictures and the paint sample. Might need to ask you all some questions, though."

Darla nodded at my dad. "Is it all right if we get this off Harley's door then?"

"I reckon so."

"Zoey, can you and Cameron go inside and get a bucket of warm water and soap and a couple of rags? We'll start there before we try something more abrasive."

Zoey nodded and pulled Cameron inside the house. "Harley," Ben asked me quietly, pulling out his phone. "Does Maggie know about this?"

Shaking my head, I answered, "No, she's been apartment hunting and wanted me to go with her. She was so stressed afterward. I didn't want to make it worse."

Ben came a little closer and gently leaned against the rail. "Harley, I know you don't want to stress Maggie out, but I think she might get stressed if she found out about it some other way and thought you were keeping it from her."

I paused, hating that he was right. "And besides," Ben continued. "I know you have Malcolm and your dad here, but something tells me that having your sister here would make you feel better, yeah?"

I nodded, my stupid face crumbling again. Still stunned, I hid my face in the crook of Malcolm's shoulder while Ben walked a little bit to call Maggie. Malcolm rubbed my back and kissed the top of my head.

"I feel so stupid," I admitted.

Malcolm leaned back to look in my eyes. "Why? Did you paint your door?"

My eyes traveled back to my door. "Of course not," I said, rolling my eyes.

"Then what could you feel stupid about?"

"Because it's just paint. It's probably just some dumb kids riding around doing something out of boredom, and here I am crying about it like some overdramatic princess."

Malcolm was shaking his head before I finished. "Harley, baby, no. This isn't you being overdramatic. Someone came to your home, your business, and painted something like that on your door? That's threatening as hell. And I don't know if it was kids or something worse, but the crew and I? We're not going anywhere."

"But Malcolm, it might not be safe. Dad said—"

"Your Dad is concerned," Malcolm interrupted. "And he has every right to be. But Harley, regardless of whatever you decide to do, which I will fully support, the crew and I are not getting chased off."

The door swung open as Zoey and Cameron, carrying two buckets of water and a stack of old rags came out on the porch.

"Hey guys, hang on a second," Davis said, jogging over with one of the camera bags from the van. When I gave him a questioning look, he said, "I know the sheriff already got pictures, but I think it's best if we get a record of this too. It won't take long."

Malcolm shrugged and looked at me. "No harm in being thorough."

I nodded consent to Davis, who pulled the camera out and took a couple of pictures before scanning the paint from top to bottom on video.

Ben walked over and talked to Darla quietly for a moment before turning to me. "Maggie's coming over. She's bringing *The Princess Bride* and she said you are not to argue."

I smiled wobbly. "Thanks Ben. Thank you all. Here, hand me a rag. I need to do something, or I'll lose my mind."

We alternated scrubbing and hosing down the door and the front porch. The paint hadn't fully dried, especially the parts that had puddled, so we were able to get most of it off. Maggie had shown up about a half hour in and started a bubble fight with Zoey and Davis. We called it a night around one in the morning and Malcolm and I collapsed into my bed, completely spent.

As my head hit the pillow and I started to succumb to the dark, I felt Malcolm hook his arm around my waist and pull me into him. I slid against him willingly, fitting in the crook of his body like the safety of Malcolm was a haven that was always meant for me.

"I'm glad you're okay, Harley." Malcolm mumbled against my hair. "I would never forgive myself if something happened to you."

I sighed dreamily as I slipped deeper into the comfort of the bed. Wanting to give comfort to Malcolm, I whispered. "You won't be here forever. I have to learn to take care of myself."

Malcolm's arm tightened around my waist as I drifted into slumber. "We'll see about that."

I was elbow-deep in biscuit batter the next morning when I heard knocking at the front door. I froze, wondering if whoever painted my door last night wanted me to leave so badly that they'd make me leave themselves. I shook myself and wiped my hands on the hand towel before striding to the door. Through the glass of the front door, I could see a striking woman with wavy brown locks pulled over one shoulder. I pulled open the door for her.

"Good morning," I said cheerily. "Please, come in. Excuse the mess," I said, indicating toward my hands. "I've been making breakfast."

"Oh, yum!" the woman said with a genuine smile. Something about her looked familiar, but I couldn't quite put a finger on it.

"Harley, honey, who's at the door?" Malcolm asked from the stairway, clomping quickly to put himself between me and whoever was at the entrance. As he rounded the corner, taking on an almost comical squaring of his shoulders to show off his height, he skidded to a halt when he saw the woman.

"You know," I said. "I actually didn't catch your name."

"Mom?" Malcolm asked, his hand going to the back of his neck.

"Ah, good," Malcolm's apparent mother said. "So, you haven't hit your head and suffered amnesia. Based on how little I've heard from you, it's nice to know you're still conscious and in control of all your faculties."

My mouth turned into an 'o' shape. "You're Malcolm's mother. Oh, boy. Um, well, I'll let you two get to chatting and catching up, and I'll be in the kitchen definitely not eavesdropping."

I turned on my heel and prepared to take a step.

"Stop," Malcolm's mother commanded. I froze as if a force was preventing my movement. I slowly spun back around to face her. "My son called you 'Honey.'"

I froze again, darting my eyes between her and Malcolm, who still looked shell-shocked at seeing his mother. She raised a perfectly arched eyebrow and merely waited.

"It seems he did, yes," I agreed.

"Is that Mama Jones I hear?" Davis's voice came from around the corner. He swept into the room, around Malcolm's lifeless body and wrapped his arms around Malcolm's mother.

"Ah, Davis, it's so good to see you!" she said, laughing as he twirled her around. "You need to come visit soon. Anita has been asking about you. You should call home more."

Davis hung his head in mock surrender. "Alas, Mama Jones, you are both a beacon of joy and a guillotine of guilt. I don't know how you do it."

"Women are great at multitasking," she said effortlessly. "Now, are you going to tell me what's going on between my son and Miss...Harley, was it?"

"Oh!" Davis said, whipping his head between the three of us. "Well, you see, Malcolm's only here for the month, so—"

"No," Malcolm said, suddenly reacting as if someone had pushed his 'on' button. "No, no. No. Nope. You," he said, pointing at his mom, "are not allowed to show up unexpectedly and start grilling my best friends about my girlfriend."

"Girlfriend?" His mother and I asked together. Both questions were of an equal tone of surprise.

"And you," Malcolm said, swiveling his finger toward Davis, "do not get to out my love life to my mother."

"And you—" Malcolm said, shifting his finger dramatically toward me.

"I'm gonna stop you right there, cowboy," I said, curling his pointer finger back into his fist. He looked down at his hand as though seeing it for the first time.

"Ah, man, that looked kind of aggressive, huh," he said, flipping his hand back and forth. "Sorry about that, Mom."

"Forgiven," she said, then mumbled under her breath, "heartless child."

"Right," I said, wanting desperately to extricate myself from the awkwardness. "Well, I still need to get those biscuits in the oven so..."

"Oh, yeah," Davis said, hooking an arm around Malcolm's mom's neck. I wondered what it said about us that I still didn't know her name. "Let's go to the kitchen. Harley here makes the best biscuits I've ever had. It's madness!"

Chapter Thirty-Six

Spirits and Mommies

Malcolm

I stood in the kitchen next to Harley as my mother and Davis sipped coffee at the breakfast nook. Pressing the cookie cutter through the dough to get the perfect size and shape for the biscuits, I listened while our surprise visitor rambled on to my friend. Taking a sip of coffee, I caught the last bit of their conversation.

"So, I decided while I was driving out of the city to visit my daughter, I might as well come see my favorite son, too," she said, waving absently in my direction.

"I'm your only son," I said, straightening up. "Besides, how did you know I was here?"

Mom shrugged, sipping on her hot coffee like it was tea with the Queen of England. I tried to follow suit and took a gentle sip in my mouth. "I'm part of the group on Facebook, the S and M's."

The moment her words traveled through to me, the small sip I was intending to take turned into a wet sputter. "I'm sorry," I said, pushing my drink far away. "You want to run that by me again? I think I misheard you."

My mother, pinnacle of posh and primness, sipped her coffee again. "I'm on Facebook now, Malcolm. Don't act so surprised. The other mothers invited me to their Facebook group Spirits and Mommies so we can all keep tabs on our children who insist on traveling around the East coast like a band of hippies."

"Spirits and Mommies?" I asked. "And you call it the S and M's?"

"Well, yes," she said, looking slightly confused. "Well, Janet started calling it that and the other mothers thought it was funny for some reason."

My mother looked at me as if she wanted me to explain, but there was no way in hell I was going to have a conversation with my mother about S&M anything.

"So, Mom, I mean, what are you doing *here*?" I asked. Catching the warning look Harley threw my way while she stirred the gravy, I amended, "Not that I'm upset, it's really good to see you, but this is just so unlike you. Is everything okay?"

Mom sniffed, sitting her coffee down on the table as she watched me cut out another row of biscuits. "I got a call from that god-awful lawyer, Richard."

I slowed my pressing of the batter. I knew she didn't like Richard, I but I still wondered if she would side with him, and ask me to get dad out of prison. I could feel Harley's eyes darting my way. "Oh?"

All of my literary training as a journalist and the only thing I could come up with was 'oh.'

"Yes," Mom said, spinning her coffee cup on the table. "He seemed to think I could convince you to sell the newspaper so your father could afford representation to get out of prison. And from the way your girlfriend isn't reacting, I'm assuming she already knows."

Harley spun around slowly, holding a gravy-covered wooden spoon, and looking at my mom. "Yes, I know what happened between Malcolm and your husband. I'm sorry you went through that. It must have been very difficult for you."

My mom nodded slowly. "It was," she said. The guilt that hit me wasn't unfamiliar, but it was stronger this time. I intentionally forced myself to not consider her feelings because if I did, I wouldn't have been able to do what had to be done. But now that all was said and done, I realized I'd left my mother to flounder on her own. Her husband in prison, her son abandoning her. All of her high society friends probably didn't stick around once the thrill of the tabloids wore off. I was a shit son.

"Mom, I'm sorry."

She walked towards me, reached up and brushed some flour off my cheek. "I know, son. I forgive you. And for what it's worth, I told Richard he could go to hell."

"Nice, Mama Jones!" Davis said from the table. As three gazes turned to look at him, Davis shrugged and wandered out of the kitchen to allow us to talk in peace.

Smiling at my mom for the first time in ages, I continued, "Thank you, Mom. I don't know what I'm going to do yet, but Dad...he did a lot of bad things, illegal things. He put you in danger. He put all those employees in danger. I can't just let the fact that he's my dad excuse that."

"I know, honey," Mom said, staring at her coffee cup on the counter. "I still love your father, but you're right, he did some bad stuff. I'm not going to ask you to do anything you don't want to do. This is something you're going to have to decide for yourself. And as for why I'm here, I decided that if my son wasn't going to come to visit me, then I was going to pack my bags and go visit my son."

I grinned because as tough as my mom was acting, I could see the hesitant look in her eye. Immediately, I dusted the flour off my hands and wrapped her up in a hug. "I'm glad you did, Mom."

I held her still although I heard the sniffle from her face near my shoulder. "I brought some of Cameron's mother's zucchini bread as added bribing if I needed it, but it's nice to see that I didn't."

A rustle came from the other side of the door as Cameron bustled through. "Hey, Mama Jones, is that zucchini bread in your purse? I'm just gonna—" Cameron reached for her purse as Mom smacked his hands away.

"Honestly Cameron, were you raised in a barn?" She pulled the saran-wrapped bread from her bag and handed it to him before he bustled back out of the kitchen.

A knock at the front door followed by the sound of the front door opening pulled Harley's eyes away from me and my mom. As I loaded the pan with the biscuits into the oven, the door to the kitchen swung open and Dorothy O'Neil sauntered in.

"Good morning," she sang grandly. "I felt a disturbance in the air that told me my services might be needed today."

Harley and I looked at each other, grins stretching across our faces. "Really?" Harley said. "I can't imagine why that would be."

"Maybe something's going on with the pumpkins?" I said, tilting my head in thought. "They haven't been feeling their best these last few days. Maybe their vines have some psychic blockage."

"That's probably it," Harley said, nodding in exaggeration. "Their horoscope is all over the place. It's my fault, I should have planted them all at the same time. Half of them are Geminis and half of them are Cancers, but I forgot which ones were which."

I tried to ignore my mom watching Harley and me with the expression on her face. It was a combination of curiosity and smugness.

"But I thought you had a threatening message on your door last night, Harley?" Dorothy said, her eyebrows furrowed in confusion.

Mom straightened. "What's this now?"

Harley waved her hand in the air and turned back toward the gravy in the pot. "It's nothing, just some local kids messing around."

"That's not what I heard," Dorothy said, before straightening up. "Um, from the spirits, of course."

"Mom, this is Dorothy O'Neil, part owner of Three Sisters' Psychic Services," I said, indicating with a flour covered hand. "Dorothy, this is my mother, Rebecca."

"A pleasure," Mom said hesitantly.

"The pleasure is mine," Dorothy said serenely.

"Ms. O'Neil, my son neglected to inform me about the threatening message left on his girlfriend's door, perhaps you would like to fill me in?"

"I'd be glad to! And Malcolm, Harley, so glad you listened to the spirits and finally made it official. Mabel and Bertha will be so pleased."

Harley snorted and poured a cup of coffee and handed it to Dorothy. Dorothy smiled, then straightened her shoulders and shuffled her hair away from her face.

"It was a dark night—" she proclaimed grandly.

"It was *last* night," Harley interrupted. "Ms. O'Neil, please don't scare Mrs. Jones. She needs to like me."

I grinned at her and nudged her shoulder.

Dorothy glared at Harley. "May I continue?"

"Ooh, yes, go on," Mom said, leaning in. Dorothy cleared her throat.

"It was last night, a *dark* night," she said, glaring pointedly at Harley who rolled her eyes. "The spirits were restless, and I was awoken by a bright light."

"A cell phone," I mumbled to Harley, who grinned back at me.

"The bright light spoke to me and told me of blood raining from the walls. No!" she shouted, causing all of us to jump and the gravy from Harley's spoon splattered against the counter. Harley glared at Dorothy, who wasn't paying attention, as her eyes were closed. I smiled and grabbed a paper towel to clean up. "Not from the walls! From a door! And not just any door! Her door!"

Dorothy's arm raised to point at the location where Harley was before Dorothy's eyes closed, but she had wandered toward the garbage can to throw away the paper towel and Dorothy was now pointing at the air. I gently grasped her wrist and moved it to point at Harley.

"There was blood?" My mother asked, completely entranced by this performance.

"There was paint," I corrected. "Someone painted "leave" on Harley's door last night."

"In blood red paint," Dorothy amended, opening her eyes.

"But it really is a nice town," Harley said, rubbing her hands nervously against a dish rag. She was obviously worried about what my mom thought about her, and it was cute.

"You know," I jumped in. "The rest of the crew will probably be filming at the museum today, but I really don't need to be there. I'm still looking for old articles about the railroad boys but why don't you come with me today while I look around town? Harley and I could show you the sights."

Dorothy perked up. "Well if it's old articles you're looking for, you should ask Sullivan. He kept a bunch of the papers from back then. He's basically a hoarder." She leaned in toward my mother. "We used to date."

"Sullivan Schneider?" Harley asked, her eyebrows raised. "When was this?"

"Oh, years and years ago." Dorothy said with a wave of her hand. "He was smitten but I had eyes for another. Now Rebecca, you come down our way while you're here and we'll give you a tarot reading on the house."

Chapter Thirty-Seven

Latte Art

Harley

T hanks for Giving Flowers was a hole-in-the-wall shop on Main Street next to Trick or Treat bakery. Along the back of the shop was a long wooden counter with a cash register flanked on either side by bouquets of flowers set for delivery. The layout was the mirror image of Jaynie's bakery next door, but that was where the similarities stopped. Sullivan Schneider's walls were the original cracked and crumbling brick with not an ounce of drywall in sight, and the floor was plain concrete. It had potential, but in its current state, it just looked depressing.

The depressing look was only heightened by the sight of Sullivan Schneider snarling from behind the counter.

"Oh, my goodness!" Rebecca said, jumping as her eyes caught Sullivan's. "I didn't see you there. This place is so...quaint!"

Sullivan grunted, glaring as he studied the three of us. He wore a set of overalls with a pair of trimming shears in the front pocket and a thick, flannel long-sleeved shirt underneath. His thinning gray hair and wrinkles on his face showed the eighty years under his belt, but it was his cold eyes that showed the misery of his years.

"We got a sale on sunflowers if you get them in a wreath," Sullivan growled from behind the counter. His voice was cracked and rough with age and his eyes narrowed at me. "I'm up to my eyeballs in them."

Malcolm chuckled. "I get it, up to your eyeballs, because they're so tall, right?"

"How the hell should I know?" Sullivan barked. "I don't grow the damn things."

"Right," I said, looking at Sullivan with what I hoped was a nice smile. "Mr. Schnieder, we were actually hoping you might have some old newspaper articles. We've been trying to find some from the nineteen-sixties to look at but no one in town seems to have them. Dorothy O'Neil mentioned you might have the ones we were looking for."

"She did, did she? Did she also mention I'm trying to run a business here? If you're not here to buy flowers, get out."

"You know what?" Malcolm said, stepping up to the counter. "I'd love a couple bouquets and one of those sunflower wreaths. And I'd even be willing to pay extra for them if I got to see a few of those newspaper clippings."

Sullivan gave Malcolm a hard look that I couldn't decipher then glanced at his empty shop and sighed. "Order the flowers now. Come back after business hours for the newspapers and you can pick up the flowers then."

Malcolm's mom and I waited outside while Malcolm finished ordering the flowers. Even the cold October air was less chilly than the cold coming from Sullivan's glare. As I waved to someone who was heading out of Jaynie's bakery next door, Malcolm's mom looked at me from the side of her eyes.

"You're not who I pictured my son with," she said suddenly. My eyes widened as my heart dropped to my feet. "Oh, shit, that sounded wrong," she said. "I'm not the best with words. That's more Malcolm and my husband's forte."

I laughed reluctantly, relieved that she was at least making jokes. "Um, well who did you picture Malcolm with?"

Rebecca tilted her head thoughtfully. "I think I always pictured him with some career reporter, someone whose nose was always to the grindstone, grilling people for a living."

"Well, if it makes you feel better, Malcolm likes to say I'd make a great reporter," I said, tucking my hair behind my ear, desperate to ask my next question but nervous all the same. "How big of a letdown was I?"

Rebecca barked out a laugh. "Heavens, no! Harley, you're a breath of fresh air. I'm relieved he's with you. He was always so serious when he lived in New York. I was starting to get concerned he'd never smile again." Rebecca's own smile melted away, lost in a memory I wasn't privy to. She turned her eyes to me and her smile came back. "The two of you joke together, tease each other. There's a comfort there that I haven't seen in him in a long time."

My attempted smile faltered. How could I explain to Malcolm's mother that I was just a stop along his road? I wasn't enough to make him want to stay. "Thank you, but—"

"Who wants lunch?" Malcolm asked as the door behind us opened and his breath formed a white mist in front of him. He rubbed his hands together in the cold before reaching a hand out to me as if it were the most natural thing in the world. I smiled as I tucked my hand into his. Maybe I wouldn't have to disappoint his mom after all.

Trick or Treat bakery was warm when we grabbed a table and yelled a 'hello' to Jaynie behind the counter. Malcolm put our orders in at the counter and introduced his mother to Jaynie before sitting next to us. I watched in amazement as Malcolm recounted his favorite places to eat in Burnt Creek, shops he thought his mother would love, and different locals that he called by their first names. Malcolm had been here two-and-a-half weeks, but he fit in like he was born here. His mother gave me a knowing look, and I know she heard the love he had for this town in his voice too.

"Malcolm, my boy!" a voice called from the entrance of the bakery. Malcolm froze, and I tore my gaze away from him to find the Jones' family lawyer walking into the bakery like it was an office in New York City. Richard wore an expensive suit under a long black trench coat and stuck out like a shark amongst goldfish.

Malcolm's face tightened and he glanced at me. "Richard, I didn't realize you were still in town."

"I wasn't planning on leaving until you agree to come back to the city with me," he said with a laugh that was designed for overcompensated men in boardrooms. He turned his attention toward me. "Ah, Miss Malone, I see you're still stealing the boy's attention. You know, I've heard you've run into some trouble down at your inn. It would be a shame if all your wandering attention gets you into some hot water with your establishment."

I felt the blood drain from my face as my mind tried to compute what Richard was saying. Malcolm's fist tightened and as I could see him getting ready to pounce, I noticed Rebecca's hand drop casually onto Malcolm's hand. Well, it looked casual, but I could see her nails subtly digging into his flesh.

"Richard," Rebecca said in a high-pitched socialite fashion. "Such a surprise to see you."

"Rebecca, looking ravishing as always," he said, his eyes as lecherous as his words. "Let me know when you're ready to leave that no-good husband of yours, I'd love to be your first call."

Rebecca chuckled good-naturedly. "Speaking of that no-good husband of mine, I'm surprised to see the money he spent in hiring your firm go to such strange use. To see a partner at the law office out doing an intern's job? Honestly, Richard, I thought playing fetch was beneath you, especially at your age."

Rebecca added a polite chuckle to the end of her cutting statement, showing what a queen she was at playing the game.

Richard's lips formed a thin line. "Well, we all must do our part to ensure your husband is able to see freedom once more. Some of us are clearly more dedicated to the pursuit of his freedom than others."

He let the words settle in the air before turning to me once more. "Miss Malone, I look forward to seeing you tomorrow at the Haunted Trail. I'm sure it will be a great memory once your inn succumbs to its financial difficulties." Richard gave a tight smile, then nodded once to Malcolm before turning and walking back out the front door.

As the door swung behind him, I felt a deep breath leave my body. Malcolm's hand found mine and gave it a squeeze. "You okay?" he asked.

I nodded. "Do you think it was him? The paint on the door? He wants you to leave, and he thinks I'm keeping you here. Maybe it was him, Malcolm."

"Take a breath, baby," Malcolm said, tilting my head to look him in the eyes and he breathed with me. "I don't know if it was him or not, but he doesn't seem the kind to get his hands dirty like that."

"We should still talk to the police, let them know to add him to the suspect list," Rebecca said, patting Malcolm on the hand. "If nothing else, it'll piss Richard off."

Jaynie shuffled around the counter, holding a tray with three mugs, and sat one down in front of me.

"Pumpkin spice latte on me, Harley, on account of that man being a dick. It's a dick latte."

I glanced down to see that there was, in fact, very profane latte art on the top of my latte. She sat one down in front of Malcolm. "A dick latte for you, sir."

Malcolm tilted his head to the side. "Oh, so that's what that is. You've given me a dick latte before, haven't you?"

Jaynie gave him her signature "you fool" look and put the third mug in front of Malcolm's mother. Jaynie hooked the serving tray against her hip and looked at Rebecca. "I was debating on getting you a dick latte. I wasn't sure you could handle it. But then I heard you cut that man down to size, and I realized you got some balls, Mrs. Jones. Now you have a dick latte to go with them."

I stared wide-eyed at Malcolm's mother as her eyes dropped to the mug in front of her with the penis foam top. Her gaze rose back to Jaynie, then she lifted the mug to her mouth, her lips touching the foam art, and took a swig of the latte.

"Jaynie," she said after a moment, "that's some good dick."

Chapter Thirty-Eight

Official Business

Malcolm

I was in equal parts of excitement and dread going to Sullivan Schneider's place for those newspaper clippings. They would be so great for the channel, but the idea of spending a lot of time in his grumpy presence was enough to have me dragging my feet. My mother was spending the night in Zoey's room and Zoey and Darla were bunking up for the night since Maggie still had my old room. When I left the house, all the girls, including my mother, were in the theatre room getting ready for Harley's sacrilege popcorn and a viewing of *The Princess Bride*.

Despite the initial shock of seeing my mom, it was really nice to spend time with her again. Even better was seeing her joke around with Harley. Harley seemed to bring out this light in everyone, it was almost blinding.

Before long, I was pulling into Sullivan's driveway and getting out of my car into the frosty autumn air. Sullivan's house was on a street with nice single-story houses, but his house stuck out like a crack house in downtown Manhattan. Previously cheery yellow paint was browned with age and peeling off of the front and sides of the house. The lawn was overgrown, and weeds climbed up the side of wire fencing that had long since fallen down. It didn't even look like anyone lived there.

I walked to the front door and put my finger out to the doorbell, but the button was hanging by a wire, so I decided knocking was the best option. Sullivan swung the door open and grunted in greeting before spinning on his feet and leading me inside.

Fine by me. I wasn't in the mood for conversation anyways.

The inside matched the outside almost exactly. Carpeting from the nineteen-sixties was worn along paths where Sullivan obviously shuffled along daily. A couch and recliner were equally tattered with the fabric worn to the point of stuffing being exposed. Although lacking in modern conveniences, the place was neat with no knickknacks cluttering up any surfaces. I was about to discount Dorothy's assumption of Sullivan being a hoarder until he led me to his spare bedroom that was stacked with piles of newspapers, photographs, announcements, and flower arrangement order forms from at least fifty years prior.

"Newspapers are over there," Sullivan growled, pointing to a stack roughly waist-high. "Grab whatcha need and don't make too much of a mess."

Sullivan hesitated by the door for a moment, staring at me as if measuring my worth, before folding his shoulders down and shuffling back to the living room. Figuring Sullivan wasn't going to give me much information on where to start, I got to work on learning the organization he used, which thankfully seemed to be chronological. I was there about an hour before finding the newspapers that listed information about the railroad boys. Surprisingly, they occupied the headlines for a few months, all the way up through their untimely disappearance along with the money they stole. There was a total of six papers mentioning Jimmy Carpenter, Bob Walker, and Pete Grant. After pulling them from the stack and neatly stacking the rest of the pile, I went to the living room where Sullivan was sitting in his recliner staring out the window.

"Mr. Schneider, would you mind if I asked you some questions about the railroad boys?"

Sullivan's eyes snapped to me, and his eyes went cold. "What for?"

"Well, you collected the newspapers, and you were at around that time. I was just wondering if you remembered anything that I wouldn't be able to find in the newspapers."

He seemed to settle at this, but he still looked at me warily. Old men always thought the world was out to get them.

"Yeah, I remember some stuff from around then," he said. "What do you wanna know?"

"Did you ever meet the guys who were trying to sell the railroad idea to the town?"

Sullivan snorted. "Yeah, I met them. Real pieces of work. They came in with their half-cocked scheme that needed dressing up with fancy words, how they were going to 'revitalize' the town with this costly 'expenditure.' I could tell from the start they were crooked, good-for-nothing troublemakers. I tried telling that to Dorothy and her sisters, but did they listen? Nope. Then they go and rob half the town and disappear."

"Well, they didn't stay disappeared, did they?" I asked. "Their bodies were found in the graveyard buried in a shallow grave."

Sullivan gave me the side-eye. "That's what I heard."

"Was any of the money recovered?"

Sullivan paused, eyeing the newspaper. "No. But if you find any of it, you let me know. I've been holding onto those damn newspapers for decades trying to figure out where they might've hidden it. That money needs to go back to the rightful owner."

I cocked my head to the side. "You mean the town?"

Sullivan nodded slowly. "Yeah, the town."

"You know, there was one more thing," I said, hesitating. Fuck, was I really going to chase down some stupid lead from a ghost? Apparently. "Have you ever heard anything about there being a fourth member of the railroad boys? Anyone else in on their scam?"

Sullivan's eyes turned hard. "No," he said, scanning my face. "Have you?"

I paused a moment, just watching him. "No," I said. "Just curious. Well, I should get going, got the Haunted Trail tomorrow night at the inn, Harley's gonna need help doing whatever it is that needs done."

"Your flowers are on the kitchen counter," he said, waving me away.

As I grabbed the two flower arrangements and the wreath, all three better than what I could ever find in the city for that price, I paused on the way out when I thought I caught a chemical smell. Sullivan must have heard me stop on the creaking floors, and he glared at me in his doorway.

"Do you smell paint?" I asked, looking around his doorway. I looked around the corner and spotted a door I hadn't seen yet.

"You think those vases paint themselves?" Sullivan snapped. "I want those newspapers back by the end of the month."

"You got it," I said, reluctantly walking out the door.

I was sitting in my car when I realized what was bothering me. I grabbed the first vase and inspected it. It was glass, not painted. I checked the second one and stared hard at Sullivan's door.

I shook my head and admonished myself for jumping at shadows trying to find who would've painted something on Harley's door. She was probably right, it was probably some kids who got too bored around town.

When I got back to the inn, I hung the wreath over the front door, looking at how well the autumn leaves and flowers expertly covered the last bit of red paint that refused to come off the white door. The girls had already finished their movie and were hanging out in the living room holding glasses of wine. I handed my mom the first bouquet with a kiss on her forehead and handed the second bouquet to Harley with a kiss on her cheek. I saw both of them beam at me like put the stars in the sky, and I felt the oddest sense of...home. In a single moment, I realized that this is what I wanted. Coming home to Harley, my friends and family spending time at the inn, going through the seasons together. I didn't want two weeks, I wanted much longer than that. Maybe forever. I just needed to get the courage to tell her as soon as all her focus on the inn was taken care of.

Lying in bed next to Harley that night, I stripped her out of her clothes and tried to show her what I wasn't sure she was ready to hear from me yet. I poured forever into each stroke, belonging into each kiss, and desire into each touch of her skin. I wanted to leave her sated, fulfilled, and completely mine.

The next morning after breakfast, the front door of the inn chimed, bringing in the only person to be met with a cold greeting from Maggie.

"What do you want, Connor?" Maggie asked.

Connor Monterey stood in the foyer of the inn wearing a shirt that was buttoned too high, pants that were too tight, and shoes that were too shiny. I was probably biased, but I didn't like guys with shoes that shiny.

"Pleasure to see you as always, Magdalene."

"What. Do. You. Want?" she asked, ice in her tone.

"I'm here on official town council business. I need to deliver a letter to Harley."

A white envelope was in his hand, and he waved it like a victory flag. "Okay, well give it here," Maggie said, holding out her hand.

Connor held the envelope away from her like a schoolyard bully. "This is for Harley's eyes only—"

I reached up and snatched the envelope out of his hand, handing it to Maggie.

"Thank you, Malcolm," Maggie said, opening the letter under the supervision of Connor's glower. She scanned the letter and cursed. "Are you for real?"

Connor's sneer turned smug. "Unfortunately. We've got it on good authority that someone has witnessed a rat infestation on the premises. If Harley can't show proof that she's hired an exterminator to investigate, the town council is required to get the health department involved. And make it a matter of public record."

Maggie's face was red and her lips thin. "This is a new low, even for you, Connor. You know that there isn't a rat problem here. What exactly are you hoping to gain from this?"

"This isn't personal, Magpie," Connor said with false sympathy. Maggie looked at him in disgust. I walked forward to lean against the desk, just a little inside Connor's personal space. He took a step back and eyed me with suspicion.

"You know, Connor," I said carefully. "I'm glad it's not personal. It's good for you that it's not personal. Because when we find out who reported the fake infestation and sue them for slander, anyone associated with them will be raked through the mud. All sorts of things come out of a lawsuit like that. Even if someone's innocent, just being mentioned in a lawsuit like that could be the death of someone's career. I couldn't imagine what that would do to someone who's a town council member."

Connor's face paled slightly, and he took another step back. "Well, you just get that to Harley. I'm just here on official business."

"So you mentioned," Maggie said, waving her hand toward the door. "Have a mediocre day."

The police were spending a lot of time in Harley's basement behind the hidden door. That little tidbit was going to make a splash on our YouTube channel, and more than that, it would put Harley's inn on the map. She wouldn't need to worry about having an empty inn after this episode goes up. Remembering the look on her face when she saw the dead body, I knew I would do anything to stop her from being afraid like that again.

Though Harley was worried about how my mother would take the news that a dead body was found at the inn, my mother was thrilled that she was in proximity of a real cold case. She pulled out her kindle and spent forty-five minutes showing Harley every true-crime and cozy mystery novel she had bought and spent a good portion of the day googling common cop phrases so she could decode what the police officers were saying.

Harley and I spent the rest of the day putting the finishing touches on the Haunted Trail so it would be ready for that evening and hanging up flyers around town for the opening. The ticket prices were posted, the scenes were planned out, props were set, and a booth for warm apple cider and baked goods was cobbled together from an old police parade float we got from Harley's dad.

The police had been quiet about the body in the basement as far as it went for the YouTube channel, but Harley sweet-talked her dad into giving us the exclusive, alluding to the story that the body in the basement was one missing preacher from the prohibition era. They were sending samples for analysis, but the two gunshot wounds to the chest indicated that someone back in the day wanted to silence the good preacher for discovering the moonshine still. Although they couldn't definitively say why the body wasn't moved, their working theory was that there was too much focus on the innkeeper at the time for him to move the body, so he just stored it.

The inn was buzzing with excitement for our best Halloween special yet. With the episode filming wrapped up, the focus was shifted to voice-overs, editing, and the Haunted Trail. Harley even mentioned that she was finally feeling like everything was going to work out. I've never been one to believe in jinxes, but even I should've known that something was going to go drastically wrong.

Chapter Thirty-Nine

Into the Woods

Harley

The Haunted Trail was in full swing and going off without a hitch. The plan was for it to go from eight to eleven at night. We ordered some of the creepiest outfits from Penny Wayward so we could jump out at unsuspecting trail walkers. There was a smaller, kid-friendly trail that Maggie and I put together where younger kids wouldn't wet their pants or be scarred for life. The kid-friendly trail didn't have any people jumping out, just little statues like a gargoyle, a pumpkin monster, and a cheap, plastic scarecrow. All with smiles, all holding bowls filled with candy for the little kids.

The adult Haunted Trail started with a few regular jump scares. A few teenagers from the theatre crew at the high school volunteered for the basic jolts to get the people ready. Some of the volunteers with cheerleading or gymnastics backgrounds got creative with exorcist-style scenes. All in all, I was really impressed with their creativity. Of course, there wasn't much to do in a small town than scare the crap out of people. But Burnt Creek lived for Halloween.

Once they got a little further down, the scenes became more elaborate, leaving the walking patrons not just frightened, but thoroughly creeped out.

Malcolm was dressed as an insane doctor, complete with fake blood, fake medical equipment, and even a gurney to which Darla was strapped as a patient with fake open gashes. When people walked by, seen in advance by a small mirror system Cameron had constructed, Malcolm would cackle loudly, and Darla thrashed against her confines, squeezing a bottle of fake blood to shoot up into the air from her torso.

Further down, dressed as a scarecrow with a realistic-looking ax sticking in his chest, Ben stood on a stump at the base of a tree that loomed over a small clearing. His arms looped over two branches to make him look like he was hung up on a post. When people walked through, indicated by a sensor that played the sounds of crows, Ben would get in position, looking like a prop until people started to pass him. Then he pulled the ax from the hook on his chest and pretended to chase the patrons.

The last station was by far the creepiest. Darla and I had hung different baby dolls from thrift stores in the trees, draping down to hang by the neck. Some of the heads were decapitated, and some of the eyes were missing. Small lights in the trees cast shadows on the heads, giving a haunted graveyard feel. Sitting underneath it was Zoey, dressed as a Victorian child playing in a graveyard of broken dolls. Her blue hair was pulled into pigtails at the nape of her neck, her face paint was pale with black makeup lining her eyes and creating black tears down her face.

When people walked by, Zoey would start singing softly to the doll in her hand, combing its hair. Then she would slowly turn and look to the walkers and open her eyes revealing contacts that made her eyes completely black. When she did that, she pushed a small button on the back of the doll that gave a Bluetooth signal to speakers in the trees that Davis had set up that let out a chorus of baby cries near the doll heads.

The guys nearly pissed themselves when we showed them.

Cameron and Davis manned the concession stand selling apple cider and doughnuts, Maggie sold small pumpkins for kids to decorate, and Malcolm's mom even jumped in to help sell tickets. When the last tour went through, we joined them at the ticket booth to figure out how well we made out.

As Malcolm's mom and Maggie collected the money, Malcolm wrapped his arms around my waist and rested his chin on my shoulder. I grabbed his hands and tucked them into the warmth of my sweater pocket. "You make a handsome doctor," I said with a grin.

"I almost became a doctor," he murmured.

"Oh?"

"Yeah, but I didn't have enough patience," he said, chuckling to himself.

I rolled my eyes. "You are such a dork."

Malcolm chuckled some more and sighed against me. "You know, I think you've made a lot of money tonight."

I leaned my head against his and sighed. "I really hope so."

"I think you might have made enough that we can start renovations on the carriage house."

Malcolm swiveled my hips to aim me at the dark outline of the carriage house just off the path. "Do you really think so?" I asked.

I felt his chin nod against my shoulder. "I do. I think we could paint it to match the inn, with red trim and a white door."

"And we could put a back porch on it to look out at the forest."

"We could put a Christmas tree inside and outside. And a porch swing," he said, kissing me on the side of the head. "I've always wanted a porch swing."

I turned my head carefully to look at him. "Porch swings can be tricky," I said slowly. "You need two people to hang them up."

Malcolm rocked his head from side to side against my shoulder. "You know, I've been thinking about that—"

"Excuse me," a young voice rushed out. "My name is Bode Jacobson and I'd like to interview you for the Burnt Creek High newspaper."

We startled apart and turned around to find a teenage boy in a red sweater with an oversized camera against his chest.

Malcolm straightened up and smiled at him. "You guys have a school newspaper? That's really cool." Malcolm led us over to the stack of hay bales near the kid's trail.

Bode shrugged as he sat down with his notebook. "Thanks, but it's actually not really that impressive. The school can't actually afford a journalism club or even a paper newspaper, so it's really just me reporting, editing, and putting together a two-page online paper that the principal posts on the school's website every two weeks."

Malcolm furrowed his brow. "That takes a lot of initiative, though. If anything, that's more impressive. Now let's do some introductions. This is Harley Malone, she owns and operates the Burnt Creek Bed and Breakfast and was responsible for putting on the Haunted Trail this year."

I grinned at Bode, and I felt like I was talking to Malcolm as a teenager. I nodded toward Malcolm. "And this is Malcolm Jones, he's been a reporter, an editor, and did a whole bunch of stuff with newspapers in the big city."

Bode's eyes widened. "Really? Like, a real newspaper?"

Malcolm chuckled. "Yeah, man, a real newspaper. So let's break down this story for your killer newspaper, add some controversy, you know? Did you know this was the first year they sold tickets to the Haunted Trail?"

I smiled and nodded as Malcolm regaled Bode with an accurate, yet dramatic retelling of the city council meeting where I heroically fought against the naysayers and brought the Haunted Trail to the Burnt Creek Bed and Breakfast. Bode took our picture, one where I insisted Malcolm sit next to me because he helped so much, and shook Malcolm's hand.

"You and Malcolm can wrap up, I'm going to do one last walk-through of the trail to make sure everything is turned off," I said, smiling at Bode. Malcolm kissed me on the cheek, and I headed toward the entrance. Night had fallen, and it was dark apart from the solar lights that dotted on the ground to show the intended path. I pulled my phone from my pocket and turned on the flashlight to find the sensors the crew had put up.

I made it past the first setting before seeing the sensor strapped to the tree, I reached down to turn it off when a rasping voice called out to me. "You need to leave."

I shrieked, holding my phone up to shine a light on the surrounding trees. I whipped the light back and forth, trying to find the source of the voice. I saw nothing in the shadows of the trees, but as I turned to carefully walk through the rest of the path toward the exit, leaves crunched underfoot in the woods to my right, as someone yelled, "leave!" A hand reached out, pushing me toward the ground. Gripping my phone in my hand, I ran through the trail, catching my foot on a root sticking up out of the ground, tumbling down, then scrambling back up. I raced through hanging branches, leaves hitting my face as I ran through them. The lights of the ticket booth glowed softly in the distance, and I ran until I found a familiar face.

Cameron, laughing with Ben on some bales of hay turned towards me and jolted to his feet.

"Harley, whoa, what's going on?"

I panted heavily, gripping his arm for support. "Someone...in the woods...said to leave...A man's voice...then someone...pushed me...I just ran."

"Harley, take a breath, you're bleeding." Cameron wiped his thumb across my cheek, and I felt a stinging for the first time. Hot tears gathered in my eyes as I leaned into him. Cameron wrapped his arms around me. "I gotcha, Harley. Ben, go get Malcolm. And call her dad, we need cops to sweep the area."

Chapter Forty

Deciding to Change

Malcolm

Once again, I found myself bathed in the blue and red of the cop cars. The lights spilled over the trees at the entrance and exit of the Haunted Trail. Two uniformed officers and one off-duty cop had been pulled out of bed and wandered into the woods about ten minutes prior, flashlights in hand, to search for clues. Harley stood with Oliver, giving her statement while her dad had her sit on a bale of hay. Harley winced as her dad rolled up her pant leg to expose cuts on her knees from her falling down. My mom came to stand next to me.

"I want you to go to Victoria's house a little early," I said. "Take my car. It's not that I don't want to spend time with you, I do, but I don't like whatever is happening here. I've already asked Harley to stay with her dad until this cools down, but she's being stubborn."

Mom nodded. "And you? What are you going to do?"

"I'm going to figure out who's behind this and fix it."

"Sometimes people don't need you to fix things. Sometimes people just need for you to be there for them."

I wasn't sure what I could say to that, so I stood in silence. Mom squeezed my arm, gave me a kiss on the cheek, and went inside to pack her bags. A few moments later, the officers emerged from the woods and bent to whisper something in the chief's ear. He secured the last bandage on Harley's knee, kissed her head, and followed them toward the woods. I walked over to him.

"What did they find?"

"Stay out of this, Malcolm, the police have it handled."

"I need to know what she's up against," I protested. "Chief, the police can't be with her twenty-four-seven."

Harley's dad gave me a hard look, then nodded his head for me to follow. I followed the officer's flashlights to the second station of the Haunted Trail where Harley had been attacked. The officer shined a light on the trees. Each of the trees were painted in red, and each of them said 'leave'.

My fists clenched at my sides. "Why the hell is someone coming after her? This doesn't make any sense."

"No, it doesn't," Harley's dad said stiffly. "I'll admit, I thought the thing on the door was someone not pleased y'all were filming here. But this here was directed at Harley."

"The timing doesn't make sense though. Why would this start after we showed up? If someone had an issue with Harley, it doesn't make sense that it would be coming out like this all of a sudden."

The chief shook his head and pointed to some officers to take pictures and to pay special attention to the forest floor in case there were any footprints with paint on them. The chief wiped his hand over his face, and I resisted the urge to put a hand on his shoulder. Harley was my girl, but she was his daughter.

When we emerged from the woods, I saw Richard in his dark coat leaning against a shining rental car. I scowled. I did not have time for this tonight.

"Malcolm, my boy," Richard said with a clap on my shoulder. My father's attorney had officially graduated to stalker status.

"Richard, what are you doing here?"

"I'm here to take you home," he said, his stony face losing some of his 'good ol' boy' routine. "Why don't we go somewhere to talk."

I turned to look for Harley. Maggie stood next to her, one arm draped over her sister's shoulders and her eyes scanning the surroundings. I wanted to be the one comforting her right now.

I sighed and walked with Richard a few feet toward the inn. "Richard, I'm not going back."

"Do you realize what you being tangled in this could do to the value of the newspaper? You need to get ahead of this."

"Richard, this town is in the middle of nowhere. They don't even have a newspaper reporting this unless you count the single kid at the high school posting two pages on the website. The closest thing they have to a news network is the geriatric grapevine. I'm still thinking about what I want to do in New York, but it's going to be on my terms and my timeline."

Richard took a good look at me. "You staying for the girl? You think this girl cares about you? She's just using your little show to save her from financial ruin."

I looked back at Richard, in his overdressed suit standing in the red and blue lights of the cop cars and squinted at him. "What do you know about Harley's financial situation?"

Richard didn't move, didn't blink, but I had seen enough of my father's lies to know. He was hiding something. "Why is it, Richard, that you make your way over here to bring me back to New York right after Harley receives a threat that could force her to close her doors?"

Richard scoffs, but I saw the tightening of his jaw, the nervous swallow. I narrow my eyes and nod at him. "So that's it then? You're trying to shut Harley down unless I leave? That's your leverage?"

"She doesn't have to worry about a thing so long as you come back to New York. I'm looking to retire, and your old man's case is a big one. I want to go out with a bang. But I need you to sell that damned newspaper so he can afford us. Or, hell, buy it from him." Red tinted my vision that had nothing to do with the lights from the cop cars. My hands fisted at my sides. Sensing the growing tension, Richard squeezed my shoulder. "Don't be so dramatic, son, it was just a little scare."

I gripped him by the front of his tacky black jacket a pushed him out of sight. I leveraged my legs to lift him up and slam him against the trunk of a tree. I didn't blink as the wind rushed out of his lungs. "Just a little scare? You scared the shit out of her. She had nothing to do with my father, with the case, with any of this. So, here's what we're going to do. I'll leave with you, and I'll do what I have to do with the newspaper, but you aren't going to come near Harley again, or I swear to God, Richard, working past retirement age will be the least of your fucking worries. Do you understand?"

I waited until Richard's old pudgy neck nodded before I released him. I would take care of this, take care of Harley, and make sure I never had to see the terrified look on her face again. Then I would find a way to bury my father for putting me through this again.

"We leave in half an hour." I spun around before hearing anything else. I would give up anything to keep Harley safe, even if I was the one putting her in danger.

Making my way to where Harley was standing, I got a glimpse at the haunted look in her eyes, and it hardened my resolve. I would fix this for her. I would be the guy she needed. Her eyes opened, so full of hope and trust as they landed on me. I gave her a deep kiss on the lips and cradled her head.

"I've gotta go, but I'll be back," I said. "I'm gonna fix this."

A look of confusion briefly crossed her face, but I didn't have time to explain. I had a plane to catch.

Walking back toward the inn, I ran through my packing list. Ben passed me coming off the porch. "Whoa, where's the fire?"

I hesitated, then faced Ben. Running my hand over my head I looked at my best friend. "Do you remember when you said that if something needed to change, we got to decide to change it?"

Ben nodded slowly. "Sure, man. Yeah."

I nodded quickly, taking stock of my time limit. "I need things to change. I haven't got it all figured out yet, but I want to buy the newspaper. I still want to research for the channel, but I won't be traveling as much. I'll tell you more soon, but I've got to go."

"Go? Where the hell are you going?" he called to me as I passed through the entryway.

I called over my shoulder. "New York."

Chapter Forty-One

Body and Soul

Harley

Maggie rubbed my arms as Dad and the other officers talked, pointing at different parts of the woods. "Come on, Harley. We still have to count the cash stuff."

"I don't know if I'm in the mood for that tonight, Mags."

"I know you're not, but nothing is going to get better by you staring off into the woods like an angsty teenager. It's cold, let's get you inside."

I followed her back toward the inn numbly, each step sending aches and pains through my legs and ribs. My hands still burned from the scrapes when I fell, and bandages lined my hands and knees like a child riding a bike for the first time. I wanted to curl up into bed and cry, to let Malcolm hold me tonight. I didn't want to be strong right now.

Darla and Zoey were sitting at the dining table when we came in, holding the card reader with the screen that had the night's credit card sales listed. They glanced up when we came in, both taking in my appearance.

"How are you holding up?" Darla asked, looking at me like I might combust any moment.

"I'm fine, just a little scratched," I said, shrugging a shoulder. I schooled my face so I wouldn't wince at the pain that movement caused. Zoey grabbed me a glass of water before sitting down again. "So, Maggie said you guys tallied up the sales for the night?"

"Yes, but as anxious as I am to see how tonight went," Maggie started, then turned to Zoey. "I need you to take those contacts out first."

I looked at Zoey, stunned that I had already grown accustomed to her fully black eyes. She tilted her head to the side like a demonic puppy and then smirked. "I'll be right back."

"Remind me what this money is going towards again?" Darla said, tapping on the card readers screen to get to end-of-day reports.

"It's going toward the restoration of the carriage house," I said with a smile, picturing the little house with my porch and Malcolm's porch swing. "I've been living in the room upstairs since before we opened and if I want the most profit when we finally get people in the doors, I'm going to need as many rooms as I can spare. That means moving out." I took a sip of water, careful to keep my hands steady.

Darla nodded with a smile. "And is Malcolm moving out with you?"

I coughed on my water and looked at her with wide eyes.

"Oh, don't act like he doesn't stay with you every night! Zoey and I have both seen him scuttling out your door every morning."

I could feel my cheeks heat up as Maggie laughed at me. "I told you they'd figure it out," Maggie said. "You two aren't nearly as clever as you think you are."

Zoey came back into the room with her face roughly scrubbed of makeup and her contacts out. Maggie was halfway through counting the cash when she handed Zoey a stack of one-dollar bills. "Double count that for me."

"Aye-aye, Mags."

As the future of my inn and my place in the town hung in the balance, I didn't feel nearly as anxious as I thought I would. I was surrounded by friends, both Malcolm's and mine, and I still had a week to go with Malcolm by my side. Maybe by the end of things, we could have more than just two weeks. I should have felt ridiculous for hoping, but what was life without a little hope?

Zoey handed Maggie the last stack of cash that she double-counted and Darla handed her the printed sales receipt for the day, circling the profit line. I sat breathless as Maggie added the two numbers and looked at me with a smile.

"Well?" I asked, scared to know the answer. "Are we on target?"

"Harley," Maggie said, her eyes beaming with pride. "We surpassed our entire goal in one night."

Silence engulfed the room as the four of us looked at each other. Suddenly, Zoey was flinging her arms around me, Maggie was crying, and Darla was dancing around the dining room.

"I can't believe we did it!" I cried, feeling my own tears streaming down my face. I hugged Zoey back, then Maggie, then Darla. "I have to go tell Malcolm! He worked so hard on this, he's gonna be amazed!"

I half-jogged-half-galloped outside, a smile stretching across my face despite my pain as I glanced at the old carriage house. I was going to make it a home. And maybe Malcolm could help me get there.

Malcolm wasn't by the woods where I had last seen him, and Ben, Davis and Cameron were all talking in hushed tones out by the parking lot. I had briefly forgotten that Malcolm said he was going to be back from somewhere, but I wasn't sure where. Probably to bed, I reasoned. With the creepy guy in my woods combined with the sales numbers we had tonight, I couldn't imagine him not being exhausted. I was ready to collapse, too. But I couldn't wait to wake him up with my appreciation.

I climbed the stairs two at a time to my bedroom where we had been sleeping every night. The bed was made the same way it was this morning. A slow sinking feeling started in my chest. Why would Malcolm be sleeping in his own room? He didn't seem to mind that his mom knew about us sleeping together. Come to think of it, I hadn't seen his mom in a while either.

I went down the hallway to his room and hesitantly knocked. When no one answered, I turned the doorknob slowly. "Malcolm?" I asked quietly.

The door swung inward, spilling the hallway light into the empty bedroom. I breathed a sigh of relief for a moment, feeling silly for thinking Malcolm was upset with me to the point where he was sleeping in a different room. It wasn't until I was about to close the door on my way out that I realized exactly how empty the room was. Malcolm's suitcase was gone. The papers and notebooks and expensive pens had vanished as if they were never there to start with.

My eyes widened as I double-checked the room number. It was definitely his room. But Malcolm was gone. I pulled out my phone and tried to call him, but my call went straight to voicemail.

I felt like I had swallowed a pile of stones with how heavy my heart was. I walked in a daze down the stairs, passing through the kitchen where Darla was pouring champagne into four flutes. Seeing my face as I passed by her, she stopped pouring and set the bottle down. "Harley, what's wrong?"

I shook my head and kept walking, aiming for the one person who could answer my question. I could hear a commotion behind me as the three women piled out of the door behind me.

"Harley," Maggie said, jogging to catch up to me. "Harley, what's going on?"

Instead of answering, I walked until my eyes caught the eyes of the one person who would know what was going on.

"Ben, where is Malcolm?" I asked quietly, hoping my desperation didn't show on my face. This wasn't how it was supposed to go. We had talked about him staying. We had talked about porch swings and holidays. And there were things I didn't have the time to say yet. I wanted to tell him I wanted him to stay. I wanted to tell him that I felt like I had known him forever, like I could tell him anything.

I wanted to tell him I loved him.

I just needed a chance to tell him, even if he didn't love me back. Ben's eyes scanned the women behind me before dropping to the ground. "Shit, Harley I'm sorry."

"Ben," I said again, stepping closer to force his eyes back to mine. "Where is Malcolm?"

Ben looked at me, his scarecrow face paint not hiding his grim expression. "He went back to New York."

I felt my heart drop into my stomach as gasps erupted behind me. "When?"

"He left about an hour ago. His family lawyer showed up."

"What does that mean?" I asked, fearing I already knew the answer.

"It means things are changing. He said he needed some things to be different. He was talking so fast, saying he was buying the newspaper. He told me he would explain everything when he could."

I broke away as the girls peppered Ben with questions and I dialed his number again. And again. And again. I turned and looked at the ruins of the carriage house, the house that had somehow morphed into *our* dream. I dialed his number again. It never even rang as I heard his voicemail over and over again.

So, it was true, then. After everything we talked about, Malcolm was going to go back to New York and take over his family newspaper company, just like he was groomed for his whole childhood.

I didn't know why I was feeling so betrayed. I knew the score. Two weeks. Two weeks of absolute bliss and then we would go our separate ways. But I didn't even get two weeks with him.

I didn't even get to say goodbye.

I ignored the voices around me as I turned to head back to the inn. My bed and breakfast. My dream. The dream I had long before Malcolm.

How was it that I had been a person, a whole person, before him but now that he's come and gone, it felt like half of me was missing?

I had wanted someone to spirit me away, body and soul. And he did. And now my spirit was gone.

Chapter Forty-Two

N.Y.C.

Malcolm

I wasn't looking forward to spending any more time with Richard. The flight back to New York was torture. Richard sat beside me in first class, shamelessly hitting on the flight attendants while wearing his wedding ring and downing overpriced mini bottles of vodka. I stared out the window and imagined what Harley was doing right then. She must have noticed I was gone.

"Cheer up, son. You're making the right decision," Richard's voice broke me from my reverie.

As hard as it was to hear from Richard of all people, I knew I was making the right decision. I spent the flight deciding what to do. I couldn't keep holding onto the past if I have any hope of a future. Not just any future, a future for me and Harley. I just hoped Harley would give me a chance to explain.

The bustle of LaGuardia airport was claustrophobic even at six in the morning as we made our way through baggage claim and finally out to the waiting car. We had arrived at the airport in the middle of the night to find that there weren't any flights for hours to New York.

As we sat down in the car, I reached for my phone in my jacket pocket, only to find my pocket empty. I gripped every pocket and fished through my bags as the car cruised to wherever Richard directed me. "Fuck, Richard I think I left my phone on the plane."

"Ah, yeah, I did that once. Took me two weeks to get it back. That was a bitch of a time for my assistant."

"Richard, we need to turn around. I need my phone."

"No can do, kiddo. I've got a bunch of people coming into the office to get the paperwork together for the sale of the newspaper. You can pick up another phone when we're done."

The car turned the corner and pulled up in front of the large office building. I got out, pulling my luggage from the trunk because that dickwad Richard didn't seem to believe I'd come here if I had the opportunity to stop at my apartment first. Prick.

Four hours later, a line of smarmy lawyers hovered in anticipation as I signed the final few pages before sliding the stack of papers toward them and tossing down the pen.

"You're making the right call, Malcolm," Richard said as he pulled the stack of papers toward his protruding gut. "Your father would be proud."

A flash of anger took hold of my stomach as I glared at Richard in contempt. "I'm not doing it for him."

Richard nodded, his slicked-back hair gleaming under the lights above. "Are you going to go see him?"

I shrugged, not wanting to give him an answer one way or another. Partially because it was none of Richard's business what I did. Also, it was because I didn't actually know what I was going to do.

"Well, it doesn't matter, champ," Richard said. "He'll be out soon enough, and I'm sure he'll want to see his boy again."

I grunted in response. "This shit is signed. You'll leave Harley alone now."

"You really did all this for the girl? I didn't realize you would get so worked up about a mouse infestation. I could've saved myself days in that shitty backward town if I would've worked with the town council from the beginning."

My eyes narrowed. "Not to mention all the other shit you did to her."

Richard tipped his head to the side. "What are you talking about?"

I sat stock-still, ignoring the confused looks of the other lawyers in the room. Then I stood to my full height and locked eyes with Richard. "Richard, for once in your life, I need total honesty here. Did you put paint on Harley's front door?"

Richard's eyebrows raised. He let out an incredulous laugh. "Why the hell would I paint her door? Can't she afford to hire someone for that?"

My heart started racing. "Did you follow Harley into the woods and push her?"

Richard's laughing stopped. "Are you fucking serious?"

"Deadly."

"No, I didn't follow a girl into the fucking woods, Malcolm. Jesus, I'm a lawyer, not a fucking criminal."

I grabbed my bag and my jacket and headed toward the elevator. "That's debatable."

My hands shook as I pounded against the down button on the elevator. I needed to find a taxi and a phone store. I ignored the curious looks that all the overly dressed people in the fancy law office gave me. Fuck the people looking at my ink-stained hands and scuffed-up shoes.

I stepped out onto the cool autumn air, dragging my suitcase behind me, and held my arm up for a cab. I hadn't slept in an age, my clothes were wrinkled, and I smelled like an airplane, but I was going to a phone store come hell or high water.

Because if Richard wasn't the one threatening Harley, then some-one else was. And now I was too far away from her to do anything about it.

I caught the taxi to the phone store, waited in line for an hour-and-a-half, then finally bought a phone that I could download all my old stuff from the cloud. It had been way past time for me to call Harley. I needed to tell her my plan, she deserved that much. But she deserved to have all of the information.

I knew what I wanted to do, but it wasn't a decision I could make alone. I pulled up my contacts and dialed.

"You know," Ben growled in answering, "now that I know you're not dead in a street somewhere, I'm really fucking pissed at you."

I ran my hand over the back of my neck. "Not dead, but I'm sorry to make you worried, Mom."

A heavy weight hung on the line until I heard him chuckle. "Ass-hole."

"I know, man. I'm sorry."

"You ready to tell me what's going on?"

"I'm still figuring things out right now, but look, Harley isn't safe. I need you to look after her while I sort through this."

Ben cursed on the other end of the line. "Malcolm, are you into some shit that I need to know about? Because you're being really fucking shady right now."

I rubbed my hand back over my head. "I—gah—I had to sign some papers with my dad's company, and I think I'm gonna go see him. I think I need to do this."

A beat of silence hung on the line. "Have you been to see him since everything happened?"

"No."

"Well, if it's what you've gotta do, then I'd be a shit friend to tell you to do anything else."

"Thanks, man. Just look after Harley for me."

"I'll do my best, but I thought you guys were over?"

"What? No, we're not over. I'm gonna take care of this, and I'll fix everything with Harley."

"Oh. Well, good luck with that."

We hung up the phone, and I looked at the suitcase filled with clothes that needed washing and old newspapers that needed scanning.

But there was something I needed to do first.

It took an hour and fifty-two minutes to reach the prison that held my father. I waited at the table, drumming my fingers as I waited for my father to come in and sit down. The door buzzed and opened, and I took in my father for the first time in two years. His face was sallow and pale, especially against the orange jumpsuit that hung loose around his thinning frame. There were no handcuffs, he just walked in, gave a smile and a thank you to the guard, and sat down across from me.

"Hey, hey, it's the prodigal son!" My dad chuckled at his own joke as he leaned back in the chair. "Richard left a message with the prison that you signed the papers. Thank you, Malcolm, I appreciate that."

I stared at him, this man that had taught me how to hold a baseball bat, how to ride a bike, how to open a door for a girl. I stared at the man who worked with the mob, who put my mother at risk, who lied to me daily. And I nodded to him.

"Dad."

He waited a moment, appraising me. "You know, son, you've got every right to be angry with me. I did something wrong, and you called me out on it. You did what your mother and I always taught you to do. You made it right."

"I don't think you get to take credit for me putting you in prison, Dad."

He raised his hands. "I'm not taking credit, Malcolm. I fucked up. And I know that you might never forgive me for doing what I did. I get that. But you're my son, and I love you. And I know this might be the only time I see you until I get out of prison, but I do love you."

I cocked my head to the side. "I put you in prison, Dad. You should be furious with me."

My father leaned back and stroked his chin. "I was. I was for a long time. But the thing about being in here is that you have nothing but time. And time grants perspective. I'm not mad at you anymore, Malcolm. You did the right thing. You did something I don't know if I would have had the strength to do."

Tears pricked at the back of my eyes, and I fisted my hands to maintain control. I waited a minute to figure out how to say what I needed to. "I don't want you to think that because I signed those papers and you're getting your lawyers back that I'm okay with it."

He paused and appraised me. "So, why'd you do it?"

"Because your fucking lawyer was threatening someone close to me."

Dad went still. "Richard?"

"Yeah, Richard. He went after my girlfriend. He worked with her ex-boyfriend to try to get her business shut down, so I would come here and sign the papers."

His lips firmed and he folded his hands together on the table. "I'm sorry, son. I didn't know that."

I nodded to him. "Well, look, I know you're trying to get out of here, but you did some horrific shit. If they ask me to testify against you at your appeal, I'm going to say yes."

Dad looked at me and slowly nodded. "All right."

"You still not pissed at me?"

My dad laughed, an actual gut-wrenching laugh. "No, Malcolm. I'm not pissed at you. You're your own man. I am pissed at Richard though. He's crossing lines that shouldn't be crossed. Anyways, tell me about this girl."

I thought of Harley and a grin spread across my face.

"Oh, man," he said, taking in my expression. "You look like a man in love."

"I don't know about that," I said, and somehow the words tasted like sawdust in my mouth. I couldn't love Harley, could I? I had only known her a few weeks. But I had felt her against me. I felt the fear when she was in danger. I felt the joy in her laugher. I felt alive when I was with her. I felt...love.

"Ah, there it is," Dad said. I looked up in confusion. "That's the look I had when I realized your mom was it for me. This must be some girl."

"Yeah, she's...she's great, Dad. You'd like her, actually," I said grinning. "She puts ranch powder on popcorn."

"An innovator!"

"A savage," I corrected, laughing. "But yeah, she's amazing. She's funny and warm, and she started her own business from the ground up. Like, she literally renovated her bed and breakfast with her own two hands."

"Your mom like her?"

"Yeah, she does. They get along great." I smiled, talking to my old man like this. It was like before. Before he became a criminal. I sighed, my smile falling away.

"Well, I should go," I said, nodding toward the door. Dad gave me a weak smile.

"Yeah, all right. But um, you know, if you happen to be in the area, I'd love to see you again. Hear more about your life."

I nodded. "Yeah, we'll see."

I stood and walked to the guard at the prison door. The door buzzed, and I went through. I turned to see my dad walking in his orange jumpsuit, his hair thinning a bit in the back, toward the prison that would probably hold him for the next few years.

When I collected my personal effects from the prison on my way out, I looked at my new phone that showed a missed call and voicemail from Harley.

As I got in my rental car, I listened to the voicemail. I smiled as Harley's voice rang out until I noticed how detached and tired it sounded.

"Um, hey Malcolm, it's Harley. I know you left, and you didn't call or answer, so I'm taking the hint that you're done with us. And that's fine, you know? We'll just call it a clean break, right? But just so you know, you really didn't need to sneak out in the middle of the night. If you would've told me you wanted out, I wouldn't have fought you. I knew the score. Two weeks, right?" I heard Harley sniffle on the recording and my heart felt like it was getting ripped out of my chest. She read it all wrong. I wanted her, I wanted us. "But I just wanted to call because even if you're okay with leaving without saying goodbye, I'm not. So, goodbye I guess."

I sank into the driver's seat clutching my phone. This wasn't how this was supposed to happen. I was leaving to save her. I didn't want someone coming after her.

But she was saying goodbye.

I tried calling her the entire drive back to the city. She never answered.

Pulling up to my apartment, I was met with the sight of my best friend, disheveled and tired on my front steps.

"Ben? How the hell did you get here so fast?"

Ben rolled his eyes. "It's like a four-hour drive. You fucking rich people always want to fly in goddamn airplanes." I wasn't going to point out that Ben was rich now, too.

"But what are you doing here? I thought you were gonna keep an eye on Harley."

"Cameron and Davis are with her, and they're keeping an eye on her. You just saw your dad for the first time in two years. I figured you needed me more right now."

I nodded and unlocked my front door and waved him inside.

Ben moved the stack of newspapers that Sullivan lent me from the couch to the coffee table.

"Have you scanned these in yet?"

I shook my head. "Not yet, I've been studying them. I feel like I'm missing something important." I pulled two bottles of beer out of the fridge. "I haven't gone grocery shopping, so this is all I have."

Ben shrugged. "It's all I need."

"How is Harley?" I asked hesitantly, as he took a swig.

"Fucking crushed, how do you think she is?" Ben asked, his eyebrows furrowed.

"Just gonna rip off the bandaid, huh?"

Ben shrugged. "I'm here for you because I know you're dealing with a lot. But if you ask me about Harley, I'm not going to let you off the hook because of your daddy issues. She's a nice girl, and you broke her heart."

"I didn't mean to break her heart, Ben! I was trying to fix everything, and everything went fucking sideways and now she won't take my calls."

Ben slammed his beer on the table and leaned forward. "Malcolm, look at me. Like really, really look at me. Do you love this girl? Because if you love Harley, and you're willing to do whatever it takes to be with her, then I'll do everything I can to help you. Because, fuck man, after everything you've been through, you deserve to be happy. But if you can't look me in the eyes and tell me you love Harley, you need to walk the fuck away from her. Because she deserves to be happy too."

"I love her, Ben," I said honestly. "She's it for me."

Ben nodded and picked up his beer again. "Then let's get to work."

Chapter Forty-Three

Halloween Special

Harley

It always amazed me how time worked. We're able to count the seconds, the minutes, the hours, but the counting of time never matches the way it feels. I could count the five days since Malcolm left. Almost a week since the opening of the Haunted Trail, since someone came after me in the woods, since Malcolm disappeared. Davis said he was in New York figuring out his life, signing papers, making changes. It felt like an eternity and the blink of an eye all at once. I could count the seven hours lying awake at night in the bed we had shared, but it felt like a year-long prison sentence. And during the daytime when I was surrounded by people, I pretended time and I were acquaintances who passed by each other with a friendly nod.

It was Halloween now, and the phones had been ringing almost non-stop since the first episode of *Spirits, Seekers, and Skeptics* Halloween Special had aired the day before. The second and last episode was set to air that day. Our online booking system was filling up faster than we could track, and I was already putting in ads to hire more help. Maggie sat behind the desk, doing her best to maintain her patience as yet another person asked if the body in the basement was, in fact, real.

"Harley, we need to update the website to include frequently asked questions. If I have to answer another of these questions about if people can expect to experience ghosts here, I might just scream."

The bell above the door jingled and we looked to find Dad and Miranda walking in, leading Gus the goose, wearing his indoor diaper, by a harness and leash.

I looked up at Dad and down at the goose again. "Happy Halloween. Is this a trick or a treat?"

"A treat, of course," Dad said. "Maggie said you could watch Gus for a few days."

I turned to Maggie. "She did, did she?"

Maggie mimed at the phone and turned back.

"Coward," I whispered. Then I turned to my dad. "Why do you need me to watch Gus?"

"Well, I'm getting a procedure done, and if something were to happen to me, I need to know that Gus is safe." My eyes started to get wide before Miranda cut in.

"For heaven's sake, Charlie, it's a colonoscopy, not open-heart surgery. You're gonna be fine," Miranda huffed. "Honestly, the way he goes on about it, you'd swear he was gonna start casket shopping."

"What happened around here?" Dad asked, nodding to the phones still ringing.

"The, uh, first episode of the ghost hunting channel thing went live yesterday. The one with the body in the basement."

Dad grunted, his frown almost hidden by his mustache. He slipped a toothpick from his pocket and wedged it in his mouth. "Well, if you'll excuse me, I need to spend some time with my goose before we say our goodbyes."

Miranda rolled her eyes. "The man gets told he has to have his ass checked and suddenly he's writing his own eulogy." I watched as Dad led Gus toward the living room, the goose's bedazzled diaper waddling behind him. Today it had a bright orange pumpkin on it. Miranda clucked as she watched them go. "You'll have to forgive your father. He might not act like it, but he's pretty torn up that Malcolm is gone."

My eyebrows raised. "What? But Dad sicced Gus on Malcolm! He didn't like him."

Miranda shrugged. "Maybe. But he liked the two of you together."

I felt my heart take root in my feet. "Well, I'm sorry to disappoint."

"Ah, Harley girl, you didn't disappoint your dad." She nudged my shoulder with hers. "Have you seen their video yet?"

I brushed away a stray tear that threatened to pour down. "Nope. And if I do, it won't be for a long time. Still too fresh, you know?"

Miranda nodded and put an arm around my shoulders. "I'm sorry, kiddo."

We both watched as my father nuzzled his goose with the affection of a new father. My father sniffed and gave Gus one more kiss on his bobbing head.

"Harley, I'm gonna have two officers checking on the Haunted Trail tonight. I'd have more, but it's Halloween and we're always short officers for the antics this town gets up to. But you'll have Gus to keep an eye on things."

"Thank you, Dad," I said, resisting the eye roll I felt coming on.

"Is the rest of that ghost hunting crew still here?" he asked, peeking around the corner.

"Yeah, they're helping me out tonight for the final night to make sure it's safe for me. They're heading out before the end of the night though. They have some filming to do in Connecticut."

Dad nodded. "You gonna be okay?"

I nodded and swallowed. "Yeah, Dad, I'm gonna be fine."

"Okay," he looked to Maggie and nodded in my direction. She gave a not-so-subtle thumbs up back to him, and I allowed the eyeroll.

After they left, I took Gus for a walk around the edge of the inn, watching as he pecked at the grass. "It's just you and me, Gus."

Gus whipped his head toward me and honked, then waddled in the other direction.

"Rude," I muttered.

My phone rang in my pocket, and I pulled it out to see Malcolm's name on the screen. I sighed and put it away again. I wasn't sure what to say to him. He left without a word, just like he promised he wouldn't do. If I talked to him, I knew I would barter heaven and earth to be with him just a little longer. At least saying goodbye now leaves me with our memories pleasant, at least until the end. I had the inn; he had his newspaper in New York. Neither one of those facts was going to change. My phone stopped ringing, and I urged Gus inside.

Night fell on the final night of the Haunted Trail. The *Spirits* crew manned their roles in the Haunted Trail while I ran the ticket booth. Cameron had taken over Malcolm's role as the crazed doctor and Davis became a scarecrow in Ben's place. Penny and Avery stepped in to help with the concession stand for the past week. In the time that we ran the Haunted Trail, nearly everyone in the town had come out at least once and we had made enough money to buy the materials and begin renovations on the carriage house. The problem was that I couldn't look at the carriage house without thinking of Malcolm.

The hours of the Haunted Trail crept by in a blur. I smiled and thanked every patron right up until we closed. As we gathered the money at the close of the trail and counted it up, Avery and Penny waved goodbye and the members of the *Spirits* crew, minus Ben and Malcolm cast hesitant glances at me.

After we counted the money, it was time for our goodbyes. I walked out to the van as they were loading their bags in the back. This is where

I would've said goodbye to Malcolm if he would have stayed. In a way, it was good that he wasn't here. I got to spend time with Darla and Zoey and the guys, giving them the goodbyes that they had earned by sticking around.

My phone rang again with Malcolm's name on my screen. I shook my head and shoved it back into my pocket.

"Is it Malcolm again?" Zoey asked, her teal hair looking more green in the dim light as she put her purse in the back seat. I nodded. "Maybe you should just talk to him. Get some closure, you know?"

I sighed and ran my hands over my face. "I don't know Zoey. He broke it off."

"Did he actually, though?" Zoey asked. "Did he tell you it was over?"

"He just left. Then he avoided me and only returned my calls after I said goodbye. He just made the decision to buy the newspaper in another state. I don't know if I want his excuses or his explanations. I don't know if I'm mad or confused or hurt or all three. I don't even know if I have the right to be upset." Zoey nodded in understanding.

"Well, what do you want?" she asked calmly.

What did I want? That was a good question. I wanted Malcolm to have never left. I wanted him to mean what he said when he told me he would stay. I wanted myself not to be so broken. I wanted to get past the heartbreak part of this.

"I want a clean break," I said finally. "I think a broken heart is like a broken bone. It takes time to heal but a clean break heals faster. And that's all I want. To heal."

Zoey nodded in understanding and put her suitcase in the back of the van. "Well, you know I'm here if you ever need to talk. You have my number. And even though I've known Malcolm for years, I'm still here for you."

"Thanks, Zo." We hugged and she climbed into the van. Darla came up to me next.

"Zoey's right, you know. You have us. Even when we're traveling, we're still just a phone call away. And we don't ever travel far." Darla shrugged a bit, uncomfortable with bearing any kind of feelings, and then gave me a quick hug. "Keep in touch, kid."

Davis sauntered over to the van, his eyes darting between me and the texts coming through on his phone, probably from Malcolm.

Davis wiped a hand over his face and groaned. "Harley, look it's not my place to be saying anything, and I can't tell you what's going through his mind. But I know he's not..."

I watched him struggle with his words impatiently. "He's not what, Davis?"

"He's not like me," he said quietly. "He's not the love 'em and leave 'em type. You mean something to him. And I don't pretend to know what's going on with the two of you, but I can't stand you thinking that you were just some out-of-town fling to him. That's not Malcolm. This is the first time in a long time that I've seen him happy, and I'd bet money that you'd had a lot to do with that."

I tried to swallow my feelings, but they tasted bitter in my mouth. When I finally spoke, it barely came out as a whisper. "Then why did he leave without saying goodbye?"

Davis wrapped an arm around my shoulders and pulled me close. "I don't know, Harley. I just know my friend, and I want you to keep an open mind about him until you figure it out."

I tried to find comfort in being held by this handsome man, but all I could think was that he didn't smell like Malcolm. All I wanted in that moment was the smell of pen ink and old paper. I wanted Malcolm, but he was gone, and he took my heart with him.

Cameron hugged me with tears in his eyes, his large, tattooed arms wrapping around me as he sniffled. "We're gonna come back and visit, okay?"

I nodded as I hugged back the burly teddy bear of a man. "You better. And when you do, bring some of your mom's bread. It's fucking delicious."

Cameron laughed and hopped in the van. As they pulled out of the driveway, Davis honked the horn in goodbye. I turned toward my inn that was once again empty, probably for the last night for a long time. Maggie took reservations until we had to turn the phone lines off. Then she headed out after checking for the fifth time that I was fine on my own.

Starting the following night, we were booked solid for almost seven months after the video had launched for Halloween, so I was determined to enjoy the time I had alone. I left Gus in the laundry room with a couple of the toys Dad left for him and headed to bed.

I pulled on my fluffy pajamas and cuddled into my blankets. The pillow that Malcolm had used was shoved in the back of my closet so I wouldn't have to smell him when I fell asleep anymore. I stared at my laptop for a moment before finally succumbing to my curiosity. Maybe it was because I was alone for the first time since he left. Maybe it was because I wanted to see the video that brought the customers flocking to my inn after a long monetary drought. Maybe I just missed him. But I turned on my computer and I opened the first episode of the Halloween special.

Tears filled my eyes when I saw him on the screen, peeking around corners in the basement. Then I watched as Ben called me downstairs and Cameron zeroed in on Malcolm's face as I walked into the room. He smiled. Even in the darkness of the shot, I could see his million-dollar smile come to life as he looked at me. I shut my laptop and tried hopelessly to fall asleep without thinking of him.

I woke in the middle of the night to the sound of my father's fucking goose honking. Growling, I pulled the covers off my legs, slipped on my slippers, and walked downstairs. Gus was hissing and shrieking, banging against the laundry room door. As I reached my hand to turn the knob on the door, I heard a sound behind me, coming from the basement. Freezing in place, I spun slowly toward the basement door.

I had a list of excuses in my mind explaining the hairs that were rising on my arms. I had watched the video where we found the corpse in the secret room of the basement before I fell asleep. Gus was panicking because he was in an unfamiliar place. But as I listened intently, I heard the sound of the false wall scraping against the wall.

Someone was in the basement.

I tried to reason with myself that the ghost hunting videos had gone live and a ton of people had seen them. Zoey had mentioned something about it trending. It was probably some local who saw the video and wanted to record something for their friends. I just had to calmly, but firmly, let them know that their being there was inappropriate.

I could call the police, but Dad already said that with Halloween they were short-staffed and the officers from the Haunted Trail had left hours ago. Maybe I could bring a weapon. I gently pushed open the door to the kitchen and grabbed the broom leaning up against the back of the door. It wasn't sharp, but it would have to do.

Gus was still shrieking in the laundry room, and I hoped that the noise from that would cover the sound of my footsteps on the basement stairs. The light wasn't on in the basement, but there was a soft glow of light from down below. I lowered my feet down onto the stairs one at a time, holding the broom behind my shoulder like a baseball bat until I reached the bottom.

As the basement came into view, I saw an old camping lantern on the floor that was casting light and shadows off the leftover artifacts in the basement, and I was reminded of all the scary movies where I yelled at the dumb woman going into a bad situation with a shitty weapon. I pulled my eyes to the false door, now open halfway, and I tightened my hands on the broom. Just as I was about to jump at the intruder in the hidden distillery room, a hand pushed at my back and the scream barely made it out of my mouth before I was draped in darkness as the door was pulled shut behind me.

Chapter Forty-Four

Headlines

Malcolm

The highway signs were getting closer and closer to the Columbia exit which would take us back to the town of Burnt Creek. Back to pumpkin-spiced lattes and autumn-themed shops. Back to Harley.

I was driving the van as Ben sat shotgun watching our latest episode that had just aired. We had a backlog of episodes that we would post after this weekend that had already been edited, but when Ben got the email from Maggie saying she needed help, Ben insisted we would use this for the Halloween episodes, despite the fast turnaround. Who would have known that only a handful of weeks ago I would have driven right by here without ever thinking of Harley?

"Have you talked to Maggie?" I asked Ben for the fifth time. Ben pressed extra hard on the pause button as he looked at me.

"Jesus, Malcolm. No, I have not talked to Maggie in the last ten minutes. She said that Harley would be fine tonight, that whoever was messing with her was probably trying to get our crew out of town."

I shook my head. "Something doesn't feel right, Ben."

"Well, royally fucking up a girl's heart will do that to you."

"I'm making it right," I insisted. Ben rolled his eyes and pressed play again.

Darla's voice crooned over my speakers as she recited the script Ben had sent her.

"Jimmy Carpenter, Bob Walker, and Peter Grant would later be known by the town as 'The Railroad Boys' after they conned the town out of over a hundred thousand dollars to build a fake railroad. The town documented the arrival of these conmen and praised their efforts to bring Burnt Creek into the 20th century."

Out of the corner of my eye, I could see the newspapers I scanned overlapping and moving across the screen as headlines from the paper were highlighted on a different graphic.

The mile marker sign reflected my headlights as I cruised down the dark highway.

Cameron's voice, one seldom ever heard on the channel, was used to read off newspaper grabs and other media texts.

"Locals help front new town expenditure!" Cameron's voice read. *"New investors to revitalize the town!"*

"Stop the video!" I said, quickly wheeling two lanes over to get off at the closest exit. A horn blared behind me as Ben yelled curse words my way.

"What the fuck, man?" he yelled, grabbing the handle on the door.

My headlights cut across the guard rails as I spun the wheel toward a gas station just off the exit. "Rewind that!" I yelled. "What did those headlines say?"

Ben must have seen the crazed look in my eye as I threw the van in park at the side of the gas station and leaned over to see the video on Ben's phone. The newspaper graphic once again ran across the screen as Cameron's voice overlayed the text.

"Locals help front new town expenditure! New investors to revitalize the town!"

"Fuck!" I yelled, yanking my seatbelt off and wrenching open the door. I had read those articles a hundred times, but this was the first time it was read aloud. I had heard those words before.

"Malcolm, what the hell is going on?" Ben shouted to me.

"Stay in the van!" I yelled back, running around the hood of the van and opening the sliding door. My suitcases had fallen over at some point during the drive, likely when I had spun the van off the exit, and I quickly grabbed one and unzipped it. Clothes went flying everywhere and I pushed that one aside and reached for the other one. "Come on," I muttered to myself. "Who's the fucking writer?"

"What writer?"

"I need to know who wrote those articles in the paper!" I said, unzipping another suitcase and flipping open the lid. The small stack of old newspapers was right on top, and I pulled them toward me, ignoring the care I normally gave to old papers, and ripped them to the articles about the railroad boys. The headline Cameron had read was staring back at me and I scanned underneath until I found the name. I cursed again as I backed out of the van and slammed the door shut.

Running back around the front of the van, I got in the driver's seat and grabbed my phone. I called Harley's phone number again as I threw the van in drive.

When she didn't answer, I stepped on the gas harder. "Ben, call Maggie."

Ben quickly pulled up Maggie's number and called, putting it on speakerphone. She picked up on the second ring.

"Ben? What's going on? It's the middle of the—"

"Maggie," I yelled across the console. "You need to go get your dad."

"Malcolm?" she said, her voice still groggy. "He's probably asleep."

"Wake him up. I know who's after Harley."

Chapter Forty-Five

Dating Advice

Harley

I felt along the dark wall in front of me as I tried to catch my bearings. Pressing my palms against the wood on the walls, I lifted myself up off the floor and felt around the space. The table with the old still for making alcohol on it was on my left and my hip slammed against it as I stood.

"Ow! Fuck!" My words reverberated off the walls surrounding me, and I spun around toward the closed door. I felt forward in the darkness until my hand connected with the false wall. I leaned my weight against the door trying to push it open, but something was in the way. "Hey!" I called. I banged my hands on the wooden wall. "Hello!"

A muffled thump sounded on the other side of the wall and a man's voice grumbled.

"I can hear you out there!" I yelled. "You realize a dead body used to be in here? It's really creepy!"

I heard the man shuffle toward the stairs before shuffling back. I held my breath as his footsteps rounded back in my direction. "I tried to tell you to leave." Ice ran through my veins. His voice was gravelly, familiar somehow, but I couldn't place it. This wasn't some local kid.

"Well, I'd love to leave now," I replied through the door. I pushed again trying to dislodge the door. "Look, just let me out of here, and we can talk about this." I waited a moment. "Please?"

The footsteps stopped moving for a moment, and I searched in the dark for my broom handle. I found it laying on the ground, and I quietly moved it to the baseball bat position. I wasn't sure who the man was that broke into my inn, but he had already thrown me into a creepy basement room and locked me in. I wasn't about to trust him.

But then I realized that he wasn't stopping because of something that I had said, he had stopped because he heard something else. A muffled voice called down the basement stairs.

"Oh, hell," the man's voice said. "What are you doing here?"

I heard the scraping sound as whatever he put in front of the false wall to keep me in was moved. I braced my free hand on the door and pushed, just as there was a push on the other side. I stumbled forward a bit, bracing myself as another body was thrown against me.

"Ooph!" A large breath of air exited as the body fell on top of me. The hidden door closed again, and I again heard the sound of a piece of furniture being moved in front of it.

"Oops, sorry about that, dear," the person on top of me said. I shuffled around in the dark, my hair getting swallowed up in her large hair.

"Ms. O'Neil?" I asked.

"Oh, please, just Dorothy is fine. No need for such formalities in a situation like this. Do you think we'll be in here long?"

"Dorothy, what the hell are you doing here?"

"Language!" Dorothy chastised. "And what am I doing here?" she asked, haughtily climbing off me. "I think the better question is what is Sullivan Schneider doing here?"

"Dorothy, I've heard you curse a million times," I protested.

"I'm as old as dirt," Dorothy sniffed. "Therefore, I've earned my dirty words."

"Wait, did you say Sullivan?" I asked, then leapt to my feet without waiting for her to answer. "Sullivan Schneider, you open this door right now!"

I heard his footsteps start to climb the stairs.

"I think he's leaving," Dorothy said with a sigh.

"How did you know I was in trouble?" I asked, still struggling to make her out in the dark.

"The spirits told me," she said wistfully.

"Did the spirits use a vessel?" I asked, rubbing my temple. Surely, Dorothy O'Neil could not be the only person who was looking for me. I could not imagine many people I would not want to be stuck in a room alone in the dark with, but Dorothy was definitely on that list.

"Well, it's possible the spirits connected with me through an intermediary."

"Who?"

"Your boyfriend," she said. "Speaking of boyfriends, Sullivan," she called out through the door. "There are better ways to obtain affection from a woman!" I felt her lean in closer to me. "We used to date," she confided.

A noise came from the other side of the door as Sullivan shifted other pieces of furniture. "How did you even know it was me?" he called. "I dyed my hair!"

"You dummy!" Dorothy called out. "You know you're one of the only men in town who used to have red hair. You should've dyed it black if you didn't want me to recognize you!"

"Dorothy, focus," I said sharply. "Do you have a phone on you?"

I heard a rustling, and a blinding light illuminated the space. I grabbed it from her hand and searched for a signal. I pulled up the text message stream between her and her sisters.

"I can explain that," she said. I rolled my eyes and quickly typed out a text and hit send.

"Okay, hopefully if the phone can pick up a signal in here, it'll send the text." I pulled up the flashlight and waved it around the space. A piece of yellow police tape draped down from the wall.

"The spirits are telling me something!" Dorothy said. "A crime took place in here!"

I slowly pulled the light from the police tape to Dorothy. "You don't say."

She nodded vigorously as we heard Sullivan shuffle back downstairs.

"Sullivan," I yelled out the door. "If I die in here, I'm haunting you so fucking hard!"

"She'll do it, too," Dorothy called. "Her boyfriend is an expert on hauntings."

"He's not my boyfriend," I mumbled.

"Oh, dear, did something happen?" Dorothy asked, sitting cross-legged on the floor like this was a day at a yoga retreat. I glanced in the light of her phone around me. I didn't really want to talk about it, but it's not like there was anything else to do.

"He left, about a week ago," I said.

Dorothy waved her hand dismissively. "I know that, I meant what *else* happened?"

"What do you mean? He left, he's gone. There's nothing else that's going to happen."

"Well, that's stupid," she huffed. "He didn't call or anything?"

"I mean, yeah, he called," I shrugged, leaning against the wall. "But I didn't really want to hear his excuses, ya know?"

"You dummy!" Dorothy said, swatting at my leg. That old lady could really swing. "He was really handsome!"

From the other side of the wall, I could hear Sullivan pause his shuffling. "He did really seem to like you," he called.

"Yeah, thanks, Sullivan," I called and rolled my eyes.

"You're welcome," he called back. Then I could hear him shuffling through the stuff again.

"So why don't you give him a call when we get out of here?" Dorothy asked. "You could invite him over for some necking."

Sullivan called back through the door. "Dorothy knows how to neck real good, Harley. She knows what she's talking about."

Dorothy primped her hair in the light. "I'm still not going on a date with you, Sullivan Schneider." She leaned in closer to me with a wink. "I might, actually. I'm just playing hard to get."

"Dorothy, he locked us in a room in a basement. He might try to kill us."

Dorothy shrugged. "When you get to be my age, dear, you let a lot of things pass inspection."

Chapter Forty-Six

A Deal with the Devil

Malcolm

I called Darla as I nervously drummed my fingers on the steering wheel. She answered on the third ring. "I'm not talking to you out of female solidarity and shit."

"Darla, please, I think Harley's in danger."

"I'm putting you on speaker." I heard the phone click and the sound of the van rumbling down the road filled my ears. "Okay, speak."

"I need you to go back to the inn. Sullivan Schneider is the one threatening Harley. He runs the flower shop."

"I'm turning around!" Davis called from the driver's seat. "And I'm not going to ask why you didn't call me instead of my sister!"

"I appreciate that," I said, rolling my eyes. "I'll be there soon, we're on our way there."

"Wait," Zoey said, pulling the phone away from Darla. "Why do you think Harley's in danger now?"

"Our video that just came out. It points to the railroad boys and the missing money. Sullivan worked at the newspaper and wrote the articles that pushed the locals to invest in the railroad. He was the one who dressed their scam up in fancy words. I thought my lawyer was the one fucking with Harley, but it was Sullivan. Sullivan was the fourth member of the railroad boys and he's been looking for the missing money."

Ben looked at me with his eyes wide. "So when we put out the video tonight—"

"We alerted everyone about the missing money and put Sullivan on a timeline. He had already been waiting for us to leave. We painted a target on Harley's back."

I heard a curse come from someone on the other side of the phone. Darla grabbed the phone back. "He must have been the one to shoot the other three. He was the one who buried them."

I gripped the steering wheel. "Zoey, I need you to call Harley. She's not answering me, but maybe she'll answer you."

We all waited with bated breath as Zoey tried over and over again to call Harley. "Malcolm, she's not answering."

It took another ten minutes of driving way too fast to arrive at the inn. As I pulled in, I turned the headlights off so I didn't alert anyone to our presence. If Harley wasn't in trouble, she probably would think I was some random man in there to murder her, but I supposed it was better I was the one scaring her rather than an actual murderer. As I opened the door, I pointed for Ben to check upstairs as I checked the main level. I nearly jumped out of my skin when I heard vicious honking from behind the laundry room door.

Of course, the fucking goose was here.

It was a smart move on the chief's part. I wasn't there to protect her anymore; she should at least have a police guard goose on the premises. The door rattled from Gus pushing against the door and he hissed.

Just as I regained my bearings and was walking toward the kitchen to check for intruders, a noise came from the basement. It was Harley, yelling. But she was yelling *at* someone. I looked at the laundry room door and cursed my luck.

I had no weapons, no time, and no idea what I was walking into. But I knew what I had to do.

Quietly opening the basement door, I peeked inside to try to get a visual. I heard voices going back and forth and I took the opportunity for the element of surprise.

Grabbing the laundry room door, I turned the handle and waited until I locked eyes with my nemesis. Gus's angry red eye zeroed in on me and I held my hands up slowly in surrender. If there was ever a moment I needed to work with the devil, this was it. Gus cocked his neck in my direction before hearing the noise in the basement. I slowly retreated out of the way and let Gus do what he was trained to do.

Gus waddled quickly toward the stairs, his diaper sparkled in the dim light like a homing beacon as he spread his wings out wide. Shrieking a battle cry that could rival a gladiator, Gus floated down the stairs like Pegasus. I followed behind him as he screeched his war cry that reverberated off the basement walls, startling a very confused Sullivan Schneider who now had flaming red hair. Sullivan raised his hands and backed away from Gus, who rapidly flew at the old man and without hesitation, took his razor-sharp monster beak and clamped it around Sullivan's privates.

As Sullivan howled in pain, the door to the secret room that was blocked by an old wooden chair was collectively pushed open by Harley and a red-faced Dorothy O'Neil, who was holding a broom like a baseball bat.

Relief coursed through me at seeing Harley safe and sound. I would ask what Dorothy was doing there later. Harley looked around the room, seeing Sullivan in a losing battle against Gus until her eyes found me. Tears started falling down her cheeks.

"You sweeping up a mess?" I asked, nodding toward the broom. Harley smirked through the tears on her face.

"You starting a petting zoo?"

Gus, who still had not let go of Sullivan's dick, was honking loudly as Ben and the other two O'Neil sisters thundered down the stairs. Holding a butcher's knife and frying pan, much more sensible weapons than the broom and mascot that Harley and I had grabbed, Ben rounded the corner and cursed. The chaos in the room grew once more as the other two O'Neil sisters barreled behind him and shoved him out of the way.

"Unhand our sister, Sullivan!" Mabel cried as she held her phone in front of her. "The spirits taught me how to live-stream and the whole town is watching!"

From my spot behind Mabel, I could see the camera app on her phone open and not even running. I ran a hand over my face. I wasn't gonna be the one to tell her.

"Aw, man," Ben complained, watching Sullivan finally remove the goose from his genitals and curl up in the fetal position on the floor. "I missed all the fucking fun."

"Language!" Dorothy corrected.

Ben sat the weapons down and turned the old lady. "Sorry, Ms. O'Neil."

Ignoring the O'Neil sisters, I walked hesitantly to Harley who was standing at the wall outside the false room and waited until I knew she wouldn't push me away. Her hands were shaking at her sides, and she leaned against the wall. Extending my arm out until I touched her, I pulled her into me until she was flush against my chest and held her. She stood stiffly for a moment, sniffling with her fists at her side until she slowly melted into my arms, and I finally allowed myself to take a breath. "I was so fucking scared I lost you, Harley."

Her arms wrapped around me, and I kissed the top of her head. Despite the goose and the murderer and the trio of old ladies, I knew tonight I was going to actually sleep because my girl was in my arms again.

The basement stairs thundered again as the police moved down, led by Chief Charlie in a pair of pajama pants with geese on them, shouting orders to put our hands up. Someone scooped Sullivan off the floor and handcuffed him. Another officer gently led Gus outside so he could be checked out by an emergency vet. The rest of us were brought to the main floor to be questioned while techs went over the scene in the basement.

I kept my hand on Harley's back the whole time. I needed to feel her, to know she was safe. I never wanted to feel her absence again. I had almost lost her, and it would have been all my fault.

An officer asked Harley to be checked out by an EMT for injuries, and despite Harley's protests that she was fine, she went willingly. Dorothy was already there explaining to an EMT that was wrapping a blood pressure cuff around her arm that Sullivan cooked up this elaborate scheme as a way to ask her out on a date. Sullivan was checked out by a separate EMT across the way, and he moaned as an ice pack was put on his chewed-up dick.

"It never would've worked between us anyway, Sully," Dorothy called across the way. Sullivan groaned louder.

The yard had been taped off by officers to keep the public back because once the O'Neil sisters had gotten the text Harley had sent when they were locked in the still room, the whole town pretty much knew what was going on. I heard some commotion at the tape line and saw Oliver, hands on his hips, as he talked with someone.

"Darla, I can't let you through, it's a crime scene."

"Move it, Dudley Do-Right!" I heard Darla say before dipping under the police tape and marching over to Harley. Oliver started after her, but the chief waved his hand.

"She's all right, Oliver."

Oliver looked at me, with a bewildered look on his face. I shrugged. "Darla's a powerhouse when it comes to people she cares about."

Oliver shook his head and grumbled to himself as he turned back to man the perimeter, "Dudley Do-Right? I'm not even Canadian."

Ben and I were pulled away by another officer who asked us questions for an hour and asked for the newspapers that led us to the understanding that it was Sullivan who was after Harley. When I walked back to where Harley had been, my stomach sank. Maggie was there. The Chief was there. But Harley was gone.

"Where is Harley?"

Harley's dad and sister looked at me, eyes hard, and the chief folded his arms on his chest and stuck a toothpick in his mouth. "She's gone."

"Gone?"

Maggie huffed at her dad. "She's visiting a relative while all this blows over. I'm taking over the inn while she's gone."

My heart sank in my chest. She didn't even say goodbye. "Do you know when she'll be back?"

Maggie narrowed her eyes at me. "She didn't know when you'd be back, now did she?"

My mind started whirling. I thought I lost her once, and I was not going to lose her again. I ran my hand over the back of my neck and racked my brain for what I could do to show her that I was here. That she was it for me. I turned to study the inn, the inn that she had lovingly restored from the ground up. Then I looked past it at the run-down carriage house, and my lips slowly grew into a grin.

I had a porch swing to put up.

Chapter Forty-Seven

Five Days Later

Harley

This month's historical society meeting was taking place in Miranda's kitchen. According to Maggie, the meeting room at the inn was filling up quickly with slots, so we would have to make sure to reserve it for the historical society meeting every four months, and the complaint about the rats mysteriously disappeared. I wasn't sure what Brandon had done to make Joanna and Connor back off from trying to sabotage my inn, but Oliver assured me it was mostly above board.

I hadn't been back to the inn since Sullivan locked me in the room, and I was equal parts excited and terrified to go back. Maggie had been my rock for the past five days as I hid from the world at Brandon's house. She ran the inn, trained the new hires, and somehow managed to keep me in the loop. I was already working on the paperwork to promote her to general manager, especially now that I could afford to give her the well-deserved pay raise.

Maggie was going to man the front desk along with her new trainee that started that day while I was at the historical society meeting. The *Spirits, Seekers, and Skeptics* Halloween two-episode special was still drumming up business for the inn and the phones have been ringing off the hook for reservations. We had to hire a new maid, a new front desk receptionist, and a part-time breakfast cook to keep up with the pending demand.

I had finally gotten everything I wanted. And I was fucking miserable.

"Earth to Harley," Penny said, waving her hand in front of my face. I jolted out of my stupor.

"Sorry," I said. "Been a bit out of it lately."

The three women clucked sympathetically, and Miranda topped off my wine glass. In a rare show of solidarity, Mabel even put her phone down.

"Honey, I think you're more than just out of it," Miranda said, patting my hand.

"What do you mean?" I asked.

"You're obviously heartbroken over the hunky ghosthunter guy," Mabel said knowingly.

I shook my head. "I don't want to think about it. Can we get to the first order of business? I've got breakfast I need to prep back at the inn."

"Your first day back?" Miranda asked.

I nodded, not really wanting to talk about it. I wasn't sure that I really wanted to go back, and not even because of the red-haired geriatric murderer who locked me in my basement. I didn't want to go back because all it reminded me of was Malcolm. My inn was tainted with memories of him. He was probably back in New York in a fancy office, rubbing at the back of his neck while he dealt with editor-in-chiefs and had meetings with advertising executives.

"Well," Penny said, a wary glance over my shoulder. "We have two new businesses opening here soon, and the owners have mentioned wanting to get more involved in the historical society."

I nodded. "That's...great. What business?"

"A newspaper," a deep voice behind me said. I froze in my seat. I knew that voice. That voice whispered dirty thoughts in my ear at night and sang terribly to the radio. I turned around slowly as Malcolm came into the room, Ben and Maggie standing in the doorway behind him.

Malcolm's hair was disheveled, and his shirt was wrinkled, but his eyes held a steadiness that I hadn't seen there before. He moved so he stood in front of me. "Malcolm?" I said, unable to reason with what I was seeing.

"I think there may have been some miscommunication," he said, getting on his knees in front of my chair. "So, please allow me to clear some things up." He took my hand in his, and every wall I had built started to crumble away. "Harley, the way I handled things was stupid. I was never going to buy the newspaper in New York. I was buying the newspaper *here*."

"Here? You're...you're moving here?" I asked breathlessly.

Malcolm suddenly looked nervous. "Yeah, that's the plan. I sold my apartment."

"Is that what you were doing in New York?" I asked, feeling stupid for ignoring his calls.

He wobbled his head back and forth. "Well, that, and I was there to sell my part of my father's newspaper. I thought Richard was the one after you. I wanted to get him as far away from you, as far away from us, as possible. I thought if I sold the newspaper he'd never have a reason to come back. I sold everything there because I want a life here, with you." Malcolm rubbed the back of his head before anxiously spilling the next words out. "I know I should've talked to you about this first, to make sure we were on the same page because I know we haven't known each other long but I'm so crazy about you, it's insane. I didn't think I could fall so fast for someone, but Harley, you're it for me. I love you. And I want to be here, helping you with the inn, doing your bidding, you putting me to work, for the rest of my days."

I hiccupped and suddenly realized tears were streaming down my face. Malcolm ran his hand over the back of his neck again. "Is that...is that something you want too?" he asked nervously.

I hiccupped again and nodded. "Hell yes. And I love you, too." I said, and went to wrap my arms around him, but drew back. "Wait, what does that mean for the *Spirits* channel?"

Malcolm looked back at Ben, and Maggie looked up at him from where she was standing. Ben cleared his throat. "Well, I'm actually the other business settling down here. I'm starting up a *Spirits, Seekers, and Skeptics* ghost tour here in Burnt Creek. If all goes well, we'll probably expand up the East coast."

"So," Maggie said, her eyes wide. "So, you're moving here too?"

He smiled at her nervously and nodded. "Yeah, can't let my best friend run wild. Someone's gotta reign him in." Malcolm chuckled and reached up to wipe more tears away from my cheeks.

My head swiveled to Maggie. "Wait, who's manning the front desk?"

Maggie grinned. "Our new hire. She's picking it up like a champ. But I told her we'd be back soon because Malcolm has to show you what he's been working on while you've been gone."

I turned to look back at Malcolm, a bashful grin covering his face. "You've been here this whole time?" I asked, a hiccup racking my torso again. I was so overwhelmed, my heart felt like it would burst in my chest.

He extended his hand to me, and I placed my hand in his. "Come on, let's go for a drive."

Malcolm navigated my car to the inn and pulled into the packed parking lot. Other than the Haunted Trail, I had never seen the inn's parking lot so full. He kissed my hand and opened the door.

"Come on, Innkeeper. I need your opinion on a few things." I opened the passenger door and stepped out. Malcolm reached me, and slid his hands around my waist. "I wanted to wait for the most romantic moment to do this, but I missed you so fucking much."

His head tilted toward mine and I relented, kissing him like my next breath would come from his lungs. It was familiar and perfect and...painful.

I broke the kiss and pulled back. Malcolm's eyebrows furrowed. "Harley, baby, what's wrong?"

"What if you leave again?" I hated how weak my voice sounded. I hated how much I needed to hear the words from him. Malcolm shook his head.

"Baby, I am never leaving you again. You have every right to doubt me, and I will spend every day proving it to you. Come on, let me show you our new place."

"Our what?" I asked, but Malcolm was already tugging me toward the inn, before taking a detour around the side. When the carriage house came into view, I stopped short, my hand covering my mouth.

What had only five days ago been a vine-covered neglected building, was now a burgeoning construction zone. Workers carried in two-by-fours and power drills were plugged into extension cords that were running in the distance. But my eyes fell on the new front porch with the roof overhang. And hanging from the ceiling of the front porch was a brand-new porch swing.

"What do you say, Harley? Can we give this a shot?"

"For another two weeks?" I asked with a hiccup.

Malcolm shook his head and pulled me in for a kiss. "I was thinking a little longer than that. How does forever sound?"

Epilogue - Five Months Later

Ben

I watched as Malcolm and Harley made goo-goo eyes at each other from across the room. I was happy for my best friend, I really was. Harley was a great girl, and I couldn't picture Malcolm with anyone else. I looked at the picture of the two of them Bode took the first night of the Haunted Trail. They deserved to be happy.

We were gathered in the newly renovated carriage house that Malcolm had worked on for the past six months. We had yet to tell Harley that as of a week ago we had found the missing money from the railroad boys. It was in one of the walls of the carriage house that we discovered while I was helping Malcolm hang the painting of a woman holding flowers that Malcolm had bought from Witches' Brew. The Railroad Boys had apparently been squatting in the carriage house before the O'Neil sisters had taken them in. We had already arranged to have the money given back to the original owners and their descendants in Harley and Maggie's name.

Things were changing. I was trying to roll with the punches. I made the decision to expand *Spirits, Seekers, and Skeptics* a few months ago, making the little town of Burnt Creek the home base. But because of intense scheduling set up almost a year in advance for the show, this month was the first time I had been back in town since the expansion announcement.

And now, here I was at an engagement party.

Of course, Harley didn't know that this was an engagement party. She thought this was a "Welcome home" party for the crew that's been on the road for the past few months. Malcolm's been a bundle of nerves all night. I don't know why; we all know Harley's going to say yes.

Davis and Darla bet money that Harley was going to cry.

Cameron bet money that Malcolm was going to cry.

I would be lying if I said I didn't get in on the action. Malcolm was always an emotional guy. Zoey was making sure to film the whole thing, discreetly, of course.

I searched the room for the one person I shouldn't be looking for. I scanned over the high school students from the journalism club that Malcolm sponsored and led. Bode had gotten some junior reporters and was excited to photograph the proposal for the school paper that was actually printed on paper now. My eyes darted over the food table and the balloons, until they finally landed on a head full of angelic blonde curls. Her sexy glasses were soft pink today, bringing out the flush in her cheeks.

My brother would've killed me for looking at Maggie Malone like this.

Maggie floated over toward Malcolm and handed him a microphone, the ambient music overhead cutting off as she switched on the mic. Maggie winked at him, and for just a flash I wanted to punch my best friend for being on the receiving end of Maggie's wink.

What is wrong with me?

"Can I have everyone's attention?" Malcolm said over the din of people in the space. Harley was dividing her attention between Malcolm and the crowd, probably expecting Malcolm to make some sort of a speech about the food or something. He rubbed the back of his neck nervously. "I wanted to thank all of you for coming tonight, it means a lot to me and Harley to have so many friends and family members here." Malcolm's eyes darted over to Harley, and I could see his eyes get misty.

Davis better get ready to fork over twenty bucks.

"I'm not sure if Harley knows this, but it's been six months to the day since I first stepped foot in this town, in this inn, and met the most incredible, funny, snarky, beautiful woman I've ever laid my eyes on." Harley's stance changed from encouraging to apprehensive. Malcolm continued on. "Harley, I know there are some people who wait years to lock down their forever, but I've known from the first month I've met you that you were it for me. I loved you then, I love you now, and I'm going to love you when we're old."

He got down on one knee, Harley gasped, it was all the things you'd expect from the perfect engagement.

"Will you marry me?" Malcolm asked. Harley nodded, wrapping her arms around him as tears fell down her face, too.

Shit. I didn't know what it meant for the betting if both of them cried. Maybe the bets were canceled out?

I lifted my beer to my lips as I scanned the crowd again for Maggie, only to find her eyes locked on me. A beautiful blush highlighted her cheeks when she realized I busted her for staring at me. My stomach flipped, seeing her eyes on mine.

This girl right here was the very reason weddings and happily-ever-afters were at the bottom of my to-do list. Because there was only one girl that was ever going to make me think of happily-ever-afters.

And that girl belonged to my dead brother.

I turned, walking out to the front porch. It was springtime. Still a little chilly to be outside without a jacket, but after being inside trapped like a sardine with all those people, I needed a reprieve.

I don't know how long I sat out there in a rocking chair before Harley and Malcolm came out, dragging Maggie behind them. I got to my feet and clapped Malcolm in a hug.

"Congratulations, man. I'm happy for you."

I turned and hugged Harley. "Congrats, girl."

"Thanks, Ben," she said, mushing herself into Malcolm's side again. "Sit, sit. You too, Mags. We need to talk with you guys about something."

I sat in the rocking chair, Maggie sitting in the one right next to me. I forced myself to ignore how right it felt, having Maggie rocking on a front porch with me. Like I could picture the next sixty years of our lives.

Malcolm smiled down at Harley before addressing Maggie and me. "We wanted to talk to you two because," Malcolm squeezed Harley's hand and she squealed with a little jump.

"We want you to be the maid of honor and best man!"

My eyebrows raised on my forehead. "Wha—of course, I'd be honored!" I said, forcing myself to smile.

Maggie clapped her hands together. "Oh, my gosh, really? I'd love to!" She clambered out of her chair and launched herself at Harley who wrapped her arms around her sister.

"Also, Malcolm and I were thinking with the influx of reservations at the inn and the renovations of the carriage house and at the newspaper, we aren't going to have as much time as we'd like to plan the wedding."

Malcolm cleared his throat and ran his hand over the back of his neck.

Oh, hell. I know what that means.

"So," Malcolm said, bashfully. "We were wondering if the two of you could team up to do some of the planning for us. Like, picking the venue, cake tasting, all of that."

Maggie and I locked eyes in shock. Electricity coursed through my veins when she looked at me like that. Planning a wedding with a girl I was crazy about but could never have? Hard pass.

"We'd love to," Maggie said, quirking her lips in a devilish grin, her eyes daring me to contradict her.

Well, it looks like my past isn't just haunting me, I'm also planning a wedding with it.

Acknowlegements

- Michelle for painstakingly editing this book and telling me it was good, even when it probably wasn't.

- Matt for getting me in touch with Michelle, without whom this book would have never been released.

- Emerson, Billy, and Roni for beta reading Spirit Me Away and talking me off the ledge when I wanted to light the book on fire.

- Stephie for being the family and support system I desperately needed when I didn't even know I needed it.

- Deborah, Dave, Kay, and Wayne for being there for me, my husband, and especially my kiddo so I could chase my dreams.

- Darleen and Brittney for using childhood anecdotes to tell me I could do this.

- Matthew (Mr. Lucky) for sacrificing time with his lovely wife (me) so I could produce this book.

I love and appreciate you all.

About Author

Jade Luck lives in the icy tundra of beautiful Michigan with her husband (Mr. Lucky), her daughter, and her dog. If you want to follow her authoring exploits, you can follow her on social media or by signing up for her newsletter on jadeluck.net.

Made in the USA
Columbia, SC
26 November 2022

71793413R00224